MARY

An Awakening of Terror

Nat Cassidy

MARY

An Awakening of Terror

NIGHTFIRE

A TOM DOHERTY ASSOCIATES BOOK
NEW YORK

For Robyn

MARY: AN AWAKENING OF TERROR

A Nightfire Book
Published by Tom Doherty Associates
120 Broadway
New York, NY 10271

www.tornightfire.com

Nightfire™ is a trademark of Macmillan Publishing Group, LLC.

Library of Congress Cataloging-in-Publication Data

Names: Cassidy, Nat, 1981– author.
Title: Mary : an awakening of terror / Nat Cassidy.
Description: First edition. | New York : Nightfire/Tom Doherty Associates, 2022. |
Identifiers: LCCN 2022008325 (print) | LCCN 2022008326 (ebook) | ISBN 9781250265234
    (trade paperback) | ISBN 9781250265227 (ebook)
Subjects: LCGFT: Horror fiction. | Novels.
Classification: LCC PS3603.A86874 M37 2022 (print) | LCC PS3603.A86874 (ebook) |
    DDC 813/.6—dc23/eng/20220225
LC record available at https://lccn.loc.gov/2022008325
LC ebook record available at https://lccn.loc.gov/2022008326

Our books may be purchased in bulk for promotional, educational, or business use. Please contact your local bookseller or the Macmillan Corporate and Premium Sales Department at 1-800-221-7945, extension 5442, or by email at MacmillanSpecialMarkets@macmillan.com.

First Edition: 2022

Printed in the United States of America

0 9 8 7 6 5 4 3 2 1

Author's Note

My mom died while I was finishing up the final draft of this book (four months to the day prior to the writing of this author's note, in fact). It's been several years since she'd been able to actually read anything, but I will forever wish that she got to at least hold a copy of it in her hands. After all, she's one of the only people who ever read my earliest attempts at writing this story, some twenty-five years ago. To put it mildly: multiple sclerosis can go fuck itself into the sun.

I wanna share with you just a quick anecdote at the top, to pay her tribute and also to shed a little light on the birth of this book—which, thankfully, you *are* able to hold in your hands (or ears or eyes or however these words are coming to you).

When I was little, one of my favorite activities was strolling up and down the Horror section of our local video store, looking at all the covers and scaring myself silly. It boggled my tiny mind how any movie, let alone an entire section of movies, could somehow sustain the garishly extreme frights promised by those images (this was before I learned that, in a lot of cases, the artwork had little to do with the actual movie itself).

There were, I suppose, more objectively disturbing covers than De Palma's *Carrie*. But, for some reason, that one messed me up *bad*. I can still see it: Sissy Spacek, drenched in red, eyes impossibly wide and white, hands frozen in a gesture of outrage. It haunted me. I saw her everywhere. Eventually, I had to do what every freaked-out seven- or eight-year-old kid does when the option's available to them: I went to my mom for help.

Robyn was a Stephen King junkie, so she was the perfect person to ask for a way to defeat Carrie so that I wouldn't have to be afraid of her anymore. Except that's not what my mom did, not quite. She sat me down and told me the story of *Carrie*, and she did so in such a way that made my heart break for this poor girl who'd been dealt such an unfair hand. She made sure I understood that Carrie wasn't so much the monster as she was surrounded by them. I'd never heard a horror story framed that way. I'd never felt sympathy—love, even—for something I thought I was supposed to fear.

My mom had also been dealt a ridiculously unfair hand, and I think on some level, she probably even envied Carrie's ability to inflict payback just a little bit. But, more than that, my mom knew the value of horror as a genre. She knew there were distinct benefits to be gained by spending time with our fears, getting to know them personally. I'm convinced her love of genre fiction was part of how she stared down a pitiless, progressive disease for decades without losing her mind. She was the strongest person I'll ever meet and, God, do I wish she didn't have to be, but I'm grateful she shared some of her tools with me.

Incidentally, for probably a year or so after that talk, whenever I was alone and afraid (which, as a latchkey kid who was already obsessed with horror, was often), I would talk to Carrie White. She became something of a matron saint for me. I have very clear memories of being home all by myself and literally whispering things, like, "I'm sorry they were so mean to you, Carrie; I'll be your friend. I won't treat you like they did. Please just keep me safe." And hey, I survived childhood. So I can't rule out that it didn't work.

A few years later, I started writing my own stories, and I had an early idea for a novel that, in part, would be something of an homage. It came from a simple question: What would happen if Carrie didn't have any special powers? Where would she be as a grown-up? Would she still have a story? I knew right away I'd even give this novel a title that acknowledged the connection. I'd call it *Mary*.

What follows is pretty far from that premise, all things considered. There's no telekinesis, no prom trauma (*prauma?*), no hyper-religious mother, no pigs' blood. Another memory from my childhood in the 1980s and early '90s was a publishing trend of direct sequels to classic works of literature (*Scarlett, Cosette*, etc.); this isn't that. But *Mary* is about bullying. The societal kind, the kind we all grow up into and begin to accept because It's Just the Way Things Are. It's about loneliness and isolation and . . . well, you'll see.

There's more I want to say about this book, the long journey of writing it, the specific things it's trying to say . . . but I'm gonna stick those thoughts in an afterword because, y'know, spoilers. While I've got you here, though, quick heads-up: this book has mutilation, animal death, and implied sexual trauma. Also misogyny. Lots of it. Internal and external, implicit and explicit, intentional and probably unintentional (though I'm immensely grateful to my sensitivity readers for their help in addressing my blind spots). There's a good reason for this, but again, you'll see. I won't say more; it just felt right to let you know ahead of time.

Okay, that's enough outta me for now. Thank you for picking this book up. I hope you enjoy it. And I'm glad you're here.

Nat Cassidy
New York, May 2021

Midway through our mortal life I'd walked
And found myself within a forest dark
                              —Dante, *The Inferno*, Canto I

Crouched on the altar-steps, a grisly band
Of women slumbers.
                              —Aeschylus, *The Eumenides*

She wanted to destroy something. The crash and clatter
were what she wanted to hear.
                              —Kate Chopin, *The Awakening*

PART ONE

THE LIFE BEFORE

APRIL 20, 1969

There's a corpse in the bathtub.

She's leaning against the wall, legs dangling over the lip of the tub. Dumped there, looks like.

She's been stripped nude, save for the pillowcase pulled over her head. A clean, almost glaringly white pillowcase, featureless other than the huge stain of dark, sopping blood in the center. The topography of what was once a face presses out of the middle of the dark, wet stain. There's so much blood the fabric clings to what's underneath like a second skin, leaving hollows where the eyes, the still-screaming mouth had been.

More blood trails out from under the pillowcase in thick rivulets, down her neck, across her chest, clotting along the basin of the tub. Stains smear the areas around the body like an aura; bloody hands having done bloody work.

Other than that, Sheriff Brannigan thinks, it's a pretty nice bathroom. At least compared to any bathroom he's ever had.

His policeman eyes pick up plenty of details that tell him a more nuanced story. The actual-gold soap dish by the sink is speckled brown with tarnish and scum. The cream-colored hand towels have a weather-beaten thinness to them. The room is like a despised relative in some opulent family: richer than sin, but not a lot of love to show for it. Exactly what you might expect for the fourth guest bathroom on the third floor of this dizzyingly large mansion.

Other than that, Mrs. Lincoln, how was the play? . . . The joke passes through his mind like a bit of trash blowing down a deserted street.

He's a thin man in his fifties. His sheriff's badge gleams like the edges of the dead woman's pillowcase: too bright, too clean for this room. His face is slimy with sweat. He's not having a good day.

The world has gone unnaturally quiet. Moments ago, it was chaos, but now . . . only the sounds of his pulse, his breath, coming in, going out, in unconscious, tidal sway. It was as if when he opened the door to this room—

there's a corpse in the bathtub

—he'd entered a bubble and now only he and this dead woman and this inauspicious bathroom existed.

Sheriff Brannigan stares at the woman, leans toward her. He's gripped by a sudden, strong urge to reach out, yank that pillowcase off her head, get that awful unveiling over with and confront her face-to-almost-face. He doesn't. He knows the horrors waiting underneath that fabric all too well. He's seen it dozens of times on dozens of morgue slabs and in dozens of crimes scenes already. Plus, his arms are beginning to feel strangely heavy and useless. So he settles for just . . . staring.

The dead woman doesn't appear to mind. Hopefully, she's past caring about such things now.

He stays this way for a long time, hands on his upper thighs, bent at the waist, regarding the body as if it were a work of inscrutable art on display—*maybe it is*—when a harried voice shouts from down the hallway.

"We found him! Sheriff!"

Brannigan doesn't jump. He doesn't twitch. Going by his body language, he doesn't appear to register a thing. The bubble around him doesn't burst so much as it begins to dissolve.

Bit by bit, reality reestablishes itself: the commotion downstairs, men shouting and barking orders, and worst of all, the *screaming*. Not a scream of pain or anguish—it's the scream of madness, an insane child realizing his favorite toy has broken.

And underneath all that, the bubbly counterpoint of a radio blaring pop music.

"We found him!" the voice yells again, louder, closer. One of his deputies, running into the room, panting either from excitement or exertion. "We—" The deputy breaks off, seeing the scene in the bathroom: the dead woman, the sheriff, bent as if ready to whisper something only for her benefit.

"Sheriff? . . . You okay?"

Brannigan doesn't turn around; something is squirming under the red center of the pillowcase and it's pulled his attention. He knows what it is, even before it emerges from the bottom of the pillowcase: an ant, curious and probing. This house appears to be full of them, and why not? Good eats aplenty around here. Ants were a common enough sight at scenes like this (more common outside, but there's something appropriate about this mansion, for all its façade of respectability, being so infested). They were drawn to the blood, and they could interfere with your forensics, but what could you do? If your murder scene had an ant problem, you might as well try to shoo sand away from the beach. Or maybe the sheriff is simply as past caring about such things as the dead woman is.

"Sheriff Brannigan?" his deputy repeats, concerned.

"How many does she make?" the sheriff asks at last, not taking his eyes off the shifting, pulsing stain. A second ant soon follows the path of the first, tracking along a rivulet of blood. The squirming underneath the fabric continues; there are more. So many more. "Is she the ninth? Tenth?"

"I-I don't know, Sheriff. But, but *we found him*! The guy, the, the—well, we *think* the guy. Come on!" The deputy makes a futile gesture toward the doorway.

This woman is actually the seventh body they've found in the mansion so far—six of them women, all stripped nude, all with something like a pillowcase pulled over their mutilated faces, matching the modus mortis of the dozens of other women they've been finding around town for the past several years, all unidentifiable. The seventh body was an exception on both counts: he was male and he was all-too-easily ID'd, despite the visual handicap of him missing most of his head.

Mayor Victor Cross. The man whose third-floor guest bathroom they were currently standing in.

Another high-pitched, manic shriek floats into the bathroom.

The guy

The guy who did

A quick mental flash—the headless mayor on the bedroom floor, the mayor they had *just* been meeting with before the screams began and the train of the world derailed, as well as the hastily written note that same mayor left on the floor by his body—and just like that, the sheriff remembers who he is and what he's here to do. He shakes his head, snapping it back and forth. It helps a little, although his arms still feel dipped in concrete. The left one in particular irregularly pulses with dark, painful alarm.

We found the guy who

"Right." The sheriff clears his throat. He sees an ant on the floor and stomps on it. "Thank Christ. Where is he?"

The deputy makes a face, half-grimace, half-plea.

"He's in the walls."

Another high, wail of insanity curls through the massive house.

The sheriff and his deputy tear out of the bathroom and throw themselves down the stairs. They pass paintings and lamps. Huge framed mirrors. They pass the giant master bedroom on the second floor, where the head-less body of Mayor Cross lies next to a shotgun and a piece of paper doused in blood and gray matter. The sheriff doesn't see more than the man's legs through the doorway, but that note is emblazoned onto his mind, indelibly, as if written by flashbulb:

"i knew"

The sheriff's lips curl in a grimace as they pass. He hates this place. Not just this mansion of horrors but this whole damn town. One of several tiny communities under his county purview, coming with the job the way unseemly in-laws come with a marriage. He knows some of the town's history—enough to have a bad taste in his mouth anytime he's forced to visit—so the way this day has developed has of course been a shock, but not necessarily a surprise. There's always been an evil energy in the air here. A poison. Maybe that's why it's so hard to breathe right now.

Brannigan and his deputy have almost made their way to the first-floor landing when the sheriff feels his heart lock in his chest. His lungs fill with sand. The pain in his arm grows new rows of teeth and bites down hard.

He wheezes: "Wait, wait. I gotta . . . I gotta sit down for a sec."

He puts a sweaty hand on the immaculate wallpaper, slowly eases his way down the steps, and sits on the bottom stairs.

"Do you need—?" his deputy starts to ask.

The sheriff angrily waves him away. *Go do your job*, the wave says. *I'll be okay*, his expression tries—fails—to add.

The deputy obeys, and Brannigan watches him continue on past the stairs and through a doorway. "I think something's wrong with Sheriff Brannigan!" the deputy is calling. There are a lot of men around—the whole countywide ad hoc task force Brannigan had assembled over the past few months showed up almost instantly when the call went out—but most of them are too focused on the task at hand to hear the deputy.

One man has come out to stare for a moment, though.

He's handsome and young, perhaps in his early forties, with ginger-red hair. If Brannigan is remembering correctly through the painfog, this man is actually a local here. That they'd received a few volunteers from this town should've perhaps softened Brannigan's opinion of the place . . . except all the men give him the same, uneasy feeling. In fact, looking at this deputy now (*His name also starts with a B, doesn't it? Burke or Burman or something.*) Brannigan feels his gorge rise in disgust. Or maybe he's about to puke from the pain. He's not even sure; his body begins to feel like someone else's.

Another shriek peals through the building. The red-haired deputy snaps to attention, but instead of running to the direction of the noise, he bolts up the stairs, pushing past the sheriff, like a man who just realized he'd left the gas on.

For the moment, the sheriff is alone again.

An ax smashes through wood in another room. On this side of the wall, a small shelf of porcelain figurines vibrates with the impact. The figurines scatter from their perch, several shattering on the floor.

The sheriff watches this, feeling oddly light and detached. Once, when he was a boy, he'd visited California with his family, and there had been an earthquake. The moment before the tremors felt similar to this: a tingling, stomach-floating, physical premonition. His arm throbs, at once dull and sharp, razor blades wrapped in wool.

California was a fun trip. Janie was alive then. Before her husband drove the two of them off the highway into that ravine. We'd had no idea what was coming for her, did we?

Why am I thinking about that?

A strange voice he doesn't quite recognize answers back: *Because we are only our memories, Owen.*

Sheriff Owen Brannigan hears the sound of men—his men—pushing themselves into the hole in the wall. The radio must be inside the walls, because as soon as they break through, the blaring music gets even louder. Brannigan has never liked that rock and roll crap. It's dissonant and charmless and too juvenile by half. But he recognizes the next song as it starts.

He doesn't remember who sings it—another dopey group with a dopey, interchangeable name—but he knows his wife, Bess, loves it. She's actually never told him that, but he can tell by the way she hums it whenever she busies herself with various tasks, by the way her head bobs and an unconscious smile curls her lips whenever the song plays over the radio. She probably knows if she confessed how much she enjoys this song, he might shake his head and look at her with his own smirk that teases, *"You're a silly woman, but I adore you."* He doesn't need her to say it. They've been married for twenty-two years, and he loves watching her and so

I knew

The sheriff's stomach pushes out of his torso and floats toward the ceiling. Liquid concrete pours into his limbs. Darkness encroaches the edges of his vision, a swarm of black ants swallowing up the world. And the song continues, not caring.

I knew

His men scream. The madman screams. Or maybe that's the punchy sound of brass accompanying the rock singer as he croons, "I love you more today than yesterday. But not as much as tomorrow. Every day's a new day of loving you."

A cluster of men round the corner. They're all blurs. They make their way to the sheriff, but as they approach, they don't become any clearer.

When he'd woken up this morning, could he have ever imagined?

I knew

Right before his sister Janie died, when her drunk of a husband randomly steered them into nothingness, could she have imagined?

I knew

Hands are on him now. The skin wrapped around his skeleton feels clammy. Is he sweating? Is he crawling with insects? He listens to the music. To the screams. To the distant volley of gunfire inside the wall. The screams stop. Yet he can still hear them.

Tears spill out of the sides of his eyes as he's laid on his back. He's dimly aware that his shirt is being ripped open. And he thinks, *Every day's a new day.*

But I can still hear the screaming.

I can still hear the screaming. (I knew.) This will never (I knew) end—

And he's right.

Nothing ever ends. Every day's a new day.

A few miles away, precisely as the sounds of gunshots finish echoing through the crawl space between the walls of the unfathomably large mansion, a pregnant woman in more modest accommodations suddenly screams with labor pains.

Her baby, a girl, is early but not alarmingly so. The doctor later jokes, clapping the woman's nervous husband on the back, "I guess she was just ready to come out."

APRIL 4, 1975

Bettina Perlmutter is hoping for a slow day. She pulls into her parking spot at the La Paz County Desert Museum, the only car in the lot, and closes her eyes for a quick early-morning prayer.

Please, Jesus, let today be quiet.

She can still hear yesterday's screams trapped in her head like ghosts in a haunted house. The museum had hosted a school field trip. An amorphous mass of more than fifteen six-year-olds roiling and shrieking down her hallways.

Please. Jesus. I'm begging you. Let no one come.

There are no other events on the calendar; today *should* be slow. It's not like the museum does a lot of business anyway. Why would it? A humble little collection of desert plants and desert animals, tucked in between a few small desert towns peppered around a desert highway? The only people this museum caters to, besides the occasional school group, are either those who can see this shit just by stepping out their front door, or random travelers passing through—the latter group only now starting to become common again since this area's troubles half a decade ago.

Plus, it's April. The brutal summer heat is already starting to crawl and scrape its way over the horizon—a person'd have to be insane to want to spend any time during the last few bearable months outside staring at their one ratty family of javelinas, or Wilson, the Sick Mountain Lion.

Bettina's not in a good mood. She has an ulcer in her mouth, just inside her right cheek, rubbing against her lower canine.

If today is a quiet day, she can draw the blinds in her office and sit in the cool dark, in silence, in her pain. Maybe she'll pull that bottle of silver tequila out of her desk and take a few sips. No guzzling, nothing her long-dead, propriety-obsessed mother would have called *mannish*. Just sips. Tiny ones to rinse the inside of her mouth with brutal, stinging alcohol. She'll be in private, so she'll be able to cry if the pain becomes too unbearable. And then, eventually, her mouth will go numb, and maybe she'll be able to think about something else for a little while.

She hates these goddamn ulcers. They spring up inside her mouth like toadstools in a dark cave—only, as far as she knows, toadstools don't radiate constant agony like little hellish fucking radio antennas. The ulcers often act as a prelude to her time of the month, too, which means even more days of barely manageable misery ahead.

"I musta done something real special in a past life," she says and then winces at the pain speaking causes. For all her grumbling, she actually loves being a woman, pains and all. She just wishes she'd been born into a world that let those pains earn a little goddamn space.

At least today she won't have to act like the sweet and patient matron she's expected to be whenever kids are around. That's always exhausting.

With a sigh and one more quick prayer (*Jesus, don't fail me now*), she pulls herself out of her boatish Studebaker and walks over to the front door. These ulcers often make it difficult to swallow, so she spits out one good-size gob into the dirt before unlocking and walking in.

Past the small lobby is a dark hallway with the first of the museum's several live insect displays. The first thing she notices is the broken glass all over the floor.

Panic immediately floods her body.

It's been six years since the murders, six years since chaos gripped the area, ending in that bloody day that saw the deaths of their county sheriff, that small-town mayor, and . . . the monster.

Except it hadn't ended. Not as far as her nervous system was concerned. Six years wasn't a long time at all, not to forget living every day waiting for some unseen fiend to leap out of the shadows and do such unspeakable things to you they couldn't even print them in the paper.

Easy, Betty, it's probably just a break-in. Or maybe God's worst creation: teen-agers.

Probably. But Betty wants no part of it. She cautiously makes her way farther into the building, ready to turn on her heels and run at the first sign of anything dangerous. She loves this museum, but she's not about to die for it. She doesn't call out like they do in the movies, no tempting "Hello?" to the psychopath who might be waiting for her in the dark. Instead, she slips her keys between her knuckles like claws, grateful she and Susan and Abby went in on those self-defense classes together last fall.

Her eyes finish adjusting from the sunlight, and now she can make out a little bit more detail in the dark hallway.

There's a small figure sitting among the broken glass, hunched over, back to the door.

A little girl.

"The fuck . . . ?" Betty whispers.

Betty cautiously moves forward. Her ears start to pick up something else: the little girl is singing. Quietly, the way kids do, more rhythm than melody. All the same, Betty recognizes the song. It's not an old song but one of those a.m. bubblegum tunes that sounds more like an early '60s Bobby Darin or Del Shannon hit than the Zeppelin or even Stones tracks her radio plays these days. The little girl's atonal recitation of the lyrics are clear in the tomb-quiet museum.

"I love you more today than yesterday," she sings. "But not as much as tomorrowwww."

It makes Betty's blood turn to ice water.

"Sweetie?" she asks, in spite of the chill. "Whatcha doing over there?"

The kid doesn't react the way Betty would expect—she doesn't flinch or jump in surprise. Instead, she just turns around where she's sitting and smiles.

When Betty gets a look at her, she has to bite down to keep from screaming. One of her top teeth slices into the ulcer, and tears flood her eyes from the momentarily mind-obliterating pain.

The little girl has a mouthful of insects. A handful, too. Some of the insect cases have been smashed open, and she's been sitting here among the glass, eating the bugs. Singing.

Betty's tears clear enough for her to see a few errant ants run across the little girl's cheek and into her hair.

She's unable to reach the girl's parents. There's no answer at the number the child gives her.

Eventually, Betty reaches the girl's aunt, a deeply unpleasant, haggish woman. Bettina hates thinking of her in those terms—men put so much effort into dehumanizing and diminishing her sex, she's loath to contribute to the effort—but there's just no other way to describe this particularly nasty specimen. Before long, the girl is retrieved and whisked away.

Betty doesn't tell anyone about the details of finding the girl. She figures the kid had just been starving and panicked. The glass is easily replaced, and none of the insects she ate were rare or anything. A lot of ants. Some worms. Betty had been momentarily horrified to see the kid had eaten some scorpions, as well, but their tails and stingers had been expertly bitten off and were left discarded in a pile.

"How'd you learn how to do all that, sweetie?" Betty had asked, after the little girl had been cleaned up and was sitting placidly in Betty's office.

The little girl shrugged, picking at a bit of fabric along the hem of her cotton dress. "He knew," she said. "'Cause of the wall spaces."

Betty didn't ask any follow-up questions. Another thing she never tells anyone is that there was something about this little girl that filled her with revulsion. And fear. And pity. From the moment she found her, Betty wanted to get this kid out of her life and forget her as soon as she can.

In time, she's able to—although the vision of that girl sitting on the floor, ants crawling over her face, palms full of squirming, undulating insects, haunts her dreams for the rest of her life. Along with visions of walking into the dark, yawning chasm of the museum and never finding her way out again.

Bettina Perlmutter doesn't have to live with these dreams for long. There's an aneurysm crouched near her brain stem, waiting for the right time to pop—roughly three and a half years from now—after which she'll leave behind two ex-husbands, a lizard named Comanche, and a humble little museum. She won't see what's to come later, forty-four years after she found that little girl, after she walked into her museum expecting to encounter a monster. A return to the chaos. A return to the horror.

But if you'd asked her, Betty would've said that, not so deep down, she knew it'd all come back.

Such things always come back, don't they? Like a recurrent canker. Like toadstools in the dark.

Because life is all about cycles.

And life, with its deadly surprises and unassuming horrors, with its mysteries and miseries, just goes on and on and

PART TWO

SINGLE SERVING

It was not despair, but it seemed to her as if life were passing by, leaving its promises broken and unfulfilled.
—Kate Chopin, *The Awakening*

"It's always the quiet ones," the cliché goes. And like many clichés, there's some truth to it. But sometimes I wonder: what comes first? Do those "quiet ones" become capable of committing an atrocity because they're shunned? Or are they shunned because there's already a sense of what they're capable of?
—Special Agent Peter Arliss, *In the Dark with the Devil: One Heroic FBI Agent's Ground Zero Account of the Arroyo Easter Massacre*

1

Textbook

APRIL 7, 2019

Beginnings are hard.

I try to explain this to the doctor in terms he'll appreciate.

It's like when you come down with a head cold. You never notice the exact moment your throat begins to hurt. Instead, it's that moment you realize your throat has been hurting for a while. It's not always clear when something begins.

"So your throat hurts?"

"No. Well, yes," I say around a bright smile. "Metaphorically."

He doesn't seem to appreciate the effort.

"Just tell me the symptoms you're experiencing that brought you in here."

So I do.

Lately—and I'm not sure for exactly how long, because, again: beginnings—I've been feeling off. Horrible moods. Crying jags. A foggy head. I barely sleep anymore, and when I do, I have this one intense, exhausting dream. My stomach is constantly upset. Clothes don't fit me the way they used to, and even when they do, I'm uncomfortable in my skin, literally and figuratively. I itch. Like there's an incessant *scratch me scratch me scratch me* humming in the back of my mind, but I can't pinpoint where exactly. I tell him I'm sorry, I know that's a lot and maybe kind of vague, and I'm rambling because I haven't seen a doctor in forever and I'm nervous, but long story short, I can't ignore that something feels wrong and also lately when I look in the mirror—

I know what he's going to ask the moment he interrupts me.

"When was your last period?"

I try not to sigh when I tell him it's been a little erratic lately. Coming and going in fits and spurts. But—

He asks how old I am. As if he didn't have my paperwork in front of him. I can appreciate that, as a free clinic, time is short, but it really wouldn't have taken that long to look down. He wants me to say it out loud, to *hear* myself say it. I swallow the sudden surge of anger.

"Forty-nine," I say. Then, begrudgingly, "Fifty in a few weeks."

The doctor, who's probably in his late thirties, nods. *Now* he looks down. Makes a note.

"I know what you're going to say," I tell him. "But this feels *different.* I know my body. I know what's normal. I really think something more is going on than just menopause."

"*Peri*menopause," he corrects. "Menopause is when it's all done. Perimenopause is the process beforehand, which actually can last for several years."

I give him a bright, patient smile. "Thank you. But I really think—"

"Are you also getting hot flashes? Night sweats?"

I concede that I am. Brutal ones. Sometimes I wake up and it's like I've wet the bed, I'm so drenched.

"Mm-hmm," the doctor concurs, blasé as paint. "Perimenopause. Pretty textbook."

Textbook.

"Actually," he continues, "I'm surprised you're only just starting to experience symptoms now. Then again, it's different for every woman. You meet one menopausal woman, you've met one menopausal woman." A laugh, more for himself than me. "What was it like for the other women in your family?"

I tell him I don't know. My only living relative is an aunt I'd rather scoop my brains out with a dull melon baller than speak to again. And my mother died when I was very young.

"Of?"

"House fire. Which shouldn't be genetic, right?"

He doesn't laugh at my joke. Instead, he clicks his pen and agrees with himself. "Textbook. Just bring this up with your gyno next time you have a checkup. They can walk you through treatment options. In the meantime, try to stay hydrated and get some rest."

But of course, I don't have a gyno. I don't have health insurance. Why does he think I've come to this *free* clinic during their *free* health fair, or whatever the hell they called it on that flyer I saw posted to my work's bulletin board? If I had a gyno, if I had any kind of doctor, I wouldn't be here.

And stay hydrated? Get some rest? Did he not hear me when I said I can barely sleep? When I said the dreams I've been having when I *do* sleep make me wake up even more exhausted than before? And then there's this throbbing, red rage I feel sometimes. I'm normally such a sweet person, a Good person, but sometimes this rage makes it impossible for me to function. And that's not even mentioning the issues I've been having with mirrors and—

"I'm sorry, ma'am. We really do have a lot of other people to see today, so . . ." I look up at the doctor. He's checking his watch. He's not trying to push me . . . but I'm being pushed all the same. "Unless you have any other questions?"

"No questions," I say through a pinhole, smiling my best Good Girl smile. "Thanks for your help!"

I tell my Loved Ones all about it when I get home. They listen patiently. Of course they do. They're little porcelain statues. What else are they going to do?

"The real curse of womanhood," I tell them as I shrug off my winter coat and snow-crusted boots, still winded from the three-story walk-up, "is that we never get to forget we have a body. And I don't just mean because we have to look or move or smell a certain way. I mean, biologically. We're so tied to these stupid, fleshy *things*." I grab my midsection. More of it in my hands than ever before. "Every month, they remind us that it's all out of our control—and we can't even see what they're up to!"

I'm ranting. Stupid, obvious observations that don't even feel like my own. Pacing around the room, pointing to my Loved Ones like some hack stand-up comedian. "The girls know what I mean. The boys might understand, but they don't know. Bodies are just the worst, cruelest things. They make promises, and they lie."

Did you tell him about the mirror? my Loved Ones ask.

"I tried to. I couldn't get much of a word in edgewise."

Did you really *try?*

"Yes! He was just . . . He was making me feel so stupid for even being there. Like this was all"—*textbook*—"totally normal. I'm not stupid. I know I'm not. Maybe I should've asked for a female doctor."

Why didn't you?

I shrug. "I didn't want to make waves."

I stop moving.

"Menopause." I say it the way someone might say *stage 4 cancer.* Or *eaten by alligators.* An unbelievable diagnosis.

Perimenopause, my Loved Ones correct me.

"Thank you."

Of course I suspected that was the culprit. I guess I just . . .

What?

I guess I just deep down thought—hoped?—that since it hadn't happened yet . . . maybe I'd be somehow exempt. Maybe it was the sort of thing that happened to other people. Like love. Or adventure.

"Fifty." I say the word through a big, fake smile. "I'm going to be fifty. How did that even happen?"

But since when did I ever care about stuff like that? Who cares how old I am? And it's not like I ever wanted children.

Another voice speaks up. It's a cold, internal voice, deep as stagnant well water at midnight. It says, *You* should *care, Mary. Your life is almost over, and you barely even lived it.*

I hate this voice. It sends a shudder through me. I'm no stranger to voices in my head—you live alone long enough, you start to develop your own personal chorus—but this particular voice? It's like . . . an undervoice. It doesn't even always speak in words. Sometimes I want to ask it, *Who are you, anyway?* Because even though it's always been with me, I recognize it as somehow separate. Alien. And lately it seems to be getting louder.

Outside, the demon dog who lives on the first floor begins barking.

I want to just watch trash TV and try to sleep. First, I want to change out of my clothes. In private. I don't want even painted, porcelain eyes on me and my stupid goddamn lying body right now. I'll close myself in my bedroom, undress, and maybe cry.

Before I do that, though, I go to the bathroom. Even though it's been happening for weeks, I want to confirm the thing with the mirror one more time. Just to prove it's still an issue.

Yep. It definitely is.

I can't look for very long. I only ever last a few seconds. Any longer than that and the world begins to gray and fall apart. It happens *fast.*

I grip the sink with both hands for balance and watch as my face begins to decompose in the glass.

My flesh sags, crumbles, oozes in clotty, rancid rivulets. My lower lip pulls down, revealing black gums and gravestone teeth. Like a corpse left to rot in the desert sun. Meanwhile, my chest is filled with hot, bitter air. My skull rings with nonsense words and phrases. *Kill rip tear peel useless mother motherf—*

Before I pass out, I look away. It all stops, like a tap spun shut, and I can breathe again. The world steadies.

The barking continues outside.

This is what's been happening to me lately.

But it's all totally normal. Right?

Textbook.

2

Blockbuster Videos

APRIL 8, 2019

It had started with the women on the street and on the subway.

I barely noticed it at first. Just small twitches. Ripples of skin. Blink-and-you'll-miss-'em tricks of the light. I don't make much prolonged eye contact with strangers as a rule anyway.

Then I started to feel queasy looking in the mirror, as if the glass itself was somehow distorting. I saw those same ripples. Twitches. It wasn't until about a week ago when I watched in horror, for the first time, as my face bloated and bulged and erupted in custardy pus, and the next thing I knew, I was staring up at the ceiling, my head aching from where it had bounced off the tile of my bathroom floor. My hands flew to my cheeks, but everything was as solid and composed as it had been before I'd looked in the mirror. I'd lost about five minutes.

I have to avoid pretty much every reflective surface now. There are more than you might think in a given day, but it's amazing what you can get used to when you seemingly don't have any other choice.

Same goes for the women I see in public. Of course, I hadn't known it was only women at first, but it's happened enough times that I've been able to nail down the pattern. The faces I've seen (*imagined*) decompose only belong to women, and more specifically, they've all appeared to be around my age. Middle age. The great and fabled Certain Age. Anyone above or below my general bracket doesn't appear to have any issues with their skin rotting away. Not that the women to whom it's happening seem bothered by it either.

Because of course they're not; it's not actually happening.

Ugh. I should've brought this up with the doctor. It was the whole point of going to that damn clinic.

What would he have said? You would have just wasted his time. Isn't wasting your own life enough? Suck it up and deal with it, you old whiner.

I'm so tired of that undervoice.

Thankfully, I'm at work now. Safe in my little basement dungeon.

I'm alone—in very little danger of dealing with facial decomposition, be it my own or a stranger's—and I'm engaging in menial, meditative work. Mind-cleansing work. The closest thing I'm getting to real rest these days.

I love it down here. The smell of wood and paper. The colors of the book spines. Even the musty carpet that hasn't been shampooed in decades. I've been working at Keats & Yeats (Independent Booksellers Since 1924!) for a long time. I've marked its changes. But the basement, like myself, has stayed stubbornly consistent.

The rest of the store, not so much.

I can hear the music upstairs on the main floor. Thudding, repetitive bass. It used to be that the first floor was all books, meant to be browsed quietly: Fiction, Children's, Bestsellers, Mystery, Photography, Employee Picks. Over the years, though, those books have given way to interlopers: stationery, expensive journals, gag gifts, even a few crates of vinyl records. The help desk at the back of the floor has been turned into cell phone repair and computer accessories. Anything to keep people coming in.

But down in the basement? These books cede no ground. They're stubborn things down here. Occult, Horror/Sci-Fi, Personal Growth, Erotica, Playscripts. The unseemly stuff customers want to be alone to browse. Occasionally, a curious straggler winds up tromping down the creaky wooden stairs to this domain—they'll either quickly realize their mistake and run back up to the land of Movie Star's Book Club and iPhone skins . . . or discover something here they didn't know they were looking for.

I'm in the middle of shelving books. This is mostly all I do at Keats & Yeats. It's vital, but invisible, work. Perfect for someone like me. Someone who blends in.

I like it this way. I've seen generations of coworkers, managers, even owners, come and go here, and at this point, I'm as functional and as unobtrusive as the wooden shelves, the rickety ladder. No one asks me to look up inventory or how to get to the nearest subway stop. It's like I don't even exist.

I've been thinking about my current dilemma. Seems to me, the cause is obvious—or at least more likely than the Delicate Nature of the Maturing Female Condition (hafuckingha). No, I still think Dr. Pen Click was wrong. I think what we're dealing with here is a side effect of sleep deprivation.

It has to be. Right?

That voice cuts in: *Don't start thinking you're special, Mary. Don't start assuming there's something unique about you. You're old; that's all this is. Besides, you know another word for* unique*? Crazy.*

I hate that word. As far as I'm concerned, it's the worst word you can call a woman. No other C-word comes close.

I shake my head clear (good thing no one's here to see me because I probably *do* look crazy in the moment). As soon as I'm done shelving this current cartful of books, I'm going to spend some time in the Personal Growth section and do a little more research. I'm allowed to take little breaks like that. I've earned them. There's a little subsection there labeled Health & Wellness where I think I'll find more information on the effects of sleep deprivation. Stress. Hallucinations. And . . . yes, maybe even on menopause. I'm going to get to the bottom of this.

Suddenly, I stop what I'm doing.

Something unfamiliar is in my hands.

I'm so used to this job I can tell when something is off, even by touch alone. Looking down, I'm not holding a trade paperback copy of *The Best Women's Stage Monologues 2014.* I'm holding an expensive, leather-bound journal, one of the ones from the artisanal stationery section upstairs. Dylan, the receiving manager, must have accidentally tossed it onto the downstairs cart. Probably while he was busy flirting with Kayla, another of my aggressively youthful coworkers.

I fan the pages open in a satisfying, cool-breeze flutter. The binding is just right, not too stiff, not at all loose. The pages are the perfect size and thickness. The leather cover feels amazing in my hand.

Maybe I should try journaling. Get my thoughts in order. Clear up some of this fog swirling around my head.

It's almost tempting to laugh at such a banal solution, but . . . maybe it *would* help?

Obviously, I wouldn't use one of these particular journals. Even with my 25 percent employee discount, I can't afford one of these. I make just enough money for rent, my MetroCard, my bills, my groceries, and, when I really scrimp and save, another Loved One once or twice a year. But maybe a cheapo notebook from Duane Reade would do the trick?

What makes you think any of your thoughts and memories are even worth exploring? Just another waste of time.

Before that thought becomes too convincing, I take this opportunity as a good excuse for a little break in my action-packed afternoon. Journal in hand, I walk to the back of the floor where there's a swinging door into the employees-only section.

I can hear Dylan and Kayla still at it. He's flirting up a storm. Maybe I'll say something like, "Get your head in the game, Dylan, you're making rookie mistakes. She'll never let you fuck her if she sees you don't know where to put things."

Sounding a little like Aunt Nadine there. I have to laugh a little. Christ, *that* woman. I wonder if she's still alive. Is death even possible for someone like Nadine? The grim reaper himself would probably spend one second with her and say—

"Excuse me, ma'am, you can't be back here."

I look up from where I was about to put the journal for the upstairs shelving carts. Malcolm, my manager, is looking at me, annoyed. He's standing by Dylan and Kayla. They're also staring at me. It takes Malcolm a beat. Then his annoyance melts as he realizes who I am. "Oh! Snap, sorry, I didn't . . ."

His eyes go wide as if he's just remembered something. "Actually," he says, "hey! Shoot, I've been meaning to talk to you. Do you have a sec?"

Talk to me? This is a first. I half-consciously clutch the journal to my chest.

He starts to lead me toward his tiny private office when Dylan says, "Don't forget, Brad and Tina are storing all the new POS computers in there."

"Shoot," Malcolm says again. "That's right, there's not a lot of room to talk in there."

He looks around, putting on a little play for me, Kayla, and Dylan: a one-man show called the Concerned Manager Tries to Find a Private Place to Talk.

There's a door under the stairs leading up to the main floor. He gestures to it.

"Would you mind?" he asks me.

"The employee bathroom?" I respond.

"It'll be quick," he says.

There's an art to smiling. I've tried to learn it over the years, practicing in the mirror (back when I could look in mirrors). Too much teeth and you look overeager. Too little teeth and you look nauseous. Too much eye and you look psychotic. Too little and you look lobotomized. I hope I'm finding the right balance as he leads me to the tiny, closet-like room.

The pull-chain light makes a metal rasp, and the bathroom isn't so much flooded with yellow light from the single bulb set in the ceiling as trickled with it. Shadows stretch under Malcolm's features. He doesn't look so babyish in here.

"Thanks," he says. "I just wanted us to have some privacy."

Right outside this room there's a hole in the basement wall that connects an ancient conveyor belt to the curb, where shipments are received. The faint sounds of cars honking and stuttering down Broadway joins the thumping bass from upstairs. Private, indeed.

Malcolm and I are practically nose to nose. That's why I'm horrified when I feel the sudden *click-click-fwoom* of whatever gas burner was recently installed in my chest. Heat rushes through me in a blast-radius wave. He'd better make this quick or I'm going to be drenched in sweat soon.

"You've been working here a long time," he says. "Right?"

I blink.

"Yes?" I reply, smile balance faltering. I try to keep the eyes active, but the lips are faltering. I tell him how long. His eyes pop a little.

"Jeez, I was only five when you—" He stops himself. Thank goodness for small favors. He tries to get back on track. "Um. Anyway. The reason I'm asking is . . ."

He pauses to gather his thoughts, and in that moment, an elaborate fantasy unspools. The reason he's asking is he's noticed how diligently I work. How I've always been here, always reliable, always low maintenance. I don't rock the boat, I don't make waves, I go along to get along, I am a Good Girl Who Knows Her Place, and the fact that I've never even asked for this before speaks to how deserving I am, so that's why he's going to offer me a raise. Maybe even a promotion. We couldn't run this store without you, Mary. And it's high time we showed you that we know it.

He resumes.

"I'm sure you've noticed the store has been going through some changes lately, right? Brad and Tina have been trying to figure out a way to transition the store into something a little less . . . old-fashioned. Something a little more competitive? Sorry if I sound nervous, I've never had to do this before, and, heh, it's actually getting a little hot in here—do you feel that? Anyway, the fact is just plain old bookstores have been going the way of Blockbuster Videos, if you know what I mean."

And I don't quite know what he means. But I do know one thing:

I'm not going to like where this is going at all.

3

How Are Things?

There's a letter stuck to my boot.

I pull it off while I stand outside my apartment door, catching my breath from the three flights of stairs, listening to the incessant barking outside coming from Demon Dog. Some of his racket followed me in and is still ricocheting up the stairwell.

The letter was placed on my welcome mat. A plain white envelope. Not personalized (other than its newly bestowed wet boot print). It simply reads "Tenants of" and the street address.

More bad news, probably. I bet our water's being turned off for a week or there'll be road construction on the block or something awful like that. No inclination to check it now. I want to get inside, away as best as can be from the dog's earsplitting yarfs. I want to tell my Loved Ones about what happened.

They're waiting for me, in all their patient, porcelain perfection. I tell them everything. Putting it all together in words, out loud, almost stuns me. What an absolutely shitty day.

"He said, 'I don't want you to think we were dissatisfied with your work here.'" I give Malcolm's voice a snotty little whine, inaccurate but deserving. "He said, 'Brad and Tina told me you've been here longer than they have!'"

So why did he fire you? they ask.

"Get this. 'It's just, the owners think we need staff that's a little more Zendaya and a little less *Jane Eyre*.' Can you fucking believe that?!"

Who's Zendaya?

"I have no idea! Which I guess proves his point: they just don't want someone old. And I'm not old! I'm—"

Going to be fifty?

Perimenopausal?

Rounding that final corner before the last sprint to—?

"Shut up. That doesn't make me old. It's called *midlife*, not . . . *end life*. Shut up. I bet I could sue them for discrimination or something."

With what lawyer? With what money?

And what if you lose? What if you learn they had every right to fire someone like you. Someone so . . .

"Anachronistic?" I sit down on the couch with a grunt. I've been holding court in the living room, but now I'm exhausted.

"I hate when I talk to you all like this, you know. I really do. You make me feel like I'm some crazy lady who just talks to the walls all day. You know how I feel about 'crazy.'"

It's the worst C-word you can call a woman.

"Exactly." I rub my temples, hoping I can stop a headache from forming. What a scene this must be, the frazzled

(*old*)

woman ranting to a shelf of tiny statues. How pathetic am I? Embarrassment swirls through me. But it's not like I think they actually reply. When you're starved for ears, a person takes what she can get, that's all.

I'm quiet for a few minutes.

Then the silence gets to me.

"It gets worse. After he fired me, he laughed in this nervous way, like, whoo-boy-you're-not-gonna-believe-this. And then he said . . . 'I feel awful, I was supposed to tell you this two weeks ago, but . . .'"

But what?

"He stopped himself. He heard what he was saying, and he stopped himself. But it's obvious what he was about to say, right?"

"But I forgot." He was supposed to fire you two weeks ago, but he forgot.

He didn't notice you were there.

Like you don't even exist.

"I am the Ghost of Bookstores Past," I say and push myself off the couch. Even though it's a freezing, wet day, I want ice cream. I pull out the carton from my freezer and help myself to a few spoonfuls.

In between the comforting blasts of sweetness, I take a deep, steadying breath. Exhale the rage and the urge to cry, like twin plumes of poisonous air. Inhale a little serenity.

"Did you know when I was, like, six years old, I got left behind during a school field trip?"

I don't know if I've ever told them this before. Truth be told, I don't know if I'd even remembered the event until this afternoon. I never think about my childhood. I barely remember any of it. I forget where I first heard this phrase, but memory is like a mansion. Full of rooms and hallways and closets. I can even picture my own memory mansion: a giant, boxy house high up in a hill. Painted yellow, with black gables. Don't know why it's yellow, it just is. Anyway. My memory mansion has a lot of burned-out bulbs. Or maybe I stopped paying the electricity bill for too long. It's mostly all dark inside. That's fine. Life is simpler that way, I think. But in this one little room, it seems as though a light has flickered on.

"We were at this little museum. I'd wandered away from the group, and when I came back to myself, I realized the lights were off and the place was too quiet. Even the person who ran the place had left. I was all alone. Like the world had just . . . moved on without me."

That was also the day my parents died, now that I'm thinking of it. The house fire that claimed them both had occurred right after I'd left for school that day. I never went home again. After spending the night at the museum, I had to live with Aunt Nadine.

That's the second time today a memory of Nadine has bubbled forth.

The ice cream doesn't taste very good to me anymore. I put the carton back in the freezer.

"Hey," I say brightly, trying to steer the mood away from the dark, dour ditch I just skidded into, "it's not all bad."

I trot over to where I dropped my purse.

"Some people get a gold watch. And some people . . ." I pull out what I've already begun to think of as my goodbye present: the expensive leather notebook I'd snuck home with me. Are they scandalized? "Ha! Screw that damn store. They're lucky I didn't swipe Dylan's box cutter. He wasn't even paying attention to it. I could've gone upstairs and cut my way through the customers! Slice and dice! Bet they'd notice me then! Bet they'd welcome a few more Jane Eyres after I gave the walls a new carotid artery paint j—"

MARY.

Stop that.

Be Good.

Their voices—the voices I give them in my head, I should say—are appalled. Their perfect little expressions now seem like grimaces of furious disappointment. For a brief moment, my nose floods with the ghostly smell of burning hair and crackling electricity. My temples ache.

"You're right," I say, chastened. "I'm being stupid."

And I am. So stupid. Pathetic and stupid.

I look at the journal in my hands. Even the little victory I felt over stealing it begins to curdle.

"I guess I shouldn't have taken it," I mutter. "That was wrong. But it wasn't totally my fault I still had it in my hands after I left the bathroom."

How do you figure that?

"Because there was a mirror in the bathroom," I say and then tell them the rest of what happened.

Malcolm didn't keep me in the bathroom much longer than it took to give me the news, but he *did* have a little prepared speech he wanted to get through. At one point, while I was mid–hot flash and he was mid-monologue about how he was sure I'd find some other place that would be happy to hire my experience and expertise (and hadn't he just told me bookstores were on the verge of extinction?), my sweaty hands twisted and lost their grip on the journal. It fell to the bathroom floor.

Malcolm didn't miss a beat. Still rambling, he stooped down, picked up the journal, and put it back in my hands.

"He put it right back in my hands," I repeat. "I didn't take it from him. I couldn't. Because I was frozen. In that split second when he bent down, I realized he was standing between me and the bathroom mirror. And so I saw . . ."

My Loved Ones know what I saw. They're in my head, too. They see the brief flash of my rotting corpse in the glass as clearly as I do.

"I ran out of the bathroom after that. I don't know if he finished his speech. I didn't even notice I still had the book in my hand until I was out on the street, trying to put my jacket on."

I sit there in silence—in almost-silence, thanks to Demon Dog.

"This sucks." I sigh.

A sudden burst of anger floods me.

Where are you going? my Loved Ones ask. I didn't even realize I was moving, but here I am, storming into the bathroom.

I'm sick of this shit. I take a deep breath and stare into the mirror above the sink.

For the briefest of seconds, my reflection is normal. Then the change begins.

My cheekbones droop. My jowls hang. My flesh becomes maggoty cake batter. It whines, *Scratch me scratch me scratch me.*

"Why?!" I demand, staring at the horror. "Why is this happening?! Why won't you just stop?!" My head and heart are filled with thunderous rage—I want to destroy this mirror-woman, tear her apart for being so hideous, hear the wet plop of her mask as it hits the floor. But just as I know it's not actually me in the glass (*it can't be!*), I know it's not me who wants this, it's someone else, some *thing* hissing, *Rip tear motherfucking useless mother—*

All this happens in a couple of seconds. I watch as small black hairs sprout from the sides of my mouth, and I realize an instant later they're not hairs, they're insect legs. An ant squirms its way out of my putrefying skin and makes its way upward to burrow into my eye.

I have to look away. I squeeze my eyes shut against the invading insect as much as the vision itself.

I'm barely standing up; my legs are jelly. The sink is the only thing holding me. My eyes are clamped shut.

"Why?!" I cry again, only my voice is a whisper, my lungs are empty. "That's not *me*! That's not . . . me . . ."

In response, that deeper, awful undervoice speaks up, and as it does, I realize what really makes it so different from the voices of my Loved Ones. They are always trying to remind me how to be better, how to be normal, how to be Good. They're always looking out for me, even when I resent them for it. But this voice tells me I'm a lost cause. It's the voice of the doctor, of Malcolm, hell, of Demon Dog if he could speak.

Of course it's you, it says.

Because you had to go and get so. fucking. old.

Because now you've become useless.

And now it's time to rot.

No.

I pull air into my lungs. Eyes still shut, I scream at this all to stop, to go away. I yell curses. I'm sure I look legitimately C-word now. I can feel the mirror staring back at me, baleful and smug, daring me to look at it. I won't look. I might not ever let myself look at it again. But I *hate* this, and so I yell so loud and long that when I finally stop, my head is ringing in the silence.

The silence.

All the damn voices in my head are quiet. No comments on my little performance.

It's bliss. For a nanosecond, it almost makes this entire god-awful day worth it.

Then I realize that ringing in my head isn't just in my head. It's coming from the kitchen. Specifically, the shelf in the corner of the room where I keep a tray for my keys, my occasional mail, and a dusty old portable phone that I never use. It hasn't rung in years. I've had the number since I moved here, back when we needed landlines in the Gilded Age, and this particular phone came bundled with my internet and cable package: a dumb little white cordless complete with—

—*Beep*—

—a voice mail box.

My voice, stumbling and shy, decades younger, comes from the speaker on the base of the phone: "Hi. Um. Thank you. For calling. Um. Please leave. A message. Thank y—"

Another beep, where I'd accidentally stopped recording the outgoing message just a hair too early.

A hacking, rusty voice, full of phlegmy venom, is in the middle of speaking. Despite coming through a small, crappy speaker, it booms as if in a cathedral.

"—sus Christ, it's like plain yogurt came to life." The speaker is racked by a hacking cough—the person speaking and the cheap answering machine speaker. Once the fit ebbs, the voice resumes. "Mary? Are you there? It's . . . it's me. Um. How are things?"

"Oh my God." *Gasping* isn't the right word for what I do. It's more of a gulp—that one final, desperate pull for air before a drowning victim sinks underwater.

It's like I conjured her forth.

It's Aunt Nadine.

This is the first time I've heard her voice in at least twenty years.

I quickly walk into the kitchen, pick up the phone, and slam it back down again.

4

Opportunity Coughs

The phone rings again a minute or so later. I've just retreated to the living room and have picked up the journal to hide it somewhere; I freeze with it in my hands as if I've been caught in a criminal act.

Beep.

The older, younger me answers, forever nervous, forever bumbling: "Hi. Um. Thank you. For calling. Um. Please leave. A message. Thank y—"

Beep.

"—bout as much personality as wet bread." Another hacking cough. Spitting.

A dog begins barking, and for a second, I panic that Nadine's calling from downstairs. Then she shouts, "Shut up!" and the dog coming through the speaker stops, while the dog outside my apartment continues. Jesus, the world is made of such awful poetry sometimes. "Mary, it's your aunt Nadine. *Again.* Where the fuck are you? Come on. I can't keep calling you, I'm not fucking made of time here. Listen. I . . . I know it's probably weird to hear my voice right now, but I'm not gonna lie to you. I need your help. Okay? There. It's been years, I know, and here I am. Begging you for help. That must feel really great, right? But it's true. Begging. I am *begging.* Mary. Are you there? Are you there? Mary? Mary. Mary. Mary. Mary." She continues saying my name, over and over in a robotic, gravelly plea.

"Mary. Mary. Mary. Mary? Mary. Mary."

And maybe it's because I empathize, or maybe it's just to put an end to the "Mary. Mary. MaryMaryMary," but against all better judgment, suddenly I'm picking up the phone.

"Yeah. Hi. Hello?" I juggle the portable receiver in my hands.

Nadine hiccups in surprise. "Wuh—Holy Jesus! Look at that! You finally decided to take pity on an old woman! How's the view from up on that high horse? You get reception up there?"

It's been literal decades, but I can still see the sneering smile that must be forming on Nadine's mouth. I wonder if she still wears those atrocious, giant plastic flowers in her hair. They're like the garish warning colors nature usually bestows on its most venomous creatures.

"H-how are you, Aunt Nadine?"

"How am I," Nadine muses. "Welp, I'm calling *you*, so must not be great, Mary. I don't get to live in a fancy New York apartment, no responsibilities, fucking and sucking like it's 1976. I'm . . . I need your help." Her voice flaps and rattles. I think of a wind sock made from dead skin. Whether she's trying to sound worse (and she does sound awful) to elicit pity, I can't tell.

"O-okay. Is Brenda okay? Isn't she still living out there with—?"

"*Brenda* isn't the solution, Mary," Nadine shouts over me, "and you can't just keep pawning your relatives off on other people!"

"But—she's your *daughter*, Aunt N—"

She interrupts me with a racking spasm of thick, phlegmy coughs. Once it passes (with the help of a hearty hock): "You hear that, Mary? I am a sick woman. I need help. I'm dying. That's the *Reader's Digest* version. I'm gonna die. Had to happen sooner or later, right? Well, here it is. And my precious daughter, Brenda, decides now's the time to take a vacation, and I am all . . . alone, dying." Oh God, is she actually crying? "I'm scared, Mary. I'm so goddamn scared."

It actually sounds sincere. I hear myself, in spite of everything, offer a sympathetic, "Oh, Aunt Nadine . . ."

She keeps going.

"So I thought, who do I know? Who do I know who, I dunno, I helped raise ever since they were a baby? Never asking for anything in return? Always being there, when her parents died or when she made the decision to move across the country and leave everyone who loved her behind? Hello? Any idea? Also, let's be honest, who do I know ain't got nothing else going on?"

"That's not true, actually," I say, barely mustering up the energy to make it sound believable. "I've got a lot going on." The journal is still in my hand. I drop it onto the kitchen counter, where I notice the envelope I tracked in.

Cradling the phone between my ear and shoulder, I pick up the envelope and rip it open while Nadine continues.

"All right, look." Her voice drops to a poisonous, conspiratorial low. "If you're gonna make me keep begging, I ain't got the time, okay? I ain't gonna spend my final hours on my knees sucking dick. I'll be more than happy to sit here, alone, in the dark, my trachea squeezing shut, drowning in my own shit and piss like a goddamn refugee. Serves me right, huh, Mary? That's the way I should go, yeah? Mary? Am I right?"

I'm barely listening. Most of my attention has gone to reading the letter I'm holding.

A plain sheet of paper, as unadorned as the envelope.

> *To our beloved tenants:*
> *As you may know, the owners of this building have been working with Sunset Properties LLC to transfer active ownership and maintain the highest standards. Please note that as of May 1, rents will be increasing to the figure below. We apologize for any inconvenience.*

The figure below is almost double what it used to be.

Gosh. At least they apologized.

The page feels like it's been faintly electrified. A numbness travels up my hand and forearm until it reaches my throat, my tongue. I can't make a sound. And outside: *barkbarkbarkbark*

Nadine takes my prolonged silence differently. I almost forgot I was on the phone with her.

"Well, shit, Mary, if you're going to play hardball," she says, suddenly clear and perfunctory, "would it sweeten the deal if I said I was willing to pay you?"

5

A New Day

APRIL 9, 2019

Beginnings are hard. Sometimes you can't tell if something is actually Beginning or if you're just sleep deprived.

The dawn light melts through my curtains. Another night of tossing and turning, and then the Dream . . . which was promptly interrupted by the unwelcome alarm clock that is Demon Dog.

Every morning, it's like this. His owners—my probably-soon-to-be-former landlords—let him out to greet the dawn like some baleful, shaggy rooster. And every morning, I lie there, staring up at the ceiling, indulging thoughts of crushing his little doggy skull in my hands, letting his pink doggy brains foam out between my fingers, feeling as decadent as eating an entire carton of ice cream in one sitting. Delicious. Mmm, have another scoop.

Of course, I have my Loved Ones to hold me back, but how someone else in the neighborhood hasn't shut that dog up by now, I will never understand.

God, I'm tired.

I've been putting this off since I hung up the phone with Nadine; time to finally get up and do it.

There are two small suitcases under my bed. They haven't been used in decades. I pull them out.

It's funny—maybe not ha ha funny—but the first thought I have upon seeing the two suitcases is: *I'm going home.*

I haven't been back to Arizona for more than thirty years. I've lived elsewhere for most of my life at this point. It's never in my mind or memories. It's not home by any stretch.

But I'm going home.

This will be good for me. Not just because of the money; I think I *need* this. I need a reset. I need to get back to myself. To Mary. Remember who I am. Why I'm Good and not useless. Why I'm not some decaying corpse in the mirror. If something really is wrong with me, what better place to start my investigation than the place I came from?

Yes. This will be a Beginning. Hard . . . but necessary.

"And remember," I say to the empty apartment, "it's just temporary. Just until Brenda gets back. If this winds up being a disaster, I'll only be there for a couple of weeks at most."

Demon Dog continues belching his barbed-wire aria outside while I pack. Into the first suitcase go a few clothes, a few toiletries.

Then I bring the other suitcase to the living room. It's already been stuffed with towels.

One by one, I pack each Loved One inside. Moving with slow, precise care. Like a midwife handling newborns. Thirty-eight of them, to be exact. They all have different names, different faces, different outfits; some feed animals, like goats or geese or puppies or birds, some are sniffing flowers or marching with bread or heading to school or trying on oversize boots or just sitting and staring as sweetly as can be. But they all have one thing in common. They're all perfect.

After they're carefully put away, my apartment suddenly seems empty. I don't think I quite realized how little I actually own or display besides my collection. My entire life in New York feels like it was just something I dreamed up. Like I never really existed here.

I spend a lot of time like this. Just looking. When I finally come back to myself, the quality of the light outside the window has changed. It's still early, but now definitely more day than night. Ugh, brain fog.

Also, I'm shivering. Freezing, in fact. Like I've been standing out in the snow without a jacket. I'd welcome a hot flash right now. Why am I so cold?

"It's time to get going," I say. "I'm losing the morning."

The sound of my voice in the empty room makes me realize how quiet things have gotten outside of my head, too. Demon Dog has finally shut up. A minor miracle.

I'm about to grab the handle of my suitcases when I notice my hands are filthy. Dirt and some clumpy dark goo. Disgusting. Must be gunk from under the bed that got on the suitcases or something. I'll need to do a more thorough cleaning when I get back.

Especially because I might need to find a new apartment.

Ignore those thoughts for now. Today, I'm going to try to be positive. Optimistic.

Beginnings are hard. But sometimes they're worth it.

"Goodbye for now," I finally manage to say to my apartment after I wash my hands and gather my things at the door. "I'll be back." And then, absurdly, stupidly, embarrassingly . . . but sincerely, "Please don't forget about me."

I close my apartment door softly, not wanting to disturb this anomalous silence, and walk out of the building.

There's a commotion in the backyard, it sounds like. Someone yelling. One of my landlord's kids. They sound frantic and upset.

Something has happened to Demon Dog, I think. Maybe that's why he's suddenly so quiet. Maybe someone finally got sick of all his noise. Maybe a brick fell on him. Maybe again and again. Maybe he'll shut up from now on.

Look at that, Mary: you *can* be optimistic.

I can't afford a cab, so I head for the subway, a little smile on my face.

6

Bloodied Mary

I am

That's as far as I get before my mind goes blank. My pen hovers over the page. I can't think of how to finish the sentence.

I am

. . . sitting in my seat in an airplane.

We've just settled into our cruising altitude, and my seatmate has begun a steady drift of his person over the armrest and into my space. I've tried asking him to close up shop, but he either doesn't hear me or he's choosing not to. So I've taken my journal out to try to christen it—and distract myself—with some opening thoughts on the beginning of this journey.

Trouble is, I have no idea what to write.

I am . . .

. . . what? I am . . . who? I am . . . going to . . . ?

"I am gonna waste a lot of pages in this damn thing, that's what," I mutter under my breath.

That's the problem with these journals: they're too nice. They put too much pressure on whatever you write to be worthy. And, as I'm so often reminded in my darkest thoughts, worthy is not something I've ever been used to thinking *I am.*

My Loved Ones are underneath me somewhere in the belly of the plane. I hate that they had to get stowed away, but I had to be smart and not pay the extra fee to keep them in the cabin with me (so many extra fees nowadays, I'm amazed I get to use this seat belt for free). If they were here, I could sound out my problems with them. At the very least, they could talk me out of jamming my pen into Mr. Manspreader's jugular next to me.

What would they say?

I suppose they'd say what they always say. Their constant reminders:

Don't be weird, Mary. Be Good, Mary. But what would that mean in this specific instance?

Let's see. I close my eyes to try to imagine them better and . . .

. . . good lord, it feels so good to close my eyes.

The adrenaline of getting to the airport and onto the plane is draining away, and my body remembers just how early it woke up today, how poorly it's been sleeping. I'd wolfed down a yogurt before leaving my apartment, but I burned through all that fuel just getting to the airport.

If they were with me right now, my Loved Ones would say: *You need sleep, Mary.*

I've never been good at sleeping in public—or even in private these days!—but . . . yes, I think I could sleep a bit now.

And without Demon Dog here to wake me up, maybe I'll get a little actual rest.

Unless I have the Dream again . . .

Too late to worry about that now. Already sliding away.

A voice follows me into the darkness:

Good Things to Good Girls . . .

And what Good Thing do you get for settling down and getting some rest? How about the Dream? Because here you are again.

It always begins the same way: in darkness. And you're running.

It's so dark you don't have any visual clues that you're running. But you feel the air break around you. You feel your muscles, your nerves, gloriously alive. It's such a real sensation you always wake up even more exhausted than when you fell asleep—but in the moment, it's exhilarating.

Those same nerves tell you, despite the expansive nothingness around you, that you're actually quite closed in. Your eyes might tell you you're running through outer space itself, but your skin understands you're wrapped in a series of dark, tight corridors. Quick turns, low ceilings, obstacles every which way, almost at random. But you're not scared; you know every twist and turn of this labyrinth. You're not Theseus. You're the minotaur. And you can move with astonishing speed. It almost feels like you're flying.

*(*I am *flying, a distant voice whispers.)*

You can actually feel dirt and the wood and the occasional sting of a nail or a splinter as your hands slap frenetically against the tight walls around you.

You round corners. You duck under pipes. You navigate the terrain as if it were the only home you've ever known.

Where is this place?

This is what you most often wonder.

And this time, a thought occurs to you.

Memory is a mansion.

That's new. You don't normally have that thought during the Dream. Then again, you're currently embarking on a voyage of self-discovery, so why not?

Back to the Dream.

Wherever this place is, it's huge. There seems to be no end to the corridors, to the ground you can explore. You almost want to weep with gratitude for finding yourself here, at once tiny and insignificant, but also supreme, comfortable, and peacefully alone. And there's music in the air. Distant and distorted, but still recognizable as peppy, up-tempo pop music from another time. A singer who loves you more today than yesterday.

You might not know where you are, but you know what you're here to do.

You're on the hunt.

You don't always get to find your prey during the Dream. Sometimes you just run through the dark, searching, until you wake up.

But sometimes—the best *times—you get a little closer than that.*

You turn an invisible, pitch-black corner, and there it is: a massive spotlight, punching an unquestionable hole in the dark.

Motes of dust float in the cone of light, making it an almost solid thing. You might be able to turn around and see the source, but you never do; to do that would break the illusion, the theatrical magic, and wouldn't that be a shame?

The spotlight thrills you and repulses you at the same time. Distantly, you feel a certain jealousy for it—wouldn't it be nice to be in the center of that glow for a change? You don't ask for much, not a billboard or a magazine cover. Just to be seen. Just to be noticed. When, if ever, will it be your turn?

Sometimes there's a figure in the center of the spotlight, but their exact identity never seems important to you. They're indistinct, barely more than blobs, and you have an understanding, a dream-understanding, that each time it's someone new. All that's consistent is your chops-slathering hunger. And that feeling that the show is about to begin.

What happens next? You don't know.

You've never made it past this point in the Dream.

But now? Now that you're getting some good, uninterrupted sleep?

You round an invisible corner, and there's the spotlight, only this time, there are three *figures in its circle of light. And they're not indistinct; they're clear as can be.*

The three figures—female bodied—are naked except they're each wearing some sort of hood. As you approach, you sense more, just like them, waiting beyond the periphery of the light.

The three figures are facing you, but now they turn and look at the darkness to their side.

Your legs take you toward them, and you begin to see hints of detail in the black. Slats and knots. It's not just featureless nothing. It's—

(Memory is a mansion, and dreams are the spaces between its walls.)

—a wall.

They're looking at a wall.

You can tell they're peering through cracks into a large, well-lit space on the other side. You pull up next to the nearest hooded woman.

You're in uncharted territory now. You've been having this Dream for months, but you've never gone this far.

There's a house on the other side. A living room. Fancy. No, that's not the right word. Extravagant. Ornate. Lavish. You can immediately picture the rest of the house: an immense box covered in peaks and gables, high up on a hill for all to look at. Not a house. A

(memory)

mansion.

"You might want to put that on," one of the women says. Her voice is ragged and whistly, a guttural buzz underneath that makes you think of insects swarming over dead meat.

You look down and realize that you're holding something. A pillowcase. You're holding it open like it's a sackful of Halloween candy. Except instead of candy—

(wet drops plip and spatter onto your foot)

—the pillowcase is filled with blood. Dark, slick, heavy. The pillowcase sags and bulges, a greedy tick ready to explode.

Why on earth would I ever want to put this on? *you want to ask but can't.*

"Because he's in here, too," another hooded woman answers as if you did. Her voice is similarly ragged, but lower in tone than the first. "And he's coming."

You feel a light tickling on your arm and notice an ant is crawling on your skin. You blow it off with a sharp puff of air and then wonder: How could I see that? I haven't been able to see any of my body in this darkness. *The answer is obvious. Some of the spotlight is finally spilling onto you, too.*

"Put it on," the third woman commands. She sounds furious, but before you can do anything to placate her, the spotlight begins to intensify. It grows brighter and brighter and brighter.

What is happening?!

"The moon moved." The first woman sighs.

But it doesn't feel like the moon. It feels like the sun. It feels like you're on the other side of a bomb blast, a brutal rising dawn scorching everything it touches.

Your skin erupts in stinging sweat, and you know, if you keep looking, in just a few moments, the blood you're carrying will begin to bubble and boil like a witch's cauldron.

It's not just the spotlight now. Other, smaller holes are opening up around it.

Someone's smashing through the darkness, coming for you, and you only recognize the pop pop pop of gunfire after you feel searing pain tear through your body and—

My eyes flutter open.

I try to catch my breath. What I just saw was so strange, so intense, that I can't process what's currently in front of my face just yet.

Barely an inch away from my nose is a thick, hairy arm.

I hear murmured pleasantries, but it's not enough to keep me from starting in my seat. I jerk away from the intruding arm, which only results in me bouncing off my seat and lurching forward again, colliding, and the next thing I know, my chest and crotch are doused in cold, stinking liquid. It's momentarily welcome, a reprieve from the hot flash that's simmering up in my chest, but then I recognize the stinging smell of vodka, the thick, peppery stench of tomato juice.

A Bloody Mary.

The man in the seat next to me and the flight attendant perform apology well. They dab me with napkins, they offer condolences. The flight attendant asks me if I'd like something to drink—and I really would—but when I look up at her, I see she's about my age, and her face instantly becomes a bloated, rotting corpse, so I go quiet, look away, dig my fingernails into my armrests.

At least I kept my journal out of the splash zone. I stow it back in my purse. No more writing today. I sit, hot, sticky, and stained. I know I should go to the bathroom and try to clean myself off, but

(there's a mirror in there)

I don't. Instead, I blast myself with the air-conditioning nozzle right above my head.

Exhaustion still grips me. I want—*need*—more rest. But now I'm too unnerved and spooked to fall back asleep. I've never had a Dream quite like that before. It started out so familiar and then . . . Who were those nude women? Why were there so many of them? What does it all mean?

Memory is a mansion.

He's coming.

The moon moved.

The man next to me, sipping on his replenished cocktail, has earbuds plugged into his armrest. My eyes drift to his screen.

He's watching some sitcom, all primary colors and exaggerated expressions. The volume is high enough that I can hear the melody of the line deliveries. He guffaws with laughter right on cue, along with the canned audience on-screen.

Most canned laughter on sitcoms is made up of dead people. I forget where I learned that. The sound cues were recorded decades and decades ago. Most everyone in that audience would be dead by now. But they're still laughing at the antics of the living. Isn't life a funny thing? Ghosts must find us hilarious.

Mr. Manspreader continues spreading his way into my seat. Metastasizing. Soon his arm is bent and jutting over our shared armrest, his legs are open wide and jouncing up and down, shaking the floor and occasionally stomping on my foot.

By the time we land, I've moved on from thoughts of stabbing him with my pen (*it would fit so nicely in his carotid artery, like one of those holes in the counter at the bank*) to wondering how many other people in the cabin I could get to as well before they finally took me down.

I watch myself get through at least a whole row or two. Stab. Stab. Stab.

And that's how a bloodied Mary arrives back in Arizona.

7

The Memory Mansion

You're bleeding," the giant cab driver says to me from the front seat, the first words out of his mouth since we got on the road.

"It's just tomato juice," I start to say. Then I feel wetness on my upper lip. The tip of my finger comes back red and shining. A pool of actual blood has begun to drip from my right nostril. Oh God.

There are tissues in my purse. I try to keep my head positioned in a way that will prevent blood from dripping anywhere while I fish one out (not that I should care—my clothes are ruined from that damn drink spilled all over me). It only takes a few dabs to blot the blood away. Just a momentary leak.

"Thank you," I say.

"Dry air," the driver says. Grunts, really. "Happens. Especially to tourists."

I'm enough of a New Yorker to quietly bristle at that; I am not a *tourist*.

You sure about that, Mary? The way you've been gawking out that window? You sure look like a tourist. You're acting like you've never seen the desert before.

That's a fair point—I guess I have been a bit enthralled. But that's also not entirely accurate. It's not like I've never seen the desert before. It's more like . . .

What?

Like I can't believe I forgot about it. How did I forget about the desert?

It stretches out, infinite and implacable, strange and yet more familiar than my own name. Its beauty is unquestionable—but I would never call it beautiful. There's a drabness, a scrubbiness to everything. Like an over-exposed Polaroid left out in the sun.

Even the man-made structures are light brown, heat-bleached. The foliage is sparse, thin, ragged. And yet, the longer you stare . . . each stubborn bush and tree, each rock and pebble . . . and that blue-white sky!

After years of trudging, head down, through New York City, I had forgotten the sky! *This* sky. So different from the one I've grown used to. There's just . . . so much of it. The New York sky is a refuge, a thing to be sought and cherished. *This* sky is dizzyingly vast. The New York sky allows towers and buildings to crowd its space. *This* sky keeps mountains, actual mountains, at bay. The first word for this sky that pops into my head:

Unapologetic.

"You know, you're lucky you found me," the driver says after another lengthy silence.

I meet his eyes in the rearview. "Why's that?"

His large neck gives a subtle tic. "Not a lot of people know Arroyo. Not a lot of people drive out this way. So you're lucky."

I don't tell him I found him after I asked several other cab services and they were all too expensive. I could see just by looking at him, at his schlubby clothes and stringy, oily hair (extruding from under a twill cap), at his hand-painted sign proclaiming simply "Taxi," that he'd be more affordable—and I was right. Truth be told, he kind of creeped me out. Still does. Those eyes have an avid look to them that's very off-putting. Especially when they flick back to find me in the rearview mirror.

"I guess I am," I say.

"Where ya coming from?" There's something unpleasant in the way he asks me this. I can't quite put my finger on why. It's like he's reading the question off a checklist.

"New York."

More silence. And even though I don't want to engage in conversation either, I add, "I'm visiting for work," a few beats later, as if I'm trying to give him an excuse to ask follow-ups.

"Work, huh," he deadpans.

"Where are *you* from?" I ask. "You're not from around here either." His accent is unmistakably Midwestern. Or maybe Canadian?

He doesn't answer at first. His eyes flick back up at me, scanning me.

At last, he says, "Bemidji."

"Come again?" That's just a collision of sounds to me.

"Minnesota."

"Oh, wow. What brought you out here? Sick of the cold?"

"Religious reasons."

"Oh." I clamp my mouth shut. I don't want to pry into personal matters. Doesn't get more personal than religion, does it?

"She's a harsh mistress," he says.

"Pardon me?"

"The desert. Nothing like the desert."

"Oh. Yes—"

"She demands sacrifice. She's cruel. She's beautiful." He says it all so matter-of-factly, he might as well be describing the technical specs of a new car. "I don't see how anyone could come out here and not . . . bow down to her. Do anything to get to get on her good side."

"Huh." I hope I sound like I'm considering what he's saying. So much talk of supplication and cruelty; I bet this guy's real special with the ladies.

But what he's saying also makes a certain amount of sense. I know there are enclaves of all sorts of religious sects scattered across the wilds of this state. And honestly? Coming back to this environment, this landscape, this heat (even now, in April, the car feels like an oven), I kinda get it. There's something primal here. Something magical. I can feel it through the window glass.

"That part of your work?" he asks. His weirdly reptilian eyes make a gesture in the rearview that seems to indicate the book in my lap.

My journal. I'd taken it out as the airport receded behind us to jot down the phrases and images from my dream on the plane that were still stubbornly stuck in my brain. "You a writer?"

I almost laugh at that. Imagine me having artistic aspirations.

Although . . . I did once, didn't I? Another faint notion I haven't thought about in years. Another flickering room in the memory mansion.

"Yes," I say, enjoying the irony, picking the journal back up and flipping to the page I'd been scribbling on. My Dream notes. "I'm a writer."

"What kinda stuff do ya write?"

I'm about to say, "Memoirs"—am, in fact, proud of this little joke—when I look down at the page and see, just beneath the phrases I wrote down (*Memory is a mansion, He's coming (who?), The moon moved*), several lines of text I cannot account for at all.

the dry and brutal all-consuming desert the sere is the truth the song of life i shall sing it truly sing it with me my brothers and sisters

What the hell does that mean? And when the hell did I write it? Did . . . did my hand write on its own while I was staring out the window?

"Mysteries," I tell the cab driver, still looking at these strange words. Then I start to feel myself getting carsick, and so I look back out the window.

Almost all signs of the metropolitan world have fallen away. Once again, I've found myself lost in the brown blur of the desert when I feel the unmistakable sensation of someone watching me. But not from the rearview mirror. From behind me. It sends a faint spark through my back and shoulders.

I turn around in time to see a dusty red sedan pass us by in another lane. Was someone . . . ?

"Shouldn't be much longer," the driver says. "Almost there."

I could've sworn I saw, for the briefest of moments, someone in the back seat of that car, hands pressed on the glass, watching me. And was it my imagination, or did they have something white pulled over their head . . . almost like a hood?

You're being stupid, Mary. You're thinking of that damn Dream.

Probably. But I crane my neck to see if I can catch a glimpse of the car one more time anyway—and then I gasp out loud.

Off in the distance is my memory mansion.

We've just crested a hill, and as we head down the sloping earth, the side of a nearby mountain, maybe fifteen or twenty miles away, is revealed. High on the side of that mountain, reaching for that unapologetic sky: an enormous, rectangular, yellow, black-gabled house.

It's the building I always picture when I think of that phrase. It's an actual, real building!

It's glaringly noticeable, even this far away. And, suddenly, in the pit of my stomach, viscerally important. I can't take my eyes off it. The way it looms over everything. It's a house that demands your attention.

"Excuse me," I ask the driver in the loudest voice I can muster. "What's that building?"

"Say again?"

"What's that building out there? The big one up on that mountain?"

"That'd be the Cross House."

The Cross House.

And in my version of the mansion—my own personal memory mansion—another light is switched on. A room I haven't visited in decades.

"It's huge," I say inanely.

"Town uses it for all kindsa things. The ground floor's the hospital. Town hall. Private school. It used to be the—"

"Mayor's house," I finish for him.

He looks back at me through the rearview again with his unnerving, avid eyes.

"Wait, did you say you've been here before?"

"I've just . . . heard about it. I know Brenda Dotson. She's a friend of mine."

Suspicious silence. Then: "All sorts of stories about that house," he says. "Myths, I guess. Fascinating place. The Cross family . . . they did some great things."

I can feel another memory trying to come to me, but the wiring is faulty. Before I can chase it down, I have that feeling of being watched again.

I look to my other side as an eighteen-wheeler barrels past us.

And was there someone looking at me in the passenger seat? Hands pressed against the glass?

Before I can get a better look, a growing swirl of dust suddenly tick-tacks against the car.

"Been a hot spring," the driver says. "Windy. Lotta dust devils. And a couple of big whaddya-call-'ems. Haboobs." He chuckles to himself, and I realize that whole little monologue was for his own benefit, not mine. "Funny word."

The dust clears, and there's the Cross House again. Getting closer . . . and closer . . .

Ten minutes or so later, after coursing through what might be residential streets or a long-abandoned ghost town, we pull to a stop in front of a forbidding-looking house behind a chain-link fence like a safari tour pulling up in front of a dangerous animal enclosure. Nadine and Brenda moved houses at some point over the past few decades, so I don't recognize the exact area . . . but the menace in the air feels familiar enough.

Before I work up the courage to open the car door, I realize I've written another completely unintentional phrase in my book.

There's a corpse in the bathtub.

8

Nadine's House

Nadine's house looks like pretty much every other house in the area: a squat, untended, one-story ranch behind a broken wire fence, everything the uniform color of dirt and neglect. There's an uneasy "knock on this door at your own peril" vibe to it. You can almost hear the house growling.

"Do you mind if I—"

The driver pitches an ear toward me. "What's that?"

"I was just . . . Do you mind waiting? I'll just be one sec, I have to go get your fare. I'll leave my bags here."

His eyes move up and down me through the mirror in a way that makes my skin crawl. Then a shrug and what might be a smile. "Do what you gotta do."

Well, *that* would be running as far away as possible, Mr. Driver Man. Telling you to step on it, let's beat tracks and get the fuck outta Dodge—

Mary, I imagine my Loved Ones saying from inside their suitcase. *Aunt Nadine needs your help. Don't be so selfish.*

Also, I remind myself as I put my journal back in my purse: I'm not just here for Nadine. I'm here for me. I'm here to reconnect with who I am. *Why* I am. I need this, too. If I'm ever going to feel normal again.

I open the car door. That dry, warm desert air hits me again. The decades since I left this town are kicked over the horizon and fade away. I vaguely remember a city, an apartment, a bookstore, but those memories seem thin and irrelevant, a dream I forgot to write down.

The gate in the chain-link fence opens with an outraged shriek.

The yard is all gravel and dirt, but there's a short path to the front door made up of broken pavement squares that give the impression of a crumbling bridge high over craggy mountaintops. There are a few spiny yucca bushes and ocotillo cacti on the outer edges of the yard and, largest of all, a crucifixion thorn tree that offers some incidental shade over the house. There's a plastic bag caught in the tree's pointy branches, and it rattles in the breeze. The tree looks dead or dying, but that's the thing about desert plants: they can look like that for a long time before springing healthily back to life upon first rainfall. Plus, no matter how close to death they might actually be . . . they can still hurt like hell.

Am I really going to do this? Not too late to turn around.

There's an aluminum screen door in front of a white wooden one. I pull the first one forward, and then I give three hollow raps on the wooden one. No answer. Only the rattling of the plastic bag in the tree behind me.

After a few moments, I knock again.

"Aunt Nadine? Hello?"

Nothing.

The doorknob turns in my hand, and I push open the door.

Two things rush at me at once: darkness and stink. It's as if someone has thrown an unwashed blanket over my head. I'm reminded of subway cars, the ones noticeably emptier than the rest of the train for reasons that become apparent the second after you step inside. My eyes will adjust; it'll take more time for my nose.

I call out again. "Hello?"

Silence.

Then I see the body. Lying facedown next to a cantered oxygen tank on the stained wall-to-wall carpeting. A garish plastic flower lies next to the scene like a hastily discarded murder weapon.

"Aunt Nadine!"

The sounds of my knees pop with firework resonance in this quiet space as I kneel next to her. I'm calling her name, shaking her, all the while my head has erupted in a dissonant chorus—

She's dead, she's dead / This is great news / This is so sad / Thank God / What do we do

—but all goes immediately silent when I hear a thick, groggy: "Wuzzuh?"

Nadine twitches, blinks, coughs a thick, phlegmy cough.

"Are, are you—" I'm going to ask, "okay?" but Nadine is already grumbling.

"The fuck you shaking me for? The fuck, *stop*."

"You were on the floor; I thought you were dead!"

"I was napping!" she grunts, swatting at me. "Dead? Jesus. Fell asleep waiting for you. Took you fucking forever."

She plucks the upside-down flower—something like a daisy, only purple and pink with an unnaturally orange heart—and sticks it into her messy, white-yet-yellow hair, behind her right ear.

"I . . . It's a long flight, and . . ." I swallow. "I have a cab waiting outside. Do, do you have any cash I could give him? I only have a little—"

"Yeah, I keep a roll of hundreds up my snatch while I sleep; it's good for my lower back."

My lip curls again. "Aunt Nadine, I just need to pay—"

"*So go pay the cab, dummy.* I didn't tell you to take a car service. You *just* got here and *already*!"

With great effort, Nadine gathers herself and her oxygen tank and heaves both into a massive recliner that looks to be made from the same fabric as the carpeting. It rocks with her weight and makes a weak, submissive squeal. I empathize.

Once Nadine settles, she reaches over to the end table with an operatic groan, picks up a pack of Capri cigarettes, pops one in her mouth, and flicks a pink lighter to life at the tip. I watch this, rapt and disgusted, as one might watch a vulture pull apart a particularly grisly bit of roadkill. Then I say with a sigh:

"Okay. This is fine, this is . . . just fine."

I make my way back out into the blinding sun.

My heart is pounding. I'm a few dollars short of the full fare. Nothing for tip. And that's officially all the cash I have. There's just my debit card and the meager balance it can conjure forth.

The driver is still sitting behind the wheel, staring out at his mistress desert. The car is idling contentedly, and the window is rolled down. "This the right place?"

"Unfortunately." I hand over the cash. "I'm really sorry, the tip is not . . . what it should be, but—"

He counts the bills, then looks back up at me. "That was a long drive, you know."

"I'm so sorry, I just wasn't expecting to—I thought Nadine would have—" My voice hitches in my throat. I suddenly feel like I'm about to start crying or screaming or I don't know what, bolt like a horse in a thunderstorm. "Please don't be mad."

He thumbs through the bills again and then leans over to the passenger seat to put the money in the glove compartment. While his head is bent, I can't help noticing a faint tattoo near the base of his neck, hidden by his collar. It looks like an eyeball. That thing was pointed back at me the whole ride.

Maybe *that's* why I felt like I was being stared at . . .

He straightens back up. "You said you're here for work, right?"

"Yes!" I exclaim a little too brightly. I want to assure him I'll have money soon, whenever I get paid, but then something in the back seat catches my attention.

Someone is sitting there. Wearing something white. A hood?

Then I blink and—no. Nothing. Just my bags.

There's a corpse in the back seat.

Ha ha. Get a grip, Mary.

"That's good," the driver says. "Then I'm sure I'll see you around."

Even though there's a threatening edge to his voice, I give him my best Good Girl smile. "Absolutely. Thank you."

I glance into the back seat one more time. Unoccupied. Probably just a cloud reflected in the glass. That unapologetic sky. I open the door and pull my bags out, and the driver barely waits for me to close the door before throwing the car in gear and peeling off. Dust kicks up and practically spits in my face. I wave it away, watching the car as it disappears, and for the second time in as many days, I have that awful forgotten-at-the-school-field-trip feeling. I'm on my own here.

Then I notice:

The Cross House.

Still visible. Even from here. Perched up the mountain. A giant, yellow monstrosity of a building. Majestic. Dominant.

I can't believe I forgot about that place.

I turn and look back at Nadine's.

"Okay," I say, sounding very much like a prayer. "Let's go see what else I forgot about."

9

Readjustments

My eyes have to readjust to the dark again. There's also a dirty haze of smoke filling the room now; it's like Nadine managed to suck up an entire pack of cigarettes in the few moments I was outside. Not out of the realm of possibility, actually.

Thick blackout curtains are drawn against the front windows. No wonder it's a tomb in here.

"Should we maybe open those up?" I ask the silhouette sitting in the massive recliner. "Get some light in h—"

"Don't you fucking dare," the shadow in Nadine's chair says back to me, smoke billowing out. "I don't need anybody snooping in here. And, by the way, don't go bringing any more strangers here either, okay? It's dangerous."

"Okay. Should . . . should you be smoking like that?" I ask.

"It's the only way I know how," she says with a purring lilt and draws a long drag. The cherry-red tip of her cigarette glows in the gloom, a single, hovering firefly.

We stare at each other. Details start to come into focus. Besides her garish plastic flower, she's wearing a faded pink sweatsuit, long-sleeved, a yellow-and-purple flamingo emblazoned on the top.

"It's good to see you," I offer.

"Yeah, it's something," Nadine muses.

She has a thin book in her lap: black, hardbound. A glowing UFO slants across the cover. I recognize it immediately. Time-Life *Mysteries of the Unknown*. She hasn't changed one bit.

She props the book up as if to read—but her eyes stay on me.

"I mean, how long has it been?" My voice pitches itself high, somehow sounding older and younger at the same time. "A few decades, at least. Can you believe it?" I'm trying too hard to be polite and conciliatory.

"Time fucking flies."

"You look good."

Nadine cocks a thin, drawn-on eyebrow. "Wanna try that again?"

"How are you feeling?"

She coughs, long and hard, then clears her throat in a loud bark. "Best shape of my life."

"How . . . how long do you . . . Did they give you a diagn—?" I can't find a polite way of asking when it is she's expected to die.

"Did you just have a stroke?" she asks flatly. "Were those words?"

"Yeah. Or no. Or— Fine." I throw my hands up. This is pointless. If I was looking for any red flags that this trip was a mistake, here's an entire goddamn flag warehouse. "I'm here. What can I do to help?"

"Maybe ease up on the questions first? Jesus. Just woke up and it's real weird seeing you, standing here. This is a lot to process."

It takes me a beat to realize I've been looking at her face without incident. Her deeply wrinkled skin, her leathery, sun-and-smoke-damaged face, look as dry and immovable as gnarled oak. Of course: she's old enough to be exempt from my little problem. Lucky me, of all the faces I can freely look at . . .

"Can we at least turn on a lamp or something? It's so dark in here, Aunt Nadine."

She leans over with another Oscar-worthy groan and turns on the floor lamp next to her chair. Soft light the color of old egg yolks fills the room.

I bite my tongue to keep from making a comment on the state of things. Holy shit.

"The maid's on vacation," Nadine says with a chuckle.

The maid's standing in front of her, I think.

There are books. Clothes. Trash. Cigarette cartons. Food wrappers. Cans.

"When was the last time you cleaned this place, Aunt Nadine?"

"That's Brenda's job, but she and me haven't been getting along too well lately, so."

Can't imagine why . . .

"This looks like a nice house, though," I say, practicing my most gracious smile. "Bigger than your last one."

"Yeah. I thought maybe more space would make Bren less crabby. Guess it worked for a little while. Try not to burn this one down, okay?"

That doesn't even make sense. She's trying so hard to be cruel. I swallow it down. A hard, hot stone lands in my gut.

To show her how little I'm affected, I start picking up the largest, most organizable items first. My knees, my back, groan in protest—bending and snatching isn't fun, especially after hours on a plane and in a car.

Everything I touch feels as if it's been lightly glazed with a still-drying layer of glue. It's disgusting.

The mess and the grime are so omnipresent that the one clean spot in the room is glaringly noticeable.

Back in my apartment, I have my sacred little bookshelf full of Loved Ones. It seems Nadine has her own sentimental real estate: a large bookcase jam-packed with books.

Not just any books, though. You can see from the spines, even at a glance, that all these books cover pretty similar territory: the occult, extraterrestrials, ghosts, demons, psychic phenomena, cryptids. There are even more than a few books on mystical religions and Celtic, Roman, Hindu, Greek mythologies (appropriate, since cleaning this place is the sort of task you call Hercules for). Then I remember: Wasn't Nadine a professor of mythology at some point in a previous life? Before she went full Cantankerous Shut-In?

"I work in a bookstore, you know. In New York. We have a whole section for books like those." From my strained and crouched position, I point to the one she's reading. "Sometimes they make me think of you. Whether I want to or not, ha ha."

I don't like how reedy and desperate that laugh sounds coming out of me. I'm nervous and overcompensating.

Nadine takes a breath to propel whatever snide comment she's got loaded in the chamber, but before that can happen, I hear the jingle of metal, and suddenly, the biggest rat I've ever seen trundles its way toward me from the shadows. I make a startled sound—"Nnyeah!"—and fall on my ass trying to back away.

It's only when the rat stops by Nadine's chair and starts growling at me that I realize it's actually some sort of dog. A Chihuahua mixed with, I don't know, an old potato?

"This is Chipotle," Nadine says. She pronounces it *chih-poddel*. "My guard dog. Thank God for him, he probably kept me alive while I was waiting for you to get here. Stop growling, you little shit." She gives the ratdog a little tap on his butt, and he obliges. He doesn't stop glaring at me, though.

His whole body shakes with unmistakable hatred. "He don't like strangers. He's just like me."

"Hi, Chipotle," I say. The name sounds clumsy in my mouth; I'm pretty sure that's not how you pronounce it. "There's a dog in my apartment building, too. He's not very friendly. Sometimes I called him—"

"Jesus, we get it, Mary. You done trying to one-up everyone yet?"

Be a Good Girl, Mary. She's stressed and sick. Don't take it out on her.

"Fine. Just—fine." I give her a you-win gesture. "Just tell me where I can put my stuff, and then . . . let me know how I can help."

"That's a real nice attitude for a caregiver, Mary. Real nice." She stubs out the rest of her thin cigarette, then pops a fresh one in her mouth. "Down that way, make a right. It's Brenda's room, so don't change anything around, she'll lose a tit."

"Thank you." I pick up my bags and head in the direction Nadine pointed. "I sure hope her vacation's quick!" I add over my shoulder.

"What?" Nadine asks.

I don't answer. I make my way down the filthy carpeted hallway to Brenda's room.

Even before I walked into this disgusting house, a deep sense of dread had settled over me. Now that dread is stretching and splaying itself out, like I'm a hot rock and it's sunning itself.

What is Brenda's room going to look like? What am I about to walk into? When was the last time she cleaned anything? Am I going to be sleeping in actual filth?

I reach the bedroom door and, already wincing at the horrors that await me, I nudge it open. It creaks, like the world's oldest tomb, and I look inside.

My breath catches in my throat.

Sometimes the simplest things seem like miracles.

The room is pristine. The bed, neatly made. There's nothing on the floor or even in the closets. Nothing. It's like no one ever lived here before.

"Thank you, Brenda." I sigh and softly shut the door behind me. If she were here, I could kiss her.

If she were here, you wouldn't be.

First, I take my journal from out of my purse and put it on the nightstand by the bed. I need to spend some more time looking at what I wrote and figuring out what it means.

But first things first.

I lift my suitcases onto the bed and look around for a flat surface. The top of the dresser is free, so I unzip my suitcase and begin to delicately place each of my Loved Ones out on the dresser. It looks like they all made the journey unharmed, thank goodness. I don't know what I'd do if one of them broke.

"Hi," I whisper to each of them. "This is only temporary. Don't be sad. This is just for now. I swear. I—"

Movement catches my peripheral vision. Someone's in here with me.

I quickly turn to see there's a brushed bronze, antique-looking standing mirror to my right, in the corner by the door. In the glass is a haggard, old, useless woman, frazzled hair, stained clothes, pathetically talking to tiny statuettes. Her skin bloats and erupts in pustulant, pinkish rivers, and the world around her begins to immediately fade. I stumble backward and throw my hands up to cover my eyes. No, no, no—

In excruciating slow motion, I realize too late I still had a Loved One in my hand, just in time to watch her fly up and out of my grip.

She's a little girl wearing a white mobcap and a red flannel dress, holding a picnic basket. Her name is Constance. She spins as she falls. I reach for her, but—

The sound her little body makes when she snaps in half against the floor pierces me in the gut.

Grief wells up in waves.

I want to cry, I want to puke—but there's no time for either. I hurry over to the bed and grab the first thing I can find: the top sheet. I throw it haphazardly over the glass. It only covers up the upper half, but at least it takes care of that horrid corpse-woman's face.

Look what you did, that awful inner voice seethes.

I want to protest: *No, it's not my fault, that's not* me *in that mirror.* Instead, I walk back to where Constance landed.

She lies there in two pieces. Blood has begun to ooze out of her, dark and red. I pick her up and feel the coppery slickness, warm and pulsing over my hands.

I blink. She's not bleeding. It's just my tears. I wipe them away, frustrated and furious with myself. Oh, Constance.

Then a curious thing happens.

In an instant, almost like one of my hallucinations, I see myself standing up, not even packing a bag, and just walking out the door. I find the nearest place of business, call another cab, and get the hell out of here. I go and live a life with no voices, no Loved Ones, no poisonous undervoice, no *commentary*. Fuck being Good. Fuck all of this. Sometimes in New York, you'll be walking down the sidewalk and a massive truck or bus drives by and blares its horn and you can feel the sound waves actually move through you, making your teeth rattle. That's what this is like, only there are no sounds, no words, just deliciously quiet certainty.

But, of course, I don't do that. I lay Constance on the shelf among the rest of my Loved Ones, their sea of perfect faces, and that vision fades away. I remember I *need* to be Good. To be grateful. Since I apparently have nothing else in my life, *that's* my purpose right now. My use. I've come here to help Nadine—I'm being selfish and awful, thinking of leaving her.

"I'm so sorry," I say. "Oh, I'm so sorry."

From the other room, Nadine lets loose a spasm of powerful, awful-sounding coughs. I crack the door open and stick my head out.

"Aunt Nadine? You okay?"

Nadine hacks some coughs that sound like an affirmative.

Chipotle must have been waiting on the other side of the door—as soon as it's open, he oozes his way into the room. He begins sniffing around until he notices my leg.

"What are you doing?" I ask him, and in response, he starts growling while lapping at the stains on my shin. I tell him to stop. I try to kick him away. His growls intensify. "Fine. Go ahead, you little jerk."

I stand there and wait for him to finish.

The covered mirror in the corner looks like a cheap haunted house ghost. I watch the damn dog in the bottom half of the glass, lapping away at my lower leg, and suddenly realize how grimy I am, coated in the remnants of the sweat and the drink and the recycled air.

"Aunt Nadine?" I call out again. "I hope you don't mind, but I'd like to hop in the shower quickly. It was a long flight."

More coughs, into which is nestled an incredulous, "You serious?"

"I'll be quick," I answer. "I just . . . I'll be quick."

Nadine hacks and spits somewhere—somewhere, no doubt, I'll have to clean later today. "Glad to see you're just as fucking weird as always. Bathroom's the next room over."

"Okay." I sigh to myself. I look back at my Loved Ones.

It looks like they're actively avoiding the dead among them.

10

Shell

As soon as I reach the bathroom door, the dog abruptly breaks off his pursuit of my legs and runs for the living room. Once I turn on the light, I can understand why. Poor thing; I'd imagine a strong sense of smell is one hell of a curse in this room.

I try to touch things as gingerly as possible—the entire room has been sprayed with mildew. The smeared and mottled taps, the slimy, splotchy shower curtain, the floor, everything. The bath mat might actually just *be* mold? The toilet bowl hasn't been cleaned in a geological age. I close the lid and flush the surprise someone left floating in the bowl.

The few decorative grace notes make the room that much grosser, acting as little reminders of what a bathroom should be. The framed drawing of a cat reaching into a fishbowl on the wall by the light switch. The—what is that, terry cloth?—toilet lid cover, pilled and faded, with calligraphic text reading *Après Moi, La Déluge,* a sentiment so unexpectedly smart yet so covertly disgusting that it could only appeal to someone like Nadine.

The tub is hidden behind a powder-blue shower curtain on rusty rings. The shower turns on, belligerently coughing water, and I realize I've come into the room unprepared.

"Are there towels?" I call out.

"There's already a towel in there!" Nadine bellows from the living room, and she's right, there's one towel hanging on the door. Old and used and soft as tree bark. "Unless you brought your own, we gotta go sharesies! Be warned: I floss it *deep*. Hahahaha!"

I force my gullet to stay where it is.

Avoiding the bathroom mirror, I drop my clothes into a pile and, Nadine's mocking laughter still ringing in my ears, stand there naked.

Suddenly, another room in my memory mansion gives a flicker. A childhood memory of shame and nudity. Laughing jeers. Cruel taunts. A feeling of deep, desperate, dizzying humiliation. And a name:

Anna-Louise Connerton.

My God, talk about a blast from the past. Anna-Louise Connerton. She used to make my life a living hell. It was her and Nadine both, working independently toward the same end of destroying every bit of self-confidence I might have once had.

Anna-Louise Connerton.

"She stole my clothes." I look down at my clothes now, hearing the shower and remembering it all in a rush.

We were eleven or twelve. I usually spent my lunch hour alone in the library, and that particular day, I'd gotten up to get another book when I bumped into a teacher—*dammit, I didn't see you there.* He spilled something all over me, coffee or soup (or maybe a Bloody Mary, ha ha), something wet and disgusting all down my hair, my neck. He didn't ask if I was okay, he just told me to go clean myself up. I went to the gym locker rooms, head down, walking quickly, trying not to be noticed, especially by the small knot of girls who were hanging out in private, giggling. Anna-Louise and her two sidekicks—what were their names? It was B-something and C-something, the ABCs, so stupidly appropriate. And the Cross House wasn't a school yet, so we were among the only children from Arroyo who went to *this* school. Our paths always inevitably crossed, no matter how I tried to avoid them, and they always made me pay.

They waited until I was in the shower, and then they stole my clothes along with any towels in the vicinity.

"I had to walk out onto the playground to find them. Buck naked. And everyone laughed and laughed . . ."

A ripple of gooseflesh covers my body, and I instinctively cover myself with my arms as I step into the shower. For the first time, I really, truly wonder if it was a mistake to come here. Maybe there are memories here I don't want to uncover.

Anna-Louise goddamn Connerton.

I run my hair under the showerhead, whisk water out of my eyes, stare at the mold-speckled tile in front of me. The warm water helps me feel a little better. My heart thuds a little less frantically.

I must zone out for a little while; there's an angry knock on the bathroom door.

"Shake a leg, Mary, that water ain't free."

Right. It's not free. It came at a cost. My standing here came at great cost. I make the water hotter.

"Anna-Louise Connerton," I whisper.

I can't believe I forgot about her. Then again, she was just one indignity among many. I can't possibly be expected to remember them all.

Suddenly, I'm overwhelmed with an intense pity for the little girl in my memory. That poor little weirdo, running naked through the hallways, crying, begging for her clothes amid a hail of laughter.

Why was she so weird? Why was she always such an easy target? Because people could sense it, smell it on her. That weirdness. That wrongness. And wasn't it at least partially her fault? She didn't try hard enough to be normal. And then all those years of isolation and loneliness, like dirt, like smog, they accumulated, layer by layer, into an invisible film. A protective shell. Like the body of an ant.

I don't want to be that way anymore. I want to be normal. Normal people have use. Normal people help others and are thanked and welcomed and cherished and loved. It won't be easy but that's the life I deserve.

I make the water hotter. As hot as it can get. I want it to be so hot it scours that shell off me.

Now there's pounding on the door. "Mary! I don't care how many folds you gotta wash, Mary, come on now!"

Okay, Aunt Nadine. I'm coming to take care of you. No matter how miserable and unpleasant you might be. I'm *here*. I am a Good person. A useful person. And I deserve Good Things.

I turn and face the water, closing my eyes from the spray, and savor one last cleansing blast. Then I shut the faucets off.

My skin tingles, raw and red. I hear the drain gurgling greedily, taking with it the old me, the shell, the insect carapace. Good riddance. I feel born anew. Ready to contribute and solve problems other than my own. Let me have them, world. *There's a corpse in the bathtub?* I've never felt more alive!

I wipe the water out of my eyes and turn around. My heart locks in my chest.

Someone is standing in the tub with me. Barely a foot away.

A woman.

Naked except for a white, bloody hood pulled over her head. A pillowcase. In the split second before I react, I see the impressions of eyes, of a mouth, the dented wetness of the gory fabric. Dark blood oozes down the woman's neck and chest in thick rivulets. She's making some sort of noise—not quite speech but I can hear a raspy voice, exhaling. I can't make any sense of it, though, because I've already begun to scream.

I stumble backward, my feet slipping. I have just enough time for one final thought in the moments between falling and cracking my head against the bathtub faucet. It follows me into featureless, pitiless black:

If only I had a shell.

11

Examinations

Two thoughts, simultaneously, like I'm caught in the middle of an argument:

I shouldn't be here I've been here before

The pain in the back of my head radiates outward like some spider, some octopus, some . . . I can't quite get a grip on the simile because the pain is too bad. But the pain's not as intense as the panic. Because, even though the world is tilted off its axis and even though I'm being squeezed by some great, multi-legged pain-thing, I know where I am.

A hospital waiting room.

And I don't have insurance.

I shouldn't be (I've been here before) here.

I'm not the only one unhappy to be here. Aunt Nadine is next to me, leg jiggling with anxious energy. She keeps nervously looking around, starting at every noise. When was the last time she was actually out of the house? She's so pale, so . . . unsocialized. I don't think I've ever seen her so out of her element like this before. So afraid.

Also, why the hell do I feel like I've been here before? I've never been here before. This hospital wasn't open when I was growing up—I only knew the Cross House as the big, boarded-up mansion on the hill. The Place Where Bad Things Happened. I never went inside—I couldn't have. Is it just that I've *emotionally* been here before, in this place of panic? That must be it. If my head didn't hurt so badly, I'd probably be halfway down the hill by now, in a full-on sprint. I can't afford a hospital visit. This is a disaster. I try to close my eyes to focus away the fog, but every time I do, I see *her* again.

The woman in the bloody cowl.

The wet gore in the center of her covered head. Every vein visible in her purple-and-green curdled skin. Her limp, sagging breasts, like balloons full of sand, hanging down over a midsection that was at once bony and soft. And her hands . . . They weren't hands at all, in fact, but red, raw, bloody talons, the fingers shredded and filed down to points that looked razor-sharp.

Just a hallucination. That's all it was, Mary. Just a holdover from that dream on the plane. You know it.

Right. Yes. True. But . . . it was so real. She was so unquestionably *there.*

"Where the fuck are you going?" Nadine asks as I lift myself out of my chair.

I don't answer. Despite the pounding in my head, I have to get up, have to move, have to get away from Nadine's antsiness.

What a strange hospital this is. We're on the ground floor, just to the left of the impressive main entrance, this massive rounded double doorway that very much looks like a mouth. It's the sort of entrance you'd expect to lead into a huge open lobby, maybe one with a giant wagon-wheel chandelier hanging from the ceiling. Instead, there's nothing; just abrupt walls forcing you to turn this way or that.

The waiting area itself is equally strange. I feel like I'm in the sitting room of some hotel or I'm resting during a walking tour of a historic land-mark. The trappings of an old home are still everywhere, in the exposed beams along the ceilings and walls, in the antique-looking furniture, in the lamp sconces above everyone's heads. Despite this, some of the room looks like a proper waiting room: a reception desk, a door leading farther into the building, presumably to exam rooms and who knows what else.

I've definitely never been in a place like this before. And yet:

I've been here before.

There are windows along one side of the room. I wander over. Beyond the Cross House's front yard the world slopes away, and the dirty, scattered buildings of Arroyo are revealed in the socket. Shards of a broken tooth.

Talk about *I've been here before.*

What new mess have I gotten myself into?

Speaking of the front yard, there's a man outside, tending to the lavender bushes, the ocotillo.

He must be a groundskeeper or a gardener or something. He stands on the large swath of extravagantly green grass stretching out in front of the main entrance—the sort of green that's only possible out here with concentrated amounts of water and chemicals. Only the elite keep their grass like this in the desert. It's an act of dominance over the nature around them.

The man stops, wipes the sweat off his brow, squints in the early afternoon sun. He's handsome in a banal, cookie-cutter way—he almost looks to me more like a politician than a gardener. That said, there's something sad and lost about his face, too. Must be because it's so hot out. And it's only April . . .

As if he hears my thoughts, he turns and looks toward the window. I could swear he turns and looks right at me. Impossible. He'd be staring into the glare of the sun. There's no way he'd see me on the inside of the glass. And yet it's like we're making eye contact.

"Hey! *Hey!*"

A woman's voice behind me makes me turn around. It's the redhead behind the reception desk. She's young, probably in her early thirties, with a round face that for some reason makes me think of the girl on the Wendy's logo.

"You can't do that in here," she's saying. I look over and see Nadine, still sitting in her chair, with a slim cigarette in her mouth, her lighter touching a trembling flame to its tip.

"You're making us wait so fucking long, I'm gonna accidentally quit cold turkey," Nadine says around the cigarette, "and then what would I do for a personality?"

"Put it out. Now." The receptionist's eyes glare at Nadine with a steeliness that makes me downright jealous.

Nadine obliges, grinding the cigarette out on a stack of magazines on an end table next to her. The ash leaves a Catholic blessing on the forehead of some generically perfect smiling idiot.

"You think that just because you're the only hospital around, you get to tell everyone what to do," Nadine is mumbling. "That's a monopoly, that's un-American, you know."

"Aunt Nadine," I say, walking toward her, "why don't we just leave? I shouldn't be here anyway, I don't have—"

"Ms. Mudgett?" a kind voice asks. I look up to see the door leading to the exam rooms has opened up, and a woman enters the waiting room. She carries a massive stack of folders. "Chantelle, can you add these to the File Pile downstairs?" She hands the receptionist the stack of manila in her hands. "I found them hiding in one of the exam room cabinets."

Chantelle accepts them with a grimace. "If that thing finally falls on me, you gotta say something nice at my funeral."

"Just hand them off to Eleanor," the woman—she must be a nurse—says. "She's the trained professional." Her voice is softly accented: a native Spanish speaker whose English is perfect. She looks back at me. She's about my age, with shining black hair tied behind her head in a bun. Several threads of gray add handsome detail. "Sorry to keep you waiting, Ms. Mudgett. We can take you back now."

Her face. The bubbling skin. The rage in my gut. I immediately break eye contact and look at the floor. Fuck.

"Okay," I squeak, barely able to hear myself.

"Be quick, Mary," Nadine grumbles to me. "We ain't safe here."

The nurse turns to her, concerned. "Did you want to come back with us?"

"I don't even wanna be *here*," Nadine sneers in response. "But at least I'm close to an exit. You gals have fun."

No fun is had, unless you consider the blood pressure machine a good time. But the nurse, who introduces herself as Nancy, is kind and sympathetic. She doesn't try to rush me or attack me with questions. I appreciate it, even though I'm hardly paying attention. All I want to do is stare at the walls, the carpet.

The exam rooms are just like the waiting room: strange double exposures of old-time hominess and medical professionalism. There's something uncanny about a gray examination table, covered in that crinkly butcher paper, sitting inside a rich, mahogany drawing room.

"You okay?" Nancy asks. "You went away for a little bit."

"I just can't believe I'm inside the Cross House," I say. "I was just admiring the building a few hours ago, and now . . ."

"Yeah," she says, a hint of dismay in her voice. "This place really is something."

I've been here before.

But no. I haven't.

Before the exam goes further, we're interrupted by a young man, tall and broad, with ginger-red hair and a close-cropped beard. He storms into the room, and the nurse jolts as if she's been caught doing something embarrassing.

"Dr. Burton, I'm still taking her—"

"It's all right," the doctor says. "Chantelle told me I should get a look at this one."

What a strange thing to say. No time to comment on it, though; he's already snapping on blue exam gloves and inspecting my head with all the care and sensitivity you might give an out-of-season melon at the grocery store.

He asks me if I'm still sore. I say a little. He asks me if I've ever fainted before. I lie and say I haven't. History of light-headedness? Low blood pressure? I can see where this is going. When was my last period? Here we go.

"Yep," he says, jotting down a note in my file, then snapping the folder shut. "It's not uncommon for menopausal women to experience the occasional vasovagal episode, especially if you like a nice hot shower. Look at putting some of those rubber nonslip pads in your bathtub for safety. Stay hydrated. Any questions?"

"Perimenopausal," I say.

"Sorry?"

"It's perimenopause. I'm not menopausal."

He stares at me with hard eyes, and for some reason, I remember the tattoo on the back of the cab driver's neck. "Right, right, no, you're correct." Then he looks at the nurse. "Pretty cut-and-dried, don't you think?"

"Her vitals all seem normal," Nancy says. I can hear she's a little flummoxed being asked like this.

The doctor turns back to me. "Ice your head, make an appointment with a gyno if anything feels particularly out of whack. But I wouldn't worry. It's a strange time for the body. A lot of changes happening. You'll be fine. You're just here visiting family, is that right?"

The change of subject is dizzying. "Um. Yes. My aunt."

"Right. So it's just the two of you now. Anyone missing you back home?"

"Um. What?"

Now his eyes are shining with either charm or malevolence—funny how similar they can look. "Just in case anyone's worried about you not feeling well. Because there's nothing to worry about." He smiles, no hint of either teeth or warmth. I try to smile back, but I seem to have forgotten how. Back to the nurse: "Finish up taking her vitals so we have them handy. But, like I said. Pretty obvious." He hands Nancy the file he was writing in and starts to leave.

I'm suddenly flush with panic. I have to say something—this could be my last doctor's appointment for the foreseeable future. I blurt out:

"But I think something's wrong with me! Like, actually wrong!"

He stops at the door. Turns. "Say again?"

How much do I tell him? All of it, I guess. Now or never. Without even taking a second to collect my thoughts, I begin to rattle off everything that has happened to me. The strange feelings, the anxiety, the hallucinations. How I can't look in the mirror or at other women anymore. How I'm writing things I don't understand. And how when I was in the shower this morning, I saw, or I thought I saw—

"Okay," he says, taking a step toward me with a hand upraised, "if you don't take a breath, you're going to pass out all over again."

I sputter to a stop.

"Good," he says, and gives a small but weary sigh, as if he's heard all this before. "Now, I'm gonna take a wild guess here. You haven't been sleeping. Right?"

"Well—"

"And you're experiencing mood swings? Sudden, intense sensations of heat? And just generally feeling like you're going crazy?"

"I'm *not* crazy," I say through gritted teeth.

"No," he says, "of course not. This is all natural, Ms.—" He looks to the nurse again.

"Mudgett," Nancy says.

"Ms. Mudgett," he says to me, not missing a beat.

"But I'm *seeing things*," I say, matching his quiet tone, but adding a brittle intensity. "Impossible things." I steal a quick look at Nancy to confirm, and, yep, her face begins to decompose right on schedule. I look back at Dr. Burton. "Is that normal?"

"Well, I wouldn't say it was normal," he replies. "But it's not abnormal. Especially if there are already underlying issues like schizophrenia; it's an exacerbatory experience." I must be making a face, because he gives me another of those tight-lipped smiles, a bad actor's approximation of kindness. "You'd know if you had those issues already, believe me. I'm sure we're not dealing with that here. Anyway, you said you're not sleeping, right? Lack of sleep can cause all sorts of hallucinations. Auditory. Peripheral. People think they're seeing insects that aren't there. Marks on skin that aren't there."

I think again of the driver's tattoo—could that have been imaginary?

"All the same," Burton continues, pulling out a prescription pad, "how about we solve this the old-fashioned way? Antianxiety? And maybe something for—"

"Trazodone," Nurse Nancy says. Dr. Burton looks up, surprised. Nancy doesn't show any embarrassment or apology from what I see in the quick glance I throw to her. "It's good for sleep and for the hot flashes." I feel her look at me. "Trust me."

"Well, you would know better than me." Burton scribbles on the pad. *Rip.* He hands me the slip of paper. "Look, I don't envy the experience," he says, and now he's talking to both women in the room. "But try to think of it as a second puberty. No fun. But natural. Glad you've come to spend some time with us in Arroyo."

He pats my arm, and like any of his other gestures of comfort, it's perfunctory, robotic. Again, I think of the driver—his small talk was the same way. Then the doctor's gone, the door closing behind him with a soft, but not considerate, click.

I sit there for a moment, numb, as if I'd just been slapped.

Nancy finishes taking my vitals, making small talk all the while. I barely hear her. Only one word rings through my ears over and over again:

textbook textbook textbook textbook

I don't realize I'm sobbing until I hear her break off what she's saying. She starts soothing me, apologizing for the doctor as if he were her responsibility. "His bedside manner sucks. Especially with women."

But, of course, it's not that. It's everything. It's too much. It's all hitting me at once. The job, the apartment, the plane ride, Nadine, her dog, my broken Loved One, the cheap Halloween ghost in Brenda's room, the goddamn dead woman in the bathroom.

I try to wave her away. "I'm okay. I'm okay. I'm okay," I keep repeating.

"Do you want me to get your aunt in here to—"

"*No, God, no!*" I sputter so abruptly that she actually laughs.

"Okay, I'm sorry, no aunt, no aunt."

That makes me laugh, too, which at least robs my sobs of their momentum.

She hands me a tissue, and we sit there in an awkward silence for a moment, me sniffling, dabbing, snorting, not making any eye contact whatsoever.

Then, around my best Good Girl apologetic grimace, I say, "I'm sorry, I'm just . . . not having a very good week. Health problems and money problems and . . ." I trail off. She's heard it all already. "I'm stupid, sorry."

"Don't apologize," she says sternly. "I know what it's like to be overwhelmed, believe me." After a moment, she adds, "If it's money, you know . . ."

"What?"

"Well, I was just going to say, you could always come work here."

"Here?"

"Well, not *here*. Downstairs, in the basement. We've got this massive pile of files down there. We call it—"

"The File Pile?"

"That's the one."

I can't tell if this offer is genuine or not. It's safer to assume she's just being polite. Besides, Brenda will be back soon; no sense in getting involved in anything other than helping Nadine.

"That's really nice of you to offer, but . . ."

"I know," she drops her voice low, "people around here can be kind of strange and . . . off. The last thing you'd want to do is spend any extra time around any of them. But it's nice and quiet down there. Just one other person, and she's really sweet. Unlike some other folks."

She doesn't know I'm from here. No reason to correct that impression.

"And actually," she continues, going to the cabinet and counter area, "I'm *trying* to make this place at least a little less unfriendly! Here!" She opens up the bottom cabinet. Next to her purse is a thick stack of paper. She pulls out a sheet and hands it to me.

It's a flyer. THE FIRST ANNUAL ARROYO EASTER EGG HUNT.

"I begged Dr. Burton to let me put it together, and he finally gave in. I actually live one town over, in Socorro, but ever since I started working here, I just wanted to try to lighten the mood, you know? Community is so important and everyone out here is so—wait a second." She goes back to my file, reads something, looks back at me. "This will be the day after your birthday! Happy almost birthday!"

I thank her.

"Well, now you *have* to come so we can sing you 'Happy Birthday.'"

"You're very kind," I say, staring at the flyer, with its adorable font and stock cartoons of eggs and rabbits. "I just . . . I don't think I'll be here that long. I'm only here to help my aunt while her daughter's on vacation. Once she comes back, I'll be heading home to New York. A week, maybe two."

There's a strange pause.

"Really?" Nancy asks. She's studying me, and I don't know why.

"What?"

"Oh. Oh, sweetie." She sounds like she just swallowed a bug.

"What is it?"

"Oh, *mi cariño*." She touches my arm as if preparing me for a terminal diagnosis. "Her daughter's Brenda, right? Brenda Dotson?"

"Yeah?"

"I don't mean to gossip, but . . . well, I *do* hear things. Everybody knows Brenda's been seeing a woman for the past few years, and I guess your aunt's, well, your aunt. Brenda's not on vacation. She and her girlfriend skipped town. For good."

"Oh?" Another Good Girl smile stretches my face. "Really?"

"Yeah," Nancy says. "I mean, I could be wrong, but . . . I'd be surprised if we ever see her again."

12

Creeps

Soft meat soaked in clotted redness.

It lands in front of me, quivering in its surrounding pool like a freshly extracted specimen on a surgeon's tray.

"Ta-da," Nadine says, lips clamped around a lit cigarette, probably raining ash down into the food. She stares at me. "What? Chicken cacciatore. Used to be your favorite, right? I figured what the fuck, maybe she still likes it."

I stammer my thanks, shocked more by the gesture than the unappetizing dish before me.

The simmering rage I've been feeling since leaving the exam room begins to abate. I've been so angry and preoccupied I didn't even notice she was cooking while I continued picking up and cleaning the living room.

"Well, don't get used to it," Nadine says, sitting down across from me. "I'm not gonna cook every night, but . . . well . . . don't nobody like going to the doctor, I know that for a fact. So. Figured you could use a little Betty fucking Crocker to the rescue. You eat up. I don't have much of an appetite anymore."

She pulls a long drag on her cigarette with a great sucking.

"Thank you," I repeat.

"Oh, you'll be thanking me, all right. I'm gonna need you on diaper duty once we're done. Been a productive day." She gives me a grin with her cracked, heavily lined lips, her teeth clamped down on the filter. *She's kidding. Please tell me she's kidding.*

I start to eat. Nadine pulls open a book with three massive letters on the cover: *ESP*.

"Yeah, nobody likes going to the doctor," she says, half to me, half to the book. "Especially not there. Hate that place. Full of creeps. This whole fucking town is full of creeps."

I take a few experimental forkfuls of food. It's not the worst thing I've ever had.

"Then why do you stay here?" I ask idly.

She looks up at me as if surprised by the question. "The whole world is full of creeps," she says. "At least I know how to stay ahead of this particular breed."

She sounds so confident, so cocksure. But there's a flimsiness to it. Thinking of her expression in the waiting room of the Cross House, too, I don't think I ever really appreciated how small and scared she is. Her cockiness is so obviously a defense mechanism. It's almost poignant. This is what the world does to some people.

I'm no different, of course. There's a reason I haven't confronted her with what Nancy told me yet, despite my boiling anger. I'm small and scared, too. But I need to say something; I can't hold this in. I take a breath and am about to speak when—

"That doctor, he's king creep, you know." Too late. "Him and his whole clan. They think they're all King Shit of Fart Mountain. I wouldn't be surprised if their family tree was a straight line."

"Nadine—"

"Oh, don't get all offended on me. They're a buncha psychopaths. And they've roped most of the whole town in on whatever they're doing. Including, hate to break it to you, that cabbie you were flirting with."

"What?! I wasn't flirting with anybody!"

"Believe me, I get no pleasure outta imagining the two of you grinding uglies. But there was some definite eye-humping happening there. Blech." She stubs out the remainder of one cigarette and lights up another.

It *was* a surprise to find him waiting in the lobby of the Cross House. I'd just come through the door from the back and was heading to the reception desk to handle my dreaded bill, and there he was, the same cap covering the same greasy, long hair, the same avid eyes, leaning over the counter and talking with Chantelle: the driver who'd taken me to Arroyo from the airport.

"Well, hi there," he said. "Guess you're seeing all the sights, huh?"

I blushed despite the unease he gave me. "Did you get another fare in town?"

"I *live* here," he said, humorless, as if I were unimaginably stupid. "How'd you think I knew the way?"

I didn't have an answer for him. Instead, I focused on not throwing up when I handed my card over to Chantelle to pay the first of, I'm sure, several fees I'll owe for this damn visit.

Ultimately, I guess it was a blessing having him be there. He was able to give us a ride back to Nadine's and save me having to carry her and her oxygen tank down the hill in the hot afternoon sun. But then, there was what he said as I got out of the cab . . .

"See you around town, Mary."

Had I ever told him my name? It felt like an icy finger briefly touching the base of my spine.

Nadine's right about one thing: creeps. They're all creepy as hell.

"Whatever," she grunts now. "At least it got us a free ride. Even though I meant what I said before: no strangers! From now on, you walk."

"It wasn't a free ride, Nadine. I had to start a tab with him. I'm going to owe him a lot of money."

"Fiscal responsibility's an important thing for someone your age to start learning."

"I'm almost fifty years old, Nadine! I'm not a child!"

"Easy, easy. Jesus, I forgot how you had no goddamn sense of humor."

We sit in silence for a moment. I pick at my food.

"I thought you said you were going to pay me for coming out here," I say into my plate.

"What was that?"

"Nothing."

Her eyes bore into me, then go back to her book. "I'm not made of money, Mary." She speaks rationally, disinterestedly. "I get my checks at the beginning of the month."

"It's already the ninth! Are you saying I'm going to be here until *May*? If I'm going to get paid at all?"

She ignores the question, turns a page.

More silence. I stab at the meat on my plate with my fork, push it around. It's now or never.

"Do you know Nurse Nancy?"

"The illegal? What about her?"

"She says there's a job. At the Cross House. For a few hours a day, doing some—"

"*No.*"

In a flash, her book is closed.

I knew she'd react like this: shocked and appalled. But at least it's a reaction.

"I have bills to pay, Nadine. Rent." Or, more likely, moving expenses.

"What the fuck were we *just* talking about?! Those people are no good! They're—"

"What? What are they up to?"

"I . . . I don't know! But it's bad shit, Mary! I need you here, with me, twenty-four-seven. It's the only thing keeping me safe."

"It'd just be for a few hours a day. I'm sure you could survive a few hours alone. You've got your guard dog, right? And you managed after—"

"I fucking said no, Mary." She bangs an open hand on the table, and my plate rattles in front of me.

Metallic adrenaline pools in my mouth.

"Are you *actually* going to be able to pay me?" I ask.

"Of course I am."

"Is Brenda *really* coming back?"

More than a beat. A (*textbook*) silence.

"Course she is."

"Are you even *really* dying—?"

I barely get the last word out. She's up in an instant, leaning over the table, and I don't even register she's slapped me until a second later when my ears start ringing with the impact.

It's not a hard slap. But it is stunning. When was the last time I was hit like that? I can't remember. *But it's not the first time, Mary.* No, it's not.

Almost as surprising as the slap is the look of guilt and regret that crosses Nadine's face.

"Shit. I shouldn't . . . I just." Something in her hardens. At the same time, I feel something in me regress. Retreat. Nadine gathers herself and straightens her spine. "No. For both our sakes. You're not taking some other job. I need you here, and that's that. You hear me?"

I do.

"I'm sorry," I say, barely above a whisper, still feeling that slap.

Nadine picks up my plate and dumps it in the sink. Her dog remains sitting under the table, where he's been this whole time, growling.

To make it up to her, I'm a Good Girl the rest of the day.

Nadine takes root in her massive chair, smoking and reading and coughing up various internal organs. I clean up the dishes and survey the sink, the counter, the kitchen floor. I make some more progress in the living room. The whole house needs a top-to-bottom scrub—maybe a light exorcism—but it's a good first dent, and I start to feel something like accomplishment.

Then I need to pee. Which is when I remember—

The bathroom.

In the tumult of everything that has just happened, I forgot about the bathroom.

My blood turns to ice water.

What do I do? Run outside to relieve myself against the side of the house? That'll be fun to explain to Nadine.

You're being ridiculous, Mary. Just go to the bathroom like a normal person. Nothing's in there. You know *this.*

The walk across the living room and down the short hallway feels miles long. Chipotle stays underfoot the entire time until, once again, I reach that specific door and he runs away, the jingle of his tags fading into the living room.

I put my ear to the door as if there's something to hear.

What am I expecting, a high, ethereal *boooo*? Someone singing in the shower? Of course it's silent. I reach out for the handle, then stop.

"What are you up to over there?" Nadine asks from her Barcalounger.

There's a corpse in the bathtub, I almost answer back.

"Just thinking about what to clean next," I finally say.

"Good luck with *that* room." Nadine chuckles. "It's fucking haunted."

I know she doesn't mean it literally. I know it's just a joke. But it spooks me just enough that I turn tail and run to Brenda's room.

I can think in here . . . and also hold myself to make the need to pee ease up a little.

Looking around, I have a moment of gratitude: at least *this* room won't require a deep clean. "Thanks for this one favor, Brend—"

Then understanding wallops me with a soft but forceful fist. I forget about the need to pee and the anxiety over the bathroom for just a moment.

Brenda left this room spotless. But it wasn't *cleaned*. It was cleaned out. Abandoned. The way a prison cell is spotless when it's time for a new inmate. Because Brenda isn't coming back. Nothing of hers remains; it's all my stuff. My suitcase still on the bed. My Loved Ones arranged on the dresser, the broken one arranged like a ritual sacrifice. My journal on the nightstand. The top sheet draped over the mirror.

It's seeing that sheet over the mirror that gets me moving again. I hate how it looks: a big, glaring neon sign, THIS WOMAN IS FULL-ON C-WORD. If I can have even one less question in my life, I'll take it. Even if the answer is that my dumb brain conjured forth an imaginary dead woman and I was pathetic enough to react as if it were real.

I head back to the bathroom. I'm sweating, so I wipe my palms on my pants before I push open the door and step inside.

The bathroom is empty.

All there is to see is the toilet, the sink, the mirror (which I keep in the periphery of my vision), and the bathtub, hiding behind its closed curtain, exactly where it was before.

I'd be lying if I said I didn't feel a kind of relief. Sure, it's probably a bad sign I had such a convincing hallucination . . . but at this point, I guess that's better than an actual dead woman. Right?

Speaking of relief, I close the door, flip up the toilet seat, sit down, and . . . *après moi, le déluge.* While I'm deluging, I look again at the tub.

Something's bothering me about that shower curtain.

A moment later, it comes to me.

Who closed it?

After I hit my head and blacked out, Nadine heard the noise and then helped me crawl out of the tub. I certainly didn't close the shower curtain. Maybe Nadine did, but it seems pretty out of character that she would have taken the time to pull it closed as neatly as it is now.

The air suddenly feels charged—and it's the kind of charge that only another body can create. Is someone—something—else in here with me?

"You're the dumbest woman in the history of dumb women, Mary," I whisper. "Stupid. Legendarily stupid."

Maybe I am.

So prove it.

"I will prove it." I walk to the tub and, with a forced laugh, pull the curtain back, still laughing. "I'll prove I'm a—"

My laughter dies.

The dead woman stands there, just as before. Naked except for the white, blood-soaked cloth covering her head. From underneath the hood, thick drips of dark, clotted blood ooze down the woman's sagging skin. Just-developed age spots freckle her flesh, rough scrub flanking the rampant rivers of her dark, purple veins. She's sallow, livid, bruised. Her breasts hang like old meat cutlets. A wine-stain birthmark capping the curve of her left shoulder, once probably loved, kissed, marveled at as so perfectly hers, now stands like an infection point, an insult, an inescapable proof that this corruption was once human.

The wet, clotted bloodstain is trained on me like an eye. A distinctly darker, wetter spot in the center acts like a pupil. She's looking right at me.

Something underneath the pillowcase is squirming. Shifting subtly.

I think I'm going to throw up.

"I'm not really seeing this." I close my eyes. Tighter. "You're not really here . . . are you?"

I open my eyes.

She's still there.

Her hands, which aren't really hands but long, red, devastatingly sharp-looking claws, flex as if they're breathing on their own.

A rattling comes from her throat. I remember in my vision on the plane how one of the hooded women gestured to my own pillowcase, the one I suddenly realized I was carrying, swollen with blood.

you might want to put that on

he's coming

"Is there something you're trying to say?" I ask and swallow hard.

Then the door explodes open behind me, and I bite back a scream.

"Outta my way! I'm gonna pop!" Nadine, her face open and wide with panic, bursts into the room and is pulling at her sweatpants while she awkwardly throws herself down onto the toilet.

"Ohhh yeah." She sighs. Then looks at me with a smirk. "Is it me, or does every trip to the bathroom become a fucking horror movie once you get to a certain age?"

PART THREE

DRY HEAT

A certain light was beginning to dawn dimly within her,—the light which, showing the way, forbids it.
—Kate Chopin, *The Awakening*

Even before the now-infamous Easter Massacre, the town knew murder and bloodshed. If I were the type of man who believed in such nonsense, I'd think the place was haunted.
—Special Agent Peter Arliss, *In the Dark with the Devil: One Heroic FBI Agent's Ground Zero Account of the Arroyo Easter Massacre*

13

Hometown Tour

APRIL 10, 2019

Running through pitch-black hallways . . .
   Manic, frantic freedom inside the cramped enclosure . . .
   Exhausting . . .
   Hunting . . . hunting . . .
   The spotlight, just ahead. Oh, how you want it. You crave it.
   Or is it the woman in the center you crave? Because she's yours if you want her . . . all yours . . . all yours . . . all—

I wake up sticky and sore and even more exhausted than when I fell asleep. The whole bed has that horrible dried-after-drenched feeling. Night sweats. Gotta love them (oh, do I really?).

I notice the door to the bedroom is cracked open a moment after I notice the smell. Unmistakable.

"You've gotta be kidding me," I mutter.

Nope. Someone has taken a small, dog-size shit in front of the dresser.

A low, rumbling growl comes from the doorway. He's looking in to see if I got his message. We make eye contact, and then he skitters away down the hall. Either Brenda always kept her door barricaded shut or this is Chipotle's way of showing me who's boss.

I feel my fists clench, imagining them around his furry little throat. "You fucking—"

Be Good, Mary. Be Good.

I force my hands to open and remind myself: Good Things come to Good Girls.

Nadine hands me a wad of somehow wet cash. I knew she had a reserve somewhere, but now I'm not eager to learn the specifics.

"Don't dawdle," she says from inside while I stand out on the front porch. She hocks and spits a massive ball of phlegm into the dirt outside before closing the door, locking herself back up in the tomb-like house.

It's a hot day, already at least in the mid-eighties, so I've taken one of Nadine's umbrellas—garish, loud, covered in an erratic print of fake flowers—to give me a little shade.

The sunshine is intense, but also, uncluttered as it is by smog and glass and steel, sweetened by a fine breeze and the scent of dry sage and creosote, it's as refreshing as cool, clear water. God, I missed the desert. How did I forget this?

That's a question I expect I'll be asking a lot today. Running errands will be a good excuse to take a little nostalgia tour around Arroyo. Prime the generators in the ol' memory mansion. Light some more rooms up in there.

I considered taking my journal with me—jotting down every memory that might flash through my head as I kick around town—but that's too much pressure. I'm just going to let whatever thoughts come, unforced, uninfluenced. That way I'll know they're real.

It's definitely not because I'm still creeped out by those mystery sentences I don't remember writing.

Despite everything—despite Chipotle's gift this morning, despite the confirmation yesterday that the persistent ghost woman in the bathtub is completely my imagination (Nadine was looking right at her when she barged in to pee, and she strikes me as someone who might say *something* if there's a corpse standing in her tub), despite the fact that I'm still sticky and grimy and can't imagine when I'm going to feel comfortable taking a shower again because of said persistent ghost woman—I'm feeling relatively good. I'm actually looking forward to meeting my hometown again.

Will I know where to go? I think so. I might lack for specific memories, but I remember the basic shape of the place.

Arroyo is like a snake. The Cross House is its rattle, held high and prominent, warning the world. Down in the foothills, the rest of the town coils in on itself, the body of the snake, a series of concentric, looping streets until you reach the head: the downtown "shopping district" and city center. Those terms are to be taken with huge barrelfuls of salt.

It's a simple enough layout, and despite the actual buildings being spread out, it's still a small enough town. If I just walk in a few concentric ovals, I should be able to hit a fair amount of real estate before winding up where I need to go. In some ways, this will be like the inverse of my Dream: wide-open spaces, walking at a leisurely pace. But still that sense of freedom. Still that sense of hunting. Zeroing in on Mary.

So, my sincerest apologies, Nadine: looks like I'm going to dawdle.

I'm so stupid.

Stupid and

(*don't say it*)

crazy.

It's an hour later. I'm walking as quickly as I can back to Nadine's now, almost jogging, huffing, balancing the umbrella handle and several plastic bags in my hand.

Why didn't I bring the journal with me? I should have brought the journal!

I leave the center of town behind me, the grocery store where I got Nadine's requested supplies, the annexed pharmacy where I filled my prescription for the trazodone (more of my money, gone). A Subway restaurant, a bar, a liquor store, a smoke store, a gun store—the paltry ingredients of Arroyo's commercial hub. The few people I saw looked just as weather-beaten and vacant as the buildings. I could hear Malcolm's voice in my head. *Blockbuster Videos . . .*

The few living people, that is.

"It's a literal ghost town," I say to myself and laugh, out of breath and more than a little manic as I hurry home like the devil's on my heels. A ghost town, that's funny.

It's accurate: the farther I get from the already sparse town center, the more it really does feel abandoned out here. The homes in the residential areas are ramshackle, ugly little things, very much like Nadine's. Most of the commercial buildings in the center of town are abandoned. Sand and trash collect in the corners of glass-and-concrete storefronts. Filthy windows look into empty commercial spaces, not even bothering to display real estate information for potential entrepreneurs. There's not even graffiti—except for a faded mural on the side of a building depicting a desert landscape at sunset with the words *"ELIAS SAVES"* and *"PURGATION"* and what looks like a target (or maybe an eyeball?) slashed over it with spray paint.

"But that's not why it's *funny*," I pant, eyes darting this way and that, on the lookout.

No, it is not.

No, the reason it's funny to say this place is a ghost town is because I've seen at least nine more dead women just like the one in Nadine's tub, standing around, watching me.

A literal ghost town, indeed.

14

Dead Women

I can't get to my journal until after dinner, when Nadine dozes off in her giant chair. I shake her awake and half drag, half escort her back to her bed. Chipotle bites at my legs the entire way.

Now I have the place to myself.

Now I can think.

I sit on Brenda's bed, my journal in my lap. Around my chest is a belt of anxiety drawn one notch too tight. I try one more time to dissolve the events of the day in the acid bath that is my rational brain.

I was just seeing things. Right? It was hot and bright out. My mind was running wild trying to come up with elusive memories of my former life here.

"Also, I hit my head *really* hard," I say to my Loved Ones and touch the still-tender spot where I collided with the tub faucet.

That all sounds reasonable. Simple. Gosh, put it that way, it's almost no wonder I saw nine dead women while out running errands today. Maybe ten.

All the same, I still want to write down every detail in case something proves useful.

Years and years ago, a shaggy-haired, bearded young man named Andy was the shipping manager at Keats & Yeats. He was barely more than five and a half feet tall and skinny as a twig, with a bafflingly deep voice. He also did an inordinate amount of drugs, and often, while he entered books into the store inventory, he'd regale the other employees with his tales of debauchery. Drinking bottles of Robitussin and running naked through Chelsea Piers. Taking mescaline and waking up confused in Co-Op City in the middle of the night. I remember overhearing him one time when he was talking about a particularly vivid evening on LSD, seeing shapes in the clouds, faces in the trees. One of the other employees asked him if the visions meant anything to him, and Andy said of course they did. They meant everything to him.

"Hallucinations are deeply personal things," he said. "There are no accidental fish in the deep sea, man."

There's a reason I'm seeing these obviously-not-there women.

There *must* be.

The first one was staring at me from a living room window as I walked past another nondescript ranch house. I had gone to seek out the spot where my parents' house had been to see if anything had ever been rebuilt on the ashes. Only problem was I couldn't quite remember where it was. I was wandering around a residential block, and I felt someone's eyes on me.

I figured I'd see some suspicious, paranoid, Nadine-like citizen of Arroyo glaring at the unfamiliar newcomer trespassing through her neighborhood. Instead, standing just inside the window, remarkably clear given the darkness inside, was a woman. Naked. Arms at her sides, hands blocked by the window frame. Fabric draped over her face, a deep, red, wet stain at the center, like Hell's own maxi pad.

It felt like an invasion—although, an invasion on me or on her I still can't say. I walked off hurriedly, telling myself I wasn't seeing what I thought I was.

The next one was far off in the distance, streets away, several minutes later. A quick and fleeting glimpse; I was almost able to convince myself the distant woman-shaped blur was a mirage. Until I walked two more blocks and there was a *third* woman standing just a few yards in front of me, next to an old, grayish-blue VW minivan cantered on two flat tires in the weed-pocked dirt.

At first I thought I must just be seeing the woman from Nadine's tub, following me like one of those wiggly blobs that can get caught in your eye from time to time. But no. This woman's body was different. More heavyset. A round belly, striped near the bottom. No wine-stain birthmark on her shoulder.

I blinked. Squeezed my eyes shut, tried to scrub them clean from the inside.

She was still there when I opened them.

I looked away. Looked back.

She was still there. Even though her face was covered, I could feel her eyes on me through her bloody fabric.

I walked away, picking up my pace, throwing glances back over my shoulder. She made no motion to follow me.

A handful of minutes later, yet another one standing on the side of the road, her nakedness, her mutilation, garish and glaring in the sunlight. Her skin was dark olive. She had a tattoo: a tiger or some other kind of snarling big cat curled around her hip. She just stood and watched me, as immobile as a streetlamp.

I'm writing down every detail now. Things like the tattoo. Or one woman's long, ugly scar along her right arm. As I do so, my heart pounds faster and faster. Seeing all this in writing, each heartbeat thrums *what is wrong with me what is wrong with me what*

Another one in the parking lot of the grocery store, peering out from a dusty station wagon. In the journal, I write, "Old car (Buick?), robin's egg fabric on head, thin gold chain around her neck. Couldn't tell if she wanted out or wanted me in."

My heart pounds faster and faster. My hands start shaking. I can't tell if I'm feeling the beginnings of a hot flash or a panic attack—they're so damn indistinguishable sometimes.

Mary. Breathe.

A reminder from my Loved Ones on the dresser. Calm. Cool. Unflappable.

Yes (*what is wrong with me?*). Breathe (*what is wrong with me?*).

You need sleep, Mary, the placid, dimpled smiles of my Loved Ones reiterate. *This will all go away after you've had some sleep. Textbook.*

Yes. I need sleep. That's all. Excitement begins to metabolize into shame. This is all just my run-down brain shooting off sparks. And what luck: I went to the pharmacy today! I almost forgot.

I bend sideways with a groan, pick up my purse from the floor, and pull out a brown paper bag. The contents inside rattle. I open up the bag and pull out a blue bottle with a white lid.

"Should I?" I ask the shelf across the room.

They look back at me as if to say, *You know the answer.*

I hate taking pills. I hate putting anything foreign into my body. But I guess now that my body itself feels so foreign, what choice do I have? I pop a little oval tablet into my mouth and try to work up some saliva. Then I gulp it down.

"Show me what you got, trazodone."

I settle against the wall and stare at my Loved Ones. Try to steady my breathing. I don't know for how long. But eventually . . .

. . . I can feel my pulse begin to slow . . .

It's like I'm an ice cube starting to melt, just a little, just enough to lose my too-rigid, anxious shape.

It's just me and my little statues. That's all that exists.

"Thank you," I whisper to my little collection.

We told you. Sleep. Don't be so dramatic. Don't be so needy. Don't be so weird.

"Be porcelain."

Exactly.

"I'm so glad I have you with me."

We know.

I started collecting my Loved Ones right after I moved to New York. I found my first one (Cynthia, the Goose Girl) in a Salvation Army while I was shopping for a heavier winter jacket. I was immediately pulled to her, I didn't know why. It was something about how calm, how sweet, how blessedly normal she looked. An oasis in that strange, bustling new place. She was just so cute, with her rosy cheeks and shiny, smooth—

"Faces." My voice is husky and slightly slurred. I feel drunk. "It all comes down to faces." The words slide out: *Dall cundannduh fazes.*

Faces. Corpses. Mirrors. Identity.

My own face—I don't recognize it in the mirror anymore. It feels alien. I wish I could peel it off. Stick a pillowcase over the bloody remains so only the clinging fabric has to know the truth.

"Sbecause . . . I look like her . . . and s'all her fault. Her fault for getting old and leaving me with him . . ."

That feels important. I try to sit up and write that down before it fades away . . .

But it's already fading and my body's too heavy and the pen is too big it's like a log I can't concentrate enough to even look at the page and this is not my body anyway my body was youthful and useful but it's okay i'll remember i'll remember because there are no accidental fish in the deep sea and i drop down and down to swim with mine.

Sometime later, my eyes flutter open. Or were they open already? Did I sleep? I don't know. I don't feel rested. I feel groggy and headachy and thirstier than a woman buried up to her head in hot desert sand.

I was supposed to remember something. What was it?

Also, what time is it? I never turned off the light, but the curtained window has been stained a slightly softer purple than before. A predawn color. Just past first light.

And my wrist . . . it's not quite a cramp, but . . . burning pain has wrapped around my wrist. I'm clutching the pen so hard it takes actual effort to let it go. When I do, I get a good look at the journal, still open on my lap, and it takes my breath away.

Pages and pages of text. Pages and pages . . . and pages.

Scrawled writing, sometimes left to right, sometimes up and down, sometimes jammed into the margins or doubled back on top of itself.

Drawings.

What have I done? The entire journal. Ruined. My God. I filled the entire book while I was in a daze. It's like the sentences I wrote in the cab, only spilling over everything. And like those sentences from my car ride, none of what I've written now makes any sense to me.

There's so much of it.

It starts out simply enough.

> *No one sees me. I am invisible. It's like I don't even exist.*

So far so normal. I recognize those sentiments. I'd imagine what follows is more insight into those nagging feelings of isolation and loneliness, but then, turn the page and . . .

> ~~The laws of God~~ *I reject*
> ~~the laws of men~~ *I reject*
> *I KNOW ONLY THE LAWS OF THE DESERT*
> *it takes it will give it demands <u>sacrifice</u>*
> *blood is the way i am the punishing hand*

That page is punctuated with a drawing of a saguaro cactus so zealously covered in spikes it almost looks hairy.

Another page is just one sentence, over and over and over again:

> *i am the observed of all observers*
> *i am the observed of all observers*
> *i am the observed of all observers*

i am the observed of all observers
i am the observed of all observers
i am the observed of all observers

Opposite that page, in huge, desperate script:

WHAT ROLE SHALL I PLAY TODAY DADDY

Something I do recognize: one page about halfway through has a drawing of an eyeball, very similar to the one I either saw or imagined I saw on the driver's neck. The eye peeks out of a jagged, zigzagging shape. An aperture in a wall or a fence post, perhaps? Surrounding the drawing, text swirls:

Ego
Identity
Begins with I
I
The Great Eye, through it, through me, through all things, what I see we see and who can prove otherwise mine are the only eyes with vision everything else is hearsay

None of it makes sense. And so many of the pages are so tightly crammed with text, in all sorts of directions, that even if I want to try, it'll take hours—days—to pore through all of it. Even longer to actually decipher it.

I slowly close the book, like closing the door on an active massacre and hoping the perpetrator doesn't notice, and set it down next to me.

I'm warm. Too warm. And, despite the grogginess and general feeling of hungover paralysis, I feel cooped up and claustrophobic. I need to move. I need cool air on my body.

I tiptoe through the house, past the sounds of Nadine and her dog snoring in concert from the other room, and out to the front yard.

Much better. The air is refreshing on my skin, in my lungs. I let out a few deep breaths. I don't feel drunk anymore, but I still feel different. Dazed. Dizzy.

Off in the distance, a yellow-painted sun that emits no light, the Cross House looks back at me. My memory mansion.

You're getting closer, Mary.

That's not my imagined voice for my Loved Ones, nor is it the under-voice, but a calmer, deeper, *realer* voice. And it's correct, isn't it?

I *am* getting closer.

I don't know to what, but I *do* know this:

I dreamed of the Cross House. Didn't I? When I was on the plane, when I first saw these mysterious hooded women and we looked through the wall into that well-appointed room? That can't be a coincidence.

"There are no accidental fishes in the deep sea," I mutter, staring at the mansion.

Every instinct in my body tells me this is so. Start *there*. Answers might be *there*. Because hallucinations are personal things.

And also because, unlike the apparitions I've seen around town or the decomposing faces, I know for a fact that the Cross House is *real*.

There's just one thing I need to do first.

If I'm brave enough.

"Huhwhuzzuh?" Nadine sputters, understandably confused when she wakes to find me crouched over her in her bed.

"Shhh." I keep both hands on the side of her face so she focuses on me.

In a calm, soothing voice, I explain to her that I'm a grown woman, that I need the space to make my own choices, that I'm here to help her out as best I can, but that doesn't mean I have to put my own well-being at risk. I appreciate her concern, but I *will* be taking the job at the Cross House. I have my reasons, and she needs to respect that. Does she understand?

"O-okay," she says. "Got it. Sounds good."

I thank her for listening and for seeing my side of things. That's what it's going to take for us to get along. Communication. Respect.

I climb off her and leave the room. Chipotle, curled in a little ball at the foot of her bed, is now also awake, and he's growling at me. His little eyes shine like polished coins.

It's not until I get back to Brenda's room (closing the door behind me in case Nadine wants to come say anything nasty to me) that I notice I have something in my hand.

My broken Loved One, Constance. Well, half of her. I'm glad I noticed because the part of her where she broke in two comes to a long, jagged point, sharp enough to slice through skin without much effort. I could have really hurt myself.

Did I have this with me in Nadine's room just now?

No. No, that would have been awful of me. That would have been Bad.

After all, if I'd had this in my hand, with the way I was holding Nadine's face? That jagged, ceramic shard would have been resting right against the soft surface of her eye.

15

First Day on the Job

APRIL 11, 2019

"I told you about this, right?" Nancy is asking me. She's picked up a flyer for the Easter egg hunt off the pile sitting on Chantelle's reception desk. Before I can answer in the affirmative, Nancy winces. "Wait, no, I already did, sorry!" She puts the flyer back down. It doesn't look like many have been taken—the stack is too neat. "I'm just trying to make sure everyone knows, and it's easy to lose track. Did you know people need to hear something seven times before they really consider it? Seven times! It's going to turn me into a robot!"

She's nervous. You'd almost think she was the one starting a new job, not me.

I can feel Chantelle's eyes boring into us as she smacks gum.

Nancy continues, "I've been reading books on marketing and advertising lately. Maybe I'll go back to school. I don't know, I'm rambling. Let's go downstairs."

I'm not looking at her face—which is why my eyes fell on that stack of flyers in the first place—but it sounds like she's blushing.

She takes me through the door leading farther into the Cross House. I fight the urge to trace my hand along the walls, feel the silken grain of its expensive, luxurious wallpaper (gold and black in vertical stripes of varying thickness). I'm here. I'm doing it. Somewhere in this house, I don't know where or what or even how, are answers.

One thing about the inside of this mansion is how unpredictable the layout is. That feels like a strange word to ascribe to a house, especially one that looks so boxy from the outside, but none of the rooms or hallways ever seem to be simple squares or rectangles. Everything is angular. Haphazard. Unnecessarily labyrinthine.

Past the exam rooms, we reach a staircase, carpeted, posts painted shiny and black. Steps climb up to a second floor, but also descend to a basement level. Nancy heads down toward the latter, but for a moment, I glance up just in time to see Dr. Burton passing by upstairs, disinterested and in a hurry.

"Burton lives on the second floor," Nancy says to me, noticing what caught my attention. "So does his family. His mom. His sister used to live there, too, but she got married and moved across town. Chantelle, from the front desk, you know."

I didn't, but I suppose the red hair was a tip-off.

"The storage room is down this way," Nancy says and starts down the stairs again. The way the wood of the stairs creaks reminds me of the basement at Keats & Yeats, and for a moment, I think, *Why is it I'm always finding myself working in basements?*

Before I follow her, I look back up to the second floor. Someone else is there now. Standing and staring down at me.

The gardener. That handsome-sad man who, for some reason, makes me think of political posters.

Is he a Burton, too? Doesn't look like it. What is he doing up there? And why is he staring at me?

"Did I lose you?" Nancy's voice called from below me.

"Sorry," I call back and hurry to catch up with her, wanting desperately to turn around and take one more look at the gardener.

I feel his eyes on me as I go.

Nancy stops as we walk through the similarly unpredictable hallways of the basement.

"By the way, I hope this is okay, but we'll need to pay you in cash."

"That's fine." Even better, all things considered.

"I actually . . ." She looks around, even though we're completely alone. "I actually didn't clear hiring you with Dr. Burton. It should be no problem; they're just weird about strangers here, so I didn't want to make a big deal about it. He won't even notice."

"That's . . . fine," I say again. It'll be like I don't even exist.

Nancy looks both ways down the winding hall. She says, "This is such a weird building, isn't it? Everything feels so indirect."

"I was just thinking that," I say, and we start walking again.

"Apparently, it was for cooling. Before the days of air-conditioning. The house was built to trap breezes and circulate them through. There's, like, a system of spaces in between the walls, like—what's the word for them?"

"Crawl spaces," I hazard.

"Yeah. I don't know how anyone lived here before AC. I grew up in the desert, too, but we were close to the gulf so at least we had nice breezes. This place is just *hot*."

I feel like she wants me to ask for more details—*Where are you from? What was it like there?*—but I don't. I'm too distracted by loud voices coming from a closed door in front of us.

"Seven severed heads were found in the refrigerators in his garage. As well as a uterus and a partially eaten spleen in the freezer in his kitchen."

"A uterus?!"

"Yup."

"Well, that's a real hyster-*yech*-tomy, huh?"

The loud, laugh-filled conversation booms in the enclosed space of the storage room. I don't know if Nancy's full-body cringe is due to the volume or the subject matter.

"Eleanor!" she calls. "Eleanor, can you turn it down?" No answer. "*Pinche chava. Eleanor!*"

From farther inside the room: "Is someone there?"

The loud conversation cuts off.

The voice again, small and high: "Is someone there?"

"Yes," Nancy says, exasperated. "Come on out here; I want you to meet somebody. You've got a coworker."

"A *what*?"

Inside the room is what appears to be a massive gray metal box. It's not until a shape emerges from one of the sides that I realize the box has been sliced into several parts capable of expanding or contracting on a track.

The shape reveals itself to be a person. My heart does a strange flutter.

It's as if one of my Loved Ones has come to life.

She can't be older than fourteen or fifteen. She has the smirk of adolescence but also a little of that round, soft flush of childhood left in her face. Wearing plain, muted, almost anachronistic clothes. Shrink her down and cast her in porcelain and she'd be right at home on my shelf. I'd name her Becky or Myrtle or—

"This is Eleanor," Nancy says. "Eleanor, this is Mary. She's going to be helping you with the File Pile, okay?"

"Hi," I say.

"Hi," Eleanor says, wearing an expression I can't interpret. Excitement? Intrigue? Surprise?

After a pause, Nancy says, "Okay, well, I have to go take care of Mr. Boisvert. He fell off a ladder into a rattler's nest, so. Try not to be jealous." She gives a laugh that all but screams, *I'm trying to be your friend!* Part of me wants to acknowledge her, but I find myself unable to look away from Eleanor's strange stare-down. She's sizing me up, from feet to head.

Then she smiles. It's an absolutely heart-melting smile, all cheeks and dimples. Her eyes scrunch up like drawings of a sun rising over a horizon.

"Thanks, Nurse Nancy," Eleanor says. "It's really good to meet you, Mary. What brings you into town?"

She takes me through the ropes, such as they are.

"I mean, the job is pretty simple."

And she's not wrong.

About ten years ago, as she explains it, three nearby county hospitals closed down due to budget cuts—including, incidentally, the hospital I would have known when I was young, before the Cross House was renovated and reopened. The Cross House was set up with some generous state funds to take those defunct hospitals' place, but unfortunately, the actual move was a haphazard one. The records rooms of all three hospitals got tossed together into one basement room in no order, no markings, no labels. The closest thing to organizing was to arrange all those files . . . into a pile.

"And, as you'll see," she says, indicating the File Pile itself, a massive wall of columns and columns of files stacked from floor to ceiling, running along one side of the room, "they go back forever. You'll find a record from ten years ago. Then you'll find a record from fifty years ago in the same pile. Sometimes in the same folder. It's a bit of a nightmare."

Eleanor goes on to explain that the File Pile sat dormant for years and years and that, even relatively recently, current patients' records would somehow make their way down here, causing even more chaos and confusion.

It wasn't until Nurse Nancy came aboard a year ago that the initiative was finally taken to clean and organize the mess.

"She's probably the best thing to happen to this town in a long time," Eleanor says. "It's too bad she . . ." Then, her eyes go wide and her face goes pink. She clamps a hand to her mouth.

"What?"

"No, nothing! I just . . ." She debates saying anything further, then gives in, speaking in a reluctant sotto voce. "I dunno, I just feel bad for her sometimes! She tries *so hard* to make people happy, you know? Like her Easter thing? Did she tell you about that?" I nod. "I mean, good luck getting people out here excited about something like that. I just hope she knows it's not personal or anything, that's all."

"She knows," I say. She's all but said as much. Even though I doubt it doesn't still *feel* personal sometimes.

"Please don't tell her I said anything!"

"I won't," I assure her.

"Ugh. Anyways." With a gee-shucks roll of the eyes that would seem cartoonish if she weren't so young and adorable, Eleanor gives me a sweet-as-sugar smile and changes the subject back to training.

"Long story short! We have to go through each one of these folders, pull out any information that's recent, which means the past seven years, and put it to the side. Everything else we have to organize and put them into the Beast."

The Beast is that massive box in the center of the room. It's a compact shelving unit: a motorized cabinet that's essentially five cabinets facing each other, able to expand or contract depending on your needs. Presumably, it saves space, but even in its compacted form, it almost fills the damn room. Eleanor shows me how it works, flipping a switch on a panel right by the shadowy wall at the back of the room. The heavy, lumbering shelves trundle toward and away from each other.

"You've gotta be careful, though," she says. "There are newer, fancier compact shelving units that have automatic sensors and junk to stop them from closing if something's in the way. But not this one." She pats the side of one of the shelves. "She almost chomped my hand right off once. There's no stopping her once she's started."

"Yikes."

"Yikes, indeed." She giggles. She's so endearing. So effortlessly young.

I find myself almost becoming jealous of her confidence, even at her young age.

"Almost." Right.

I invite that voice to shut up.

Did you notice how she made records from fifty years ago sound like ancient relics?

Shut. Up.

"How do we know who's a recent patient and who's not?" I ask.

"Ready to see a time machine?" She points me toward a computer on the same side as the door. "Ta-da."

The monitor is a huge, chunky tan box with a brown screen and a blinking, golden cursor.

"It takes forever, but you can access all the records from the past seven years here. And, I mean, that's pretty much it." She gives the room a sweep of her hand. "The hardest part is just how tedious it gets. It's like getting to go to the beach but then having to just sit there and count sand. Which is why . . ." A wicked grin crosses her face, paradoxically making her look more innocent. ". . . I've developed a system."

"Which is?"

"Well, it's very complicated, Mary." She puts on a haughty air. "Basically, I work for five minutes, and then I take a thirty-minute break so I don't kill myself."

I can't help smiling. "That's really funny."

Eleanor throws her hands up in a mock-modest shrug. "Also I listen to podcasts. Do you listen to podcasts?"

I don't even know what one is. She explains it to me and then informs me that she's mostly drawn to true crime. "That's my favorite genre. Do you know what *that* is?"

I don't know if she means *genre* or *True Crime,* but I tell her, "I actually work in a bookstore in New York City. We have an entire True Crime section."

Eleanor's eyes go wide. "New York City? Whoa."

You're bragging, I can imagine my Loved Ones reprimanding. *And why are you acting like you still work there? That's pathetic and weird.*

Embarrassment sets my cheeks to burning. I wave her admiration away. "Why don't we get to work?"

She gives a great sigh and says, "Okay. Prepare thyself. Do you mind if I pick up where I left off?"

She presses Play on the podcast she was listening to: a chat show with two peppy, sarcastic, female hosts who are currently talking about a serial killer nicknamed the Crossbow Cannibal. It's gory, unpleasant stuff, but the hosts are so gleeful, so delighted, you'd think they were talking about an old Buster Keaton routine.

"Oh! One last thing!" Eleanor shouts over the broadcast. "There's a box of surgical gloves right over there in case you find any folders that are extra moldy or anything! It happens!"

Great. I pull a file off the File Pile. I can see hundreds of files already in the compact shelving unit, but that barely appears to be a dent in the overall number of files still yet to be gone through. Eleanor's right; this will be tedious, mind-numbing work. That's the kind of work I'm made for, though; I bet I could have this done in a month at most if I got into a groove.

I'm definitely not in a groove now, though. I'm too busy watching Eleanor while she works. I just met her, and already I'm fascinated by the hidden edges to her. She looks nothing like the sort of person who I'd imagine enjoys hearing about dismemberment, cannibalism. I find myself wondering if I was ever so confident and comfortable at that age. Where does that come from? And where does it go?

She gets through two more files before she announces, "Break time!" She presses Pause on her podcast. Then she gives an appreciative jut of her chin toward the single folder I've still got in my hands. "Look at you, a real addition to the team."

My cheeks flush at the teasing. But also at being included as part of "the team." I think that's a first for me.

"What do you do on your breaks?" I ask.

Eleanor bounds over to her pile of personal things. "Sometimes I'll read. But also, I like to work on my own stuff." In a corner of the room is a crumpled, plain backpack. She pulls from it a small sketch pad. "I like to draw. Sketches and stuff. I'm pretty good, I guess."

"I'd love to see some of your work."

A suspicious beat. "Yeah?"

"Yes."

She smiles like her fondest wish has been granted. Then her face hardens. "I've gotta warn you, though—my work's a little dark."

"I don't mind dark."

The smile returns, dimples and all. "Then maybe you and me are gonna get along fine. Okay. Don't judge."

She turns her sketch pad around to show me.

I look at her drawing for a long, long time. Time doesn't so much stop as I feel it begin a new chapter: everything after this moment will be different.

I think I say, "Oh my God." Or maybe I just imagine it because it's the sort of thing someone says when they feel like the world lurches out from under them and they're left somehow seasick in midair. I blink, just to make sure I'm really seeing what I'm seeing.

I am.

"It's one in a series," she's saying from far away. "I call them *Victims*."

She's very talented. The drawing is almost photorealistic, while still also maintaining an abstract artistry beyond simple mimicry.

Before I can stop myself, the words tumble out of my mouth in a hoarse whisper:

"You see them, too?"

She's handed me a drawing of a naked woman with a blood-soaked pillow-case pulled over her head.

16

Bath Time

"Put your back into it, Mary, I feel like I'm being tongue-fucked by a German shepherd with a brain injury."

Water sloshes out of the tub, getting my thighs wet. How did I let Nadine talk me into giving her a bath?

Oh, right, because I've been in a daze since I got home.

Daze. More like I've been walloped with a two-by-four.

"Jesus, Mary, focus. Come on, this shouldn't be hard!"

Easy for her to say. She's not constantly rerunning the conversation I had with Eleanor after seeing those drawings a few hours ago.

She's also not trying to warily watch out for the ghost woman currently hovering in a corner of the bathroom. Honestly, it's a wonder I'm able to do *anything* else.

I lift up Nadine's arm and clean underneath it with a thick yellow sponge. She could do this herself, I have zero doubt, but the sooner I get her out of this tub, the sooner I can steal some private time to think more about everything that's happened.

"Know what I've decided, though?" Nadine is saying. "This is a good thing."

"What's a good thing?"

"You going to that fucking house. I mean, I definitely don't like being left on my own, but as long as I've got Chipotle to watch out for intruders, at least I'm not totally helpless."

"Don't you have any weapons?" I ask, disinterested, the way you humor an annoying child telling you about his invisible friend for the hundredth time.

"Of course I don't have any w—wait." She pauses. Considers. "I *do* have a hammer in my bucket of tools under the sink. I guess that could work. Yeah, I could bash a fucking skull or two, sure."

"Well, there you go."

"Yeah." She volleys a wet, ripping cough and spits a wad of gray-green phlegm into the water. "Anyway, I always wanted to know what goes on up there. Now you can tell me all about it. I got myself a little spy. A weird-as-shit little spy. See? It's a good thing."

"Sure, Nadine." I move on to her other arm.

I still can't believe what happened. I can't believe I said what I said to Eleanor . . . *You see them, too?*

And then the way I tried to cover it up afterward? I must have sounded like such an idiot. Is Eleanor laughing at me right now? In her own home, where she's no doubt surrounded by the comfort and ease that produces a teenager as well put-together as she? Is she telling her friends, her family, about the crazy old (*not old!*) lady she has to work with in the basement now, who probably smells and says crazy old lady things like—

"Ow, don't twist my arm like that!"

"Sorry, Aunt Na—"

"Give me the damn sponge; I'll do it myself. Just make sure I don't drown."

I sit back while Nadine rubs the sponge against herself. Meanwhile, the ghost woman watches us from the corner of the room. So strange to see her out of the tub like this.

It was pretty remarkable: when Nadine trundled into the bathroom and yanked the shower curtain open, the ghost almost reflexively floated backward, toes dragging against the floor, to accommodate Nadine getting in. I guess that answers the question of how Nadine has gotten by with her invisible spectral roommate all these years.

One question down, only a hundred more to go.

Always assuming, of course, you're not just imagining all of this. Yesterday, you'd concluded this was all in your head, remember?

Right. But that was before I saw—

What? A drawing by a child you just met?

That's not fair; she's not just a child. She's special. Even besides her talent, she's wise beyond her years. That much was obvious: just look at how she listened to me, took me seriously, asked questions only when they made sense to be asked . . . and said the three words I needed most to hear: "*I believe you.*"

Of course, I didn't know she would at first. I tried desperately to backtrack after "You see them, too?" flopped out of my stupid mouth. She looked at me as if I'd suddenly started speaking ancient Latin.

"Ha ha," I stammered, "I mean, *seen*, you've *seen*, um, photos of . . . them, those women?"

"Photos?" she asked. "No. No one's seen photos of them. What are you talking about?"

I started to sweat. Not hot-flash sweat. Panic sweat. I tried to play the whole thing off as a mistake, change the subject—oh, silly me, I must have been thinking of something else never mind anyway gosh your drawing is so good did you do it yourself is that pen or pencil? She knew well enough to not say a thing, let me hang myself with words and twist in the wind. Twist I did. And all it took was a glance down at the picture again, to really confirm I was seeing what I was seeing, and I broke into tears. I couldn't help it, it was all too much, the surprise, the confusion, the *relief.*

She reached out and touched my arm. "I'm sorry," she said, genuinely distressed and probably confused. "I told you my work was kinda dark."

"It's not that," I replied.

"Then what?" she asked. And her face was so sweet, so sincere, so porcelain perfect. Before I could stop myself . . . I told her. Everything.

Well, almost everything. I didn't tell her about my problems with faces or with mirrors—more out of embarrassment than anything. But I told her about what I saw in Nadine's tub, what I saw on the street. I even told her about filling my journal with nonsense.

And when I was finished, Eleanor said those three beautiful, desperately needed words. She believed me. Or at least she said she did.

Then she asked me if I knew what these drawings were actually of.

And when I said I didn't . . . she told me.

Nadine sits up and starts working the sponge in some more private areas. "Brenda used to think I was nuts," she says. "She told me I was being paranoid. I told her she was being dumb as a hairnet full of diarrhea. You just gotta be careful, Mary. Don't trust anybody over there. You don't know this world like I do. You gotta rely on me as much as I rely on you, okay? We'll keep each other safe. This town ain't safe for women like us. But if you keep your eyes and ears open, maybe we'll be just—"

"What do you know about Damon Cross?" I ask her.

Sploosh. She turns around in the tub to look at me. The goodwill in her face drains away.

"What'd you just say?"

"Damon Cross. The serial killer. What do you know about him?"

She's silent for several beats longer than I'm comfortable with. When she finally speaks, her voice is low and gravelly.

"What the fuck is wrong with you? You fucking asshole. Get me out of the tub."

She doesn't wait for me to help. She awkwardly lifts herself up, water splashing everywhere, cascading off her in sheets, and stares down at me, her bare body slick and intimidating.

"Fucking unbelievable," she sneers at me.

I try to help her out of the tub, but she slaps my hand away, eases herself out in an awkward, graceless crawl, then snatches the towel from off its hook and rubs herself semidry. Under the rustle of fabric, she says, "You'd better not be starting your shit again. You'd better have outgrown all that. You'd better not make me regret having you come here."

She sounds furious. She sounds scared.

Still dripping, she thump-pads her way out of the bathroom. I hear Chipotle's tags as he stirs from his resting place outside the bathroom door and follows her farther into the house.

There are two options one has in moments like this: attack or retreat. Go and demand answers, or swallow the incident down and hope when the time comes for it to pass, its edges have been worn down as smooth as a river rock.

I do the latter.

I always do the latter.

You'd better not be starting your shit again. What does that even mean?

The answer is obvious: more paranoia. She's even worse than I remember, seeing enemies everywhere. It'd be sad if she weren't so vulgar and unpleasant. Getting old is indignity upon indignity—a race to obsolescence between body and mind.

I have just enough time to wonder if maybe I should take this opportunity to bathe my own increasingly obsolescent self in the currently vacant tub, when I look up and gasp.

The dead woman is already back in the bath. Standing right in the middle of the water. Almost defiant. Dammit. She was too quick.

"So you'll move out of the way for other people but not me?"

No answer.

"Why?"

No answer.

"Were you just trying to avoid Nadine? Can't blame you there."

I cautiously reach over and activate the drain latch, then quickly lean back, way too close for comfort to her red, gnarled claws. As the water gurgles down, I look at the way blood oozes, thick and clotting, almost black, like inky tree sap between her breasts. Something else, too. Trickling down her neck around the rivulets of blood, but not a liquid. It's an insect. An ant.

I shudder, repulsed. Nope. No way I'm getting in with that thing. I'll just have to figure out bathing another day.

I go to leave. Then stop.

"I know what you are," I say to the ghost. "I don't know much else, but . . ."

Her head tilts the tiniest bit at that. Like a dog hearing a strange noise.

"You're a victim of Damon Cross."

The sentence hangs there. In the silence, before I step out and close the door on the dead woman floating in the middle of the draining tub, the conversation with Eleanor replays in my mind. The way she'd said his name. The way, for just a moment, it wasn't like lights went on in my memory mansion; it was like a whole stadium's worth of floodlights blared in white luminescence.

Damon Cross.

"That's why I call the series *Victims*," Eleanor had said. "And it sounds like maybe, for some reason, you came back to Arroyo and . . . now you're seeing their ghosts."

"But why?" My voice was a pinprick whistle. Even harder to hear than usual. "Why would that be happening to me? What would that mean?"

"That I don't know," Eleanor replied, closing up her sketch pad. She waggled her eyebrows enticingly. "But maybe we can find out together."

17

Investigations

APRIL 12, 2019

The Cross House lumbers toward me, getting larger and larger with every step. They're my steps—I'm just finishing my walk up the hill, staring up at the massive house from under my umbrella—but I can't shake the impression that it's approaching me instead of the other way around.

What secrets will you reveal to me, you strange, inscrutable house? What mental crawl spaces will we explore in the memory mansion today?

You can only get to the Cross House via a paved road that runs up into its parking lot, which is situated parallel to the front of the building. This means you approach almost coyly, like you might just keep walking past if you're of a mind to. If you *were* to keep walking, you'd either hit the rocky side of the mountain slope or you could hook around to the eastern side of the building, which is the entrance for the small school that serves the children of Arroyo. As I enter the parking lot now, I can just see the edge of the school's tiny playground around the corner.

I'm so curious what the school here is like. Before I head into the hospital entrance, I keep walking.

Recess is in session, it appears; children are out in the yard. But there's none of the usual chaos I would expect during recess time. These kids seem remarkably disciplined, mostly standing in clumps, talking. Then again, it's an unseasonably hot day. I wouldn't want to be running around either.

A moment later, I realize something else is strange about them, too: they're all wearing similar clothes. Not *the same* clothes, but similar. Similar fabrics, similar muted colors. No logos, no cartoon characters, no pop culture merit badges. If they're not handmade, they're at least purposefully generic. Now that I think of it, Eleanor wears the same kind of style, too. Curious.

Probably off-the-rack, Walmart-type stuff. People aren't exactly rolling in cash out here.

I find myself looking past the children to see if the gardener is also out and about. He intrigues me, too. I think it's something about his combination of good looks and sadness. What's his deal?

If he *is* here today, I don't see him. But as I get a little closer, I do see an adult woman, weaving her way around the playground. An authority figure of some kind.

Maybe that's why, when she looks my way, a rush of adrenaline floods through me like I've just gotten caught doing something naughty. The woman adjusts the white tennis visor she's wearing to keep the sun out of her eyes, and I get a better look at her face to see—

"Oh my God," I gasp.

Now I'm running back toward the hospital entrance as inconspicuously as possible. *Ohmigod, ohmigod.*

Carole.

That was her name. One of Anna-Louise's sidekicks. Carole fucking Huff.

Mary, Mary, face is scary, when will your titties grow?

I stop inside the hospital. Catch my breath. Fumble in my attempt to close my umbrella. Bad luck. Almost as bad as running into Carole fucking Huff.

Mary, Mary, pits are hairy, how does your period flow?

And, as if remembering one name was the key to remembering the other, the third member of their little girl gang comes to me, too.

"Bonnie Franks," I mutter.

Anna-Louise Connerton, Bonnie Franks, and Carole fucking Huff. Those three girls, laser focused on me. Making my life even more miserable than it already was. With their childish, taunting voices, their hallway shoves, their chants about things they probably didn't even understand at that age; they just knew the language of abuse.

The only people who noticed me.

"You okay over there?" Chantelle asks disinterestedly from behind her desk, smacking her gum. Her desk radio is playing soft rock, that song about summer breezes.

Yup. Doing great, Chantelle. Just realizing that the prospect of running into Anna-Louise in this town at some point now feels less hypothetical and more like an ominous cloud overhead, loaded with lightning.

I give Chantelle a bright Good Girl smile. "Heading to the basement."

I hurry toward the stairs, eager to have something less upsetting than Carole fucking Huff to focus on.

"So, Damon Cross was sometimes known as the 'Jane Doe Killer,'" Eleanor says, "because he'd remove pretty much all identifiable traces of his victims: fingerprints, teeth . . . faces. Then he'd scatter the bodies all around—in cars, in empty houses, in this town, in nearby towns like Socorro, Welcome, Salome. So the police were totally baffled, right? Because they had all these bodies, but they didn't know who they were. And he was *thorough,* too. Did his research. He got to know each of his victims first. He took his time. Befriended them. Made sure they didn't have any real connections—you know, no family, no close friends, no one missing them back home. That way, no one would be looking for them or report they were missing. He was brilliant."

Her face is flush with the excitement of getting to tell a grown-up everything she knows about a favorite subject.

"And you learned all this from your podcasts?" I ask.

She shrugs, then intones in a mock commercial announcer voice, "They're fun, informative, and free!"

"But why did he do it? And why did he cover them up after he . . . you know . . ." My voice sticks before I can say *skinned their faces.* Almost like words can't do the act justice.

"Well, the thinking is, that way he could hold on to the bodies for however long he wanted—confuse the time of death, make their disappearances even harder to trace. Same with making them, like, anonymous. He basically turned them all into dead ends—if you can't identify the victims, it's that much harder to find the killer in their lives. As for the covering?" She pauses. Holding something back. She has her own theories, but she doesn't want to share them. It's almost kind of endearing to see her become self-conscious, even if just for a moment. "Nobody really knows. Probably just one more way to make them hard to identify."

"I guess it wasn't enough in the end, though, right?"

"What do you mean?"

"Well, he got caught."

Her face hardens a little. She jabs a finger towards me.

"*That* was just a fluke! They never should have caught him, but . . . You know his brother was the mayor, right? And the cops just happened to be here, giving his brother an update on their search, when things went wrong. It was all a total coincidence."

"Wait, he was caught here? In this house?"

"Yup. They gunned him down before he could get away. I think somewhere near the back of the first floor. He didn't even get a chance to explain why he did what he did."

"You almost sound disappointed."

She lifts her shoulders, lets them drop, her mouth a thin sliver in her sweet face. It almost looks comical—her expression is so serious and glum.

We've been talking for a while. "Should we get back to work?" I ask.

She sighs and stretches. "Let's make the world a more boring place."

We both pull a few files off the Pile, organize them, enter any data that needs to be entered. Eleanor puts on another podcast, filling the room with giggling repartee discussing the so-called Vampire of Dusseldorf. Exsanguination never sounded so hilarious.

But soon it's time to stop again. Turn off the podcast. Get to our *real* work.

"So," I say with a grin, "I brought something . . ."

"Do go on," she says, delighted.

I hurry over to my purse.

Something about that podcast has gotten into my bones. I feel giddy, gossipy, rebellious. I want to share what I did, which was very much not Good of me. Not to mention risky.

When I left Nadine this morning, she was sitting in her massive chair with her hammer in hand, ratlike attack dog at her feet, and, truth be told, she actually did look intimidating. Frail, old, paranoid woman though she may be, I wouldn't want to be an intruder in that house. Or someone who stole some of her prized possessions.

Not stole. Borrowed. Just for the afternoon. And hopefully, the house is dim and dark enough that she won't notice a few of the slim volumes missing from her shelves.

I pull Nadine's books out of my purse, and Eleanor coos in wonder.

Our break goes on longer than usual. We sit on the floor, the books I borrowed piled between us. *Ghosts and Spirits. Haunted Places. Psychic Phenomena. Paranormal Messages.* We leaf through pages. We volley theories and interesting tidbits. Facts about poltergeists. Haunted roads. Cold spots.

Funnel ghosts. Ecto-mist. Crisis apparitions. ESP. Each subject opens up new questions—why the autowriting, why now, why me, why, why, why? Do you have a relationship with the deceased? No. Have you ever seen a ghost before? Not that I know of, but New York is pretty crowded.

"Huh," Eleanor says at one point, reading.

"What?"

"According to some dude named Lafcardio Hearn—great name—'The common fear of ghosts is the fear of being *touched* by ghosts—or, in other words, that the imagined supernatural is dreaded mainly because of its imagined power to touch.' Ew." She looks up at me. "Have they ever tried to touch you?"

I think of the incident in the tub with Nadine. "No. I don't think they *want* to be touched."

"Oh yeah? These ghosts have boundary issues, huh?"

She's got a smirk on her face. It occurs to me—and not for the first time, if I'm being honest—that she might totally just be humoring me. Maybe even making fun of me. This whole investigation could just be indulging the crazy old lady for a little entertainment.

I stuff that fear down as far as I can. I've just got bullies on the brain, that's all. That's

(*Mary, Mary, face is scary*)

all.

I meet her grin with my own best approximation. "Maybe they do," I say. I tell her about bath time. How the ghost quickly got out of the way when Nadine trundled toward her. I don't mention the fact that the ghost immediately got back in once Nadine was gone. I still can't quite wrap my mind around that part.

"Also," I continue a little sheepishly, "I threw a rock at one."

She shifts her sitting position, her grin intensifying. "Um. What?"

I tell her about how, that first day I began seeing them—my day of errands—at one point, I threw a few pebbles at a ghost who was across the street from me. Just to see if I could make her disappear.

"I'm a horrible shot, and I was a little shaken up, so it took a few tries, but . . ."

"But what?" Eleanor asks, breathless and delighted.

I try to explain. It was like the woman was there . . . and then the instant before the rock would have made contact, she zigged to the side, only to right herself another split second after. The movement was so jagged and unnatural it made my head ache. It reminded me of an old VHS tape momentarily losing its tracking, a reference I do not make in front of Eleanor so as to not sound a million years old.

Instead, she's giggling. "Wow. You are a brave woman, my friend. Mary the Ghost Slayer."

That makes me smile. I try to suppress it, just in case she's being sarcastic. But the smile is too strong to subdue. Mary the Ghost Slayer. I like it. Although, I'd settle for the Ghost Understander.

We read for a little while longer, but eventually, we both come to the same conclusion: fascinating as these books might be, they don't offer many answers for my particular problems.

"They're just too"—she searches for the word—"anecdotal. You know what I mean? They're more about stories than cold hard facts."

I do know what she means. These books are pointing us in directions but not giving us any sort of road map beyond that.

"What about your journal? Think there are any clues in there?"

The subject drops a stone into my gut.

"I . . . don't know. It's all pretty hard to read and nonsensical." Insane, more like. I desperately don't want her to see how C-word that book looks. Not yet, at least. If I can help it.

"Maybe you should bring it in for us to go over!"

"Yeah, maybe. I'll . . . give it another look. What about that?" I point to the boxy computer. "Is there internet on that thing? Maybe we could look for, I dunno, ghost websites?"

She groans. "I wish. It's only hooked up to a local network. Dr. B. made it so you can't browse or download anything. He's pretty obsessed with security and privacy. Actually, pretty much everyone here is. Most of the town is off-line, you know? Probably because the mountains make service pretty crappy."

"It's a cowboy town," I say. She looks at me, not understanding. I explain, "A lot of people out here probably don't want to be connected to the world on purpose. They live here *because* it's so isolated."

"That's exactly it. That's this town to a T."

She starts to gather up the books. I quickly go over to help. It's the closest I've gotten physically so far, and I'm unable to mistake the subtle little lip curl she gives when I get next to her. Her hand goes to her nose. It's totally involuntary, I know—that just makes it worse.

"Oh no," I moan, stepping backward.

"What?"

"I stink, don't I?" I try to get a good whiff of my armpit while still holding the books.

"You—no," she says. But she's already taken a few steps back, as well.

"I do! Oh, I'm sorry." I was hoping it wasn't as bad as I thought. Between the night sweats and the desert sweats and the grime in Nadine's house and who knows what else, I probably smell like a fully stocked refrigerator after two weeks of no power. "I haven't been able to shower, because of the—"

"Yeah, no, I get it, it's totally not a problem. Just . . . close quarters, that's all."

"I'm going to keep my distance, I promise." It feels like my face is about to burst into flames. Fire is cleansing, right? Maybe that'll get the stench out.

"Hey." Eleanor says to my back as I fit the books into my purse. "I've got a crazy idea."

"No!" I quickly look back at her. "Not crazy."

"Um . . . what?"

"Don't call yourself crazy. That's a word people use to make you small. Don't do it for them."

She nods, taking the point. "I have a *wacky* idea. There is *one* place I know of with good internet . . ."

"Where?"

"My house. My stepdad is town comptroller, so he needs a good connection for, y'know, the comptrolling? And he and my mom are going to be gone tomorrow night. So why don't you come over? We can do some actual research on an actual computer, away from this gross basement. And you can use our shower!"

"Oh?" My face must be beet red. Tomorrow is Saturday; that would mean not only interacting with Eleanor outside of the basement but doing so on a day when we wouldn't even normally be seeing each other anyway.

"Plus," she adds, "it'd be a good excuse to actually just hang out and talk more! I haven't gotten to know *you* at all yet, you know?"

"There's not much to know," I say with an awkward shrug.

"Hey!" She says, pointing. "Don't make yourself small."

She's got me there. Her offer is incredibly tempting. But . . . there's Nadine to think about. And also . . .

The undervoice pipes up.

Call it what it is, Mary. You're scared shitless. You have no idea how to have a friend; you never really had any practice.

That's not true!

Name one friend in your life—one that's not ceramic. I'll wait.

Frowning, I look at Eleanor.

"That's so kind of you," I say. "But . . . no. I'm sorry. I just don't think I can."

She blinks. She's silent for a second. "Okay. It was just an idea." Then, after another excruciating pause: "I guess we should get back to the grind?" She gives me a polite smile, then grabs a file and gives me some distance.

Good job, Mary. You wrecked that relationship in record time.

Now I feel like shit.

I want to cry. I want to apologize.

I pull a file off the Pile and absently open it. My eyes are on the page, but I'm not really processing anything. God, I'm so stupid. Stupid and strange.

Something tickles my arm. I look down, then flinch, barely managing to not cry out.

An ant is crawling on my wrist. Thick and black. I whip my hand, whisking the nasty thing off me. It must have been hiding in the file. Great. Now we have to worry about an infestation down here, too.

I give the folder a little shake and then look at the contents inside just to make sure there are no stragglers. No more ants, but there's a photograph paper-clipped to the patient's file. My eyes fall on the picture and a moment later I process what I'm looking at.

For the second time today, I gasp. "Oh my God."

Eleanor looks up from what she's doing. "What?"

When I'm able to find my voice again: "You said you have good internet at your house, right?"

"Yeah?"

"I might have something else for us to investigate." I hand her the file. "This is the dead woman in Nadine's tub."

18

Women's Stories

APRIL 13, 2019

For the next thirty-odd hours, I'm as Good as can be, trying to betray none of the Fourth of July fireworks going on inside me. The time passes in a blur—I didn't even really notice the chores, the insults, the new pile of dog shit left for me by Chipotle when I woke up in the morning.

I only give myself one moment to indulge: a prolonged stare at the shower curtain. I don't open it, I just breathe it in . . . and I whisper, "I might know who you are," in a voice so quiet even a ghost wouldn't hear it.

At last, Saturday evening arrives. Obviously, Nadine would pitch a fit if I tell her I have plans tonight, but I came up with a solution hours ago.

"This tastes chalky," she says of her banana pudding after dinner.

"No, it doesn't," I tell her.

Fifteen minutes later, she's passed out in her massive chair, snoring in wet, ripping waves. Chipotle is licking her feet, trying to rouse her, in between shooting growls and glares my way. Her hammer is propped up against the side of her chair. One trazodone knocked me out for about six hours. I figure two will keep Nadine nice and comfortable for the evening.

If an intruder comes along and murders her while I'm away, I'll owe her an apology.

Eleanor is full of questions from the moment she picks me up in a dusty red station wagon (windows not so subtly cracked open).

Is Nadine okay with you coming out tonight? How did you get her to let you go?

Her eyes bulge, scandalized, when I tell her.

"I'm not going to let Nadine hold me back from doing the things I want to do," I say with a casual shrug. I'm playacting. But it's a role I'd like to believe I can lose myself in. For a little while. With enough practice.

The next question is: Why Is Nadine the Way She Is? I give a brief recap of Nadine's life. How she used to teach at a small college in Phoenix. How her husband had an affair with another teacher and the ensuing confrontation resulted in Nadine getting fired. How Nadine eventually moved herself and her young daughter, Brenda, to be by her only sister, just in time for that sister and her husband to die in a fire. How Nadine found herself raising her niece. How, over the years, Nadine got more and more paranoid, more obsessed with conspiracies, while her health deteriorated. As I talk, I start to feel some pity for Nadine. Guilt, even. So much happened *to* her. Not her fault at all.

Soon Eleanor's questions turn to me, though, and I wish we were still talking about Nadine.

When did you move to New York? What's your apartment like? Is it scary living in the big city?

The undervoice is alive and well as I attempt to answer all of Eleanor's questions. I wish I were more interesting. I wish I were worthy of conversation.

Why did you move there? What do you do for fun? Do you have anyone missing you back home? Anyone you're seeing?

One of my answers surprises me. I'd almost completely forgotten how, when I first moved to New York, I'd actually entertained ideas of becoming an actress. Mostly when I think of why I moved there, it's because I wanted as big a change from Arroyo as I could get. I wanted winter, I wanted ocean, I wanted crowds. But, no, I *did* think that performing was in my cards at one point, didn't I? I was just too scared to ever really try. I never went on auditions. I never got pictures taken or took classes. I got my bookstore job that paid just enough to live on, and, with both hands, I dug myself a comfy little rut and forgot my stupid fantasies.

Remembering all this makes me feel even crappier. My hand slips into my purse to graze the soft, cottony bundle I've secreted along with me. One of my Loved Ones, wrapped in a T-shirt. A little ceramic security blanket. I imagine its porcelain face now saying, *Mary, relax. Just be normal. Don't be weird.* Good advice. I take my hand out, keep the rest of my answers chipper and short.

Eventually, we pull up in front of a large, well-tended house. A mid-length walkway, traversing through tasteful landscaping, white rock, smartly arranged cacti and bushes underlit by small, soft lamps.

"You said your parents are out tonight, right?"

"Yup," Eleanor says over the whip-whir of our seat belts as they disengage. "They're both on the town council, and they're having a meeting to prep for a big event later this month."

"Nurse Nancy's Easter egg hunt?"

Instead of an answer, Eleanor laughs and gets out of the car.

The shower is a blessing. I could stay in here for hours.

There's a little guilt using their products, but it's all so much nicer than what's available to me at Nadine's that the guilt doesn't last long.

When I turn around to rinse the shampoo out of my hair, though, I experience a moment of sheer terror. Will there be another bloodied, naked woman standing in front of me after I close my eyes again? Another victim?

I take a deep breath to steel myself, lean back, and stick my head under the water—and then quickly pull my head back out and whip the water from my face.

The tub remains empty. Just me. Me and this body of mine.

I soap myself up.

It's been a while since I was able to look at my body in such good, bright lighting. It feels as though I'm looking at it through two sets of eyes. One that recognizes it as mine, feels ownership, pride. Then another set, critical, mean, cruel. I pinch the places that didn't use to be pinchable. I prod the soft areas that used to be firmer. Random explosions of purple veins in some spots, pebbled splotches in others. Is this really me? Where did my body go? I think of Eleanor's perfect youth and feel a kind of resentment, as if aging was a thing I did by mistake.

Soon I'm toweling off on the soft, pink bath mat.

My fog-shrouded reflection mimics my movements in the bathroom mirror, and I watch the indistinct shape as it moves. The closest I've gotten to voluntarily looking into a mirror in quite a long time.

"You're doing okay, Mary," I tell that hazy shape. I hope she hears me.

I don't mean to snoop.

Well. Maybe I do. Just a little. Let's say I take the scenic route on my way from the bathroom to Eleanor's bedroom.

Eleanor's parents have minimalist taste. There's not a lot on the walls, beyond some teal and turquoise abstract art. In the corner of one hallway is a large sandstone vase with thin cactus branches made out of metal sticking out. A clump of petrified wood under an off-the-rack Hopi basket on another wall.

One framed photo catches my eye. A woman in her thirties. Familiar, but I can't remember why. Another photo of a child. Eleanor. So small and doll-like. Wearing a little empire-waisted dress. Again I'm struck by how, if you threw a mobcap on her, she'd make an achingly perfect little ceramic statue.

At the end of one hallway is what can only be a master bedroom. The door is open. I peek inside. There's a king-size bed (*God that bed looks good I could just climb in and sleep like a middle-aged Goldilocks*), flanked by matching night tables.

On one of the nightstands, a large book lies tented open, like it was put down in the middle of reading. It's a soft blue, like a robin's egg. Hardcover, buckram bound, no dust jacket. Looks independently published.

Something familiar-looking is embossed on the cover.

I'm about to step forward to investigate when Eleanor's voice jolts me from elsewhere in the house.

"Hey, you want anything to drink? Where'd you go?"

I quickly leave the room, reminding myself that I probably imagined that tattoo of an eye on the cab driver's neck. There's no reason the same image would be on some book cover, too.

Her name was Jane Mayhew.

She lived in a place called Quartzsite, a few towns over from here. Her medical history was unremarkable, but she had very fair skin and freckles and was concerned about skin cancer. She had a large wine-stain birthmark on her shoulder and was having it checked to make sure its borders hadn't spread. The yellowing photograph of her shoulder paper-clipped to her records was how I recognized her.

Unsurprisingly, there's not much of a web presence for a middle-aged woman who died more than half a century ago. However, there is one surprising, immediate result: an Amazon page.

A book. Written by Jane Mayhew.

"Think it's the same person?" Eleanor asks.

Only one way to find out. Click.

An author photo, black and white.

"Wow," I say, a hand unintentionally going to the base of my throat. Eleanor looks at me, curious. "If that *is* her, I've just . . . never seen her face." I only know the bloody cowl that replaced it.

The photo shows a woman in her forties. Short hair. A wry smile. Looks to have been taken in the mid-1960s, which would be right as far as the time line goes.

"I think this might really be her."

"Looks like she was a poet," Eleanor reads. There are three original collections under her name: *Distant Messages Unheard, The Peacock,* and *Amor Crepuscular.* Her paltry bio says she was born and raised in New Mexico. Nothing more. No mention of family. No mention of her moving to Arizona. No mention of her death. But of course not, Jane would have just been marked as "disappeared," if anyone even reported her absence at all. The sadness of such a fate hits me in the gut. The unfairness.

Another book reveals another author photo. This time, she's wearing a black tank top, holding the reins of a dark and shiny horse, shielding her eyes against the sun. Her birthmark is plainly visible. It's her.

"Guess she didn't have to worry about that cancer, huh," Eleanor says.

"Can we order a copy?" I ask.

"Only if you wanna drop a couple hundred bucks."

The copies on Amazon are laughably expensive—out of print, small houses. However, I watched our receiving managers at Keats & Yeats track down books over the years. I know a few tricks.

"Do you mind if I . . . ?" I gesture to her keyboard. It feels a little like an invasion, which is maybe why she doesn't move just yet.

"Are you sure about this?" Eleanor asks. "Getting a copy, I mean? What's it really gonna solve?"

"I don't know." I actually *do* know, I just can't articulate it. "There's . . .

Haven't the books and things we've looked at all said that one of the reasons people see ghosts is that the ghosts want something from the living?"

"You think all the ghosts want you to read their poetry?"

"No. Just. Maybe there's a clue in there, or, I don't . . ." She's making me feel stupid. I know she doesn't mean to—if anything, it's my fault for just *being* stupid—but my instincts are very loud here.

She suddenly smiles at me. Eleanor's demeanor becomes bright and cheery again.

"Then go for it." She gives up her seat.

I move her mouse around. Start to type. One finger, hunt and peck. "I'll warn you, I'm not the fastest typer." My cheeks warm. God, I wish I weren't so lame. Do kids her age even use that word anymore?

"Actually," she says, "I'm going to make some more tea. Want some?"

"Sure," I say.

She leaves—practically skipping. I watch her go, and then I take in her room again.

It's bigger than my city apartment bedroom and living room combined. Full of soft pinks and golds. As sparsely decorated as the rest of the house, which, now that I'm alone to think about it, is kind of strange for a teenager's bedroom, right? No stuffed animals, no posters of pop stars. It's not overflowing with expressions of rebellion or individuality.

There's only one exception: in various spots on the walls are a few sheets of paper torn carefully from a sketch pad. Eleanor's artwork. Once again, I'm struck by her talent. And not just a little envious.

There's a drawing of a tree, bare branches against a mountainous backdrop. One of a bird; looks like a cactus wren. A rather majestic lynx. On opposite sides of her door, like sentries, are two striking drawings of angels, floating against white, cloud-lined nothingness. Beautiful. Reverent. Imposing. One has the name Zepar written underneath, the other Azazel.

Then I remember something the cab driver said to me on the way from the airport. He moved out here for "religious reasons." *Here* turned out to be Arroyo.

Is Arroyo a religious town? Does that explain all the modest clothing? The minimalism? The general insularity?

Seems like the most obvious answer. Although, I don't remember religion playing a part in my childhood here at all.

You don't remember anything about your childhood here at all.

Fair point. But I'd think I'd remember something like *that*. And, if this *is* such a religious place, why wouldn't they be more excited about Easter? Maybe it's one of those no-fun religions? The kind that doesn't allow you to have holidays or birthdays or—

I hear clinking and humming far away in the kitchen.

Back on task. I copy the ISBNs of the poetry books I can find and then search all the independent book retailers I know of. Worst-case scenario, I can check their publishing house sites and order them direct, but I also have a feeling . . . ah, bingo. I find a copy of one of Jane's poetry books for just a few dollars, used.

Before I buy it, I open up a new tab to search for another of her collections in case I can combine the order. Unfortunately, besides being a slow typer, I'm also a clumsy one, and as I'm punching in the name of the book, my finger slips, and I accidentally hit Enter.

A page of search results begins to load, and I realize the browser must have filled in something from Eleanor's previous history.

The window fills up with images.

Red, bloody muscle. Gleaming eyeballs and teeth. Stretched and pulled skin.

These are all pictures of various stages of facial reconstruction surgery. Jesus.

My gorge rises . . . and then my heart shatters once I realize what this must mean. Oh, Eleanor. You poor, perfect girl. How awful must it be to navigate all the insecurities inflicted on a girl her age, even in this tiny town? Here she is, researching facial reconstruction surgery! Despite having a face without a single flaw! I could cry at this thought. It's just not fair. It's just—

"You know, this is actually kind of huge."

I jump in my seat at the voice behind me. I quickly, guiltily close the tab and swivel around in her desk chair. Eleanor's back, holding two mugs of steaming tea.

"I mean," she continues, "we might be the first people to have identified one of Damon Cross's victims ever." She hands me a mug. I must be making some sort of face because as I take it, she asks, "You okay? You look . . . ha, I was going to say you look like you've seen a ghost, but that's why we're here."

"No, I'm fine." I try to slow my heart from a gallop to at least a manageable trot. "I was just going to ask if you think it'd be okay if I had something shipped to the Cross House." I indicate the monitor, where the order form for one of Jane's books is up, all the skinless faces safely hidden.

"Why not?" She shrugs. "I mean, we do get the mail out here, city girl."

I fill in my credit card info and use the Cross House as the shipping address: the first purchase I've made here that hasn't made me cringe. "I just don't want Nadine to know I'm getting any packages, you know?" Also, unsaid, still forming in my head: I don't want any book of Jane's near her own ghost. I fear it might cause some sort of reaction. What kind exactly, I can't say. An odd, half-formed warning flashes in my mind: *The fear of ghosts is that they'll touch you.*

Eleanor sits on the edge of her neatly made bed, sipping her tea. When I'm finished at the computer, I turn around and look at her.

I have to say something. Something pithy and wise. Something worthy of a mentor. I settle for:

"You know you're perfect, right?"

Her eyes narrow. "Uh . . ."

Smooth, Mary. Real great job.

"I just. I mean. It's been really nice hanging out with you, and it's making me remember what it was like for me at your age and . . . it's hard. It was hard then, and I can only imagine how hard it is now. With magazines and television and . . . I used to stare at magazine covers a lot and wonder why I couldn't be like the women in those pictures. And I had bullies. Girls at school, and Nadine at home, and so my head is kinda full of voices even now, telling me what's wrong with me, how I should be better than I am. It's . . . it's awful. And I guess I'm just saying I really hope *you* don't feel that way, Eleanor. Because I think you're really great, and you shouldn't change a thing." Drowning. I'm drowning. I've shared too much.

"That's . . . wow." Her eyes dart to the sides of the room, to her tea, to my face. "That's a lot. That's—"

"I'm sorry." My throat is suddenly very dry, but the tea is too hot to sip. "I'm stupid. I'm so bad at this."

"At what?"

I resist the urge to bury my head in my hands. Instead, I throw them upward in helpless surrender. "Socializing? Interacting with people? Words? All of it? I shouldn't have said anything, I'm—"

"No!" She surprises me with her forcefulness. "You're great! I really appreciate it. I . . . I actually needed to hear all that."

"You did?"

"Yeah." Her brows set themselves. Her whole demeanor suddenly becomes very serious, as if she's puzzling this out for herself for the first time. "My mom has a really hard time letting me do, well, anything. She always treats me like a kid. 'You're too young,' 'You're not ready for that,' blah blah blah. It actually . . ." Her voice breaks a little. "It actually really hurts. I hate not feeling like I'm a part of things. You know what I mean? It's the worst feeling in the world. I want to *scream* sometimes."

"I do know what you mean." I know it very well.

"I want to be a part of things. I want to be a good member of this community. I want to *count*. I take my studies seriously. I take our worship seriously. I'm sick of being written off as this stupid little baby who's not ready yet. Who's *never* ready. I get so mad thinking about it sometimes. I just want to *show* them sometimes."

"You should!" I say. My heart is pounding. Am I helping? I think I'm helping! "You should show them! Don't let them write you off just because you're young!" Of course, I'm giving advice I would never take in a thousand lifetimes. But it feels good! "Eleanor, do you know how special you are? Look at those drawings on the wall! Are those something someone who's just *young* could do? No! There's wisdom there. Skill. A point of view. And you know something else? I bet if you were a boy, they'd already be entrusting you with all sorts of new responsibilities."

Her eyes meet mine. "You're not wrong. This town's pretty complicated when it comes to women."

"This town and every town. It's like background radiation—we don't even notice it most of the time." *Wow, Mary, I hope you did some calf stretches before getting on that soapbox.* "But you know what, Eleanor? Fuck 'em. Fuck 'em right in their dumb faces."

Her eyes go wide with scandal. I relish it. I start thinking of every aphorism I encountered while skimming the various Personal Growth books at the bookstore.

"You should never wait for their permission to live your dreams. You are ready because you are you! Focus on what makes you Eleanor, not what your mom says, not what she lets you do or not do. You're living your own story, and you get to be the main character. Okay?"

Her eyes shine with tears. Actual tears! *And the award for Best Actress goes to . . .*

"Thank you," she says, nodding firmly. "You're right, I *am* ready."

We've definitely drifted away from the topic of reconstructive surgery, but this is Good. I've done a Good thing. I've made her feel more confident, more sure of her worth. Me! I did that. My heart's still pounding, an excited, triumphant drumbeat.

"I'm sorry you were bullied," she says, wiping tears. "That really sucks. Girls are the worst."

No, they're not, I almost say. *Don't buy into that thinking.* But I've lectured her enough. Instead, I laugh. "It's weird. I think I forgot a lot of it. I'm only really remembering some of it now. On one hand, it feels really present to me, like it never stopped, and on the other, it's like I'm learning details about, I don't know, a past life or something." I give another chuckle, aiming for nonchalant, landing more in the high, reedy territory.

Now she's looking at me funny.

"What?" I ask, stomach turning. What's that expression on her face? "What did I say?"

She speaks slowly. "Okay. Go with me here. This is a really strange idea. Maybe stupid. Maybe crazy—"

"Don't say crazy!"

"But, Mary, this actually might be!" She takes a dramatic breath, a swallow, resetting herself. "I don't know, this first popped into my head earlier, when we were looking up stuff about auto writing and one of the books made a little offhand reference." She stares at me again. I feel like a specimen suddenly. "I've just been sitting here, trying to think of why you might be seeing these ghosts, what is it about you, what is it about them. And you said what you just said, and then I realized . . . we never talked about Damon Cross's type, did we?"

"His type?"

"The thing all his victims had in common. Not just his MO but *who* he picked. He had a *type*." She gets up from the bed. "Shove over and let me drive."

We switch places at the computer. A low rumbling noise gets louder outside. Am I imagining that? Eleanor doesn't seem to notice. She's typing into a search bar.

"Maybe we're going at this all wrong. Maybe there's something else we should be researching. Maybe it's not just ghosts but something even bigger, and I'm not saying you're *her,* this Jane woman, but maybe you're *one* of them. I don't know. We've been so focused on what *they* are . . . but maybe it's *you*."

"Eleanor, I don't understand what you're saying." The rumbling has gotten louder. It's right outside.

The whir of a garage door. The sound of car doors shutting.

Finally, Eleanor hears it, too. "Oh shit. My mom's home. Come on. I probably shouldn't get caught with a freshly showered grown-up in my bedroom, you know?"

I'm so turned around. "Wait, but what were you saying? What—?" I take a look at the screen, where Eleanor's latest search has gone through:

SIGNS OF REINCARNATION

She catches my expression. She shrugs, a massive smile plastered to her perfect face. She's enjoying this.

"What if you're one of Damon Cross's victims reincarnated?" she asks. "What if that's why you can see them? Because you've finally come home?"

She says this so casually. The way you'd say *Maybe lie down and take a nap* to someone who complains of being tired, or *Let's go to the store* when someone says they're out of milk.

What if you're one of Damon Cross's victims reincarnated?

Once again, suspicion rears its head: Is she making fun of me?

"Come on," she says, "we can talk about this more later. It's just a *craaaazy* idea."

I expect this will be the only thing I will be able to think about for the foreseeable future. It's such a massive idea, such a strange, compelling, baffling, impossible idea, there's no way I'll have the bandwidth for anything else tonight.

Then we walk out into the living room, and there's Eleanor's mom, and my mind goes completely blank.

Because Eleanor's mom is standing there with Carole fucking Huff.

Because Eleanor's mom is Bonnie Franks.

19

Mary, Mary, Face Is Scary

The fight happens around me, but I'm having a hard time catching any of it. All I really see and hear is Bonnie and Carole, not even as two separate entities but one conjoined monstrosity, Bonnieandcarole.

I can only look at them for the briefest of moments, but they stick in my brain like Polaroids.

Carole: prim, pretty face, though with a droopy, doe-eyed downturn that no amount of cosmetic subterfuge could ever make up for. It's the face of a perpetual also-ran. A second-place face.

Bonnie: rail thin, lean muscled, the sort of body I can picture doing yoga in the sunrise before going for a jog with free weights in hand. But what was once muscle tone is becoming stringiness, and she's put highlights in her hair just to keep her perfect tan from becoming monochromatic with her brown dye job. A bruiser. An enforcer.

Next to Bonnie is an utterly generic-looking man in a gray blazer with blue slacks, and a white button-down shirt open at the throat. Weak chin. Pink, wet lips. Tiny, dark, button eyes. Eleanor alluded to a stepfather before. Here's the living embodiment.

"You won't let me do *anything*!" Eleanor is whining.

"And this is why. You're too emotional," her mother explains. Calm. Even-toned. But all I hear every time she opens her oh-so-reasonable mouth is *Mary, Mary, face is scary, when will your titties grow?*

Carole butts in. "Your mother's right; there's a proper way we do things. We can't be impulsive."

"This is what I was talking about," Bonnie says to Carole, and Carole nods, an instant conspiracy. I can feel rage sizzling off Eleanor even from where I'm standing, in the hallway between Eleanor's room and the living room.

"I'm just trying to be *useful*, Carole," Eleanor says, loading the word with venom. "'Let the women among you have *use*,' right? And what do *you* do again? What's *your* point?"

Carole is shocked. "Excuse me?"

Bonnie is appalled. "Eleanor!"

It even stings *me* to hear.

"No, seriously," Eleanor insists, approaching Carole, getting a taste for cruelty, "you're not married, you never had kids. What do you give back to this community? What is your *use*, Carole?"

Bonnie steps in front of her daughter. "What has gotten into you?!"

"Okay," the stepfather says, "that does it." His voice is higher than I'd expect, a nauseating frog-like croak. He pulls Eleanor by the arm into another hallway to reprimand her in private. Eleanor shoots me a helpless look before she disappears.

Bonnie is about to follow, but first she says, "Carole, would you mind—?" She gestures to me in such a patronizing, dehumanizing way—the first real acknowledgment of my presence—that now I'm pissed, too. I suddenly want to start jumping on her couch, ripping up her cushions, tipping over her glass coffee table, shitting all over her cream-colored carpet, grabbing her fake metal cactus art and doing unspeakable acts with it. The teenager and I aren't so different, it appears.

Instead, I quietly follow Carole out to her car.

I wish I hadn't showered. At least then I'd be able to stink up Carole's car a little.

"That kid," Carole mutters. "She's so smart, but she's so angry sometimes."

Angry. Yes. That's exactly how I feel right now.

Other than that one comment, we drive in silence, Carole's radio softly filling the car with the twang of country pop. My nails are digging into my knees. I'm *so* fucking angry. At Carole, at Bonnie . . . and yes, even at Eleanor.

Especially at Eleanor.

Eleanor is Bonnie's *daughter.* Did her mother tell her about me? Is this all some sort of trap?

Maybe you're one of Damon Cross's victims, she'd said, and was there a double meaning to that? Was she making fun of me? Using this all as an excuse to ask me question after question, find all the vulnerabilities she can and then share them with Bonnieandcarole? Make me the perpetual victim once again?

You're being paranoid, Mary, my Loved One urges from my purse. But, how could I not be?! A thousand context-free memories flit by in my mind: the time they poured glue in my hair, the balled-up cannon-wads of paper, the taunts. *We didn't even* have *tits yet and they made fun of me!*

I stare straight ahead. I don't want to look out the window to my right for fear of catching a glimpse of myself in the rearview. Looking down at my hands makes me carsick. And I *can't* look at Carole. I can't do anything.

I want to ask Carole if she remembers me. No—more than that, I want to ask her if *Anna-Louise* still lives in town, and does *she* remember me? Do they still see each other? Do they still hang out and make innocent people's lives miserable? Do they visit each other's houses—nice, comfortable, elegant houses like Bonnie's, such a contrast to my isolated, cramped little life?

A movie of resentment plays in my head, scored by a soundtrack of Eleanor's incessant questions and my pathetic answers. Yes, Eleanor *must* have known. Why else would she have asked so many questions carefully designed to make me feel bad about myself? She stripped me nude just as Anna-Louise, Bonnie, and Carole did the day they stole my clothes and made me parade myself naked in front of the school to get them. They're all giggling now, Eleanor included: *I can't believe she thinks you're her friend. I can't believe she's falling for it. I can't believe how pathetic she still is. I—*

Carole pulls to a stop in front of Nadine's house.

Two things happen at the same time. First, I begin digging in my purse for my keys and notice the Loved One I brought with me has come unwrapped from her shirt. It's Constance. Or, rather, the upper half of her. Once again, I guess I accidentally grabbed her in my rush to get ready. I seriously need to be careful—she's too sharp and jagged to keep mishandling like this.

Second: the music on Carole's radio changes. No longer country pop. Something a little older. A song from the '60s—familiar, but in a very strange way. The singer begins:

I don't remember what day it was . . . I didn't notice what time it was . . .

"Thank you for the ride," I say, still staring into my purse at Constance.

"You know . . . I still think of you sometimes," Carole says.

"You do?" I look up. So she *does* remember who I am. And now I suddenly can't recall: Did I tell her how to get to Nadine's house?

"I *see* your name a lot."

"Why would you see my name?"

"At the Cross House. When we were young—"

"We didn't go to school at the Cross House," I say, too quickly, pouncing on the fact to assure myself that it's correct.

"Right, but don't you remember? They laid the foundation for the school when we were in first or second grade? When they started the renovations? All the kids in town got to put their hands in the concrete. Sign their names. It was cute. You probably don't remember. I'm sure your life's a lot more exciting wherever you moved off to."

She's making fun of me.

"It *is* exciting," I tell her. "I moved to the biggest city, and . . . I help manage a bookstore and also write mysteries on the side." I know I shouldn't do it, but I risk looking up at her face, just for a moment. I want to see her expression when I say in as snide and loaded a voice as I can: "*I'm* very useful, Carole."

She looks startled. Good.

That startled look quickly dissembles as her face erupts in broken, oozing pustules. The skin, like cottage cheese under a heat lamp, yellowing, drooping, dripping, not even palatable for worms. I blink and look away, but in the half second when my eyes are closed, the screen of Eleanor's search history fills my vision.

Am I sure I didn't type that in that image search myself?

Mary, Mary, mind is scary, where do the crazy kids go?

On the radio, the singer croons: "I love you more today than yesterday . . ."

I shake my head a little.

I get out of the car.

I stand there in the cool night air.

I've never felt like this before, so capable of doing something awful. Because they're all against me. They're all actors, only I'm not the audience, I'm just a prop.

I feel the Cross House staring down at me.

I watch Carole drive away.

I imagine what it would have been like to pull out Constance and scrape Carole's decaying face off with the serrated edge, pop an eye out, the optic nerve trailing like wires because she's not real, a lie, remove all the pretense from that fake pretender, that bad actor, that bully, that useless woman. I *see* this happen. I smell it. I taste the coppery promise of violence. I slice her throat open and drive her car out into the desert, singing in triumph under the moon.

Jesus. What is wrong with me?

I need to lie down and either pretend to sleep . . . or dream of the hunt.

PART FOUR

VICTIMS

But the beginning of things, of a world especially, is necessarily vague, chaotic, and exceedingly disturbing. How few of us ever emerge from such beginning! How many souls perish in its tumult! The voice of the sea is seductive.

—Kate Chopin, *The Awakening*

I knew Arroyo would be a strange town by the way it treated its (previously) most famous monster. There are a lot of places like Arroyo out West. Technically speaking, Arroyo wasn't even a town per se, but a CDP, or Census-Designated Place, within La Paz County. There are fifteen such CDPs, each with their own council-led government and law enforcement, inside that county, and three-hundred and sixty throughout the entire state of Arizona. But most communities with a Damon Cross in their history try to capitalize on it in one way or another. Museums. Tours. Local Boy Made Evil. Not Arroyo. Arroyo wanted to remain invisible and forgotten.

—Special Agent Peter Arliss, *In the Dark with the Devil: One Heroic FBI Agent's Ground Zero Account of the Arroyo Easter Massacre*

20

Every Open Door Reveals
Another to Be Opened

APRIL 14, 2019

I'm going to murder Nadine's dog.

I feel downright nostalgic for Demon Dog back in New York—God help me, this little rat is a thousand times worse.

He left me yet another present this morning. I almost stepped in it first thing. The door to Brenda's room doesn't stay shut very well and he keeps managing to squirm his way in before I wake up. I'm tempted to barricade the door, but I'm worried about Nadine needing me in the middle of the night and me hurting myself in the dark. Took me almost fifteen minutes to scrub the stain out of the area rug under the bed.

I debate all the ways I could do it. Superglue his snout shut? Feed him to a rattlesnake? Throw him into a cactus patch and watch him try to crawl out? The desert is cruel, but oh how that cruelty can be *useful* sometimes.

"What the jolly Christfuck are you singing?" Nadine snaps.

"Huh?" I ask, looking up from my coffee cup on the kitchen counter. I've been lost in thought, watching the swirls and streaks of Lactaid resist incorporating themselves into the coffee.

Nadine is sitting at the table situated in the narrow no-man's-land between the kitchen and the living room. Yesterday's trazodone really knocked her out. She's slumped over the mostly untouched plate of eggs I just made her. She's miserable. She barely has enough energy to spit venom; mostly it just dribbles down her chin. "You're singing to yourself. It's creepy."

"I am?"

"Yes!" She mumblesings an ugly, sped-up snippet back to me: "'I love you more today than yesterday.' Knock it off."

"Sorry. I didn't know."

She grunts. Drops her fork. "Feel like shit anyway. Going back to bed. Better not be getting sick."

She pushes herself away from the table and drags herself back to the bedroom, drunkenly bumping a wall as she leaves.

Chipotle avoids her chair—he's been sitting next to her, glaring at me with eerily human suspicion. *You're responsible for this,* his eyes say. *I'm onto you, pal.*

I glare back at him.

"Stop pooping in Brenda's room," I hiss.

He gives a snarl and runs to join Nadine. From where I'm leaning against the kitchen counter, I hear her settle back into her bed, followed by a grunt and a jingle from the dog and his tags as he leaps up to join her.

I open up my palm, revealing two trazodone. I don't want the pills to get sweaty and ruined, so I slip them back to my pocket. They were just a precaution anyway—something to maybe sprinkle into Nadine's yogurt or something in case she started getting argumentative. I'm in no mood for arguments.

I hardly slept last night. I tossed and turned, head jangling with recriminating thoughts about Eleanor, visions of hurting Carole. When I finally *did* drop off, I had the Dream again, only this time, inside the spotlight were Bonnie and Carole . . . and a little girl just barely visible in the shadows I knew to be Anna-Louise. She was grinning. Full of malevolence.

Or maybe she was Eleanor.

Fucking Eleanor.

I'm grateful it's Sunday. I don't have to go anywhere, and I don't have to see anyone, particularly any daughters of former bullies who might be plotting behind my back. I'm glad I have a day to sort through these developments on my own.

As Nadine's wet snores softly roll through the house, I find the book I'm looking for in the living room and slip it off the shelf. Will this one hold any answers? I sure hope so. I really feel like every opened door just reveals another to be opened. Rooms within rooms. Walls within walls.

"Reincarnation."

I say the word to the ghost in the bathtub. If it means anything to her, she doesn't show it. She just stands there, like always. I show her the cover of the book in my hands: *The Journey of the Soul: Amazing Stories of Past Lives and Metempsychosis.*

"Is that what this is?" I ask. No response. "Am I one of you, reincarnated? I don't know if I even believe in this stuff. Then again, I don't know if I believed in ghosts before you came along."

No response.

"I guess it would explain some things, huh? But what a letdown, winding up living my life! If you get murdered by a serial killer, you should at least get to be reborn as, like . . . Arnold Schwarzenegger or something."

No response.

"Anyway. I just wanted to say it all out loud, and you seemed like the best person to say it to. Er, former person." I swallow. My throat is dry; I can hear it click. "I just . . . I don't think I can trust Eleanor anymore. I feel awful saying that. It makes me so sad. But . . . she's Bonnie's daughter, for God's sake. Why didn't she tell me? Why—never mind. This is personal stuff; you don't care."

No response.

"The books all say that ghosts want something. Do you want something?"

No response.

"Is your name Jane?" A question I haven't had the nerve to ask her yet. Now seems as good a time as any. "Jane Mayh—"

It's barely out of my mouth when: *whoosh!* Less like air being pushed toward me and more like air being sucked out of the way.

She's suddenly right in front of me, out of the tub and *right in front of me.* I smell burned ozone and meat with freezer burn and the faint odor of hot, coppery blood. All I can think of are her razor fingers. All I can see is the deep, somehow-still-oozing blood in the middle of her face covering.

I stumble backward, quickly escaping the bathroom and shutting the door. My heart thunders in my throat as I run to Brenda's room and shut myself inside. Fear and adrenaline pound through me.

Only after staring at the doorknob for a good minute, waiting to see if it will turn, do I feel like I can breathe again.

The reincarnation book is more complicated than I would have guessed. This is a good thing; it takes my mind off what just happened in the bathroom. There are charts—circles connecting circles, arranged in a tree—and data tables and even a few maps, these latter displaying evidence for, I guess, a documented case of reincarnation after a plane crash. There are thick, impenetrable quotes from gnostics and Manicheans, from Cathars and Hindus. Bolded terms like *gilgul* and *neshamot* and *samsara*.

It's a relief to stumble upon the more casually readable—*anecdotal,* to borrow the word from Eleanor—paragraphs sprinkled about like sugar.

Tales of child prodigies, expert piano players still in diapers, children with picture-perfect recall of events they had no way of witnessing, adults treated for injuries they've only dreamed about. One little boy in Taiwan apparently knew the punch line to every dirty joke imaginable, despite having no idea what any of the terms meant. Shirley MacLaine was a Moorish peasant who slept with Charlemagne (who himself would be reborn as Napoléon). Tina Turner was an Egyptian queen. Phil Collins died at the Alamo.

I don't see anything anywhere about seeing ghosts. Which means, joke or not, Eleanor's theory might be another dead end.

Then something catches my eye. A journalist turned psychic named Ruth Montgomery, herself able to trace her lives back to, of all things, witnessing Jesus Christ's circumcision (how's that for bragging rights?). She was a big believer in channeling spirits, and her preferred method . . . was automatic writing. I keep flipping and find several more references to the practice. Trancelike states with pencils or pens. Previous identities, as Montgomery puts it, "shining through."

I put the reincarnation book down. I've been avoiding looking at my journal for days. Now, I pick it up.

Truth be told, I'm embarrassed by it. The compact lunacy, the pages crammed with text, the drawings. It all makes me dizzy—and not in the way a mirror does. This is more like the ledge of a very tall building.

But Eleanor's right; there could be a clue in here somewhere. Maybe it was the result of communication with another plane of existence. A previous identity shining through.

"Or maybe it's Maybelline," I mutter to my Loved Ones, flipping through the pages. "I mean, was the woman I used to be a schizophrenic? Most of these pages don't even have punctuation at all! Make sense of this!" I rotate the journal in my hand as I read some spiraling text aloud: "'*Yea tho mortal man is not mortal no more though a morsel for your show.*' I mean, what?"

I flip to another passage.

"Of course, then I'll see something like . . ." I point to the page. "'*I am alone. I am so desperately alone. No one understands this existence but me, and I shut myself away for as long as I can as if to reinforce that. Some days, I can almost convince myself it's like I don't even exist.*'" That phrase, that oh-so-familiar phrase, sends a shiver through me.

"But then it dissolves into more nonsense! Like, look: '*Wind and sky i know that i am more than he will ever be no no no i call upon the desert the laws of the desert i call upon the avenging spirits to cleanse me of his shit of his reek of the stain of him i call upon Azazel and i call upon Zepar the A–Z of the universe, I call upon them to teach me how to scrub mys—*'"

Wait.

Those two names snag me like hooks. I read them again.

Zepar and Azazel.

The same names as Eleanor's drawings.

"How did I know those names?" I ask my Loved Ones. "I *didn't* know those names. I'd never heard of those names before."

They stare back at me, begging to differ.

I look back down at the sprawling, bottomless pages.

"Rooms within rooms," I mutter, and then my stomach sinks. "I guess I'm gonna need Eleanor's help after all. Fuck."

21

Mood Swings

APRIL 15, 2019

There's a sign taped to the door of the hospital.

Come Join Us!
TUESDAY, April 16th
TOWN HALL MEETING
8–9 p.m.
Brannigan Auditorium
You are cordially invited to join your friends and neighbors to help plan Arroyo's First Annual Easter Egg Hunt! We'll be discussing assignments and organizing to make this the Best Easter Ever! (Next week! Sunday, April 21st)
Any questions? Ask Nurse Nancy!
Please enter through the east entrance and proceed to the auditorium.
Light refreshments will be served.

Tuesday. That's tomorrow night.

Good for you, Mary, you can still keep track of what day it is.

It's too bright out today. Too hot for April.

Recess has just begun; the sound of children filing onto the playground wraps around the corner.

I quickly slip through the hospital entrance, terrified of the prospect of running into Carole. I want to get as far away from her as possible.

All the same, I pause at the top of the stairs to the basement. I have to give myself one more moment of quiet devastation over my conflicted feelings toward Eleanor, as well . . .

(*i need her*)

(*i can't trust her*)

(*i don't deserve her*)

   . . . and then, head down, I head down.

Eleanor is a giddy whirl of energy.

Even before I can put my purse down:

"That was so fun the other night. *So* fun. And fascinating! I can't stop thinking about it! And I'm so sorry about my mom; that was so not cool. I'm so embarrassed. She's . . . ugh! But I think we've got something really huge to chew on, you know? I love it, the whole idea of it: having someone else's energy living on inside you, having, like, a destiny! I want to read more and more about it. I am wiped out, though. I barely slept. I just kept thinking about, well, everything. Especially what you said."

What I said? I barely remember anything of what I said.

She's already gone through a record number of files, too, even though the day has only just begun. Talk about having energy living inside you.

Her erratic ping-ponging between subjects almost reminds me of the way the words in my journal swirl and collide and ramble on and on—which makes my desire to ask her thoughts about what I just discovered in those words burn brighter.

She stops, mid-filing, and faces me dead-on. "But seriously. Thank you again for coming over. I know it probably wasn't the easiest thing to leave your aunt for the night. I just really appreciate it. Thanks for . . . you know, listening to me. I'm sorry again for how it ended."

I tell her it was my pleasure, and she beams. Once again, I'm struck by how young she is. Barely more than a child.

She won't stop staring at me.

"What?" I ask, clutching my purse harder than I'd like to. I haven't even had a chance to set it down yet.

"Nothing. Just . . . thanks. Again." She goes back to what she was doing before I walked in. "Do you mind if—?" She indicates her phone, her short-hand for playing one of her podcasts. I tell her to go ahead, and the voices of those two giggling hosts, halfway through a description of a man named the Night Stalker hacking a hapless victim with a machete, fill the room.

(*Carole's face in pieces*)

(*rip, slice*)

I blink that image away. Now it's my turn to stare at Eleanor.

I'm starting to feel like a real asshole. What am I doing? Look at how excited she was to hang out with me. Visions of Carole's mangled face begin to be replaced by Eleanor's innocent one. Her devastation when her parents showed up. Her vulnerability when she confessed her frustrations at always being treated like a child. How could I be so stupid as to think Eleanor is in on some sort of conspiracy against me? No one is that good an actor.

I'm a bad person. I have bad instincts. I can't recognize goodness in others.

Not the undervoice. *My* voice thinks those words.

All Eleanor has ever wanted is to be taken seriously.

Let's see if I can make it up to her.

"Eleanor?"

"Yeah?" She pauses the podcast.

"I need your help."

I told myself I was just bringing the journal with me to have something to look at while we were on our breaks. But here I am, handing it over to the girl who, not five minutes ago, I was almost certain was at best a patsy and at worst a secret enemy.

Mary, you really are something.

Eleanor fans through the pages. "Whoa. You weren't kidding. This is"—she rotates the book to follow a line of text—"this is *intense*."

"I can't read it. I try, but it makes me . . . kind of dizzy. It's just too much."

"Yeah, I can imagine."

Deep breath.

"Will you read it for me? Tell me what you think some of it means?" She looks up, agog. "There are things in it I don't understand . . . but you might."

"But . . . *you* wrote it."

Did I really? I want to say. Instead, I just tell her how she's the only person I can trust. I make sure I emphasize that. This is an exclusive opportunity. A real For Eleanor's Eyes Only sort of deal.

Those eyes sparkle, a slot machine processing a jackpot. She takes the book reverently, and I know I've made the right decision. She'll never forget this, being included like this.

"You can *totally* trust me," she says, drawing a zipper across her mouth. Then she unzips it. "What kind of things don't you get? What should I look out for?"

I'm opening my mouth to tell her about Azazel and Zepar when the storage room door bursts opens.

Dr. Burton steps into the room. He snaps his fingers and points at me.

"Can I talk to you outside, please?"

It's so unexpected I don't process his question. He has to repeat it. Not good. Meanwhile, Eleanor has sprung to attention like a soldier, holding my journal behind her back.

When Burton and I are out in the basement hallway, he looks me up and down for a moment. My skin crawls. I want to cover myself. As if I'm standing here nude and being laughed at.

"I need a favor," he says. He looks tired. Annoyed. "You're good with kids, right?"

I stammer a response: "I-I don't— Why? And why do you assume I'm—?"

"We need someone at the school to help out with recess for the next couple of hours," he says. His voice takes on an echo in the concrete space. It makes me feel the weight of the house pressing down on us. "Carole didn't show up this morning. Nobody knows where she is."

We walk outside and then around the corner. Burton explains that recess lasts for three periods. The children come out in shifts, from eldest to youngest. This is so the older kids can be back inside and ready to help watch over the younger as they come back in, as well. The school tends to children from kindergarten through eighth grade and then offers something called *structured guidance* to the high school–aged teenagers of Arroyo's paltry population, which explains why Eleanor never has to go to any proper classes, I imagine.

It's fascinating to glimpse the details of this education system, so different from the more generic, institutional public schools I was filtered through. That's the word for it, too. Institutional. The faint memories I can conjure are all fluorescent, tiled, antiseptic, nothing like the warmth and grandeur of the Cross House.

What kind of lessons do these buddingly religious townschildren receive, anyway? Are they learning math and biology and reading *Anne of Green*

Gables? Or is it more like a day care–slash-seminary, where they have things like "Let the women among you have use" drilled into their soft little heads? I should ask Eleanor.

Whatever they're learning, it definitely keeps them well-behaved. Once again, I find the relative calmness of the playground remarkable compared to those I'm more familiar with.

That said, I'm told it'll be my job to wander around and "make sure there's nothing Mrs. Burton isn't seeing." She's the *real* disciplinarian. Sitting in the only patch of shade under the eaves of the building like the world's oldest lifeguard, leaving the rest of us to swim in the hot, sun-drenched dirt.

Elvira Burton. Dr. Burton's mother and Arroyo's primary school teacher. With her white hair still faintly stained as red as an old crime scene and eyes that follow you wherever you turn like some haunted portrait in a cobwebbed attic. Her whip-crack voice barks orders from her shaded perch, and the children she reprimands immediately stop. Am I good with kids? I honestly don't know. But Mrs. Burton (and she definitely stays *Mrs. Burton*, no matter how old you are) seems to have it all well under control.

"It used to be she could handle them all on her own," Dr. Burton says, "but every now and then, there's a troublemaker in the group, and I don't want her running around in this heat."

"Got it," I say.

Dr. Burton gives his mother a cursory glance and, from yards away, she gives him a barely perceptible nod. Then he turns and leaves me, heads back to the hospital. No introductions. No proper greetings. Just, here's that furniture you ordered, see you later.

A few minutes after the oldest children go back inside and the middle group of children comes out (a change heralded by a harsh, earsplitting blast from a whistle around Mrs. Burton's neck), it occurs to me that of course it's not Eleanor I should be suspicious of. It's Carole. She's up to something, not showing up like this.

Probably she drove back to Bonnie's last night, and the two of them decided to start planning *something*. What, I don't know, but something cruel. I bet they even called Anna-Louise up, getting the band back together, let's get Mary, Mary, pits are hairy; no, don't worry, I'll stay home from work today so we can really plan it out.

I know these are Nadine-thoughts. It's bad enough I'm seeing ghosts; I hate that I'm starting to see enemies everywhere, too.

But it's hard to shake these suspicions. It's almost like, by forcing myself to trust Eleanor again, I've shifted more paranoia onto everyone else.

You're all over the place, Mary.

I wind my way through the playground, barely paying attention to the strange, serene children. An apt visual metaphor: I've never belonged, even when I was their age.

Have you ever tried just relaxing, *Mary? Jesus. It's exhausting. You're suspicious, then you're not, then you are again. You don't remember bullies, and then that's all you can think of. You're as all over the place as that damn book. Maybe you* did *write it all on your own.*

I take a deep breath and let it out slowly. God, it's hot.

Movement catches my eye in the distance. I look up just in time to see someone disappear around the back of the building. The gardener. Had he been watching me? He's probably just tending the grounds. But looking at the wall he disappeared behind reminds me of something Carole said last night.

"You know . . . . I still think of you sometimes." Because we'd laid our hands in the foundation when we were small and the school was being constructed.

I'm suddenly gripped by an overwhelming desire to see if Carole was telling the truth. If I find out she was lying, then, yes, I can allow myself to feel as paranoid about her as I want. Another observable, objective experiment, like throwing rocks at ghosts. Or saying Jane's name out loud.

Because that *worked so well, Mary.*

I let myself drift around the perimeter of the playground, pretending to watch the kids but really trying to scan the concrete at the base of the mansion.

When I'm a few yards away from the wall, I spot what looks like a set of tiny indentations in the gray ground. And another. And another. They're faint from this distance. Almost looks like the base of the building has been gingerly nibbled on. Children's handprints. Must be.

I feel Mrs. Burton's eyes on me again and freeze. I look over at her. Her raptor eyes are focused on a cluster of preteen girls who might potentially be on the brink of having fun. All the same, I wait for this shift of children to start heading back inside and the youngest group to come out before I take the opportunity to get closer to the wall.

Sure enough, lines of children's handprints decorate the base of the school. They're hardly prominent—like whoever planned this knew it was a bad idea—tucked away on the side of this massive building, not even facing the main walkway. The hands and text are sun-bleached, worn away by time and indifference. I suppose it's meant to look cute and endearing. Instead, it's ominous and ugly, like the memorial to a massacre or something.

Desert Strong & Ready to Be of Use! reads a cursive engraving. Then there's a flurry of handprints and names, written in increasingly clunky, finger-driven script, as the children get younger and younger. I scan for my name. There's no date, so I'm not sure how young I'd be, and I have no memory of the event.

It's taking me too long. Mrs. Burton is going to yell at me, I just know it.

Finally, I find Bonnie and Carole and Anna-Louise, all clustered together, some three headed, six-handed monster. But where am I?

Nowhere. I reach the end of the names. I'm nowhere to be found. Like I didn't even exist.

So Carole *was* making fun of me. Pranking me. Making me feel like I had a history, a past, knowing that I'd check and be humiliated. I knew it. That fucking bitch. A tide of anger almost blots out my vision. I wish I *had* carved her face into little fucking ribbons.

Then I notice there's one more imprint. Far off from the others, at the very, very end of the wall they all share. Almost at the very corner of the building where the back wall joins.

Two little hands.

Jagged script.

Etched in concrete.

MARY

I *did* exist. I *did* have a childhood.

And apparently I was always an outcast. A sculptor couldn't have designed a better memorial to my isolation.

Nadine's voice whispers in my head: *You'd better not be starting your shit again. You'd better have outgrown all that.*

From a thousand miles away, I hear Mrs. Burton squawk. "Where did she go?!"

She's right here, I think. *She's always been right here.*

Eleanor has left for the day by the time I get back to the basement. Probably for the best. I'm in a sad mood now, thinking of bullies and names and other things that define us. If Eleanor were still here I'd probably just tell her to throw my journal away. Why bother reading it? This is all a lost cause. Mary, Mary, brain needs repair-y.

All the same, I say a silent prayer: *I hope you can help me, Eleanor. I feel more lost than ever.*

I pick up my purse, but before I head for the door, I notice something on the ground, black and crawling.

Another ant. A pretty big one.

Ugh. There'd better not be any in my purse now.

Then I notice something is off—the bug isn't moving normally. At first, I think maybe it's been injured, but then . . . no.

It's crawling backward.

My stomach lurches. It's an unnerving image to process. The ant's head is facing me, almost beckoning me, and it inches its way backward to the File Pile. Like footage run in reverse.

Eventually, it reaches the File Pile and turns around before scaling the wall of manila and white. It finds a specific spot close to the top and slips inside.

Then I remember . . . it was an ant that led me to Jane's folder.

Grimacing, I pull the top files off. Dozens of ants spill to the ground, an ant waterfall, and I shriek, lifting my feet. But when I look down, they've all disappeared. They must have scuttled back into the safety of the Pile almost before I could blink.

"Is this all really happening?" I ask the room.

You'd better not be starting your shit again.

I shake the folders I'm holding, just to make sure there are no more bugs inside.

"Are there more things I'm supposed to find in here?"

Silence.

"I'd really like to start getting some actual answers, please."

Jane bursting from the tub flashes in my mind again.

Am I really going to do this?

I guess I am.

Once I'm sure the folders are insect-free, I start stuffing them in my purse.

I feel very tired . . . and very certain something awful is going to happen soon.

22

Shreds

APRIL 16, 2019

I pause while scrubbing at the clumpy puddle of wet, runny shit and give my shoulders a rest.

Right on cue, I hear a growling. Chipotle is watching me from the doorway.

"You proud of yourself?" I ask. He lifts his upper lip in response. Shows me his nasty little teeth. Not as nasty as what he left for me, not just in Brenda's room this time but smack-dab *on the bed while I was in the kitchen making Nadine breakfast.*

The smell is absolutely rancid, enough to make me gag. Nadine has a washing machine, but she insists it's broken. More likely, she just doesn't want her water bill going up. So here I am, forced to spot clean as best I can. What it really needs is something big enough to soak in. Like the tub. The tub I am currently still too unnerved to use.

I guess on some level I should be grateful he chose to shit on the bed and not on the folders I snuck home from work. I took way too many with me yesterday. I even went so far as to stuff some folders in between my pants and shirt once my purse was too full. It's going to be tricky bringing them back in as covertly as possible—I could probably get in serious trouble for stealing other people's personal information like this.

Right now, the folders are all scattered on the floor after I threw them aside in frustration last night. No recognizable info in any of them so far (I've made it through probably half). If I still had my journal with me, I could double-check some of my ghost notes and maybe figure out the importance— if any—of this batch of folders, but for now, my little act of larceny has yielded no additional answers, no additional insights, just mounting feelings of desperation, loneliness, confusion.

And rage.

That's why something in me has kind of snapped. I want answers for *something*. I'm tired of feeling held hostage by my weirdness.

Which means—

Experiment time.

I throw the next wad of shit-smeared paper towels into the plastic shopping bag by my side and then quickly scoop up the snarling ratdog before he can run away.

"We're going to go see Jane."

When I really think about it, I'm only basing my aversion to using the tub on two things: my natural revulsion of the dead woman, and also one sentence Eleanor read in one book a few days ago that said it's a bad idea to ever touch a ghost. I can get over the first thing (or at least compartmentalize it—I'm a pro at that). The second thing is actually a pretty flimsy reason when you really think about it. Today we're going to find out just *how* flimsy.

I like this. I like objective, analytical activity. It helps me feel grounded. It helps me feel less scattered and overwhelmed.

Chipotle squirms in my hands. He wants to bite me and he wants to bark at me, but he can't quite commit to one or the other yet.

"Shhhh," I say. "Don't wake Nadine."

She's currently having an after-breakfast nap in her recliner in the living room. It's an honest nap; I didn't dope her this morning or anything. She's in much better shape than yesterday, which is good since I'll need to give her more pills tonight if I want to go to that town hall meeting. Probably shouldn't get too reliant on drugging her when I want to do social things—it can't be good for her. But for now, I'm just glad to know she seems to bounce back to normal after almost two days or so.

She'd been awake fifteen or twenty minutes ago when I first stormed out of the bedroom to get cleaning supplies.

"What just happened?" she blurted.

"Your dog left me a surprise. *On the bed*."

"Heheh." She went back to her book on Stonehenge. "That's a good dog."

Now she's snoring softly, and her good dog is growling. His squirms get more desperate when we reach the bathroom.

I close the door behind us and put him on the floor. He immediately scampers to the door and starts to try to paw it open. His nails sound insectile on the tiles.

"Relax," I tell him. "You're going to be fine." Of course, I don't *know* that.

I pull open the shower curtain.

"Jane, meet Chipotle. Chipotle, meet Jane." The dog hugs as close to the crack in the door as he can get.

The dead woman stares back at us, no sign that she's in any way invested in what's going on.

"I'm here to see how scared of you I need to be," I explain. "I notice you didn't do your in-your-face thing when I said your name this time. That's progress, I guess. I appreciate that."

Chipotle doesn't appreciate it. He's plenty scared, scratching at the door, whining. When I pick him back up, I can feel his little heart jackhammering through his body. Sorry, puppers. You started this fight. I'm sure whatever ectoplasm or ghost snot or whatever you might get coated with won't compare to your runny diarrhea, though.

I bring him over to the ghost and attempt to facilitate a meeting.

"What happens if you're touched, Jane?"

I push the dog forward.

He moves every which way he can to escape my grasp. And now Jane is also making things difficult. Every time I push the dog forward, she dodges out of the way—nothing dramatic, just enough to not make contact.

I whine in frustration. "Come on!"

Finally, the dog has enough. He manages to weasel his little body around and clamp his teeth into my hand. The pain is white hot. I don't drop him, though, so he bites again, tearing farther into my already-punctured skin.

My mind is blotted out with rage. All that remains is the undervoice, seething, *FUCK IT, I'LL DO IT,* and the next thing I know, I'm watching as if a bystander as my hands lightly toss the dog toward the ghost like a beach ball.

Oh God, no, no, NO.

He's going to pass right through her and break his legs in the tub. I can see it happen. Gravity is about to spike him down into the merciless porcelain of the tub basin. There will be a snap and an earsplitting yelp. Nadine will rush in and I'll have to explain to her what I've done. It's going to be a nightmare.

Except he doesn't yelp.

He doesn't get the chance.

The world slows down. This all happens with terrible clarity.

Jane plucks him out of the air and I have plenty of time to think: What would it look like if someone came in to see this right now? Would it look like this dog—this mean, ugly, ratlike creature—was floating in midair? Would it look like I was levitating him?

I half expect Chipotle to try to bite at the apparition holding him, but that doesn't happen. Slowed-down world or not, there's no time for that.

The noise. Like scissors in the air. Only not metal. It's an organic noise. *Shlkkh*. Fleshy. Wet.

Because it isn't actually Jane's fingers I'm hearing. It's the dog's body.

It's not the sound of something tearing meat; it's meat *being torn*. A difference so small but so profoundly unsettling.

Before I can see what that really looks like, though, I run out of the room, wanting to scream, wanting to sob, wanting to puke, but my throat is sealed up in horror. Somehow, I manage to pull the bathroom door closed behind me just in time to hear what sounds like a trash bag full of water break open all over the tile . . . and then a silence. A horrible, final silence. I stumble across the hallway into Brenda's bedroom.

I blink, staring at the plastic bag, the paper towels on the bed. Did that just happen?

I'm drenched in sweat. I look down and see fine red dots covering my skin in a mist. Not sweat after all. Oh God.

I whip off my clothes and blot myself as clean as I can, hoping I'm not spreading it around and making it worse. I need to clean myself. And the bathroom. I can't use that bathroom ever again. And I can't let Nadine use it either. She might not be able to see Jane, but she'll sure as hell see what Jane can do.

What have I done? Why did I do that? (*I didn't it wasn't me it was the undervoice*)

From the living room, groggy, waking up: "Mary? Did you just slam a door?"

I call back, "My stomach is upset. Um, you might want to stay out of the bathroom for a little bit."

Nadine laughs appreciatively. "Gross!" A moment of silence, then: "I wanna take a bath later, though, so . . . light some matches or something."

"Good idea!" A Good Girl smile strong enough to split my face in two. Tears spill down my cheeks from the effort. "We can do that!" I'm astounded my voice can squeeze out, with my heart thudding so frantically in my throat. I finish putting on fresh clothes, then grab a handful of pills. "How about some ice cream first?"

23

The Sound

Shlkkh!

I can't stop hearing it.

My whole walk up the hill to the Cross House, it follows me.

As I pass Chantelle—who's having a very intense phone conversation at the reception desk—I hear it.

I even hear it as I reach the stairs, despite the fact that Dr. Burton is in the middle of shouting at someone on the second floor. He's furious. I didn't know he could show so much emotion . . . but all I really can hear is the sound of the dog's flesh severing into a shower of viscera and hot blood.

Shlkkh!

It's even worse when I get down to the basement. Eleanor's not there. There's no one to distract me, no one to play loud podcasts where insouciant people laugh about horrible things that I didn't have to witness.

Where is she? Why isn't she here? I was hoping for a friendly face to take my mind off—

Shlkkh!

Ripping. Shredding. Blood splashing the tile in a burst. The faintest whimper before vocal cords were severed—or maybe it was my own voice, caught in terror as the breath flew out of me.

I can't stay down here alone. I go back upstairs to see if I'm needed to help out with recess again. I am. Carole still hasn't shown up, from what I can gather (although everyone seems very distracted today, and not very talkative). For once, I'm actually eager to help, to be distracted by the sun and the children and even the anxiety-provoking presence of Mrs. Burton.

It doesn't work for long. It's too easy to imagine little bodies bursting into fireworks displays of blood and viscera, torn to shreds by invisible claws. Soon enough, I'm back in the not-silent silence of the basement.

Shlkkh!

I don't know what to do. Do I go back to Nadine's? Do I run? Do I . . . organize some files? Seems stupid, but menial work has always helped clear my mind before.

Looking at the File Pile, I realize I forgot to bring any stolen files back with me. I'll have to remember to do that tomorrow. I don't like thinking of them lying around in Brenda's room. Something could happen to them, like the dog could—

No. The dog *couldn't.* Because the dog is—

Shlkkh!

Splash.

I try to get a little work done.

I'm successful for about fifteen minutes. Then I notice the first ant.

I stare at it. It's doing its unnerving, walking-backward thing. A chilliness comes over me and, rather than watch where it's going, I lift my foot up and bring it down onto the bug. Hard.

Slam!

When I lift my foot up again, nothing's there.

No, there it is. It somehow evaded my foot by a few centimeters. I stomp again—*Slam!!*—hard enough to feel the impact in my teeth.

I missed it. Just barely.

So I try again.

And again.

And now I see more of them. A whole cluster. Crawling backward from the File Pile toward the compact shelving unit.

Just like that, the fury is back on me. Killing these ants is now the most important thing in the world. I start stepping as hard as I can on them. Each time, unsuccessfully—they're too quick. They move in a tightly knit unit, but as soon as my foot comes down, they scatter.

"You little fuckers!" I shout, breathing heavily. "Quit moving!"

Slam, slam, slam!!

The ants all disappear behind the compact shelving.

"Fuck you!"

Wait. Eleanor showed me how to work the control console that operates the shelves. It's right here on the wall. I fiddle with the buttons. The motor roars to life, a truly apocalyptic noise, half flooded engine, half hydraulic press.

A few false starts as I remember which thing does what, but then with a deafening clatter, all the shelves on the track move away from the wall, revealing an empty gap save for the tracks above and below. Looks very much like a mouth missing a tooth.

It's dark over here, but then I see a little segmented knot against the dim concrete. It's like they were waiting for me.

"Gotcha," I say.

This time, though, before I can squish them, they disappear into a crack in the wall.

"No!"

I stand there, panting, enraged beyond reason. I thought the cliché was "seeing red"; I'm so furious, *every* color seems more vibrant. My eyes are bulging.

The crack the ants slipped into is just barely visible. Hardly a hair's width. They're gone for good. But then, I notice something interesting. The crack goes straight up, vertically. Then cuts a ninety-degree angle to the right about three feet off the ground.

It's not a crack. It's . . .

"A door?" I whisper.

I fumble at the possible-door like I fumbled at the control panel of the compact shelving.

I don't exactly know how it works, but some instinctual knowledge guides my hand. I can't get my nails in to pry, and there's no handle, but the right amount of pressure at the right spot and—

Click.

The tiny door pops open an inch.

I swing it open all the way.

It's as if I've opened up a portal to space itself. Or, no—it's as if I were in a submarine in the deepest ocean and I've just opened up a hatch, only instead of water rushing in, it's cold, musty air. The black beyond is featureless. Pure, inky nothingness. Profound and chilling.

I have time for one thought—

The Dream. I was inside the walls in my Dream. This is how you get inside the walls.

—and then I hear scraping. Dragging. And the temperature plummets even further in the room.

Maybe I'm still thinking of submarines because what emerges from the secret door reminds me of some sort of red, gnarled crab. Then more follows: an arm, a shoulder, a foot, a leg . . . and a cream-colored, blood-saturated pillow-case for a head. The dead woman's heavy breasts swing pendulously against her chest as she pulls herself to a standing position on the other side of the door.

My side.

I back into the metal bookcase behind me. A choice: peel to the right or left. The ghost is right in front of me. Rasping. Her claws flexing. I hear that sound again—*Shlkkh!*—but in the air or in my mind? Has she sliced me already? Would my nerves even know it?

I move to the right. Bad move. I should've moved left; I would have been next to the console to control the shelves, I could've moved the shelves back into place and blocked the door. Now I have to circle around the entire shelving unit.

But she shouldn't want *to touch me, right? Jane avoided the dog until I threw him at her.*

Unless . . . maybe they have a taste for blood now . . .

I make a weak noise. An attempt to tell the ghost I'm sorry, that whatever I did was a mistake, I'm not trying to rile her, or any of them, up. The air is too cold and thin to carry words.

I keep backing up. She pursues steadily. I skid over a stack of files. Manage to stay upright, but barely. Paper spins out everywhere.

By the time I circle around the shelving unit to the control side, my heart is ready to burst out of my throat. *Be calm, just don't touch her.* I try to punch in the commands to close the shelves and block the wall.

Another woman has emerged from the wall.

She's growling, from deep in her throat. A cat's warning.

Behind her, another one. I can hear the pinhole whistle of her breathing and she steps through.

My fingers shake. I'm sweating even though the basement is freezing. I punch the wrong buttons, and the compact shelving moves one way, then another, shuddering, shaking, confused by my contradictory commands.

Another dead woman appears. Christ, how many are in the wall?

I smash my hands on the console, then throw myself backward to avoid yet another ghost (baby-blue pillowcase, claws up in full menacing display, in a gesture that reminds me of a doctor after scrubbing for surgery). As the shelving unit goes haywire, I land full force against the File Pile and scramble in every direction I can, trying for purchase. Files explode and scatter everywhere. I throw some more in self-defense. It works, at least as subterfuge, and I run forward, slipping and sliding in paper.

I dart to one side and manage to avoid another woman, only to realize in horror as a shelf bears down on me that I've run *into* the compact shelving unit. I escape barely in time to avoid the closing shelf, then run into yet *another* dead woman. I dive back into a newly opened space in the motorized shelves. I trip and fall over the tracks, slamming my knee down into the concrete, and grab on to the shelves for support. I'm spilling files and folders everywhere. The commotion causes the other shelves to rock and drop their contents. Paper rains down, and the dead women's livid, necrotic feet drag through the sheets.

I'm going to be either torn apart or crushed.

I try to crawl to the other side. A dead woman waits for me there. I turn on my butt and try to backtrack. The way is momentarily clear, and I try to get free. Suddenly, I can't move.

There's a tremendous groaning. At first, I think it's some sort of cry from the ghosts, a howl of rage. Then I realize my ankle is on fire. My foot is caught in between two shelves. The noise is the engine of the compact shelves, outraged that it can't close farther. I try to pry myself free, but I only succeed in awkwardly jamming my foot further.

The room is freezing now. How many women are in here? They cast no shadows, yet I can feel their looming presence fall on me as if they did. Closer and closer. I hear the rasp of their broken throats, the twin whistles of crushed tracheas and shattered teeth.

I look up and there's at least half a dozen. This close, I can see more de-tails on each of them. Bruises pepper their skin. One appears to have been socked heavily in the gut. Scrapes abrade them everywhere.

One woman is barely holding in her intestines with one red, taloned hand. Another limps, her other leg bent in a ninety-degree angle halfway down the shin. One bears bite marks up and down her arms. Different headcloths cover each of them—pillowcases, shirts, even a window curtain—but they are all clotted with blood, wet and obscene, raw.

"Please," I finally manage to gasp. "Don't. I'm . . . I'm one of you."

They don't care. Or maybe they *do.* Maybe that's the entire point; they've come to make good on our shared destiny. I'm being claimed. A fellow Victim, like in Eleanor's portraits. Goodbye, Mary. She was so invisible she was killed by ghosts, how fucking fitting. At least it will be quick. Will I even know when it happens? Or will I wink out and wake up with no memory of this pathetic existence save for some nagging dreams?

"Close your eyes! Close your fucking eyes!"

I do, without question.

It's a man's voice. Firm. Angry. And suddenly, he's hurling insults. "Fuck off. You stupid piece of shit. Get the fuck out of here. You worthless, ugly bitch. Go on! Nobody needs you. Go rot, you ugly cunt." Takes me a moment to realize he's yelling at the ghost women. Corralling them, like some sort of cowboy. Only with insults instead of a lasso.

I don't know how long I lie there, eyes shut, heart pounding, breath burning in my throat. All I know is that breath never stops. I never feel the slice of razors through my skin and bone.

"They're gone," the man's voice says at last.

To punctuate that fact, I hear the door in the wall shut with a firm *click*.

I open my eyes. The man is telling the truth; the dead women are gone. But he's nowhere to be found either. I twist awkwardly, trying to free myself from the jammed shelving unit. Did he go into the wall with the ghosts?

Then he comes around from the other side of the shelving unit, and I lose my breath all over again.

The gardener stares down at me.

"You see them, too?" For the second time in a week, I'm gasping these words in the basement. Only this time, I'm in the most prone, vulnerable position I've ever been in, still trapped in the shelving unit, ankle shrieking, knee throbbing, elbows digging into the dirty floor.

"Of course I see them," he says.

"I . . . I think they were going to kill me. This morning, I saw one of them do something horrible and I think they wanted to—"

"You dumb fucking bitch," he says abruptly. "This was your fault."

"What do you mean?" I try to wriggle free, but it's still no use. "Can you help me?"

He doesn't move. He just stares down at me with his blandly handsome face. "You need to understand something about them," he says. Then he crouches onto his heels so he's closer to my level. His knees don't pop. "They need your attention. Okay? It *feeds* them. So you've gotta stop all this. Talking to them, asking questions about them, all of it. It only makes them mad. And strong."

"But—"

"*Ignore* them." His voice is firm. His blue eyes flash with anger. "Put them in their place and then ignore them."

"How?!" Images of Chipotle in the bathroom, his eyes bulging in brief, intense terror before I ran out of the bathroom and heard that wet, horrifying *burst*. "I've seen what they can do! It's not safe to ig—"

"*Listen to me,*" he says, with no hint of camaraderie. Just unquestionable seriousness. "They're used to it. They *deserve* it. Without your eyes on them, they'll go back to behaving real quick."

"Fine. Okay." My ankle, my back, my elbows, are all starting to scream in pain. "Can you please help me out of this?"

But he's making his way to the door.

"Wait!" I yell.

He doesn't wait. He's out of my line of sight now.

"Come back!" I shout at him. "You fucking asshole!"

Silence. He's gone.

I'm not totally alone, though. I look down and see an ant crawling over my forearm.

24

Fish

When I hear the rasping, scratching noise outside, of course I assume they've come back to finish the job.

The front door to the storage room creaks open and I brace myself for an entire army of dead women, ready to fall on me in a wheezing, gibbering mass.

But when I turn my head from its awkward angle on the floor, a solitary woman, both clothed and alive, is standing in the doorway.

"Oh my God!" she exclaims, running to me. "What happened? Are you okay?"

It's Nurse Nancy.

"My foot," I manage.

She hurries around the compact shelving unit and finds the control panel. A few button pushes and the shelf, which was still making a grunting, groaning whine and pulsing against my ankle like toothless gums chewing, whirs backward. I'm free.

I pull myself out. The pains in my ankle and knee are magnificent, but now that the adrenaline has receded, I can feel I'm aching everywhere. Nancy keeps asking me what happened, over and over. All I can think to say is, "The shelving unit went haywire." Not a story that will hold up, but I don't care because now I'm getting a clear-eyed look at what's happened.

The entire basement is in ruin. It's like a bomb went off.

Papers are everywhere. A good portion of the File Pile, as well as much of the shelves' contents, is now spread out along the floor: an ocean of manila.

Nancy looks at the machine. Kicks it lightly, waits to see if it reacts. "We have to get rid of this thing; you could've been seriously hurt. Wait. *Are* you seriously hurt?"

I shake my head, remembering what the gardener said. "My fault. It's . . . I must have done something wrong. But I don't know what."

"No, no, no, Burton buys old junk all the time. He loves antiques. It's dangerous."

I can't stop staring at the mess. The folders. The wreckage. The reality of the situation is starting to sink in.

"All that work. I ruined it." My voice chokes with shame. "Eleanor is going to hate me."

"What? She's not going to hate—"

"And now *they* hate me, too. What am I going to do?"

"They who? Mary, what are you talking about?"

I shrug, still staring at the mess. All these papers. I'm so *stupid*.

Nancy gives me a sympathetic head tilt. "Why don't we get you some ice and some Tylenol?"

I give a weak nod. I'm so fucking stupid.

"You're okay now," she says. "Do you mind if I touch you?"

Before I answer, she carefully reaches out and squeezes my shoulder.

I continue to feel that squeeze even as we make our way up to an exam room. I try to take comfort and strength from it but, the whole way there, I'm a skittish wreck, jumping and starting at every shadow and corner.

I move as quickly as my bruised body allows, head down but eyes peeled, ready to bolt at the first sight of anything. Aches and pains pound through my nerves as steadily as questions pound through my skull: *Why, why, why?* Why did they attack me? Why does the gardener see them, too? *Why did he leave me like that?*

"Here we are again," Nancy says as she hands me an ice pack. Another exam room, another cold compress after another unexpected spectral run-in (not that she'd know that last part). I have to give a small, defeated laugh. Funny how the extraordinary can begin to seem mundane after a while. Circles. Cycles.

Next she riffles through a cabinet to retrieve some Tylenol.

Her eyes linger on me after she puts the painkillers in my hand.

"Okay, I'm just going to ask," she says after a moment. "Mary, are you okay? Is there something going on with you? And I don't just mean today. I mean, you won't even look at me."

"Sorry," I say, very much not looking at her. "I just—"

"You don't have to be sorry, I just want to know if you're okay. Have you been using the trazodone? You look exhausted."

I think of Nadine, snoring away in her bed, and nod. "It works really well. Knocks me out."

"Hm." She doesn't sound convinced.

I want to bring my eyes up to meet hers. I really do. "I'm just going through a very strange time right now. It's hard being back here. And Nadine. And . . . I just haven't been feeling myself." Not exactly the truth, but certainly not lying.

"I get that." She's silent for a moment. "Dr. Burton probably wouldn't approve of this, but . . ." I watch her back as she goes to the counter, finds a notepad, scribbles something, and tears off a page. As soon as her face is facing me again, I look away.

She's holding a piece of paper out.

"You know that little strip mall over on Mariposa Street, close to the highway?"

I do. It's about an hour's walk from here.

"There's a pretty special store there," she continues. "They sell a lot of holistic stuff. Home remedies. Teas. Even crystals and incense, if you're into that sort of stuff. It's not a substitute for medicine, but . . . I wrote down a few suggestions. Black cohosh. Ginseng. Kava. CBD. It all can help."

"Oh?"

"Plus, talking, Mary. Talking helps." She comes over and leans against the exam table next to me. "Look, I don't know you, Mary. But you're weird, right? You're a weird person?"

I blink. "What?"

"Nothing wrong with weird. Weird is great! And I have a feeling you like to do things on your own. Or maybe you don't *like* it, but that's what you're used to. I get it. I'm the same way, actually. It's easier. It's comfortable. But there are some things you go through . . . You know, I had to have a hysterectomy when I was thirty-eight. They found a growth, they took everything out just to be safe, and, whoo, the emotional journey that was? It was a lot. And I was not someone who liked to rely on her family for help—I like my space. But . . . if I hadn't had my mother and my sisters to talk with during that adjustment, I don't know what I would have done. Just because things are *easier* one way doesn't mean they're always *better*. It's like my grandfather used to tell me when I was small, whenever I complained about doing something I didn't want to do: *el que quiera peces, que se moje el culo.*"

"What does that mean?" I ask.

"Basically? The real good stuff takes effort. And it can be uncomfortable, but . . . if you want to eat fish, you gotta get your ass wet."

"That's really funny."

"It is funny. But it's also true. Relying on other people is messy. But some mess is necessary. So just . . . don't try to go it alone, okay?"

"Okay. Thank you."

She pats my leg, then moves off the table, all business. "Now. That damn shelf thing. If you want, I can talk to Dr. Burton tomorrow, see if he'll be willing to—what's the phrase? Put it to pasture?"

"No, please, I don't want to be a bother."

"Mary, you were almost eaten alive! You don't have to apologize for it!"

"I'm just trying to be Good." I wonder if she hears the capital letter.

"Good? Good this: good riddance to that machine." Nancy claps her hands together like a farmer dusting dirt off. Then, after a beat: "I mean, no promises. He doesn't exactly *listen* to my suggestions. Some days, he looks right through me, you know? Like I'm a ghost."

I look up at her for a moment. Her kind face, smiling, trying to make me laugh. Then her face crumbles into wet, maggoty ruin, and I look away.

"Like you don't exist," I say. "I know the feeling."

She points at me, excited. "Exactly! Like I don't exist. Women our age get to know that feeling well, huh? Although"—she gives a wry chuckle—"it's a little different when you're brown. In this country, when you're brown, you don't exist until something goes wrong. Then you really, *really* exist, you know what I mean?"

I don't know how to respond to that, so I give her a tight-lipped smile and say, "I'm sorry."

She laughs—a genuine laugh—and throws her hands up to the sky in mock ecstasy. "Finally! Apology accepted." Pause. "I'm just playing with you, Mary."

"Oh. I'm sorry."

She groans. "You mentioned that." I've become boring, predictable. She goes to the counter and tidies things up. "*I'm* sorry," she says. "I shouldn't joke. Everyone's stressed out right now, and I . . . It's a nervous habit of mine, joking. I had a boyfriend once who said I was the only person he knew who cracked more jokes during our breakup than our relationship."

"Why is everyone stressed right now?" I remember Burton's yelling, Chantelle's intense phone call, that feeling of tension in the air a million years ago when I first arrived this morning. "Is it because of Easter or something?"

"Oh, sure. That and the murder."

My mouth goes dry. "The what?"

I feel Nancy's eyes on me.

"Did you not—? Everyone is talking about it, so I just . . ." She collects herself. But I somehow know what's she's going to say before she says it. "That woman who works at the school. Worked. The blond one?"

(*Her face*)

"Carole," I say.

(*Porcelain slicing into that horrid, decomposing, oh-so-satisfying-to-peel flesh*)

"Right. Carole. It's awful. Some kids from Socorro found her car out by the highway last night. And . . . *her*. I almost thought about canceling the town hall meeting tonight, but Dr. Burton said he wanted to say a few words at it. Are you going to be there?" She sounds almost hopeful, despite the news she's relaying.

I mumble something about, yeah sure, I was planning on it. "But," I almost interrupt myself, "what happened?"

She shrugs. "That's all I know. Well . . . I overheard a little more than that—Chantelle has been on the phone all day, and she gets a little loud sometimes. But . . . I don't know if you want to hear this. Did you know her or—?"

"What did you hear?"

"Just . . . Chantelle kept talking about her face. I guess something had been done to her face. Like, 'He tried to take her face,' I think she said. 'He tried to take it and he messed it up,' or something." She shudders, grimaces. "I don't know why that's extra horrifying to me. I mean, can you imagine? Something awful happening to your face like that? Ugh!"

25

The Best Defense

Nadine's bathroom is a horror show. Blood everywhere. Fur. Bits of flesh. The first thing that comes to mind is that it's like someone turned on an industrial-size food processor full of spaghetti sauce and toupees. The metallic, meaty smell makes me want to gag. Poor dog. I can't believe I did this. Except, no, *I* didn't. It was the undervoice. With a little help, of course . . .

The shower curtain is closed. She must be back in her usual spot. For now, at least.

The room feels ten degrees colder than I remember it feeling.

I put the mop and bucket and other cleaning supplies down on the floor quietly.

Nadine's drugged, wet snores roll through the house. Otherwise, it's deathly silent.

Except inside my head. Inside my head, it's chaos.

For once all the voices in my head are in agreement. The undervoice, my Loved Ones, my own voice, all of them are shouting: *This is a horrible idea, this is Capital-C Crazy, Mary, don't do this, get out of there already!*

I ignore them.

Not because they're wrong but because they're right. This *is* a horrible idea. But I have to do it. I have to try.

The whole walk home—more of a limping drag than a walk—I couldn't stop looking around frantically. All my senses felt heightened. They were, I knew, the senses of a wounded animal in the midst of predators. They were the senses of *prey*.

So I tried to focus, to wrap my head around everything that's happened so far during this strange and horrific day. Chipotle. The women in the walls. The gardener. The news about Carole.

It all led me to the same conclusion.

I'm fucked.

Well and truly fucked.

For starters, there's a murderer out there. A mad killer judging by what he did to Carole. And I know it in my bones that I'm likely next on his list.

You don't know that, the voices all say.

No. But I do know Carole was murdered right after dropping me off. That timing is too notable. And I also know Carole was a Woman of a Certain Age, just like me. We're a type, to quote Eleanor. And I've listened to enough of Eleanor's podcasts to know these kinds of murders are never isolated incidents. There will be more. Maybe I won't be *exactly* next on the list . . . but if there's a list I'm definitely on it.

Plus, I mean . . . I'm a reincarnated Victim, right? Isn't that my destiny? My inheritance? So, of course I'm a target.

And let's not forget the ghosts. They're *also* out to get me. They would have killed me this afternoon if it weren't for the gardener's last-minute rescue.

So that's double the chances of Victimhood right there. If the murderer doesn't get me, the ghosts will.

All of which means I'm fucked.

Unless . . .

I realized what I had to do about halfway to Nadine's house.

The closer I got, the scarier that idea became, and the surer I became that there's no other way. After all, if I want to eat fish, I've got to get my ass wet.

You're going to get your ass killed, the voices say.

I start in on cleaning Nadine's bathroom.

Some time later, I've made a good dent in the nauseating work. My plan is to clean as much of the blood and dog bits as I can, then unscrew all but maybe one of the vanity lights in the mirror just enough so that the room is effectively dark. That plus the fact that this was never a spotless room to begin with should hopefully cover up all signs of what happened here.

As always, the menial activity helps clear my mind a little . . . although, this time I can't quite lose myself in it because I'm always casting a nervous glance at the tub. Will she leap out at me the way those women oozed out the hole in the basement wall, talons flashing?

The water in the bucket sloshes as the mop goes in, comes out. Nadine's distant, thick, rhythmic snores add to the feeling of tidal push and pull.

Nadine was the final tumbler that fell into place when I made the decision to run this little experiment.

She'll need to use this bathroom soon enough. I can't keep drugging her forever. It *had* to be cleaned.

But that wasn't the only reason.

When I finally dragged myself inside, after my long, painful walk back from the Cross House, I realized I had three options, where initially I thought I only had two. The first was to just resign myself to Victimhood, change nothing and let whatever method of death was going to get me get me. The second was to recklessly conduct the experiment I'm about to conduct. But now there was another choice that stared me in the face. I could live like Nadine.

My eyes had fallen on her living room bookcase of prized reading material, so very much like my own shelf of Loved Ones: a museum piece preserving the last vestiges of our individuality. The final bits of ourselves the scouring winds of the world couldn't blast away. I looked at those books and I imagined how easy it would be to shut myself away in here. See enemies everywhere. Jump at shadows. Curse and theorize and withdraw. I'd have an amazing teacher—the best, really. And I know she'd relish the company.

I looked at those books and I thought:

Abuse is its own kind of reincarnation, isn't it? We become the ones who made us.

I don't want to be like Nadine.

I'd rather die than let that happen.

Looking at the shower curtain now, in this inordinately cold, blood-smeared room, I think: I might just get my wish.

I close my eyes, remember the gardener, and pull open the curtain.

The dead woman stands in the tub and stares at me through her bloody cloth. Her broken throat gives a faint whistle. Her claws flex. They're even redder than before, as if the dog's blood isn't just coating them, it's giving them life, giving them the power to take on brighter shades, and now those claws are going to reach out and carve me into ribbons, drink deep in my blood, too, and pulse an even richer red than—

"G-go away, you pathetic idiot," I say, eyes focusing on the rim of the tub. "You dumb piece of shit. Get your worthless shit self away from me before I puke."

I'm not looking at Jane . . . but I sense her pause. Even the coldness in the room feels as if it's holding its breath.

You have to do better than that, Mary. Think of That Tone—the one you're so afraid people will take with you.

"I've gotta clean up this fucking mess—no idea how it happened, but whoever did it is a real dumb bitch."

No. That's not quite right. You don't need to play dumb or act like you don't see her. You need her to know she's not worthy of being seen.

"Go back to whatever sad, lonely shithole you came from, you depressing, stupid waste of space. I want to say you're nothing, but you can't even do that much. You're worse than nothing. 'Nothing' would be an improvement. 'Nothing' would be a fucking delight. You make 'nothing' feel like a visit from the fucking Queen."

The room begins to feel slightly warmer. She's physically moving farther and farther away from me. It's working.

"I never should have looked into your past, your stupid name. Thank God it's so forgettable. I can't wait to forget you. It'll be the easiest thing I've ever done." Then a realization: "I know why you hide in your stupid tub. You *know* you're worthless. And guess what? You're right. Get the fuck out of my space!"

She's out of the tub now and fully retreated into a corner of the room. It's working! Thank God, it's working! I might just have one less thing to worry about after all!

I dump the water from my mop bucket into the tub, refill it, rinse the mop out, and so on. The tub is all mine. The whole time, it's like my back is on fire, an icy kind of fire, with my nerves trying to alert me of the danger I'm exposing myself to, but I ignore it all. Because nothing's there. Nothing worth caring about, at least.

"Yeah," I say, acting like I'm talking to myself. "That's better. Much better. That's the kinda world I want to live in. It's just like you don't . . ."

But I can't bring myself to finish that sentence. It sticks in my throat like sand.

It's just like you don't even exist.

26

Meeting

Darkness turns the town upside down.

At the top of the hill, I look at the community spread out beneath me. Very few lights, besides the occasional streetlamp. Some spots, you could almost convince yourself you're looking into the past, to a time before electricity. Up above, though, the stars and the moon burn with astonishing busyness. There's only the faintest wisps of cloud tonight, and so it becomes an image of a nighttime cityscape turned on its head: the stars are apartment buildings and office windows and streetlights; the town is just a dark, featureless wash.

The parking lot is full. I can even hear the people inside the school from where I'm standing, some twenty yards from the entrance.

A sudden flush of anxiety washes through me. So many people—more than I've been around since I arrived here.

I wonder if Carole's murderer is here tonight. Will he be watching me? Will he follow me home? Will he choose a different victim tonight and save me for later?

Another thought on the heels of these: And what about Anna-Louise? What if *she's* here? What if tonight's the night *we* finally meet again?

I suppress my shudders by remembering that none of that matters for my purposes—I'm only here for one person. The damn gardener. Somehow he knew what to do about the ghost women, and I want answers. I *deserve* answers. I'm going to demand them.

I decide to wait until the meeting is already underway before I slip in. That way, I can avoid undesirable run-ins and also get a good lay of the land. With a little more time to kill, I make my way past the playground and, before I know it, I'm looking at my handprints in concrete again.

They're clearer in the starlight. The shadows and purple light deepen the usually sun-washed contrast. The distance between my hands and all the others feels even vaster now. I can't believe I strayed this far away from the rest of the kids. More than that, I can't believe the adults let me. Then again, these were the same adults who let me wander off during that field trip at the museum, who didn't notice I wasn't there when they left.

A few more stragglers arrive and enter the school. The meeting is in the auditorium, which is farther inside the building, so I don't hear the meeting when it starts, I just hear the silence that suddenly falls over the building. The halls are clear. It's just me and the night now.

I'm about to head in myself when I hear noise from around the corner of the building.

An animal? A human?

Now I should *definitely* go inside. Could be a coyote. Or a mountain lion. Or a murderer.

The noise gets closer. Stops. Just around the corner from me. I try my best not to crunch gravel as I tiptoe around the building to see.

It's him. Looking up at the sky.

Just the man I came to see.

We stare at each other in the moonlight. The moon is bright, half-full and growing.

What's my opener? You come here often? How 'bout that moon? It sure moves, from what I hear.

"Hi," I say. "I was hoping I'd run into you."

He looks otherworldly in this light. His strong, dimpled chin. His tense brow. His tired, wet, sad eyes. So handsome, yet so defeated. The face of someone who should be the center of attention, and yet here he is in the shadows.

I swallow. "I wanted to thank you for what you did today. I've been so scared lately, and now I feel a little safer. I'm very grateful. But." Deep breath. Here's the hard part. "I need answers. I need to know h—"

He takes off running in the opposite direction. Full sprint.

My brain literally cannot process it for a few seconds. He just . . . ran away?

Who fucking does that?

Then I remember how he left me trapped in the shelving unit. Injured.

Vulnerable. I could still be trapped down there for all he cared. I don't want him to have the satisfaction of ignoring me. I want to ruin his night.

I strap on anger like a jet pack and follow him.

I regret this immediately.

I'm sore. I'm not in great shape. My ankle still hurts. My jet pack runs out of fuel pretty quick.

A stitch sets its teeth into my side. My breath whistles. My joints feel set in concrete. Good God, I've never felt heavier, clumsier. The only thing that keeps me going is I'm pretty sure I'd collapse if I stopped or tried to change direction.

"Leave me alone!" he shouts back at me.

What a goddamn baby!

Unfortunately, I can't will myself to be faster than he is. He easily outpaces me. But then I see him hook around the next corner of the mansion and realize he's just running a circle around the building. I lose him about halfway, but just by following the arc in my breathless, pained walk-run, soon I find myself right back where we started.

The sonofabitch is kneeling by my handprints. What is he doing to my handprints?

His silhouette begins to merge with the building's. I use the final bit of energy I have stored up and, without a second thought, I charge at him, shoulder down, full speed. We both collapse into the dirt.

He scrambles to a squatting position. If I had my umbrella with me, I'd swat him, trip him. Someone is laughing, and it's only when more air whoops into my lungs that I realize it's me. This is suddenly the funniest thing that's ever happened to me, tackling a stranger in the moonlight.

Unfortunately, I come back to my senses too late. He's back at the wall, and he's opened some invisible aperture because just like that, he disappears. Vanishes. Like he was never here.

My laughter dies immediately.

"No!" I wheeze.

I crawl to the spot where he disappeared, my adult hands laid over my tiny childhood ones. I bang on the side of the building.

"Where did you go? What did you do?"

No answer. Of course. I sit back and catch my breath. Regroup. Look at my tiny handprints and ragged name. Feel generally like a pathetic reject.

Then I notice something. The A in my name. It looks . . . abnormal. It's childish handwriting made even cruder by the medium of finger and concrete, sure, but it's tilted and pointed in such a noticeable way that . . . it looks more like it's pointing somewhere specific than just an accident of sloppy script.

I follow the point's direction and feel along the wall. I push and push along the base until—

Click.

A door. Accessible with the right amount of pressure in the right spot. Even more invisible than the one in the basement. The siding of the wall is slatted and the seams of the door are matched with the grooves—you'd never have known there was an opening here. Unless—

Memory, like a flash of light. A strobe.

"I've been here before," I whisper. "In the crawl space."

Flash.

"When I was little."

Flash.

The crawl space.

The crawl space that, for all I know, is teeming with dead women. Dead women and living spiders. Snakes. Who knows what nasties could be hiding in the darkness of this old house? I'm not seriously going to follow him in there, am I?

But I know I am. Even more than following him, I'm going to follow that feeling, that flash of memory.

I give myself one more moment to breathe the clean night air and then, for the second time today, I go after my fish.

27

Crawl Space

Bad idea.

This was a bad, bad idea.

Oh God, what am I doing?

If I thought it the basement crawl space looked dark, then this is beyond darkness. This is living, suffocating blackness the likes of which I've never experienced before. No. Not entirely true. I've seen it in dreams. But I never thought darkness like this could exist in waking life.

I'm on my hands and knees, so the gritty concrete against my palms is the only reference point I have. I have no idea how low the ceiling is or where I can go.

Worse than that, I also don't know what's in here with me. I can smell dry, fetid earth and wood. I feel the cottony wisp of spiderwebs and imagine black widows (*their bites can paralyze you*), brown recluses (*their venom dissolves your skin like acid*), any other sort of deadly creatures hanging nearby waiting to strike.

There could be a nest of snakes in the corner. Or a wounded coyote, rabid and insane from hunger and from being lost in the dark. Any moment now, I'll hear it growling and pulling itself toward me across the floor.

Panic starts to set in. I turn around to find my way out again, but I can't even see my hand in front of my face. It's totally disorienting. I find the wall again, but I'm not sure if it's the same part of the wall I came in through. I feel for the door, but nothing budges.

I stop. Breathing heavily. Trying to concentrate on what I do have, not what I don't.

I can *hear* . . .

. . . scraping, shuffling footsteps. Human footsteps.

I put my hand up, carefully, wincingly, expecting to end up wrist-deep in spiderweb. No. The ceiling is higher here; I can stand. Okay. I get to my feet. Hold still again; wait for another audio clue. There he is. Hands in front of me like a blind woman, I do my best to follow the sounds. Now for refuge, not just pursuit.

Mary, has it occurred to you yet that he *is the killer? That this is a trap he's led you into?*

Then why did he save me earlier? Sport? Doesn't matter—right now, he's the only definable thing in here, and I'm just going to have to take my chances or float away into nothingness like an untethered astronaut.

My hands hit concrete. The walls of the crawl space have been finished—I remember Nancy saying these were essentially old-time air-conditioning ducts. The concrete is certainly cold to the touch. A horrible image comes to me: these smooth, hard walls are teeth. Soon they'll move toward me, set in a splintery pair of jaws, the house coming alive, finally claiming me as prey.

Where are we? Am I walking farther into the house? Farther along the perimeter? A sharp turn. Suddenly—*wham!* The space in front of me becomes unyielding brick and wood. Thankfully, my foot hits it before my face.

The sound of footsteps to my left tells me which way to turn. What I hope is a nail scrapes across my hand, drawing blood. My hiss turns into a whimper. What if it was a claw? I guess one good thing is that it'd be easier to ignore the ghosts in this darkness—I can't see a goddamn thing.

Another turn and I give a quick glance behind, as if that will help me get oriented; it's just as black and featureless in that direction. It's dizzying, not knowing anything about where I came from or where I'm going. How do I even know there's air in here? Was I really once here before as a child? Where did that memory come from? And how did I escape? How could a person ever find their way out of this darkness? Another spiderweb brushes its sticky strands against my face. I hear breath, frantic and hot, close to madness. Mine.

What if I can't get out? It's not like anyone would hear my screams even if I were right in front of them. The only thing that will prevent me from living out the rest of my days as a blind, pale, hairless, wall-licking lunatic will be when some charitably poisonous creature puts me out of my misery.

Almost in response to that thought, I walk through another web, and this time I feel the solid, horrible round body of something skittering across the back of my neck. Impossibly needle-thin legs race across my skin, down

into my shirt, and that's when I lose all pretense of composure. I scream.
I flail. I beat at whatever poisonous thing has just launched itself into my
clothes.

"*Shut up!*" a voice whispers surprisingly close to me. "They'll hear you."

The nothingness turns into invisible hands, clammy and hot, that suddenly clamp onto my arm.

"Spiders," I stammer stupidly.

"Of course there are spiders. And there are worse than spiders. So don't
get bit, and shut up."

Now I'm being pulled. Guided.

I might as well be upside down for all I know which direction I'm heading. The floor begins to incline, and I realize we've reached stairs of some
kind.

Little bits of light occasionally stab through the darkness now. Like stars.
Tiny peepholes, I realize.

At another point, we come to an abrupt stop. I hear him grunt and the unmistakable rattle of a locked doorknob. He says something under his breath I
don't quite catch, but it sounds like, "I always forget this is here." We move on.

Something curious has begun to happen. From the moment his hands
grabbed on to me, the panic started to dissipate. Maybe it's because I'm
no longer alone, but it's also . . . How to explain? Once I read about inch-
worms. They can learn to navigate a maze, then be ground up and fed to
another worm who suddenly can also navigate that same maze on its first
try, having somehow absorbed the information. It's like I can feel the logic
of the path in front of us, flowing through his palms and into my skin. More
rooms in the memory mansion—or, rather, rooms within rooms.

I start to feel so confident that at one point, I even break away from his
grasp when I hear angry, shouting voices on the other side of the wall.

The town hall meeting. We must be passing by the auditorium.

There's another tiny hole in the wall for me to peer through. We're off to
the side and several yards away, but I'm able to see a bit of the stage, where
Dr. Burton is currently holding forth. Members of the audience are arguing
with him, their voices raw and outraged:

"How could this have happened?"

"You need to do something!"

Burton is waving his hands at them, trying to tamp their fury down from
afar.

"I promise," he's saying, "we're looking into who is responsible for this. We're going to get through this. We're going to be fine."

A man's voice, rough and deep yet scared as a child: "But the fucking *feds*, Bill? We've got the fucking feds coming in?"

Another voice: "This is a disaster."

More shouts and accusations. Burton calmly, but resolutely, talks over them. "Don't answer any questions. Don't give any leads. Treat him like the outsider he is and we'll be fine."

"The feds?" the gardener whispers next to me. "Jesus."

"Because of Carole?" I ask him. He doesn't respond.

I can see Nancy, miserable, ignored, not at all having the town meeting she was expecting. She looks toward us—not at us, the aperture is too small for her to see from where she's standing, but she clearly senses something. I wonder if she'll even get to say a single word about her Easter festivities.

I want to stay, but the gardener is pulling me once again. "Let's go," he says, and we move away.

Minutes pass. Maybe hours, years, entire lifetimes. Until finally, a square of purplish gray opens up in the black.

A door! Or an opening, at the very least.

He crawls through, and then I'm yanked through after him.

Even though this new room is also dark, my eyes have to adjust to so much more light. There are actual windows, not in this room but nearby, and the contrast is immense.

It takes me a moment to realize we're in one of the hallways by the waiting room of the hospital, next to Chantelle's desk. Around the corner is the door to the waiting room and outside entrance. Around a different corner, the stairs to the basement, as well as the stairs leading to the second floor.

The black-and-gold wallpaper we just came out of is seamless—I don't think there'd be any possible way to know there was a passageway there had I not just seen it close. How many other hidden openings are in this house?

"You should be able to find your way out from here," he says, looking at me very contemptuously. "Now leave me alone."

"Why are you running away from me?" I ask. Besides the relief of finally being back in a proper room . . . I also feel exhilarated. Shaky and hungry, in that just-got-off-a-roller-coaster sort of way. I almost want to go back for more, beg him to take me through it again like a bouncy younger sister. "And why did you save me? Twice?"

"My job," he mutters.

"What does that mean?"

He doesn't answer. He turns and starts to walk away.

"Jesus. You're gonna run away again? What are you, five?" And I can't think of anything else to say, so I blurt out: "You owe me!"

That actually stops him. He turns around, his expression now a mixture of contempt and confusion. "I *owe* you? Why would I owe you anything?"

"Because!" I swallow. "Because without me, you're all alone. No one else sees these things. Just you and me. And I don't think you like being alone. *That's* why you look so sad all the time."

That makes him laugh, a short, bitter sound. "I *am* alone. Doesn't matter if I like it or not. It's what I earned."

"I'm not impressed, you know."

He blinks at that. He's not used to being challenged. "Impressed with what?"

"With your moodiness or whatever. And with your not liking me. I've gotten far worse from people way more interesting than you."

He gives me a strange smile. "You don't know a fucking thing."

From far away, the sound of a crowd gurgles up the throat of the building and then gets belched through another set of doors. The assembly is letting out.

"So fill me in!" I say. "I'm so dumb? Tell me what you know. Then I'll leave you alone, I promise." He's stone-faced, but I sense him considering. *"Please."*

"What do you want to know?" he asks at last.

Oh God, so many things. I need a moment to try to get my questions in order, but the sound of crunching gravel, of voices outside, freezes my blood. Someone's coming this way. We have to make this quick.

"How can you see them? The ghosts. What's your connection? If I can see them because I was one in a past life, is that your story? Were you a victim, too?"

He lets out an abrupt, barking guffaw. Like he's just heard the best joke in months.

"What's so funny?" I demand. The footsteps and voices get closer.

"'In a past life'?" the gardener repeats. "'One of *them*'? Jesus, you really are crazy."

"Don't call me crazy." I have the sudden urge to claw his eyes out.

He's still laughing. "You're not one of them! God, no."

"Then what am I?" I ask. I demand. I flat-out fucking *plead.* My voice breaks with emotion in a way I'd be embarrassed about if I didn't feel so urgent.

His laughter stops, though a smirk remains. His head tilts in a mockery of empathy.

"A punch line," he says.

Before I can respond—and I have such curses ready—the door to the hospital opens. The sound of two voices engaged in a heated argument bursts into the building. I can't place the first voice, though he sounds familiar, but I recognize the other right away. Dr. Burton. He can't find me standing here, after hours, having a chat with the damn groundskeeper, that'd be impossible to explain.

"We need to hide," I say. The gardener laughs again, like a fucking asshole. "We're not done here."

"Ooo, okay," he says, hands raised in mock defense.

Dr. Burton and his companion storm through the door from the waiting room. Only a wall with an open door separates us now and, depending on where they're going, they could be in this area in a heartbeat. I do the only thing I can think of and throw myself under Chantelle's desk. I pull her rolling chair forward, covering me, hoping the gardener has done something similar.

From what I'm able to see around the chair, he hasn't. He's still standing there, laughing.

Burton comes into the room, and then I'm able to catch a glimpse of his companion. It's Bonnie's husband, he of the wet lips and weak chin. No wonder he sounded familiar.

They're both walking so fast they're about to run right into the gardener. At the very least, I expect them to stop and ask him what he's doing there, laughing in the middle of the room.

"I don't fucking know, Steve, we're going to have to figure it out," Burton says.

Steve is in a panic. "You keep saying that, but what does that *mean*?"

Burton stops. Rounds on Steve. "I also keep saying I don't fucking know. What do you think that means? Give me some fucking space!"

"Okay! It's just . . . there are like half a dozen people outside; they say they won't leave until they get answers."

"Well, I hope they brought sleeping bags."

"What about me? Can you just tell me? You know I won't say anything. What happened? How come the FBI is—"

"Her fucking face was mutilated, Steve." Burton is calm, even-toned. It's like he's explaining how he chose what shirt to wear this morning. "Like someone was trying to take it off. And afterward, her head was covered."

Steve is appalled. "Jesus. Was she covered with a—?"

"No. Just her shirt. Must have been a rush job. But whatever idiotic highway patrolman found her still recognized the signature, called the feds, and now they're treating it like a copycat killer." He sounds fit to tear his hair out in frustration. "So, like I said, we just have to play nice, say we don't know anything, and he'll be gone in no time. Our ancestors literally prepared us for this."

"But it must have been someone here, right? One of us?"

"I would imagine so."

"Christ. What do we do about this Easter thing?" Steve asks. "Make her cancel?"

Burton scoffs. "No one's coming to that; I really couldn't care less. Might even be a good look for the town. Subterfuge."

Steve's voice drops. "And what about the—?" He says a word here that I don't quite catch. It sounds like *market*. Or *harvest*.

Burton puts his hands on Steve's shoulders. He speaks calmly, but there's no mistaking the venom in his throat. "People wait for it all year, Steve. It's why a lot of them live here. It's why a lot of them behave."

"But—"

"I don't care how many outsiders are sniffing around. I don't care if they bring the whole fucking bureau riding in on J. Edgar's reanimated corpse. This is our town, and there's no changing that." He breaks away from Steve. For a heart-stopping moment, I think he's looking in my direction, but no, it's toward the front door and the crowd on the other side. "I want you to pay attention, Steve. Watch everyone. See how they react to the fed. We'll find the sonofabitch who did this, and we'll take care of him ourselves. Like we do everything."

Burton leaves. Steve follows, asking if he has any ideas who it might be.

If I'm really listening, I can hear other voices outside, the people waiting for Burton to come out and give them more information. But I'm not really listening. I'm too busy staring at the gardener.

He's still standing in the middle of the room.

Burton and Steve just blasted past him. No acknowledgment. Not even an attempt to change their demeanor, and I *know* Burton wouldn't let someone like a gardener see him be so frazzled.

It's like they didn't see him.

No. It's like . . . they *couldn't* see him.

Like he's invisible. Like he's . . .

"I told you," the gardener says to me. I'm still hiding, but I can see his face pointed toward my direction. His deep-set eyes glimmer with a baleful intensity. Broken glass next to bare feet. "You don't know a fucking thing."

28

Files

APRIL 17, 2019

Well, that doesn't look comfortable at all."

I snap awake. Eleanor is standing over me. What the—where am I?

Oh, right. The basement. I peel myself off the wall against which I fell asleep.

"What are you doing here?" Eleanor asks. She sets her bag and sketch pad down in their usual spot.

Slowly, awkwardly, I get to my feet. I feel . . . oh God, I feel a million years old. The soreness from everything yesterday, capped off by a night spent sleeping on concrete. I'm also coated in sweat. Old sweat, sour and cakey. Must have had hot flashes something fierce while I slept, but the cool floor kept me from waking up.

How did I get here? I replay the events of last night as quickly as my sluggish brain allows. After Burton and Steve went off to continue their argument, I heard the sounds of a crowd outside: more townspeople, wanting answers from the doctor. I couldn't escape through the front without being noticed, so I hid in the only place I could think—the one room where I assumed no one was likely to come visit. Despite the horrors I'd encountered here earlier in the day, I also figured the compact shelving was an effective enough barrier to keep the crawl space door closed from any ghosts who felt particularly un-ignorable.

Ghosts . . . like the gardener?

You don't know a fucking thing.

"I, uh, got here early," I lie. "To try to . . . fix things. I guess I must have fallen asleep."

It's almost like I'm seeing the destruction of the room for the first time now that Eleanor is here. It's even worse than I remembered. The room is an utter horror show of papers. Poor Eleanor; what must it be to walk in here and see me sleeping among the wreckage of all her hard work? Now that I think of it, I don't even know how long she'd been working here before I showed up. It could be an entire year of effort down the toilet. No wonder she looks paler than usual.

"Nurse Nancy warned me upstairs," she says, "but I didn't think . . ."

"I'm so sorry," I whisper. Whimper.

"So the machine just . . . went psycho?"

I want to tell her everything. The only thing that stops me is sheer exhaustion. I don't have the energy to relive it all right now, even through words. I *will* tell her, all of it, but I just can't now. So I don't say anything. I just nod and look sad.

"Are *you* okay?" she asks next. "That's the most important thing."

My face burns underneath the layer of sweat. "Just a little sore." I hope it's not obvious I'm wearing last night's clothes. I'm suddenly self-conscious. The wet-plaster feel of my hair on my neck. My stale breath.

Meanwhile, Eleanor is kicking at some of the scattered folders. "I guess it was for the best anyways."

"What do you mean?"

"Well, you were getting a little too good at organizing. We were gonna finish too quick, and I'd be out of a job."

She's kidding—at least, the rhythm of her words suggests so—but she's not smiling. She's not even looking at me. She wants to say something she's not ready to say yet.

"I'm so sorry," I say again. "Please don't hate me." A dumb, pathetic thing to say. It deserves a disingenuous, automatic response, like, *Of course I don't hate you, don't be silly.*

I don't get that. My stomach sinks.

"Welp," Eleanor eventually sighs, "you know what they say about a journey of a thousand miles, right?"

"You've gotta get your ass wet," I reply. She snorts a short laugh, but her eyebrows knit. *Something is wrong with you, lady,* those eyebrows say.

———

We start with a jolly lesson about John Wayne Gacy and his famous "rope trick."

Eleanor moves to one quadrant of the room, picking up and examining the scattered folders. I'm working near the compact shelving. She's either avoiding the machine, because she's scared of it, or me, because I must stink. My mouth tastes thick and gummy—I make a mental note to keep it closed as much as possible until I can rinse it out with something.

She already hates you. Bad breath isn't going to change that.

But she must know it was an accident, right?

She knows enough about you to know it's no accident. You're a train wreck of a human being. You're *the accident.*

A punch line. His voice in my head. *You don't know a fucking thing.*

I need to ask Eleanor about this new ghost. Did Damon Cross have any male victims? Or maybe, didn't she say something about his brother dying somewhere in this mansion?

The podcast is too loud for me to ask just yet—now a gleeful, excited discussion of famous killer clowns and whether or not Gacy should be considered a "pop culture pioneer." I'll have to wait until we take a break.

Or never. Because she hates you. She hates your tragic inconvenience.

When I see another ant among the ruins of the File Pile, I want to laugh and I want to cry. These little fuckers really don't take the hint, do they?

I prepare to kill it—or, *attempt* to kill it—as surreptitiously as possible. Instead of going into the Pile or to the secret wall entrance, though, it begins pacing back and forth in a tight little line at the bottom of one of the compact shelves. *Here,* it seems to be saying, *here, here.*

And it looks like there's a file under the shelf, caught between the tracks.

Exhausted beyond words, I stoop down, grunting a bit, and try to pull the paper out from under the shelf.

The paper doesn't want to come. It's really wedged under the shelf. Because of the podcast, Eleanor can't hear me. Unfortunately, that also means I can't hear the paper ripping until I'm suddenly flung backward onto my ass. The pain is a short, sharp shock. I narrowly avoid biting my tongue in half.

Eleanor doesn't notice; she's trying to match some loose sheets with a folder.

I quickly look back to the ripped page. I'm holding the upper-right corner of one sheet, yellowed with age. Oh, I hope it wasn't anything important. Clumsy Mary. It would be just my luck that this folder was some major clue I've been searching for. It's a man's name, I bet; a clue as to who the gardener once was. Why am I such an—

Everything stops.

My heart. The world. Everything. It all goes silent.

Because I'm looking at my own name on this scrap of paper.

I don't know if I gasp. I don't know if I speak. I don't know anything that happens for the next several seconds. All I know is what's on the page. Blotting out the world. Like the wake of a shotgun blast. A few typewritten letters. And a stamp, right under my name.

Patient's Name: Mary Mudgett.

Referred to Clearview, underneath.

Stunned isn't even the word for it. I'm knocked into a different dimension. I'm . . . I'm . . . I want to say something, to call out, to scream, to get Eleanor to come look, come confirm with me. I shut my eyes, open them again, and yes, it's still true. My name.

"Mary."

My name.

"Hey, Mary?"

I slowly drop back down into my body.

Everything is still silent.

I wasn't imagining it—it's silent because the podcast has been turned off.

Eleanor is speaking to me.

"What did you say?" I ask, my voice barely a ghost of itself.

"I said . . . I'm sorry I've been weird. I need to talk to you."

"Weird? You haven't—"

"I just couldn't figure out how to bring this up, so I got kinda awkward. It's about your journal." She looks very, very serious. Almost sick.

"What about it?" I ask as if I'm not holding the most important thing I've yet discovered during this entire cursed trip.

Before she can answer, the door to the storage room opens.

Mrs. Burton stands there. Hunched. Gnarled.

"Are you going to come help me or what?" Then Mrs. Burton takes a moment and looks at the state of the room. "What in God's name happened in here?"

I'm not really here.

I'm down in the basement, talking with Eleanor, hearing her thoughts on my journal, telling her about all I learned yesterday. Then the two of us rescue my file and read it together. We start figuring me out. Finally.

Unfortunately, my body disagrees. The sun on my shoulders. The dirt under my shoes. The dry air on my skin. My body, my stupid fucking liar of a body, is outside, standing by the playground, but all I can think about is:

My file. I found my file.

I feel like I'm going to faint.

Of course you do, dummy. You haven't eaten in probably twelve hours. You've barely slept. I don't remember the last time you drank water.

Yes. I've pushed myself to the limit. Too much walking. Not enough self-care. Not enough sleep. Scattered. Fractaled. Is that a word? My eyes can barely focus, let alone my brain. And isn't it funny, then, that the words on my file my mind keeps coming back to, stamped there under my name: "*Referred to Clearview.*"

My view is anything but clear right now. But it will be. As soon as I get back downstairs.

My file.

"Referred to Clearview." I whisper the words into the hot air. What is Clearview? What does it mean? A new avenue to pursue. Whatever this Clearview is, maybe they have records, too. More pieces of me.

The first group of children, the oldest, are out right now. Only a handful. The boys do pull-ups on the jungle gym to impress each other—the sun-heated rungs must be scalding their hands. The girls cluster and gossip. A blink reveals that they're my bookstore coworkers. Malcolm. Devin. Kayla. Were those their names? I don't even remember. I'm used to shedding my past the moment it's behind me. It's the best way to keep a clear view of the future. But I have *records* now. Even better than handprints in concrete.

Another blink and my coworkers are headed inside. Recess round two begins.

I'm starting to feel angry. I don't want to be here. I want to be back inside. I want to get back to my discovery. I want to find out what Eleanor was so hesitant to talk to me about. I don't care about any of these little brats. I want to care about myself for a change.

Eleanor said she wants to talk to me about my journal. How appropriate— my thoughts feel as cluttered and chaotic as the pages of that little book:

I'm so hungry. So thirsty. I don't feel good. I feel faint. When was the last time I ate? Why do they expect me to help out like this? Why don't I get to sit in the shade, too?

What does Clearview mean? You're so stupid, Mary. Why can't you remember these things? This is your life—even you aren't interested in your own life, you pathetic hag.

Was he a ghost? Should I ignore him, too, then? Is he just as dangerous? He doesn't have claw hands. Why does he help me sometimes, taunt me others?

"The other day? I found a scorpion? In my room?" A little voice is speaking to my hip. It even pronounces that last word as *woom*.

The second group of kids has gone in, and now the third group is out. The youngest. Thank God, we're almost done. Except, unfortunately, this little boy won't stop talking to me. His name is Wallace, and I hate him. It seems I've been on the playground just enough times that now he's comfortable approaching me, and he won't shut up. Like a dog outside my window, *yarfyarfyarf.*

An autopilot part of my brain takes over. He doesn't care that I obviously sound disinterested. He just wants attention, no matter how robotic.

"I got bit by a scorpion once," Wallace tells me, his little eyes wide.

I tell him that's very scary. That must have hurt.

"I bet you didn't know they bite with their tails. Sometimes? I'll go outside and look for them at night? My dad lets me use his black light? And you know what?"

"They glow," we say at the same time.

He's frustrated I know this. My preempting of his answer has upset him.

As if I can't know things. As if I'm not a thousand times older than he is and worthy of knowledge. I am worthy of knowledge, you little yelping dog, and you're keeping me from the knowledge I've been searching for.

I tell him you can eat scorpions. It's true. You just have to bite off their tails where the poison is. You can live off bugs for days. His eyes expand with little-boy wonder.

"Can you eat spiders?"

"No. But you can eat scorpions and worms and ants and all sorts of insects if you have to." If you get trapped in a crawl space . . . or left in a museum overnight.

"You're weird." *Wee-uhd,* he pronounces it. "You smell funny, too." Then he abruptly announces, with the confidence only someone his age can own: "I have to pee."

Boys usually get to keep that confidence, I think; girls have to give it back like it never really belonged to them.

I give a quick glance to Mrs. Burton. She's not looking at me—she's staring at some other children like a vulture watching a legless man drag himself across the endless desert.

I take Wallace to the back side of the building where he can pee in private. No one can see us here. The noise of the playground might as well be a movie played in another room.

He continues talking. I continue hating every second of it.

"I bet I know more about bugs than you," he says as he pulls his pants down and tucks his shirt under his chin.

Looking off into the mountains, I tell him he probably does. But I'm starting to feel that rage again. The rage of throwing the dog, of stomping on ants until my shins ripple in my teeth, of tackling the gardener. That fucking gardener who called me a punch line, who sneered and patronized me—*you don't know a fucking thing.* No, maybe I don't know a fucking thing because I've always been pulled away to attend to the needs of others. This kid, this brat, little Wallace, is no different from the gardener—taunting me with what I don't know as if it's my fault. It's *not* my fault!

"Did you know? Spiders and scorpions aren't bugs? They're arachnids." *Awack-nits.* Yes, I fucking knew that, Wallace. I know things. I know there's a secret entrance where you're pissing, right now. I know what it's like in the crawl space. In fact, I know it so well I didn't even remember I knew it at your age!

But no, I can't know these things, right? I'm just a stupid old lady. What if I left you behind in a museum, smarty-pants? What if I stuffed you in that dark, secret crawl space entrance?

He *keeps talking,* and I imagine myself hunched over an old, black, sooty stove. A fairy-tale crone, stuffing a naughty little boy into bottomless darkness. A stove. A crawl space. Doesn't matter, just enjoy the silence. Blissful. Like that morning Demon Dog finally stopped yapping. Ice cream—mmmm, smother that shit in chocolate syrup.

How long have we been standing here?

God, I feel so dizzy. I really should go sit down. Conserve my energy.

A drop of rain hits my hand.

Oh, thank the lord! Except—that's weird. There's not a cloud in the sky. And it's definitely not monsoon season, that time when aggressively intense storms suddenly appear out of nowhere and dump a week's worth of rain onto the ground within minutes. I look down as another droplet spatters onto my hand.

Not rain.

Blood.

Blood is dripping onto my hand. What the—

I swipe up at my nose with the heel of my hand. It comes away stained with a dark, wet red. My nose is bleeding. Not just bleeding—gushing.

"God*dammit,*" I mutter. I've had a few more dry-air nosebleeds since I've been back, but they've been nonevents, usually taken care of with a few dabs of tissue. This one is a gusher already. Why is blood so unpredictable?

"I'll be right back," I say. Wallace doesn't respond. Or maybe he does and I don't hear, who cares. I quickly walk back around the corner to the playground, leaving Wallace without a second thought. I need to see if Mrs. Burton has tissues or anything, before the front of my shirt becomes blotted with blood.

I go around the corner and then—

Oh no.

I suddenly don't care if I'm doused in blood, even as I dimly feel the warm-then-cold gush of thick fluid down my upper lip and chin.

Oh no no no.

I can't believe what I'm seeing, even as understanding hits me.

I didn't go home last night. In the fog and excitement of this morning, I failed to realize what that meant. I never gave Nadine another pill.

I watch, horrified, as Nadine crests the hill, wheezing, dry heaving, and reaches the hospital entrance. Her arms are full. She's carrying as many of the files I stole as she can, and I know exactly what she's about to do with them.

29

Shards

Nadine tells me I can open up the curtains in the living room if I want to. A huge concession for her. It's cooler today, she says. Maybe some light would be nice.

I don't move.

It's silent for a long time.

A long, long time.

"You ain't seen Chipotle around lately, have you?" She pulls out a pack of cigarettes, puts one in her mouth. "Sometimes he hides when he's mad at me; I been sleeping so much maybe he's pissy, but . . . I'm starting to get worried. Maybe he dug out the yard and I didn't notice."

I tell her I'm sure he's around here somewhere.

I'm sitting on the couch, staring straight ahead. Forward. The same kind of soft focus I've learned whenever there's a mirror nearby. There's no mirror here, unless you count the twisted face of Nadine. A fun house mirror. A monster mirror.

She sits in her chair. Her throne. Rocking ever so slightly. A book tucked under her arm I guess in case she gets bored. She stuck a teal plastic peony into her hair before marching up the hill and ruining my life. The effort made her work up a sweat, so now the fake flower is sagging listlessly above her ear. She doesn't fix it. She's allowed to be as messy as she wants. It's the rest of us who have to be perfect.

Finally, after an eternity—an eternity that somehow isn't long enough—she grunts.

"You should fucking be thanking me."

She says it low, maybe even to herself. But I hear it, and I flinch as if I've just been splashed in the face with human waste. "Excuse me?"

She tries to light her cigarette, but her hands appear to be shaking. "Ugh.

Still feel like shit." She looks at me. "And you look like shit, by the way. What the hell happened to your nose? You should go clean yourself up."

"I should be *thanking you*?" I repeat, my voice low.

"Try to keep up with the conversation, Mary." She puts the unlit cigarette down.

My whole body is vibrating, ready to explode, to coat the walls with my hot, steaming guts. "Why . . . should I be thanking you, Nadine? You just got me fired. I was humiliated. I probably can't ever go back there." I don't add: *And I had* just *found the thing I've practically waited my whole life to find.*

Nadine shrugs. She may be feeling sick, but she'll probably be able to muster that snide smile of hers even on the embalming table.

"Well, first off," she says, "you already have a job. A job you've been seriously slacking on. I mean, have you been in the bathroom lately? Smells like hot meat in there, and all the bulbs are burned out. But secondly—"

I bolt to my feet. I don't want to hear any of this.

Nadine is suddenly holding her hammer, both hands on the handle, clutching it to her chest, sinking into her chair. She must have been sitting on it, hiding it in the cushions. "Don't you attack me again!" she cries. "Don't you come near me!"

"I wasn't going to attack you," I say through gritted teeth.

"*Second of all*," Nadine continues, still glistening with sweat, "I don't know what you were getting up to with all those files, but it couldn't have been good. I'm . . . I'm worried about you."

"Yeah, you're a real saint, Nadine," I say, and I walk out of the room.

I don't even realize I'm in the bathroom, scrubbing the blood off until the cold water splashes onto my face and hands. I walked right in here without even thinking of you-know-who. Good. She's probably still in the tub behind the curtain, but I block her out of my mind. As far as I'm concerned, she doesn't exist. If only this tactic worked with the living.

I strip off my shirt and dab at the small amount of blood that soaked through to my chest.

"Seriously, though, where is the dog?"

I jump.

"Nadine!" I cover myself with my arms. She's behind me, holding herself up against the doorway. "I don't have a shirt on!"

"Like it's nothing I haven't seen." She looks down at my chest and gives a chuckle. "I see you've met my old friend, gravity."

I storm past her out of the bathroom and make my way to Brenda's room. She follows.

"I'm just *joking* with—Look!" She says, "I don't want you being mad at me, Mary, I really don't." She's still carrying the hammer. Maybe absently. Or maybe just in case. Either way, it's a real picture of love and affection. "I'm still your aunt, you know. Whether you like it or not, I have a duty to look out for you. And I never shoulda let you spend time in that damn house. That place is full of—"

"Please cut the conspiracy bullshit, Nadine, I'm begging you." I start looking through my few clothes for something to wear. Nothing feels right.

"Conspiracy nothing! I'm not talking about conspiracy here! Although . . ." She drops her voice low. "I *have* told you my theory, right? I think it's Satan worship. This whole town. Wouldn't be the first; I've got a book all about—"

"Oh my God, *shut up*!"

"Fine!" She throws her hands up. "I don't wanna be fucking fighting with you! Okay? I want you to clean yourself up, take a damn breath, make us some food, and chill out. I'm sick of this agitation. I don't feel good, and you know what, I deserve some peace and quiet!"

"Oh, I'll give you peace and quiet."

I'm not sure if I actually say it or just think it. My Loved Ones catch my eye. *Careful, Mary. Don't get overexcited. Be porcelain.* God, I'm so sick of these reminders. Why can't I just be angry?!

I find a shirt that I'm willing to wear—a purple cotton tee that feels too colorful for how I'm feeling—and, as I put it on, I take a deep breath. I stare down at the floor.

"I will *never* forgive you for this, Nadine. It's bad enough you lied to me to get me to come here. But I need money, and I need personal space, and you just took everything from me. Everything. You're like a vampire. Bleeding me dry." I'm not going to cry. I keep my breath steady. "I have an apartment, I have bills, I have—"

"You're right."

It's like being slapped. "What?"

"You're right. I'm sorry."

"I . . . *What?!*"

"I said I'm fucking sorry! Jesus Christ! You think I enjoy this? You think I liked having to go up to that fucking house and do that to you?"

"Yes."

"Of course." Now, *she* starts to cry. One of her final tactics. "You're such a nasty piece of work. Of course that's what you think. It took a lot for me to walk up there. I'm already not doing good. I'm old, I'm *infirm,* and I'm getting sicker. But I saw those files, and I've seen the way you've been acting lately, and . . . Mary, something ain't right. I mean—why is that mirror covered up? What is going on with you?" She indicates the mirror in the corner of the room.

"Leave me alone, Nadine. I don't want to see you. Make your own lunch, I know you can."

But the performance must continue. "Ohhh," she sighs, "I never shoulda asked you to come back here. I just got desperate. I didn't have anyone else to call after Bren left. I'm all alone—and bad things happen to women who are alone out here. I didn't think you were like this anymore. I thought they fixed you. I thought you've been doing okay on your own, out in New York, so what they did to you musta worked—"

"Wait, what? *They* who? Who fixed me?"

She rolls her eyes. "Can't you for once in your life stop being so *weird*?"

"I don't know what you're talking about, Nadine!"

A pause. She looks me up and down. "You're serious? Oh my God, you really are serious?"

I swallow. "What's Clearview?"

She doesn't move from the doorway. I don't move from where I stand in the bedroom. We're both fixed poles. We've been made inorganic by the moment—no bodily discomfort, no need to sit or lean. Nadine's answer was a magic spell that turned us both into statues.

"Clearview's where you lived, Mary."

"I lived here. In your old house. With you and Brenda."

"For a couple years, yeah. We couldn't keep you here for long. You had too many problems; it wasn't safe."

"Wasn't safe?"

"First it was just the bed-wetting and the talking to yourself. Then it was the fires. And the animals. I mean, I was already worried about the fire that got your mom and dad; we were never sure if that was an accident or what—"

"I *never*—don't you dare—"

"But then when we'd find the rabbits. The rats. The bugs. Like you were collecting them. Or parts of them, at least. And you started getting into trouble with other kids. No one knew what to do with you."

A thousand indignities flash before my eyes. Running the halls, screaming for help. Glue down my shirt, in my hair. Paper missiles, extended feet, cutting comments. The incident in the gym, when Anna-Louise and her posse stole my clothes and made me parade naked through the playground, occurs to me. Was it all retaliatory? Worse: Was it even me? Or was I the one—?

No. Stop it. I know that happened to me.

"Of course I was disturbed, Nadine," I say firmly. "I was bullied. By you. By the other kids. I had no one looking out for me. No one protecting me."

"Bullied?" She gives a sad exhale. "Oh, Mary, *you* were the—"

Anger is making the world turn red. As red as the bloodstains on my clothes. "So you had me, what, committed? You just threw me into a padded cell and wiped your hands of me?"

"We didn't do shit but try to keep you from hurting anybody. Including yourself. And then you were eighteen and they let you go and you basically disappeared. I didn't know where you were until I got a call from you from fucking New York City, and you said you were gonna be an actor in the big city. I thought, well, actors are crazy anyway. But I figured they'd fixed you up. Gave you meds. Taught you how to be Good." She doesn't capitalize the G in her inflection, but that's how I hear it. Because I realize that's exactly what they did. Be Good, be Good. "I guess Clearview had a bit of a reputation for doping kids up, y'know, but, shit, it kept you calm, it kept you happy, it kept you safe."

Another sudden flash. Little, perfect boys and girls, faces pristine, sitting in chairs, lying in beds, shuffling in rooms. Except for those moments when they weren't perfect, and then it was needles in the arm, pills down the throat.

My eyes fall on my display of Loved Ones. My friends. My perfect little reminders: *Be Good. Be porcelain.*

"No wonder I can't remember my life," I hear myself saying. "I never had one."

Nadine says, "What does that mean? You can't remember your life?"

I look at her. Her brow is all scrunched up in dumb—or maybe pretend—confusion.

"No," I say. "No, this isn't right."

I have to consider the source. This is Nadine. This is the woman who refuses to leave her house because of conspiracies she thinks are out to get her. I'm basing this revelation off a stamp on a ripped piece of paper and the ravings of a paranoid shut-in.

"*You* were the bully," I say again, my voice a low but rising growl. "And if I really did wind up in Clearview, it's because you threw me there. Because I was inconvenient. Because I was sad and difficult, and that's too much for someone like you. You don't care about anything but yourself."

"See? This is what I'm talking about, Mary. Something in your brain is broke. And going to work in that house was no good for you. *I warned you.*" She points the hammer at me. Shoves it in my direction. The exertion, on top of the yelling, causes her to fall into a coughing fit. When she gets ahold of herself, her voice rumbles, "There is an evil in that house. You can think I'm stupid for believing in that kinda stuff, but that don't mean it's not true. God, when you were little, you were obsessed with that house. You used to draw it all the time. I'd catch you outside, just staring at it. That house does bad things to people. I don't know what or why, but it sure seems to drive you crazy."

"Don't call me crazy."

"*Crazier*, I should say. You were already crazy to begin with. Crazy enough to burn your own house down, kill your mom and dad. Crazy enough to wind up in the nuthouse. And apparently, I'm just as crazy from bringing your crazy ass back here—"

That vibration in my bones, it finally reaches critical mass. "*Shut the fuck up, you hideous, useless bitch!*" I scream. "You paranoid, stupid piece of shit! You fat, ugly waste of flesh!" Now I'm close, in her face. "It's no wonder your husband left you. It's no wonder your daughter left you. All you do is make up stuff about other people so that you can feel like there's something interesting about you. But there's not, Nadine. You're a fucking joke. You're worse than a fucking joke, because there's nothing funny about you. You're as fake as those stupid flowers you put in your hair. Your whole existence is as empty and rotten as a corpse's cunt."

I want to hurt her. I want to find some entryway past her thick skin and draw blood. I want her to cry real tears. I want to carve into her like I imagined carving into Carole. I want to stuff her into the dark, like I imagined stuffing little Wallace away.

Her eyes are wide. They shimmer. Her lined lips are pulled down in a pout. Good. Capital fucking *G*.

"You—you fucking—y—" she stammers in a shocked hush. Just random noises, unable to commit to being words. "J—f—"

I feel elation. I did it. I finally gave her as good as she deserves. For this split second, I almost don't mind having been fired, just to have gotten to this moment.

Then . . .

I see the moment when inspiration strikes her, but I'm not fast enough to stop it. I can only watch in horror as she brings that hammer down. Onto the dresser. Onto the heads of the Loved Ones within reach. *Smash. Smash.*

The other statues jump in terror.

Smash.

She begins to laugh. A bully's laugh. A look-what-you-made-me-do laugh. Stop hitting yourself.

Smash.

I'm still a statue. No longer of porcelain or stone, but of ice. I start shivering all over.

Smash.

Somehow, one of my ice-statue hands is able to reach out and grab the hammer away from her. And then I slap her.

As hard as I can.

The report it makes might as well be a gunshot, the way it rings in my ears afterward.

She and I both stare at each other. Wide-eyed. Mirrored reflections.

This is about to get real Bad.

I put my hands on her shoulders and push-walk her backward, down the hallway, back to her chair, where I let gravity take her. Neither of us blinks. Neither of us speaks. Neither of us breathes.

Then I go back to the bedroom. Close the door. Look at my massacred shelf. And sob.

30

Let the Women Among You Have Use

I should get up and feed Nadine.

Nadine needs to eat.

It's dinnertime. Or maybe breakfast. I don't know how long it's been.

I don't remember what day it was.
I didn't notice what time it was.

I can't get that song out of my head.

The room is dark, and I don't want to get up.

Let her fend for herself. Let her starve to death. Let her run outside and get killed by the mob she's so sure is after her.

My ears won't stop ringing.

I should get up and feed her.

Nadine needs to eat something.

31

Peace Offering

APRIL 18, 2019

Be Good . . .

Be Good, Mary . . .

Even though their voices are faint, garbled, blood-clotted . . . I know they're right.

My poor smashed and shattered Loves.

Hunger eventually gets me out of bed.

Stumbling out into the headache-inducing dimness of the living room, I see Nadine is asleep in her chair. Her wet, whistling breath is steady and low.

I set about preparing some peanut butter and jelly sandwiches for both of us as quietly as I can, lit only by the light above the oven and the occasional campfire relief thrown by the refrigerator. The blackout curtains on every window do their jobs well—I have no idea what time it is—but the microwave says 8:18. Pretty sure that's a.m.

I feel better when I get some food in me. I figure Nadine will be asleep for a little while yet, so I put her sandwich in the fridge.

There are some dishes in the sink. I wash them, enjoying the hot water on my hands, moving slowly so as to not make too much noise. When I'm finished, I look at the back of Nadine's chair some more and listen to her soft, wet snores.

Poor thing. She's probably as exhausted and starved as I am. Looking at her like this, a dark, sleeping lump in her massive chair, it's hard not to pity her. Life has been hard on her. I was not Good to her.

I don't want to fight. She's my only source of information now—skewed though she may be—when it comes to my past. I want things to be calmer so we can talk. Put our disagreements aside. Share a cup of tea.

An idea comes to me.

"I'm going to run an errand, Aunt Nadine." My voice is barely a whisper. "I'll be right back. You've got breakfast ready in the fridge if you want it."

She might be mad if she wakes up and finds me gone.

That's okay.

I'm going to come home with a peace offering.

Of course it's not true. Any of what she said. I know that. I set myself up by mentioning Clearview—she saw it was something I was feeling vulnerable about, so she made up a mean story to hurt me.

I'm not going to let her bully me.

I'm going to be her friend. In a way, she's no different from the ghost women. If I just ignore her cruelty, she'll lose her power.

It's a long walk. Another hot, bright day. The birds are incredibly loud.

I feel the Cross House staring down at me. I don't look at it. I stay focused.

My pain keeps me centered. Every throbbing ache in my legs, my head, tells me I know what's real, I know what's true.

Just as Nurse Nancy described, the storefront is tucked away in a corner of a completely faceless, mostly empty strip mall. I'm in luck: according to the sign on the door, the store opens at 10:00 a.m. I arrive just after opening.

Approaching the door and its tinted windows, you might expect to enter an insurance company, a carpet seller, a travel agency. Instead, you walk in and you're blinded by an array of crystals, some as huge as a dustbuster. There's a bubbling fountain to the right of the door: a little stone fixture that almost looks like an end table, except the top isn't flat; it has a little gurgling pond with a gray Buddha who overlooks the reservoir smilingly. At least I think it's a Buddha.

The store is an assault of teal and turquoise. Of geodes and feathers. Chimes—wooden, metal, stone—hang from the ceiling everywhere. Over one area of the store, bodiless fairy wings. Over another, dream catchers. The soft sounds of windpipes and synthesizers coo and curl from hidden speakers. Keats & Yeats used to pump in music onto the sales floor, too, although it was never music this soothing and shapeless. There's even an occasional distant wolf howl.

It's an immediately relaxing place. Maybe that's why I feel so put off by it. It's almost too pleasant. Too colorful. Too . . . considerate. Nothing else in Arroyo is remotely like it.

"Hello?" A voice from a back room behind the counter. "Is someone—? Oh! Someone's here." An older woman has emerged. Looks to be in her seventies. Long white hair pulled into a ponytail. Flowing lavender dress. She smiles at me while she sets herself onto a stool behind the register. "I thought I heard someone. You let me know if you need any help, okay? I don't see too good, but my hearing's fine."

I tell her thanks.

The store isn't very large, but the clutter makes taking it all in a challenge. There's an entire wall dedicated to small, shiny rocks—not gems or jewelry, just rocks. Smooth, polished rocks, almost like the skin of my Loved Ones. I remember how they shattered under hammer blows, and I quickly move on. There's a display of numerous different decks of cards. Not playing cards; they're the kind you tell fortunes with. I didn't realize there were so many different kinds. I wonder if your fortune is different with each deck. Maybe one deck says you're going to die in a horrible accident, and one says you're going to meet the love of your life. Which deck wins?

The song playing on the speakers fades and a new song begins. More of the same: synths and chimes and—had I called them *windpipes* earlier? I meant panpipes.

"You from around here?" the old woman behind the counter asks. Pleasantly, not obtrusively.

"A few towns away," I lie. "Just passing through."

"How wonderful. Are you looking for anything in particular?"

"A gift. For my aunt."

"That's very sweet. You must love her very much."

No comment.

"Is there anything she likes in particular?" the old woman asks.

Cigarettes and conspiracy theories? Salisbury steaks and making you smell her farts? Destroying the only precious things you have in the world?

"She's got pretty wide tastes. I guess I'm just looking for something that will make her happy. Improve her mood. Mine, too, if I'm being honest. We've had a rough couple of weeks."

Her face brightens. "Does she drink tea?"

"That's exactly what I was thinking," I say.

A bend, around the display of stones and bushels of incense, leads to a corner stocked full of herbs in glass apothecary jars. Some of the jars are huge, holding entire branches inside them. Some of the jars are small and packed with brightly monochromatic plant matter ground as fine as dirt. There are oils and diffusers. There's even a coffee percolator and an electric kettle for tea.

I don't even know where to begin. The old woman's eyesight might not be good, but she must sense my hesitance.

"So you want a mood improver, right?" She starts gesturing toward various jars. "I would recommend valerian, ginger, saffron, turmeric, or lemongrass. You can mix and match to find a blend of flavors, or you can try them on their own. In fact, we've got some unique blends already prepared, as well, over here." More jars. Names like Blissful Morning, Calming Breeze, Cinnamon Storm.

I make a show of nodding, considering.

"Here, try this." She hands me a small clear plastic cup full of yellowish water, pulled from a glass jug filled with liquid, ice, and plant matter. "This is one of our more popular blends, so we keep it handy. It's called Good Talk tea. It's meant to facilitate peace, conversation. Pretty tasty, right?"

It's pleasant. Softly citrus, a hint of lavender. Mountain air and wild grass. I nod and smile. Just imagine, me and Nadine, sitting at the table, two Good Girls having a Good Talk.

It must work, though, because I decide to ask a more personal question.

"Do you have any that are good for insomnia? Or . . . um"—I drop my voice even though we appear to be alone—"hot flashes?"

She grins. "Thought you'd never ask. Got a few minutes?"

I think of Nadine snoring away again and say sure. She goes about preparing a few different herbs like an ancient apothecary.

"Feel free to keep looking around while the water heats up," she tells me, then tips me a wink. "I'll find you."

I say a silent prayer that the tea she's making isn't too expensive as I turn and notice, on the other side of the store, a huge bookshelf. Floor to ceiling. Full of books. Force of habit: I walk closer to check out the titles.

"Anything strike your fancy?" the old woman asks.

"Maybe," I say. "My aunt loves to read."

One book cover, facing out, grabs my attention: a drawing of a man speaking with a robed figure, white and ethereal, who almost looks like a ghost. Is this a book about communicating with spirits? No, it's—

"Dante," the old woman says next to me. She moved so quickly and quietly I almost gasp. "I don't see great, but I do know these shelves like the back of my hand. You a fan?"

"I've never read him."

"The greatest work of art ever written about a midlife crisis. Guess being middle-aged wasn't any easier in the twelfth century."

I give a polite, breathy laugh. As I put the book back, I notice there's a whole shelf dedicated to reincarnation. There's even a hand-painted sign on the wall: CRYSTAL READINGS * PALMISTRY * TAROT * PAST LIVES

I reach out for the closest book in that section. *Cycle of Souls* by Celia Gayheart.

"We've got a great selection, if I do say so myself," the old woman is saying. "I know it's not the sort of store you might expect to find around these parts, but that's why my daughter and I set up shop in the first place." She looks at the book in my hand. "Is that Gayheart? That's a fun read."

"It's . . . I have a friend who has been going through something very strange, and this is the only thing we could think of. So I've been reading up."

"What sort of something? Do you mind if I ask?"

"Well—" A thin, high-pitched shrieking begins to emanate from the back. Like someone far away, running toward us. I jump a little.

"Hold that thought. I'll get us some of that tea, and you can tell me all about your friend. If you don't mind."

"Maybe I can get some advice," I say. A distant wolf howls. Windpipes flourish. I mean, *panpipes*.

"I'm always happy to be of use," she calls over her shoulder as she walks to the tea station. "What's your name, by the way?"

I don't overthink it. "Jane," I say.

"It's lovely to meet you, Jane. My name's Barb." She goes about preparing two mugs of tea. "And actually, if you want some advice, it's my daughter you want to talk to. She's the real expert."

"The more the merrier," I say.

So Barb calls for her daughter.

When she says her name, my heart stops. If I'd been holding the mug Barb is preparing for me, I would have dropped it.

Maybe I misheard? Maybe it's just a common name?

Her daughter walks out from the back room.

Flowing red-and-brown dress. Graying hair, similarly pulled into a ponytail. A shawl over her shoulders. Hands clasped in front of her midsection. Nothing like she used to be, and I can only look at her face for a moment, but there's no mistaking her.

It's Anna-Louise Connerton.

32

Bully

I have the sudden, unmistakable sensation of being naked, shamed, laughed at. I want to cover myself up. My body has just begun to change, and I don't recognize it, it's not for anybody's eyes, this isn't right, it's not fair, not funny—

I imagine myself running. Pushing past rocks and feathers and crystals in this overpacked store, bumping into the Buddha fountain and sloshing water onto the floor, bursting out into the parking lot, thinking, absurdly, of the gardener and how it was his instinct to sprint away from me the other night.

You don't know a fucking thing.

I don't realize I actually *have* run out until I turn around to see the outside of the crystal and herb shop, and then the world begins to gray. The sudden exertion has made me very dizzy. I've been holding my breath too long.

The last thing I see is the front door opening and Anna-Louise, as flowy as a wraith, coming out of her shop, shouting over her shoulder, "Momma! She's dropping!"

Then the pavement rushes up to greet me, and I—

"Thank God you crumpled and didn't just fall down onto your head," the old woman is saying, feeling around my head in a way that's reminiscent of Dr. Burton checking my skull for lumps. Only this time, the hands are caring, soft, slow. They're checking for pain, not for imperfections.

We're sitting in the back room/private office of the store, through the door just behind the checkout counter. I wonder if they've locked the front door, or if they just don't get enough visitors to worry about that.

"I'm very lucky," I say automatically.

I can't look at Anna-Louise. But I also can't stop trying to stare at her.

Grown-up Anna-Louise.

Cruel, calculating Anna-Louise.

She hands me a mug of tea.

"Has this ever happened before?" My (former?) bully asks. "You . . ." She appears to search for the word. "Fanning?"

"Fainting," her mother corrects.

"Fainting," Anna-Louise says. It's an exchange with no sense of reprimand, like they barely even notice it. "Has that ever happened before?"

Gosh, only when I look in the mirror. Or see a dead woman in the bathtub for the first time. Or a woman about your age, Anna-Louise.

"Must have been the sun," I say weakly.

"It's been awful lately," Anna-Louise agrees. "So harp."

"Hot," her mother adds.

"Yes," I say. I flick my eyes up from the mug in my hands to Anna-Louise's face. There's something strange going on there I keep noticing. I'm pretty sure it's not my usual hallucination.

"But," Barb continues, "we don't want to keep you. If you have to leave. You ran out of here so fast—"

My face flushes. I must have seemed so ridiculous, tearing out of here like that. "No, I'm sorry, I just . . . remembered my phone was in the car. And I was expecting a . . . phone call." I swallow.

"Oh," Barb says. "Do you still need to—"

"No. No, it's okay. I think it . . . was actually for a different day."

Barb and Anna-Louise exchange a look. A look I recognize. *She's crazy,* that look says. I'm not crazy. I'm just not a good liar. Sue me.

I stifle my anger.

"Well," Barb says. "There's one crisis averted." She gives me a patient smile.

"Crisis averted," Anna-Louise echoes. She puts a hand on my knee. My flesh crawls under her touch. "What's your name?"

"Jane," her mom says before I can.

"Jane," Anna-Louise repeats. "It's lively to meet you."

Her mom lets that one go.

But here's something I can't let go: Anna-Louise *really* doesn't seem to recognize me. Neither does her mother, who at least admitted her eyesight wasn't great. But Anna-Louise . . . Wasn't she warned by Bonnie or Carole that I was in town? Do they not talk anymore?

I quickly dart my eyes back up at her face. Something is definitely going on there. A slight tremble of her lips. One eye slightly cocked off to the side. Not necessarily immediately noticeable. Same goes for the dimpling on her skin, like old acne scarring. But perfect Anna-Louise never had acne . . .

"It's okay if you're a little on edge, Jane," Barb says. "We're all a little on edge here these days."

"The *murder*," Anna-Louise says with relish, slowly, enunciating it like it's something she's been practicing to get right.

"Have you heard about it where you live?"

I nod. "I have. It's awful."

"Awful is right. Something's screwed up. It's not supposed to be this way."

"No," I agree. Odd way to phrase that, though.

"You know, yesterday," Barb continues, "I was even interviewed by some damn fool from the FBI? Can you imagine? The FBI! Came right in here to the store with his little notepad out, asking what I knew. Just unbelievable what's been allowed to happen here."

"Unbelievable," Anna-Louise concurs.

We sit in silence for an awkward beat, Barb worryingly knitting her fingers together, Anna-Louise staring glassy-eyed into the space between us. I can't tell if I'm supposed to say more or have an opinion or what. Then Barb turns to her daughter.

"Jane says she has a friend with regression issues."

"Cooool!"

"I caught her looking at one of Celia Gayheart's books."

"Oh!" Anna-Louise turns to me. I note again how one eye is looking just past me. "Do you podcow? Know her?" She screws her face up for a moment. Focuses. "Do. You. Know. Her. Podcats. Cast. Her *podcast*?"

"No."

"She's great. I don't read well, but she's on Audible. And pod. Casts."

Barb pats her daughter's shoulder supportively, then turns back to me. "What's going on with your friend?"

I tell them the hits, this time in third person. Strange dreams. A general feeling of unease. Unfamiliar impulses. Visions. Auto writing.

"Auto writing? That's great," Barb says with the savor of a professional wine taster.

"So great." Anna-Louise nods. "That's a *big* lawn."

"Sign."

"Sign."

I tell them how my friend has seen doctors, but they all seem unwilling to take her complaints seriously.

"Western medicine." Barb shakes her head, like someone lamenting the predictably bad behavior of a deviant friend. "Not surprising. But this sounds pretty textbook."

"Textbook," Anna-Louise agrees.

Textbook.

Mostly, though, I tell them, my friend is worried.

"About what?"

"She knows that, in her past life"—and it's still hard for me to say such things definitively—"she knows that she was murdered. She's scared she's destined to . . . you know . . . end the same way."

Barb and Anna-Louise exchange glances.

"Does your friend live around here?" Barb asks.

"Socorro."

"Hm. Well, murder is on a lot of people's minds, I guess," Barb says. I nod. "Be that as it may, destiny is a much different topic than reincarnation."

"Tell her about the cup," Anna-Louise whispers.

"She's not going to want to hear about—"

"Then *I* will." I feel her eyes fall on me. I briefly meet them and, before I have to look away, I once again marvel how crooked her expression is. The effect is as of a just slightly subpar portrait artist, getting the alignment of her features just a smidge wrong—you might not even notice all the time. But in the right light, at the right angle, there's an uncanniness, like her eyes and nose are at risk of sliding off to one side or the other. What happened to her? A dozen dark, gleeful scenarios flit through my mind: drug problems, a horrible accident, an abusive spouse. Poor, cruel Anna-Louise, life wasn't as perfect as she'd acted like it would have to be.

"The cup," Anna-Louise is saying, "is my own, um . . ." She turns to her mother for the word.

"Theory," Barb supplies. "Well, no, not quite theory. It's how Anna-Louise likes to think of the universal life force."

"Think of life, all of it . . . as a *sea*." She moves her arms around the air, signifying a vast body of calm water. Her bracelets clackle and klangle excitedly. "And each living body, whether it's a plant, a germ, a bort—"

"Bug," Barb says.

"Bug. A human. Each living body is like a little cup." She forms a cup with her hand. "Every birth? That cup dips into the sea and holds some life for a little while. Every death?" She overturns her cupped hand and pours the imaginary water back out.

The sea. It sends a shiver through me. *There are no accidental fishes . . .*

"So," she continues, occasionally wincing when she gets to a word she can't quite remember, but generally speaking with more ease on this complicated subject than anything else she's said so far, "basically, life . . . is life. Being human isn't all that special. And an . . . identity doesn't jump from body to body like some, some—" She waggles her thumb like someone trying to flag down a ride.

"Hitchhiker?" I say. She nods.

"It's the same idea behind you can't draw the exact same water from a well you've just poured into," Barb says.

"We're all made up of so *many* past lives," Anna-Louise continues. "We just spread it around and mix it up. Water into water. Except sometimes . . ." I'm not looking at her face, but I can hear the devilish grin in her words. "Sometimes a life is *sticky*. Like oil. It gets scooped out more whole than usual. Maybe not all of it, but most of it. That's when you get recall, or talent, or, or . . . you know, things your friend has."

Barb puts a hand on Anna-Louise as if to say, *Don't get overexcited.* "Of course, there are still also things like social influence, life experience, friends and family. Nature, nurture." She shrugs. I get a momentary—but strong—impression that she really doesn't put as much stock into the metaphysical as her daughter does. "What it all comes down to is we are all part of one life force. Every living thing. We are all just vessels, and death is impossible because we are all forever living one life together. One big 'I.'"

Anna-Louise nods. "It's what our relitivision teaches us. No. *Religion*."

That's when I notice there are images of angels on one of the cluttered back-office walls. I'm too far away from the pictures to see if they have names, but I think I can guess what they might be. Azazel. Zepar. *This town . . .*

"Anyway," Barb says, "I don't think your friend has too much to worry about. Past lives are more like echoes than threats. Although she's more than welcome to come here for a reading. I'm a certified hypnotist for just these sorts of occasions, you know."

"We also do auras and chakras!"

"But hypnosis is the best," Barb says. "That's where you really start to peel layers away."

These are the witches on the outskirts of the village, I think.

Anna-Louise leans toward me and asks, "Are you done with your tree? Top? Tap." She smacks her thigh in frustration, which seems to jar the word loose. *"Tea?"*

I tell her I am and that I'd love to buy some for my aunt. I hand her my mug, and she quickly shuffles out of the room to take the dirty dish away, leaving me and Barb alone.

Before I can ask anything, Barb says to me, "They call it TBI. Traumatic brain injury. Happened when she was about twelve. Gives her aphasia. Occasional memory lapses. Especially around strangers."

When she was twelve? "What happened?" I ask, certain the bald question is rude but not caring.

"She was in a horrible accident."

"It wasn't an accident," Anna-Louise calls from the other room. A moment later, she's coming back into the office, a small brown bag of tea in her hand. "I got beat up real bad."

"What happened?" I ask again. It sounds more like a statement this time. My mouth has gone dry.

"Baseball bat. Bang, bam. Right in the face." She points at her head. I notice again the faint divots in her skin, like chicken pox scarring. "Wound up in a cactus patch. Can you reheat that? They had a big ol' cactus patch right by our playmate. Ground. Playground. She whacked me into the cactuses and just kept . . . bam bam bam."

Her mother shifts in her seat, uncomfortable with the memory.

"She?" I ask.

"There was this girl," Barb says. "A horrible girl—"

This time, Anna-Louise puts a hand on her mother, silencing her. "I did a bad thing," she tells me.

Yes. Good. Confess. Admit it, you bully.

I might even be smiling.

"You did no such thing," Barb says to her daughter. "She was horrible, and there's not a day goes by I don't curse her memory."

"She was dist—disturbed. She scared everyone. And you know kids: sometimes they pick on what they don't understand. So my friends and I teased her. And one day, we went . . . too far."

A curious thing happens, almost like the inverse of an echo. In the space before she finishes her sentence, an image flashes before me: an equipment rack right by a gymnasium door. The sort of door I would have had to walk through after Anna-Louise and her friends stole my clothes and made me march naked and dripping out to the playground to get them back. The rack is full of items like tennis rackets, badminton paddles . . . baseball bats. Easily grabbable before one might step outside.

But . . . they're not talking about me, are they? No, absolutely not. There could have been another kid—she just admitted she and her friends were bullies.

Nadine's voice, phlegmy and mocking: *Oh, Mary,* you *were the*—

"What happened to her?" I ask. "To the girl who did it, I mean."

"After she almost killed Anna-Louise, they sent her away to the nuthouse," Barb says, her tone dripping. "People finally had enough of her, I think. After that, who knows? Desert has a way of swallowing people up. I can only hope that's what happened."

"Mother, don't be indicative," Anna-Louise reprimands.

"Vindictive," her mother corrects. "And if you had a daughter, you'd understand."

Anna-Louise waves her away, and the bracelets on her wrist jangle with a pleasant plastic clackiting.

The nuthouse.

Clearview.

Oh, Mary, *you* were the bully—

No. No, this is absurd. Besides, what if *they're* the ones remembering it wrong? What if they think it was the wrong person? Anna-Louise has memory problems; Barb is just plain old. Unreliable witnesses if ever there were a pair. How do I even know what they're talking about is accurate?

"Do you remember her name?" I ask. Dreading the answer. Knowing what it will be.

Suddenly—

"Hello?"

—a voice comes from the front of the store.

"I'll get it," Anna-Louise says and heads out of the room.

Barb grumbles. "Better not be another damn FBI agent."

That possibility is enough to keep me here in the back office for the moment. Still, I could be in a very bad spot here if they realize who I am while also thinking I'm someone I'm not. My heart is beating fast now. Despite just having tea, my mouth feels slimy and thick. I want to get out of here. As soon as this new visitor leaves.

"How much do I owe you for the tea?" I ask Barb. She jumps slightly, as if she'd forgotten I was there.

She tells me, and I pay her. As soon as the money crosses hands, she looks at me afresh.

"Have we ever met before? Is this your first time stopping by?"

"No. I mean, yes. No, we haven't. Yes, it is."

"Hmm." She stuffs the money away in a lockbox on the cluttered desk. "Well, you should bring your friend by sometime. Especially if she's . . . you know . . . a woman your age. That's why we set up this store, for women like you. There are so few spaces for women after a certain point, don't you think?" She flashes me a toothy grin, and I'm suddenly unnerved. It doesn't quite reach her eyes. Were all her smiles like this during our little visit? I can't remember.

I tell her yes, I do think that.

"Some days, I think we only have each other to rely on. It's good your friend has you."

"Yes." A question floats to the surface of my thoughts—a question I think was originally Dr. Burton's but I'm realizing has been asked of me several times by several different people. *Is there anyone missing you back home?* She's about to ask it, too, isn't she?

"Tell me," she begins. "Is there—"

Before she can finish, Anna-Louise comes back into the office, voicing a small moan in despair.

"What is it?" her mother asks. "Who stopped by?"

"That was—oh God, now I'm forgetting her name." Anna-Louise rubs her temples, frustrated, and I see she's got some sheets of paper in her hands. "Uh, skin—thinny—grocer—"

"The skinny girl from the grocery store," Barb translates. "Tania?"

Anna-Louise nods. "And her husband, Ruh—Ruh—"

"Ronald."

Anna-Louise awkwardly thrusts the pages at Barb. She's upset. "They gave me a buncha these to put up." Barb bobbles the pages, and a few of them fly around the office. I attempt to grab the copies that float my way. Barb does the same and, as she's scooping a page off the floor, I happen to get a peek down the front of Barb's flowy dress. Totally accidental, I'm not meaning to look, but I catch a glimpse something just above her left breast. Something round. Drawn in dark ink.

Almost looks like an eyeball.

As soon as Barb reads what's on the pages—all of which are xeroxed copies of the same sheet—she says quietly, "Oh no."

Another victim, I think, and I'm soon proven right. Sort of.

Meanwhile, Anna-Louise is still rubbing her temples. "I wish I wasn't like this! I wish I could think of words! I didn't know what to say to them, to make them feel better!"

"Oh, honey." Barb reaches out to rub her daughter's arm. "You try. That's enough." She looks back at the sheets in her hand. "What the hell is going on in this town?!"

On the page is a photo of a little boy who's not very comfortable smiling for a camera. **Missing! Please help!** screams the header. At the bottom, his parents' contact info.

I recognize the photo. It'd be hard not to. I just saw him the other day, pestering me with trivia about bugs he assumed there was no way I could know.

His name is Wallace.

33

Clear View

Nadine is laughing. From the moment I walk in the door, her throaty chuckle rolls out of the shadows toward me like marbles on the floor, like trash pushed by a soft breeze. The house is its usual dark and forbidding self, and my eyes are half-blind by the adjustment from high sunshine to gloom, so all I see is her form in her chair. But there's no mistaking that laugh.

Heh-heh-heh.

"Hi," I say, stepping inside and closing the door. My voice is soft. Humbled. Choking on all the things I want to say: *It was true; everything you told me was true.* "I'm back."

My walk from the store was painful, all my aches and abuses keeping pace. And with every slow step, every scuff of the dirt with my exhausted feet, my mind attempted to rationalize what I've learned only to be met with the *tonk!* of a baseball bat against a young girl's skull. The vibration of impact raced up my arm into my teeth. By the time I got closer to the residential streets and started seeing more flyers for the missing child, that vibration became constant, the sounds of impact both more furious and less solid as bone gave way to mush.

Tonk!

Surely, there has to be a reasonable explanation—

Tonk!

Some other girl Anna-Louise tortured—

Tonk!

Maybe Carole had enemies—

Tonk!

Maybe Wallace ran away—

Tonk tonk tonk tonk crunch!

I walk past Nadine into the kitchen.

"I . . . I got us some tea," I say. "It's good. I think you'll like it. I got it from that crystal shop over on Mariposa. You ever been?"

Heh-heh-heh.

A wet, gurgling laugh. A knowing laugh. She knows exactly what I learned at that store. She knew I'd come face-to-face with the girl I'd almost beaten to death and, one way or another, I'd be unable to run from the truth anymore.

Tonk!

I have the sudden urge to drop myself at Nadine's feet and cry. Sob. Maybe then she'll be forced to do something—put her hand in my hair, rub my back, tell me it's okay, even if it's just to shut me up, I don't care, I just need *someone,* a mommy. But I don't have a mommy, do I? She burned up in a fire, and that was probably my fault, too. Nurse Nancy's voice in my head: *If I hadn't had my mother and my sisters . . . don't try to do this alone . . .* Barb's: *We only have each other to rely on . . .*

I have discovered new depths of feeling alone. A disorienting discovery for someone who's always been lonely.

"Can we have some tea and talk, Nadine? I . . . I'm ready to talk. I'll leave the room dark if you want, I just . . . need to talk." My voice drops to a whisper. It's too horrible to say full-throatedly just yet. "You were right. About everything. I'm . . . I'm so sorry."

And even though there's no way she heard me, she gives me another chuckle, short and percussive as a burp. *Heh.*

She's loving my torment. She'll never let me live this down. But hasn't she earned the right to gloat? She *told* me. I didn't believe her, but she told me. And even after all that, she was willing to let me come back home to her.

I prepare the tea. Fill the kettle with water and set it on a burner. The sounds of the mugs being set on the counter feels very loud. Louder than normal, actually.

Something feels wrong.

You. You're the one who's wrong. You've always been wrong.

That's true. But . . . something *else* feels wrong. From my vantage point at the counter, staring at the back of Nadine's chair and the living room around her, I feel like I'm looking at one of those cartoons where you're supposed to Spot the Difference. Something is wrong with what I'm seeing and, combined with Nadine's throaty, delighted-yet-subdued laughter, it fills me with a feeling I can't quite name.

Yes, I can name it. Dread. Stomach-twisting, back-prickling dread.

You're just looking for something to let you run away from the truth right now. You're being crazy, Mary. And you deserve *that word now.*

"I'm scared, Nadine," I whisper again.

I turn on the burner under the kettle. Click-click-*fwoom*.

"I'll be right back."

In Brenda's bedroom, I drop my purse on the floor and try to shake this feeling off. *I'm okay,* I tell myself, *I'm okay. I'm just having a bad day, I'm learning unpleasant information, but I'm okay, my feet are still on the ground.*

Time for another round of Spot the Difference. My Loved Ones on the dresser. This one's easy, the Difference is they're still standing among the massacre of porcelain Nadine wrought. Brian, Pamela, Eunice, Peter, all used to be whole and perfect, not jagged edges and powdery bursts. Same for Melissa, Troy, Fra—wait a minute. Where is Frannie? Or Llewyn? Or, or, or—

Something's wrong. *Very* wrong. Some of my Loved Ones are missing. Not just the ones Nadine pulverized.

"No," I whisper. "Oh, Nadine. You *bitch*."

Is she stealing from me? Is that why she's laughing?

"Is that why you're laughing, Nadine?" I call out.

I hear her chuckling from her plushy throne in the living room. A horrible sound. Low and gurgly, full of phlegm and smugness. Waiting for—daring—me to come confront her.

Heheheheheh.

And just behind the surface of my mind—in my own mental crawl space—dread begins to skitter frantically in the dark.

Where are they?" I ask, standing in the entryway to the living room. "This isn't funny. Please. I'm trying to be as honest and vulnerable as I can with you. Please don't play games, not today."

Hehehehehe.

"It's bad enough you destroyed some of them. Please don't hide them from me. Is this because I borrowed your books a couple times? Did you find out and now you're paying me back? I'm sorry. I was careful with them, I didn't do anything bad to them. Where are my figurines, Nadine?"

Heheh.

Heart pounding but still outwardly calm, I pull one of her books off the shelf.

"I can destroy your things, too. So you'd better tell me."

I give her enough time to respond. She doesn't.

Riiiiiip.

First one page. Then another. Calmly. Waiting for her to explode in anger.

I let the pages drop to the floor. This makes me think of the basement in the Cross House, and for just a moment the dread animal in my mind becomes the rage animal and I'm pulling more and more pages from their binding, rip, riiiiip, tossing them to the carpet in delight at the distraction. Is this how I felt when I was bashing that little girl's head in with a baseball bat? Delirious and giddy and context-free? If so, I can see the appeal!

Then the moment is over. The dread returns, stronger than ever.

Paper litters the floor.

Nadine hasn't reacted at all.

Apologies bubbling in my throat, I bend down to start picking pages up . . . then stop short.

The Difference. The thing about this scene that has been bugging and eluding me since I got back. I've spotted it.

There's a dark lump on the floor next to Nadine's feet that's not usually there.

"Nadine?"

Only a soft, snide gurgle in response.

I'm already on my hands and knees, so I crawl forward. Reach out and grab the shadowy lump.

It's a plastic flower. The kind Nadine always wears in her hair. The kind she would never let fall to the floor without immediately picking it back up and sticking it in its place.

"Nadine?" I ask again. The dread animal is now in full frenzy behind the walls of my mind, racing up and down, to and fro. "Nadine, I'm going to turn on the light, okay?"

No answer. Just her wet, gurgling grumble. And I realize there's another sound I haven't heard in a little while. The intake hiss of her oxygen tank.

I try to flick on the living room light from the wall plate, but the bulb has burned out. She never turned that light on anyway; whenever she did light up the living room, it was with floor lamps.

I approach Nadine, waiting for, *willing* the sound of her oxygen tank to softly pull some air into her nostrils. Nothing.

She could still be trying to fool me; maybe even scare me . . .

Yeah. Maybe. I reach over her to turn on the lamp by her chair with a slow, cautious hand.

The lamp clicks on. I make the mistake of staring at it when the bulb flares to life and I'm momentarily blinded. I have to blink away layers of light from my retinas.

Blink. Blink. Blink.

When I can finally see—when I get a good look at what's sitting in Nadine's chair—I start to scream. From the kitchen, the teakettle finally reaches a boil and joins me.

34

Much to Swallow

This is what I rehearsed saying to Nadine on my walk back from the crystal shop:

> *I'm scared, Nadine.*
>
> *Somehow, I managed to forget everything. About my past. About my present. How can I know who I am if I don't know who I've been?*
>
> *I've been thinking a lot about past lives and destiny and . . . I don't know, is change even possible? Can a person ever start a new life, or is it always out of our hands because we're just running a track that's already been laid down in front of us? Barb said they're two different things, destiny and past lives, but are they really?*

It plays on a loop in my head now as I stare at what's left of my aunt.

Meanwhile, the teakettle continues to shriek. When I'm finally able to get my body to work, I go to the kitchen and turn off the burner. The kettle dies down.

Maybe it'll be different now. Maybe I just needed to look away for a moment, give myself the visual equivalent of a palate cleanser. Maybe I won't see the obscene horror waiting for me in Nadine's chair.

I walk back to the recliner.

Nope. Still there. Unquestionable in the lamplight.

Nadine is sitting in her usual spot, but she's looking up at the ceiling. Her cheeks are veiny and mottled, but also puffed and smooth, the inflated surface of a balloon. Her skin is slick, sweating like deli meat left out in the heat.

Her mouth is open, and the rim is frosted with the strawberry jam and cottage cheese of dried foamy spittle and clotted blood. Her throat bulges with sharp, unnatural angles. Blood courses down her mouth onto her neck, highlighting the shapes. She almost looks like a duck caught in the process of swallowing bread. But it's not bread.

Blue and yellow legs stick out of her pale, puffed lips.

Someone has been forcing her to eat the little statues.

Or, rather, small, broken fragments of the statues. Swallowable fragments. Choke-able fragments.

At her feet, resting in a spray of powder, is her hammer, along with pieces of a jagged torso I recognize as Arthur, the little boy carrying his books to school.

The inside of Nadine's mouth and throat must be lacerated to hell. Her throat must be a drowning pool of porcelain and blood.

Her eyes roll toward me, wide and helpless and maybe insane with misery.

She makes another laughing noise. *Huhhhhuhuhuh.* But it's not an actual laugh. More like a guttural gurgle. This whole time, she was never really laughing. She's been trying to talk while gravity and muscle memory pulled sharp shards of porcelain down her throat, scraping and lodging . . . deeper and deeper. *Huhuh huhme.* Weaker now. Winding down like the teakettle just did.

"Hold on, Nadine," I say. "We're going to get you help. We're going to make this right. We're going to get the person who did this to you."

But I don't move. I'm standing stone-still, looking down at this horrid, pathetic sight. Because I *know* who did this to her.

It's the feet sticking out of her mouth that eventually breaks my paralysis.

I reach a tentative hand out toward her mouth.

With my other hand, I touch the back of Nadine's head. There's a pulverized wetness there and, in a flash, I remember slapping her after she began to smash my Loved Ones with her hammer. Did I actually slap her? Or had I grabbed the hammer from her at that point? One smash deserving of another.

Bracing her head, I gently pinch the statue sticking out of her mouth between two fingers.

"I'm sorry, Nadine," I say, and then I begin to pull the shard out. The noise it makes reminds me of the sound a tub makes when the water is just about all gone down the drain. A rushing, gurgling exhale. Her voice comes along with it in a pained *huuhhhhh,* followed by another laugh-like, miserable gurgle.

Blood and mucus and saliva hang on the porcelain in globby strands, still wet but with a gelatinous tenacity, as clotted as old soup. It drips onto her barely moving chest. She's wearing a sweatshirt with a flamingo on it; the flamingo gets coated.

There are too many other shards in there for her throat to lose its bulge just yet. I'll have to keep digging. Maybe some of the statues are salvageable. I recognize the fragment I'm currently holding as the bottom half of Nathan, the little boy with a palette and paintbrush.

I've just about dragged the upper half of Nathan past Nadine's teeth when there's a knock on the front door.

Nadine's wild eyes roll to meet mine. Does she comprehend what's going on? Hell, do I? Who could be knocking on the door at this moment? No one ever comes to visit Nadine.

I hold very still.

Just when I think it's safe, that maybe it was just a mailman or a salesman or any number of other solicitors who have other stops to make and take a lack of response as a clear invitation to keep on moving . . . *thump!* Nadine's oxygen tank falls to the ground. It lands hard enough to roll forward and, with an appallingly loud *tonk!* that might remind one of an aluminum bat hitting bone, smacks against the leg of the nearby coffee table. She must have kicked it. One final act of defiance. Nadine, you absolute piece of—

"Hello? Someone in there?" A man's unfamiliar voice outside. He heard the noise. I wince. Do I stay silent? He knocks again.

"Just a minute," I call back, wiping my hands on Nadine's sweatshirt and trying to check in the lamplight how much, if any, blood is on me.

It takes my eyes a moment to adjust to the short, balding man on the porch.

"Oh, hi," he says, surprised to see someone at the door, as if he hadn't just been repeatedly knocking on it. "I'm Special Agent Peter Arliss with the FBI. Have a minute?"

Hot day. Nice, but, whoo, I don't know how you all do it, living out here in the sun!"

He's immediately unlikable. There's just something about the sound of his voice, the unctuous way he smiles. It's hard to put a finger on—maybe that's why the first word that comes to mind is *squirmy.*

I give him a taste of the ol' Good Girl classic. No words, just teeth.

"So anyway," he begins. "I—" Then his own grin falters as his eyes creep down my shirt. There's a red stain near the bottom, obvious in the sunlight.

Think fast.

"I'm sorry," I say evenly, clasping my hands behind my back in case they're also stained, mind flailing for the quickest way to inspire this man to leave. "I'm currently going through menopause, and my menstrual cycle is very erratic."

He's wearing sunglasses, but I can see his eyes bulge behind the tinted glass. "Oh. Oh, it's not, don't . . . don't worry about that. I won't keep you." He twitches as if given a low-voltage jolt, waving his hands with a no-no-no gesture. He's so uncomfortable I almost can't repress a laugh.

Then I realize Nadine's lamp is still on and he has a direct line of sight into the living room, and the urge to laugh evaporates. I step farther out onto the porch and shut the door behind me.

"Anyway." He regains his composure. "I was just making my way around town, knocking on doors and chasing leads. I wonder if I might be able to ask you a few questions?"

"Of course."

"Great." He takes off his sunglasses, folds them into the neck of his polo shirt, makes a show out of flipping open a notebook. I realize in an instant he's the sort of man who became an investigator as much for the costume and props as for the solving of crimes.

My heart is beating strongly and steadily. My body hasn't quite made the decision to panic; it's just waiting out this initial first stage of the encounter, ready for anything.

The FBI agent proceeds to ask me a series of banal questions: if I'm aware of the murder of Carole Huff (yes, I've heard rumors), if I've seen anything suspicious (not at all).

It feels like he's sufficiently convinced of my uselessness when, from inside: a thump, this one sounding like a foot being stomped down onto carpet.

His eyebrows raise. "Is everything okay in there?"

"My aunt is very sick. She gets hungry around this time, so I'll need to finish feeding her."

"Hey, I'd love to chat with her, too, if that's possible!"

"No. She doesn't leave the house or talk to strangers. She wouldn't know anything about what's going on."

"Gotcha." He makes a note. Or maybe just a doodle where a note would go. "Just a few more questions and I'll let you go."

"It's a horrible thing," I say, eager to have him gone. "What happened. To Carole."

"You can say that again. And now this little boy going missing? *So* horrible. What do you know about Damon Cross?"

Now my heart begins to actually pound.

"That name . . . sounds familiar. He used to live around here, right? In that big house up on the hill? He was a killer from a long time ago?" I almost add: he killed women like me.

He looks at me. "You must not be from around here." He chuckles at my confused expression. "I've always been fascinated by little towns like this. No one trusts anyone from 'the Outside.'" He makes little finger quotes in the air. "Honestly, you just admitted to knowing more about Damon Cross than anyone else I've spoken to this entire trip. Even though I'm willing to bet everyone here knows *exactly* who Damon Cross is! Heck, they probably have all sorts of inside info I could never dream of! But any question I ask, no matter how basic, they all play dumb—if they even bother responding at all. Like I said: fascinating!"

"Oh," I say. "Well, yes, I'm . . . from out of town. I'm just here visiting my aunt."

As if on cue, another thump comes from inside. Do I have to worry about Nadine getting up and walking to the door? She's way too far gone for that . . . right? My heartbeat increases. I need to wrap this up.

"Hey, can I ask you something? Is your aunt religious?" He drops his voice as if there's anyone around to hear. "Is she from *that* part of town?"

"*That* part?"

"Do you not know the history of this place?"

He doesn't wait for me to respond. He bounces a little on the balls of his feet, giddy to tell someone all he knows. I'm immediately reminded of precocious little Wallace, and a whole complicated raft of feelings washes through me.

"Well, like a lot of the really teeny towns around these parts, actually, Arroyo was founded way back in the day by basically a splinter group of a splinter

group of a splinter group of religious fundamentalists who were fleeing perse-
cution. You know, the town wasn't even called Arroyo then, it was—what was
it?—oh yeah: Fertile Ground. Can you believe that? I love those weird little
town names. Anyway, it's pretty safe to say they barely bore a resemblance to
any established religion by a factor of two or three by that point. I mean, these
people were so extreme that whatever they were doing was untenable for the
other extremists who were too extreme for *their* religion in the first place!"
He's so excited, a little spit bubble pops in the corner of his mouth. *Please wrap
this up,* I beg with my eyes. I shift my weight impatiently.

"We don't know much more about those original settlers because there was
very little contact with"—again the finger quotes—"'the Outside.' I mean,
that was the point for setting up the town to begin with, right? Until the
day . . . they found ore in the mountains. Hello, Outsiders! Eventually, that
mining boom went bust—when the ground literally stopped being Fertile,
ha ha—and everyone pulled up stakes. Except two groups of people: religious nuts and stubborn, antisocial loners. I'm sure you can guess which side
the *Cross* family comes from, huh? Someone—who knows who—renamed
the town Arroyo, which, as I understand it, is like a dried-up old gulch, I
guess to signify those two distinct sides, and bing bang boom, here we are.
I mean, obviously, I'm oversimplifying a bit; I'm sure after a while, people
started intermingling, and it's not so segregated between the religious
nuts and the . . . Oh. Wait. I'm sorry, I wasn't trying to imply your aunt was
a stubborn loner!"

"Of course not." As eager as I am to shoo this man away, it is somewhat
gratifying to learn a little more about the history of this town. And while
Nadine was never religious, it occurs to me I don't know a thing about my
father's side. Could that be why he and my mother were out here?

The FBI agent wipes sweat from his face. "Oh well. One of these days,
I'm going to actually land an interview with an insider here. I wrote a paper
about towns like this back at the academy, but what I'd really love is to write
a book. *The Secret Small Towns of the Still-Wild West,* or something. Just
fascinating stuff."

Another thump from the living room, bigger than either of the previous
ones. What is going on in there? Is she coming closer? I want to see, but I
don't want to give the impression something is wrong.

My palms start to slicken. "I really should get—"

"Yeah, not a lot of people know about the Cross murders to begin with," he muses, now squinting off into the distance. "I don't know why; he just never was one of the more famous of the '70s golden era, you know? Maybe because he died before he could ever be questioned and turned into one of those 'sexy' serial killers some people are so obsessed with nowadays? But when we got the call that there might be a potential copycat, I jumped at the chance to head down here. I have a theory there's some sort of nexus where religious fanaticism and serial killing intersect." He links his hands to show what he means. "After all, what is a copycat killer but a fellow worshipper, really? You know what I mean? Hybristophilia is just another way to scratch that godhead itch. And with the anniversary coming up, I dunno, my instincts are telling me there might be something ritualistic about the killing. Ah, jeez, look at me, you get me blathering on like I'm the one being interviewed—"

I should let it end. I should let him leave. But I can't help myself.

"What anniversary? What's coming up?"

He gives me another excited-to-lecture smile.

"This Saturday. It's the anniversary of Damon Cross's death. The fiftieth, to be exact."

"Oh." My throat has suddenly become very dry.

Because this Saturday is my birthday.

My fiftieth.

To be exact.

The door clicks shut, and I'm back in the gloom.

Click.

Pieces of the puzzle falling into place.

Click. Click. I'm shaking a little, like my blood sugar is low. I put my forehead against the door.

It occurs to me: I can stop myself from putting this all together *right now*. This might, in fact, be my last chance. It will take effort, but I can do it. I can stuff these revelations back into my mental crawl space and continue on living, eventually forgetting what I've just learned. Or *think* I've learned.

I turn around, suddenly remembering the thumps. "Aunt Nadine?"

She's lying facedown on the carpet, having fallen out of her chair. A grim parody of how I found her oh so long ago when I first arrived back in town. I quickly move to her, though with less urgency than that previous time.

Her body is completely still, not even the barely perceptible hum of blood circulating beneath skin. She's not cold yet, but she's distinctly not warm. It's an unnerving room-temperature feel. She must have made one desperate move for the door and then . . .

I roll her over. Her eyes stare up at nothing, glassy, sightless. Might as well be painted on.

Speaking of, she vomited out some shards in her fall. Three bits of statue lie on the carpet, resting in red, foamy spew that smells vaguely of standing water: metallic, fetid.

Three heads.

I pick them up, wipe them off on the carpet.

I'm feeling very strange. Disconnected. It feels like forever ago since I last communed with my figurines for advice.

It's not too late. You can stop right now. You can keep living your simple, explainable life and leave these pieces scattered.

But I think it *is* too late.

"What if Eleanor and I had it wrong?" I ask the little, broken, stained faces.

Are you sure you want to do this? they implore.

"What if I'm not the reincarnation of one of Damon Cross's *victims?* What if . . ."

Last chance . . .

I look at one of the shards in my hand. Bettylou, the little girl feeding sheep (although those sheep are nowhere to be found; they're probably grazing somewhere between Nadine's trachea and stomach at this point). Bettylou's neck comes to a sharp, jagged crag. A perfect cutting instrument.

"What if . . . in a past life . . . I was . . . Damon Cross?"

Tonk! The sound of puzzle pieces *really* clicking into place.

I replay what I imagined doing to Carole. Had it only been a fantasy? Or was it something I kept myself from remembering? The same way I've apparently kept so much from myself over the years?

But how would you have gotten home that night, then? And what about the bloody clothes? How could you have hidden all the evidence?

I don't know.

And what about the fact that apparently whoever tried to slice Carole's face off didn't know what they were doing?

I look at Nadine's prone face, then back to the razor-sharp edge of Betty-lou's neck.

Should I try it? Here, now, fully aware?

Could I slip this porcelain tip into flesh, perhaps just under where I imagine her lower jawline would be, and trace a shape around the face, slip under that thick top layer, puncturing fat, separating muscle, pull away a strip of skin that'd look a little like when you were a kid, taking bites out of a slice of bologna to make eyes and a mouth? A dark, thrumming instinct tells me: yes, I could. In fact, I bet I'd be surprisingly good at it for a newbie. You might think I had an inexplicable talent for such things. Like a prodigy.

Someone who was born with it.

I move over to Nadine, porcelain in hand, ready to test my theory.

What stops me is an ant. It bubbles out from Nadine's mouth and crawls down her chin toward her neck. A second emerges . . . and then two more. Nadine's cheeks ripple ever so slightly. There are more ants in there—none of them real, of course, none of this is real, but I don't want to give them the satisfaction of seeing me upset.

I'm not upset.

I calmly put the porcelain heads down, cover Nadine with the ratty blue fleece blanket from the couch, and walk out the front door.

I collapse into a sitting position in the yard, soaking in the bright sunshine.

I sit here for a very long time. The baked gravel bites into my skin. It's a real feeling, and I appreciate it. Things are only real in the sun. The sun burns things down to their purest, truest essences. Everything gets put into perspective. I'm safe in the sun.

Eventually, though, the sun begins to dip past the mountains, turning the sky a blinding yellow red that will soon soften into pinks and purples.

I hear footsteps approaching.

A shadow appears against the sun. I have to squint.

"Hey," its voice speaks. "Are you okay?"

The shadow grows features.

Of course it's her. She's come to claim me.

"Hi, Anna-Louise."

My former bully. My former victim. Her flowing silhouette has the shape of an angel, but the sun behind her turns her into a negative image in charcoal relief.

Not real. None of this is real. It's all pretend.

"Hi, Mary," Anna-Louise says. "I think . . . we have to talk. About this."

She's holding something in her hands. It takes me a moment to blink enough sight into my eyes to make it out clearly.

Clasped in front of her, just below the bracelets that have slid down to her skinny wrists, is a book. A book I haven't seen since I gave it to my dear friend Eleanor.

My journal.

35

Roundtable

That feeling of unreality doesn't go away when, following Anna-Louise to a parked car around the corner, I discover Eleanor and Barb waiting for me. Eleanor, in the driver's seat, gripping the wheel in a strangely tense way. Barb, in the back, staring straight ahead and—

Nope, not anymore. Barb is pushing the door open and barreling out toward me.

"You filthy fucking liar," she seethes. "How dare you come into our store and lie to our faces!"

"Mother—" Anna-Louise gets in between us and puts a hand on Barb's shoulder. Barb doesn't shake her off, but I can see she wants to. Instead, she settles for shooting dagger after dagger at me with her eyes.

"I should bash your head in right now, shouldn't I? Serve you right. I wish *I* had a baseball bat."

"Mother. *Please.* You promised."

Barb finally looks at Anna-Louise, then back at me, her wrinkled mouth drawn down in a severe frown. Her tongue runs against the insides of her cheeks, and then she spits at my feet.

Anna-Louise begins to apologize on her behalf, but Barb cuts her off. "Don't you dare say sorry to her. She's lucky she's getting off with her head intact."

Eleanor has climbed out of the car and is standing by the driver's seat. "I'm the one who's sorry," she says to me. "I didn't know who else to talk to about this." She's keeping her distance. Something feels immediately different about her. She seems heavier. Not in weight but in years. Like she's aged since last I saw her.

"What's going on?" I ask.

The sun has finally sunk behind the mountains, and the dull matte of dusk drapes over us. Everything begins to grow a deepening shade of blue, as if we're all asphyxiating and don't know it.

The three women look at each other. Then Eleanor says, "Should we get out of here? Go somewhere more private to talk?" She focuses squarely on me. "Maybe work your magic on your aunt and let us borrow you for the night?"

"My aunt's not going to be a problem," I say.

"Great." Eleanor shrugs. "So let's—"

Suddenly, Barb grabs the journal from Anna-Louise's hands, causing Anna-Louise to give a soft yelp.

"What is this?!" Barb demands of me, furious. "How did you do it?!" She glares at me with such fury it practically glows in the twilight.

"I don't know what you're asking me."

"Where did you get a copy of our text?!"

"Your . . . text?"

"You're the friend, aren't you?" Anna-Louise interjects. I turn to her, let my eyes bounce off her face to the dirt at her feet.

"What?" Another one of her aphasic mysteries?

"The *friend*. With the problems. At the . . . the store. You said. The friend?"

"Your *lie*," Barb says. "You 'had a friend who has been going through something very strange.' It's you. Right? 'Jane'?" Her voice is curdled with disgust.

"Yes," I say, remembering. Then I look at Eleanor. "Eleanor, what's going on? What's happening right now?"

Eleanor throws her hands up, not in defeat but in impotence. "Like I said! I didn't know who else to go to."

"Go to about what?"

Finally, she takes a step away from the car and toward me. "Mary. What you wrote. It's . . . Jesus, it's crazy."

The night sky briefly turns red. My fingers curl into fists. "Don't you call me crazy."

Barb is still on me. "Tell the truth! Did you copy this down somewhere? Did you steal a copy? Or your godforsaken aunt, maybe—did she get ahold of our text at some point over the years?"

I'm punch-drunk. Slow and sluggish and stupid and reeling. "I don't know what you're talking about." I want to insist more vehemently, but I barely have the energy.

"Then how did you write it all down? Word for word in some places!" She brandishes the book like a preacher delivering a fiery sermon.

"I don't . . . I don't know wh—"

"Well, you had to have seen it somewhere! This just doesn't make sense!"

And just like that, I whipsaw from fatigue and dizziness back to bright, crackling rage. My voice splits the night, high, reedy, desperate. *I know it doesn't make sense! That's why I came to you all for help!*"

A thin breeze rattles the thorn tree like bones. I try to calm down. I don't want to hyperventilate, but I'm so very close to doing so.

"Like I've been saying, I don't know what you're talking about. Everything in that book, I wrote. Or, not me. Something through me, I don't know, I don't understand what's in it, but it came from me, just me, just . . ." My lungs run out of air, and I gulp at the night for replenishment.

It's almost full dark now. Stars have begun their brilliant display above us, the same constellations and galaxies, the same show as always, and isn't that nice, because nothing down here makes any sense anymore.

"We have to take her to the council," Barb says at last.

Eleanor gapes. "What? No way! They'll never believe—"

"We have to take her to the council and explain it as best we can. Let them decide."

"They might decide to straight-up kill her! She's an outsider."

By the light of the stars, Barb's venomous smile is downright radioactive. "Oh well."

"Mother," Anna-Louise says hesitatingly. "What if she . . . *is*, though?"

"What if I'm what?" I ask. For a second, nobody answers. That silence tells me everything. "Damon Cross? Is that what you're talking about? What if I'm Damon Cross? Not one of his victims, like Eleanor and I thought, but *him*? Reincarnated?"

They all turn to me. Something about it being stated so bluntly, so inelegantly, focuses the group like a slap in the face.

"Yes," Barb says, barely able to squeeze her hateful voice out above a whisper. She sounds like she's swallowed vomit. "I suppose that is the hypothesis we're debating at this moment. But we are also taking into consideration the fact that you are clearly unwell and that you have also already proven yourself to be . . . untrustworthy. Not to mention the fact that, I mean . . . how could someone like *you* be . . . ?" She gives a high, disbelieving laugh.

"Mother," Anna-Louise says quietly. Tenderly. "Don't you believe? I know you don't as much as I do. But even a little? Don't you?"

"I'm sorry I lied in the store," I say to Barb. The fatigue has returned. I just want this confrontation over with. "I didn't know what else to do. I don't know anything. I'm stupid and bad and wrong and I've done bad things and I don't know why. I just wanted help figuring out who I am and why these things are happening to me."

Barb continues to stare at her daughter, not at me. But I feel eyes burning through me all the same, and when I turn my head, I see it's Eleanor. She's locked onto me, wearing an unreadable expression. Maybe disgust? Maybe it's just the darkness making shadows on her face.

Finally, Barb sighs.

"We will take her to the council and explain the situation." Anna-Louise begins to protest, and her mother holds up a hand. "But. I will make sure Burton and the rest of them treat her fairly. I will make sure they understand this is serious. Insane. But serious. I'm not going to throw her to the wolves. If this is what we think it *might* be, we all need to know."

"They're not going to be happy about us interrupting their meeting," Eleanor says. "It's been a tense couple of days."

She turns back to the car and opens up the driver's-side door.

"What are they meeting about?" I ask. My stomach feels heavy. My skin feels chilled. I'd welcome the warm embrace of a hot flash right about now. "I'm going to assume it's not about the Easter egg hunt."

Eleanor sniffs and gets behind the wheel. "Mary, my friend? You're about to learn a whole lot about what really goes on here in Arroyo."

36

Council

A dozen cars and trucks are parked along the side of the road outside Eleanor's house, semi-visible in the night like insects gathered on a dark log.

Anna-Louise, Barb, and Eleanor spring out of the car and, for a moment, I'm alone. I want nothing more than to stay here, strapped to my seat. I don't want to go into that house. I miss my Loved Ones. I miss my boring, predictable life. I miss my safe solitude. This all seems like a horrible idea.

Eleanor raps her knuckles on the window. "Come on," she says.

Inside, there's the unmistakable sense that something's happening in another room. Nobody around, but the house feels full.

Voices from elsewhere in the house, phrases barely audible.

Eleanor, Barb, Anna-Louise, and I stand in the foyer.

"How should we do this?" Barb asks Eleanor, pulling my journal out from her purse. "Do you want to go talk to them, or should I?" Eleanor suddenly looks very young. She gulps. Even though I'm sure Eleanor is about to bravely volunteer, Barb touches her shoulder sweetly. "Let's do it together."

Then, all sweetness gone, Barb turns to me. "Wait here." She looks at her daughter, then back at me. A warning. I'm not trusted.

With that, she and Eleanor disappear farther into the house, leaving the former bully and her victim—but which is which, ha ha—alone.

Should I say something? Apologize? Hey, sorry I ruined your life? I maybe remembered our relationship a little backward? She looks back at me, smiling her crooked smile. I avert my gaze before her face changes.

The voices in the other room stop. It's deathly silent. Listening.

I'm knitting my fingers. Rubbing the pads of my thumbs. I wonder if it's snowing in New York right now.

"I *knew* you looked familiar," she says, surprising me.

"Oh," I say guiltily. I'm about to tell her how sorry I am when she continues, "It's *him*. I see him. In your eyes." She speaks with a hushed love that befits her glassy, detached demeanor. It sends a chill through me. Once again, I think, *What is this town?*

The voices are suddenly louder now. An argument like a wave crests and then settles back to quiet. Outrage. Explanation.

"Are we sure I should be here?" I can't help asking.

"Don't be skinned," she says. She scrunches her face, finds the right word. "Scared."

Don't be skinned. Good advice.

Then something occurs to me. Why aren't *they* scared? Eleanor, Barb, Anna-Louise, they just learned that I'm likely responsible for murder. Why aren't they treating me with the horror, the disgust, the *fear* I deserve?

A realization is beginning to form. Not quite solid yet . . . but almost . . .

"Anna-Louise?" I say, very tentatively.

"Yes?" she asks, bright and chipper.

"Do you have any tattoos?"

"Just the one," she says, shrugging, as if it's a given, as if I asked her how many noses she has. I suppose it is a given; I even know exactly what it will be.

"The eye," I say.

"See?" she says warmly. "You do belong here."

All things considered, that phrase shouldn't affect me. But it does. I belong here. It dispels the brutal loneliness clouding my chest. For just a moment, it's like a sunburst.

Then a door opens, and I hear the urgent murmur of footsteps. A lot of footsteps. Something like ten, fifteen, twenty people round a corner and advance toward us. Dr. Burton leads the way, but behind him I can make out other faces I've seen lately: Mrs. Burton, Chantelle, the pharmacist, even the cab driver. Loneliness clouds over me again.

Dr. Burton is holding my journal now. Quite a journey that little book has had. Only he's treating it like some trashy magazine he found in a teenager's bedroom, something he's about to throw away in a show of disapproval. If only he knew how much it went for at Keats & Yeats.

He looks at me, then back at Barb and Eleanor. He swats his palm with the journal in his hand.

"No, but seriously," he says to the room, "this is a fucking joke, right?"

Rough hands—sourceless, anonymous—grab me and hustle me into a large den farther inside the house. Rooms within rooms.

An argument has exploded around me. Swirls of outrage, confusion, excitement. Despite the room's size, it's oppressively claustrophobic. Too many bodies, too much emotion.

And they're all talking about me.

"This is fucking crazy." A common sentiment.

"Hold on, hold on, hold on." Another one.

"I'm so confused." Yet another.

My journal is passed around, hands flipping through it, violently looking for answers or confirmation or God knows what.

"She copied it, right?"

"Had to've!"

"We should just fucking kill her."

Barb attempts to direct the conversation, fielding questions about our impossible hypothesis. Burton, unsurprisingly, leads the opposition. I can barely hold on to any of it myself. Their words have become greased and lubricated, like sweat, like oil, like blood, and it all slips through my hands whenever I try to hold on.

"We can't honestly be debating this, can we?"

"Do we even *believe* in reincarnation?"

"Just fucking crazy!" someone repeats.

I've been sat on a leather ottoman next to a bracket of dark brown leather couches. The furniture complements the dark, burgundy walls, made even darker by the fact that there are no windows. The only lighting is courtesy of a few wall sconces, glowing yellow with their soft bulbs, and faces as leathery as the upholstery leer at me in the low light.

Occasionally, the knot of heads and faces move in such a way that I can see a framed portrait on the wall across from me. A grim, sepia-tinted painting of an old man with hair the color of dirty cotton. He glares at me with contempt. Even the artwork knows I don't belong.

"Actually, there's nothing in our belief system that says this isn't possible," Barb says, hands held over the crowd in an attempt to lower their volume. "Quite the opposite, in fact—"

"Working at that store has gone to your head," Burton says. "We set you up there as a scout, Barb, not as a shaman."

She folds her arms against her chest. "And how many courses and classes did you have me take so I could learn all about past life readings in the first damn place?"

"That was to attract a certain kind of customer. Not for *this* kind of bull-shit!"

Burton's mother's strident, teacher voice whip-cracks across the room. "It is a fundamental tenant of our gospel that bodies are vessels, William."

That changes the temperature in the room. Everyone is looking at Burton now, challenging him. He bristles under the pressure.

"Of course I know that, Mother. Don't patronize me."

"I *will* patronize you if you're acting like a child."

Eleanor suddenly pipes up from where she's been leaning against a wall. "Maybe we should explain some of this to Mary? Maybe that would be—"

"And why the fuck is there an *actual* child here?" Dr. Burton cuts her a devastating look.

I hear Bonnie gasp in offense, but whether it's at Burton or Eleanor I don't know. Burton continues, back at Barb, "There is a goddamn FBI agent sniffing around our business like a dog. I'm not going to start spilling secrets to strangers."

"She's not a stranger," Barb says, "she's *from* here."

"She hasn't lived here in forty fucking years, give me a break. And she is not a member of *our* community."

Another man—I don't know his name, but he has a spotty auburn mustache that's barely visible in his bronzed skin, and when he opens his mouth, I can see he's missing a tooth from his bottom row—agrees loudly, "How do we know she's not with the feds?"

Another voice, from a man so thin he looks like a sentient walking stick and who's holding a bottle of neon-pink Pepto Bismol like a beer at a barbecue: "If she copied one of our books, that's entrapment!"

If only Nadine socialized more, she'd have found out she has more in common with these people than she'd thought.

Bonnie's husband, Steve, pipes up. "*When* were you born?" he asks me, the inflection making it sound like something he just realized he didn't realize.

I tell them. There's a collective intake of breath.

Burton is unimpressed. "So what? Where is it written that the day of birth even matters?"

Barb replies, "Actually, Talmudic commentary states that the *nefesh*, the life force, of a baby doesn't enter the body until it takes its first breath of air outside the mother—"

"Oh, fuck the Talmud!" Burton barks. "We're not here to discuss the goddamn Talmud."

"Somatic echo," Anna-Louise says suddenly.

Burton whips around, stares at her. "What?"

"Somatic echo."

An incredibly heavyset man grunts. "Is this another one of her brain things?"

"Mind sharts," the Pepto-drinking man says with a chuckle.

Barb snaps: "Fuck you, Charles."

"Somatic echo," Anna-Louise repeats, deliberately, as if the effort is costing her. "It's when there's a, a, a . . ." She gestures to her body, wiping her hands across her torso. Barb, takes over, putting a hand on her daughter's shoulder.

"Somatic echo," Barb says. "It's when there's a physical manifestation of a previous life. Sometimes it's literal, like there was a two-day-old baby whose arm became red and swollen in the exact same spot where a tourniquet had been applied to his uncle before he bled to death. Or a little German girl whose throat always became red and raw whenever she described dreams of being strangled. Sometimes it's a phobic response—a little kid inexplicably freaks out whenever an old song is played because it was playing when they died."

Dr. Burton scoffs. "What do you suggest we do, shoot her and see if she reacts badly to it?"

"No," Barb says. "You didn't let me finish. Sometimes it can manifest more abstractly. In birthmarks or moles where old wounds were received and—"

"Birthmarks," Anna-Louise says, nodding furiously. My face grows hot. Oh God, I know what she's getting to.

Her mother thinks it's just another repetition. "Yes, exactly," trying to wave away the interruption. But Anna-Louise shakes her head.

"She *has*."

"What?"

"Birthm . . . uhs."

"She has birthmarks?"

Nod, nod. "I remember. From before."

"Honey, how can you remember that?"

We make the briefest eye contact. Anna-Louise smiles a crooked, painful smile. I watch it form before I have to look away.

"One of my last real, clear memories," she says, her eyes still on me. "Before the bat."

Barb is staring at me, too. But soon she turns back to Burton. "We know where he was shot. We have the coroner's report. We know—"

"I know what we know, Barbara. Better than you, I'd imagine. But this isn't going to prove anything."

"It's a start," Steve says across the room. Burton is fighting it, but I can see on the faces of others, slowly but surely, with every reference and ten-dollar term, the rest of the room is being won over. Or at least becoming more curious.

Hands suddenly grab me from behind. I feel my shirt tugged up, my pants tugged down. I start to scream in protest, "Don't! Stop! Let me go!"

"Relax," a man chuckles, "he's a doctor."

"It's not like any of us wanna see it," another man adds, laughing cruelly.

I have the briefest of physical memory flashes—arms held backward, struggling, being poked and prodded and examined—and feel tears slip down my cheeks.

"No," I say, "please, I don't want this, I don't want this," and now Burton is in front of me, ready to expose my body to the room, and I'm drowning in misery, in embarrassment, in loneliness. I don't want their eyes on me. My arms try to get loose, but the grips are like iron, I'm not strong enough to stop this from happening.

Then, barely perceptible, I hear—*feel*—a voice in my head. For a moment, I think it's the undervoice, that voice I'm so oppressively familiar with that I don't always even know when I'm hearing it . . . but no, it can't be. This voice is so very different from the undervoice. It's reassuring. Loving. *Kind.*

It's okay. You're not alone. Let them see.

Who is this?

It's okay.

I stop resisting. My shirt is pulled above my breasts. My pants are pushed down past my knees.

Burton leans in. The room has gotten unnaturally cold, and I begin to shiver. I want to throw up. But I know exactly what he's looking at. Because I do have birthmarks. Several, randomly scattered across my torso and upper thighs. I never gave them much thought before, but I suppose the pattern could resemble something if you're really looking for it.

Something like bullet spray.

"Okay," Burton says at last. I'm let go, free to put my clothes to right, which I do, hoping the shivers will go away.

"Well?" Steve says.

Burton rubs his brow. "We know he was hit in the heart, the lower lobe of the left lung, the femoral artery . . ."

"And?"

"Maybe there's a correlation," Burton grumbles. But if his skepticism is cracking, it's only making him madder. "But this doesn't prove anything, Barbara! And my patience is getting really thin here."

"I know one thing we can try that might tell us all we need to know," Barb says. "Might even show you why she might be useful to keep around."

"What's that?"

"Haven't you ever wished you could talk to the prophet? Get his impressions on things? His guidance?"

"What the hell are you—"

"Have you forgotten, Bill? I'm a trained hypnotist." She sounds venomously pleased. "So let me ask her some questions. See how much—if any—of our prophet lives inside her."

And now I see her plan. Her cruel—but fair—method of getting revenge on me. Because if I fail this little audition, I'm dead. And if I don't . . .

Once again, that soft, new yet naggingly familiar voice:

It's okay. I'm here with you. Don't worry.

"Are you that good a hypnotist, you can knock her out even with everyone around her like this? You just happen to have a pocket watch ready to go?"

Barb gives him a look that, to him, must read as confidence. To me, it reads as *no skin off my ass if I fail.*

"Don't be so cliché, *Doctor.*" She turns to Bonnie. "Do you mind if I run to your bedroom for a moment?"

The rest of the room has been watching, rapt. Bonnie snaps to attention and assents. Barb hustles out.

The crowd gathers around me, pinning me even further to my spot. Through them, the portrait of the severe old man sneers down at me, through time, through paint. I try to shift positions and realize another man is holding a hunting knife out, not too far away from my face. The light from the wall sconces gleams off the blade.

"Don't try to move," he sneers.

Claustrophobia begins to set in, I'm going to panic, but then—

It's okay. You're going to be okay. We're going to get through this.

But who is this? Who is this voice?

Just stay calm.

And despite everything, I listen. What choice do I have?

I stay calm, even when I hear Barb come back proclaiming, "Found it," and walking through the crowd. I stay calm as I hear the murmur of the unfriendly crowd follow her to me.

I stay calm right up until I see the object she's brought into the room with her.

A mirror.

37

Reflections

I'm bucking in my seat as if I've been electrocuted.

The disembodied hands holding me down push harder. Concerned questions ricochet off each other above my head: What's happening? What's wrong with her? What is she doing?

It's just a hand mirror, they assure me—but they don't know, they don't know, I can't, I don't want to see what's there.

The lights have been turned off, a candle has been lit. More hands hold my head in place to prevent me from looking away, and so I squeeze my eyes shut.

Barb tries to soothe me. I can hear her hypnosis shit, *you're relaxing, you're getting sleepy, you're lifting into the air,* but it's not working, I don't want to see that hideous, shifting face in the glass. More than that, I don't want to pass out in this room, among these people! I might never wake up. That horrid, rancid, crumbling face could be the last thing I ever—

Then that voice again. That new but almost recognizable voice. Louder this time. It almost sounds like it's coming from outside my head.

Like it's coming from the glass.

"Mary," it says. Calm, yet commanding. Enough to make me settle for a moment and listen. "Just look at *me*. Let them do whatever they're doing. Just look at me."

The din continues around me. No one else seems to hear this voice.

I'm tempted to look, but—

No, it's a trick, I'm not going to look, I'm not—

"It's not a trick, Mary. It's okay. Don't look at yourself. Look *juuust* behind you."

So I do. My eyes open and flick to the glass, keeping my face firmly in the periphery, and . . .

"Good. Like I said, you're okay."

The hypnosis must be working. Either that or—

"You're not going crazy. You're just letting yourself see. For the first time."

There's a face behind me in the mirror. I see it . . . and I don't. My eyes are soft-focused, in that way I've learned to look past myself in reflective surfaces. So I see nothing clearly, and yet I see him clearly. A face I have never seen before.

"That's because I'm not *outside* of you, Mary," he says.

It's . . .

"Yes."

You.

"You can say my name."

Damon Cross.

I think on some level, I expected to see the gardener standing there. That mysterious *other* ghost of mine. But, while the men have a certain similarity, they're clearly two different people. Damon has none of the whiz-bang handsomeness of the gardener—I suppose that would be a liability for someone who did what Damon did. Instead, he has a plain, almost featureless face. Instantly forgettable.

"The gardener, as you like to think of him . . . That's Victor. My brother. He's been looking out for you and keeping us both safe. He always loved taking care of things for me. And he always loved that house. It's no wonder he's still there. Personally, I always kinda hated that place. Except for one part. You know which one?"

The crawl space.

"Exactly. Let's go there now, okay? Leave this group of idiots behind. What do you say?"

Okay.

The noise around us continues; they're not privy to this private conversation.

"You're not alone, Mary. That's how I always felt, too. My whole life. But we'll have each other, okay?"

Okay.

"So let's go."

And I feel myself fall backward into unconsciousness.

———

No. Not unconsciousness. I'm still awake, still aware. It's . . . How to describe . . .

The consciousness behind consciousness. The crawl space of consciousness.

Yes. That's it. I can hear the murmurs of the people interrogating me after they'd noticed I calmed down—but it's a wah-wah, muted trumpet, Charlie Brown grown-ups sort of noise. Like a next-door neighbor has a TV up too loud.

Let them ask whatever they want. They'll be no closer to learning the truth, my companion says. *Our truth.*

Do we need to worry about what they're asking?

No. They're simpleminded people. They just want the confirmation of trivia. Muscle memory can take care of that. What do you want, Mary?

I want to feel whole again. I want to feel at peace in my own skin. I don't want to feel so lonely.

How funny that you ever thought you were alone . . .

Follow me.

And now we're running through the darkness, like Tarzan swinging through vines, knowing when to duck, when to spin, when to step lightly. It's a delicious, free feeling, unencumbered by a slow, blind, weak, frightened body.

This is like my Dream. Just like my Dream.

We're hunting, Mary!

As we speed past nothingness, occasional apertures spill pinpricks of light into our path, and I can pull aside and peek into moments if I want.

I see a little girl, owl-faced, chubby cheeks, trying to lay her hands in cement along with a gaggle of other children. They push her out of the way like newborn puppies fighting for their mother's nipple, leaving the runt to starve. The little girl finds her own deserted corner and, after writing her name in wet cement by herself, wipes her dirty hands on the wall. A panel pops out and, sparing a glance back at her peers, the little girl dips into the darkness. I know, somehow, that little girl will be lost in the darkness for hours until . . .

You weren't alone then. I helped you find your way out again.

Another stretch of nothingness. Another peephole. Now that strange little girl is in a dark museum, closed for the night. She's all alone and scared and hungry and—

Not alone. I helped you. I showed you how to eat. I sang to you.

"I love you more today than yesterday . . ."

More darkness. More obscured glimpses into the life of a little girl receiving a strange, intimate, imaginary education.

I was with you when we found that jackrabbit and decided to see what made it move. I was with you when you discovered that book of matches. I was with you when you had to sit all alone, every lunch, every recess, because even though the children didn't always know why, they had an instinct to avoid you. And I was with you when you fought back. I taught you how to fight back.

The little girl, naked and tear-streaked now, finds a rack of sports equipment and slides a bat from out of its slot before exiting into blinding sunlight.

Then they tried to take me from you . . .

I peer in to see the little girl strapped to a chair, arms tied painfully back, while a man sporting a large black mustache and a white lab coat tells her if she's not going to be Good, she's going to get the needles and the shocks. Only Good Girls get Good Things like no needles. His arms become a mess of syringes, like the arms of a cactus, and he jabs them all into the little girl, and she screams in resistance but it's no use, she can't move, she can't escape, until soon whatever's in those syringes courses through her veins and the girl's skin begins to slicken and harden and then . . . she's made entirely of porcelain. Perfect and Good.

But even then, I was with you. You felt so alone because they tried to drive me from you. But I was there, waiting. You were just acting. You've always been such a good actor. You're so good, you disappear into your role. But, Mary, that's not you. You're not quiet. You're not forgettable. You're not invisible.

What am I, then? A punch line, right?

No. You're the inheritor of something great and powerful. You're a desert creature: barbed and venomous and dangerous.

I feel as if I'm supposed to be finding comfort in all this. But something nags at me. Some unresolved chord I can't quite articulate just yet.

Another pinhole light. Suddenly, the little girl is all grown up. Years and years and years of her life have blinked by, and she's barely even noticed. She's still porcelain, but there are cracks appearing all over. Cracks from being sat on by subway passengers. Cracks from being pushed aside in line. So many little cracks from moments too mundane to catalog. And she's in a small bathroom, barely bigger than a closet. She's being fired by a boss young enough to be her child, and she's realizing she let her whole life pass and it might be too late to turn it around. She looks into the mirror and—

Don't.

This time, instead of my moving on, he pulls me away.

Why? What's wrong?

Don't revisit those memories.

There's an edge to his voice.

Again, I feel that unresolved chord. Something isn't quite right. What's wrong with those memories? And how did so much of my life go by unnoticed? Where did the rest of it go?

Because the past is like the moon, isn't it? It's always there, but it shifts, it's never the same when you revisit it.

It moves. The moon moves.

Yes! That's exactly right. So why are we wasting time on the past? Mary. We have our future to plan.

The murmur of the voices on the other side of consciousness continues. It's always been there. Ever-present, no matter how far we've traveled into the darkness.

What are they talking about now?

They're still not convinced. We've answered all their questions, but some of them are still not convinced.

I hear faint music. Far away but getting closer. The blare of horns. A descending bass line. A singer claiming every day's a new day; that, if all his dreams come true, he will be spending time with me.

How do we make them believe? How do we convince them?

My father used to have a saying. Actions speak louder than words, he would say.

That's a very father thing to say.

Fathers are the worst. Who needs them? Let's make them accept you. What do you say?

I want to say yes. But I also want to say let's make sure it's nothing too Bad, because I'm not ready to give up my training just yet, I would still so very much like to be Good.

I want to say that. But it's too late.

Our actions have begun speaking, and the saying holds true enough: it'd be impossible to hear my words right now.

Because of all the screaming.

38

Cleanup

The air is thick with the smells of blood and smoke. The smoke is from the candle, which had been knocked over—no fire, thankfully, only the curling ghost of a just-extinguished wick. As for the blood . . .

Someone is moaning. Whimpering. Badly wounded from the sound of it. A woman.

Lights are turned on. A clump of bodies attends to someone who has been hustled over to the couch in the corner.

There's blood everywhere. An astounding amount. Splashed across the coffee table, the chair, my lap, my upper arms. It's drying, along with my sweat, in a maddeningly itchy film. There's broken shards of something on the floor, too.

Porcelain, I think wildly. *I've finally, fully cracked.*

But no, that's not porcelain. It's glass. And there's a not-too-deep slash on my right palm.

I try to remember the visions I saw just now in the mirror. They're elusive, the way dreams are. Slipping away. All I remember is:

You're not alone. We have our future *to plan.*

People are shouting. I can't make out just what they're saying exactly. But the urgency is undeniable. This feels like a war room.

"Can I help?" I offer weakly. No one takes me up on it. No one hears me. "Should I help clean up?"

A hand falls on my shoulder, and I jump. It's Eleanor. When I look at her, she flinches like I'm about to strike her. After she's sure I'm not going to, she says, "Let's get you cleaned up," in a tone that tells me I should get out of this room and quick.

She pushes me past a cluster of people who stare at me with eyes the size of headlights.

Guess you passed the test," she says, handing me a white dish towel in the kitchen.

"I'm going to ruin this," I say, taking the towel and drying my just-washed, stinging hand. The cut has begun to scab over, and the pain helps keep me steady.

"Whatever." She shrugs. She stares at me for a beat too long. "Are you . . . ?"

"Am I what?"

"Are you okay? Are you all the way awake? I . . . That was intense."

"I think I'm okay. A little dizzy. And thirsty."

She pulls open one of the two large, silver doors of their massive fridge and removes a plastic bottle of water. She hands it to me. "Unless you want a beer? Or wine? Or . . . ?"

"This is fine," I say, and swallow half of the bottle in one go. After I gasp for breath again: "What happened?"

She proceeds to tell me while I wet the dish towel and try to wipe my arms clean. Mostly the blood smears across my arms and turns the towel a ruddy maroon. As Eleanor describes the scene, I expect my stomach to fill with guilt. It doesn't. I just hear those words again: *You're not alone.*

And I think, *Serves them right for doubting me.*

And the towel gets redder.

According to Eleanor, my demeanor changed completely while I was under. My voice. My face. I began answering their questions, confidently, accurately, questions only Damon Cross would know the answers to . . . but then something changed. I stopped answering and I started laughing.

"Really laughing. Like it was the funniest thing you'd ever seen in your life. And then . . ."

Before anyone could stop me, I'd reached out and grabbed the hand mirror. I smashed it against the side of the coffee table and used a particularly long shard to start slashing.

Laughing the entire time.

"Who did I get?" I ask.

"You got Ronnie's arm pretty good—he was one of the ones holding you. But the one who got it worst . . . was Anna-Louise. I guess her reflexes were the slowest." Eleanor swallows, grimaces. "I think I could see her teeth through her cheek you got her so bad."

I finish the rest of the bottle of water. Then:

"Eleanor, what is all this? This . . . place? This community? How many are you?"

She blinks as if she'd just woken up from the world's quickest nap. "What? Oh. Um. Well, Arroyo is a little less than a hundred people. And our flock is about sixty."

I really don't like the way she's staring at me. It's like she's been split into two consciousnesses: one that is answering my questions and the other that wants to throw me onto this marble kitchen island and dissect me with a carving knife.

"And you worship Damon Cross?"

"Not exactly. He was our prophet. We worship . . . well, we worship the desert."

"The desert," I repeat, though more for myself than for her. I have so many more questions. I settle for the most pressing. "And what are you all going to do with me?"

The look on her face tells me she doesn't know, but another voice cuts in before she can say as much.

"What are you doing?" It's Bonnie. She's just walked into the kitchen, arms crossed.

Eleanor goes red. "I was just telling her about—"

"Ah-ah-ah. Come on." She waves a well-manicured hand at us to follow her back.

Eleanor protests. "I think she's proven herself, Mom. Jesus, why can't we just tell her?"

"That's not for you to decide, Eleanor. You shouldn't even be watching all this, so just. *Be quiet.*" She points a finger at her daughter and speaks through clenched teeth. No arguments allowed. She also keeps her distance from me. In case I find another shard, I guess.

We make our way back to the meeting room. The war room atmosphere has dissipated. It's as silent as a tomb, save for the wet whimpers of Anna-Louise and the cooing tones of her mother.

Everyone stares at me. There's nothing funny about it, but I've suddenly got to suppress the urge to start laughing once again. Nervous giggles.

It's a long time before anyone speaks.

"So what do we do about this?" It's Steve. "What does this mean?"

"I don't know." Dr. Burton sighs. He sounds thoroughly defeated. He's pressing a white hand towel to Anna-Louise's face.

Then a voice from the crowd: "He has come back to us."

Another voice: "Almost fifty years to the day."

And another: "He has more to teach us."

There's a hushed murmur of agreement, so reverent that it doesn't seem to come from any one mouth.

"We're not really going to act like this is real, are we?" Dr. Burton protests. But there's no fight in his voice. His resistance is a weak pantomime, already doomed.

I empathize. My first impulse—immeasurably strong—is to apologize for all of this. As if I've done something wrong. Sorry to inconvenience you all.

I look at the broken shards of glass on the floor. Was what I saw real? Or was it all in my head?

Then . . . *his* voice, calm and serene and not just a little menacing:

Just because it's in your head doesn't mean it's not real, Mary.

Besides. Isn't this what you always wanted?

They're looking *at you now.*

And, boy howdy, is that ever true. I've never felt so many eyes on me before. I bet every ear would hear me if I said something, too.

A wild thought careens through me: *Is this what Jane and the other ghosts feel when attention gives them power?*

Don't think about them. This is *my* time. Even though I feel like this is all a mistake, even though I feel like the world's greatest imposter, I also feel drunk on their eyes. In this moment, I could fall to my knees in relief. I *exist.* I can set my handprint in this concrete reality and write my name underneath with my finger. M A R Y. You were wrong, Nadine, when you said they'd all hate me. You were wrong, and that's why you're going to rot in your living room while I—

Anna-Louise moans in pain, and the moment dissipates. But the image of Nadine makes me think of something. You could even call it a test.

"Help me get her up," Burton is saying, lifting Anna-Louise into a more upright position. I stop him with my voice.

"I'd like to make a request."

"Jesus," Dr. Burton groans. And then someone actually reprimands him. One of the other men. On my behalf.

"Bill, come on, hear her out."

Burton sighs. "Fine, but make it quick. We have to get her to the hospital."

I ignore his attitude. For him, this is probably as close to subservient as he'll ever get.

"Funny you should mention that," I say. I take a deep breath and then speak my request through the smile that's beginning to form on my lips.

PART FIVE

MURDERERS

She had all her life long been accustomed to harbor thoughts and emotions which never voiced themselves.

—Kate Chopin, *The Awakening*

39

One Word

I wake up to knocking.

I'm more disoriented by the fact that I slept—deep, dreamless, restful sleep—than by my strange surroundings.

No. Not strange. Just . . . unexpected. I can't believe I'm not waking up in Brenda's room. I can't believe I'm here.

That means everything last night . . . *happened*. Either that or I've really gone off the deep end and am now fully committed to my fantasy world.

Wouldn't be the first time in my life I was fully committed, ha ha.

Sun irradiates the lace curtains. The musty room hasn't been turned over in a while, but it's comfortable in a way I've never experienced before. It's *rich* comfortable. Quality material. I fell asleep before I managed to get under the covers, but I can feel their softness, their luxuriousness. Even the stale air feels well made.

That's not the only reason I feel so comfortable here.

I stretch, spreading myself across the large bed, wishing I could wrap all the way around it, invert my joints and become some giant hand that refuses to let go of this bed, this room, this turn of events.

More knocking on the door. Oops. Almost forgot.

I'm still dressed, so I don't need to throw anything on, but my hands go to my shirt as if I'm wearing an open robe. Memories of last night, of the way I had to expose myself to that strange, leering crowd, crawl across my skin. I smooth my hair down.

It's the giant cab driver.

He actually takes off his cap when he talks to me. The top of his long hair is balding in such a way that it makes me think his head has been used as an eraser. I bite back a smile.

"Sleep okay there?" he asks me. I tell him I did. "You hungry?" I tell him I am. "Someone's rustling up some breakfast for you." Someone cooking for me? Can't remember the last time that happened.

He looks behind me into the room for a beat too long, then comes back to himself. "Sorry, just never seen in there before. These rooms aren't exactly for public viewing, you know."

I do know that. I can smell how exclusive this room is. It's a wonderful, almost basement-y smell. And, of course, there was also the way Dr. Burton blanched when I told him of my request—my *order*—last night.

"I want to live in the Cross House," I told him, head held high. And the room hushed for Burton's response.

As we entered the mansion last night and began our walk up the stairs (splitting off from Burton and everyone else helping him admit Anna-Louise to a hospital room), Stepdad Steve informed me, "The top floor has been kept exactly as it was when the last living members of the Cross family died. The state fought us. Wanted to gut the whole place. We compromised and argued there was historical value to the top floor. Thankfully, they didn't push it."

When we walked up to the upper floor, a wave of vertigo hit me, so strong it practically knocked me off my feet. It was like stepping out of a pressure lock into a different altitude, and in the silence created by that dizziness, I heard one word in my head, barely audible, as soft as an arterial pulse. One word. It made me smile.

It still does.

The driver is holding something in his huge hands. A little brown rectangle.

"This came for you, by the way. Dr. Burton told me to bring it to you." He hands it over. The sender is a company called the Book Basement. Could it be what I think it is? The timing is almost laughable. "Also," the driver continues, "he wants you to come down to his office on the second floor as soon as you're ready."

"Okay. Can I ask you something?"

"Sure."

"Dr. Burton. He's not . . . just a doctor, is he? To the town, I mean?"

"Of course. He's our leader."

"Like a *spiritual* leader, right?" I search for the name Eleanor used last night. "Of . . . the flock?"

The driver purses his lips, looks down the hall. "I probably should leave it up to him to say." He puts his cap back on his worn-down head. "I'll see you tomorrow."

Tomorrow. *The anniversary,* I remember the FBI agent calling it. What exactly is going to happen?

I open my mouth to ask, but the driver is already walking away.

I watch him go, then take in the hallway for a few more moments, remembering again how it felt to be let into this sacred area last night.

Everything up here is a rich, warm brown, with purple and gold accents, unlike anything I've ever seen before and yet undeniably familiar. Paintings and photographs of old Cross relatives, as well as the occasional decorative mirror, hang on the walls. I didn't see any images of Damon hung up anywhere, but every mirror we passed, I could swear he was there, just out of sight. Keeping pace.

Electric candlestick wall sconces keep the path lit. There are also small tables and stands, draped in doilies, some bearing vases or framed photos. One such table made me stop in my tracks, forget to breathe—

"What is it?" Bonnie asked. I probably looked as if I was about to faint.

"Nothing," I said, although I don't know if I actually made a sound.

I was staring down at a small stand with a half dozen ceramic statuettes. Perfect, porcelain little children.

I can see that table now from my bedroom doorway. An earlier generation of Loved Ones. Separated by distance and time—entire lives, in fact—but inextricably linked. I let them be the last thing I stare at before stepping back into the room and closing the door.

No one told me which bedroom had been Damon's. One final test, I suppose. By that point in the evening, Burton had come up to join us, no doubt eager to see if I passed.

"Take whichever room you want," he said. I chose a small bedroom a few doors down from where we were standing. I went straight to it. My chaperones all exchanged glances. I didn't even need confirmation—their expressions said it all.

It's a very modest room considering the opulence of the mansion. Nothing like the stripped-and-deserted way Brenda's room had been, though;

this room is just fundamentally simple and spare. The person who lived here liked it this way. Reminds me of my apartment in the city, actually.

Maybe that's why one particular item seemed so out of place when I first entered the room. "This didn't use to be here, did it?" I pointed to the large radio on the floor by the door.

It did my heart good to see Burton's face redden. He started to stammer an excuse about how it was put there temporarily and forgotten about—I cut him off.

"It's okay. I don't mind. I could just . . . tell it was out of place."

"We can take it out now—"

"No, leave it. Maybe I'll plug it in and see if it works."

And maybe I will. But if I'm being entirely honest with myself, I also didn't want to be a bother. Old habits die hard. If death even is a thing anymore.

There's one other item of note in this room. Propped on an otherwise bare dresser is a smallish rectangular mirror in a dull metal frame.

My first instinct was to cover it up . . . but then I stopped. I wasn't—still am not—brave enough to look into it . . . but it sits there, unobstructed, all the same. I can avoid looking at it if I have to. Or look just off to the side of me, where I know I can find *him*, as if he's standing just behind me in the room. But looking directly at my reflection—seeing whether or not I can face myself now that I've been accepted and embraced—is my true final test. One I'm not ready to take just yet. Maybe tomorrow. A birthday present to myself.

For now, I have an appointment to keep.

I put my package down on the nightstand. I'll open it when I get back. I sit in the silence of this room, my room, and I hear that one word again.

One word, whispering in the tiny blood vessels inside my ears, soft as a pulse.

Home.

Home.

Yes.

This all very much feels like coming home.

That feeling starts to dissipate as I descend to the second floor. I'm scared of Burton. I don't like to admit that, but there's also no denying it.

I reach his office door just as someone is scuttling out of it. A young woman. Pretty, at least by Arroyo standards. She avoids my gaze as she rushes away, and I understand immediately women like her must be a perk to being the town's "spiritual leader." One of the ways he ensures they stay useful. My gorge rises a little bit at the thought, actually.

I wait for a few moments in the hallway to let him collect himself. Then I knock on the door.

"Enter," he says, and I roll my eyes before complying.

He pretends like he's glad to see me, but he doesn't get up.

He has me sit in a chair in front of his large, commanding, shiningly oaken desk. A mayor's desk.

"I'm going to be blunt, Mary." He folds his hands on the blotter and knits his brows in concern. "Our community is not very welcoming to outsiders. We're very protective of our secrets. So I'm going to make you an offer." He looks down at his hands for a moment. "Well, no, that's imprecise. This isn't so much an offer as it is a series of questions. And I think you're smart enough to understand the consequences of your answers." He looks back up at me, his expression blank and chilling.

A thought, unbidden: I don't hear a thing outside of this office. No sound from any other room or area of the mansion. This room is soundproof. Would anyone hear me if I screamed?

Home. Home, this is my—

"Can we trust you?" he asks. "Are you prepared to become part of our flock? I still have no goddamn idea how you'll fit in here, but judging by your behavior, by your . . . tendencies . . . I'm inclined to believe there's some place for you."

What does that mean?

Either way, the choice is clear: I don't really have a choice.

Don't be so glum. They will worship you. He just wants to intimidate you because he knows that's true. He's gotta put you in your place as soon as possible.

"Yes," I say. "You can trust me." Then after a beat: "I don't have anyone else to tell."

"What about your aunt?" he says coolly. Not a question, but a challenge.

"She's dead."

He stares at me. For a while. He wants to ask for more information, but he also doesn't want to afford me the power of knowing I surprised him. Eventually, he gets up and goes to a locked armoire in a corner. I take the opportunity to look around his office.

Behind Burton's desk are what appear to be framed medical degrees. On another wall, in a golden frame, is a large painted portrait of a stern old man with ruddy white hair. Takes me a few seconds before I realize this is the same stern old man whose portrait is up in Bonnie and Steve's home. But this man is not a Cross—there are no images of him upstairs.

Burton's back, handing me a thick, blue, buckram book. This, too, I recognize from Bonnie's house. I saw a copy of it in her bedroom a few days ago. Embossed on the spine is an eye. On the cover are two words:

CROSS
BURTON

"Read it," he says. "Familiarize yourself with its contents before tomorrow. Tomorrow is our most sacred day."

"My birthday?" I say dryly.

He looks at me, unamused. "Our harvest day."

Harvest? What kind of crop could even grow out here?

I open the book, flip through pages. Dense, single-spaced, small-font text stares unblinkingly back at me.

"That is our gospel," Burton intones. "Interpretations. Rituals. All based, of course, on Damon Cross's sacred texts."

My page-flipping stops as I come upon what I first think are illustrations, then realize are photo reproductions. I bring the book up for a closer look, unable to believe it at first.

"Oh my God." I don't mean to gasp. I can't help it.

He leans over to see what I'm looking at. "Yes," he says without any joy, as if remembering he's due for a colonoscopy.

I stammer, pointing to the pages in front of me: "But this is . . ."

"Did you seriously not know?" He sounds genuinely curious.

I don't answer. I'm too busy staring at the page . . . and the next . . . and the next. I suppose I *knew* what to expect after the fracas yesterday. But there's knowing, and then there's seeing.

Maybe this is *actually happening.*

Yes, I don't think I truly appreciated how much I've been operating under the assumption that maybe I've simply been losing my mind up to this point. Here it is, spelled out in front of me, that maybe this is actually real.

Pages and pages and pages of *my* journal. Bound and reproduced in a book that's clearly decades old. I don't need to even read the words; I recognize the shapes. The scrawl of letters up and down the margins. The occasional doodles. Everything I wrote while in my stupor.

"These are the . . . sacred texts?"

"Mmm."

"And what about the rest of it? The 'interpretations,' and all this other writing, and, and—"

"Written by my father," he says grandly and shifts himself on his chair to acknowledge the portrait I'd been looking at. So that's his father, then? "He was a great man, too, you know. He rescued Cross's journals on the day Cross was martyred. My father had been studying Cross's actions and had been eager to better understand them. He recognized that these texts are occasionally disjointed and often obscure—but, when properly interpreted in the context of our town's prior legacies, they are revelatory. He saw that Cross was a prophet."

"A prophet," I say. "Of . . . the desert, right?"

He raises his eyebrows slightly, impressed. "That's correct. More or less."

"How . . . What . . . ?" I can't figure out how to ask the questions churning in my brain. He seems patient enough with me for the moment. "What does that mean?"

"Can you tell me what is more deserving of worship than the desert? What is more beautiful? What is crueler? The desert demands humility. It asks for great sacrifice, but it rewards by burning away your excesses and making you stronger than you could have ever imagined. Like our ancestors who had to survive without any of our modern creature comforts. To worship the desert is to be made strong and also worthy of strength. In the desert, everything has use. Because only the useful can survive."

Let the women among you . . . , I think, and a shiver runs through me.

"Perhaps that sounds cruel," he continues, "but I promise you, ours is a loving religion. We accept all. We judge nothing—no urge, no history—as long as you are useful. We offer, like the desert, a purgation of sin. Sins aren't useful. Guilt isn't useful. If you are to survive here, the desert demands that you give those burdens up, and that is what we offer. Release. Purgation. Acceptance. There's a reason all the great religions have two things in common, you know: a great man and a desert. Joseph Smith, Jesus, Muhammad, Moses, Abraham . . ."

"Damon Cross." I complete his list.

Burton's patience begins to visibly drain out of him. "That's correct."

"I guess I thought he was just—"

"What, some serial murderer? That ridiculous, narrow-minded classification for the morbid rubbernecker? See, this is why I have such a hard time understanding you. You seem to know so much and yet you know so little. Damon Cross wasn't some *killer*. He was gifted with visions. He saw spirits. He saw angels."

My mouth goes dry. "He . . . saw spirits?" Does that mean like ghosts? *You are the inheritor of a great legacy.* That had been whispered to me during my hypnotized state last night, and it comes floating back to me now.

Burton is looking me up and down again. A predator's appraisal. He leans back in his chair, crosses his arms over his chest. "Are you going to tell me you see spirits, too?"

I swallow with great effort. "Would you believe me if I did?"

He has no answer for that, so we stare at each other. I suppose I should leave now, while he's still at least intrigued. I give a polite smile, then get up and head for the door.

He stops me with his voice.

"One last question. The little boy. What did you do to him? And *why*? With Carole, I understand; she fit Cross's type to a tee. But the little boy? What were you thinking?" He doesn't ask it reproachfully. I almost wish he did. Instead, it's with a syrupy curiosity between peers, two tradespeople sharing shoptalk. It makes my skin crawl.

"I—"

"I should say," he interrupts, "it would be best if you don't do anything like that again. We can't afford to be impulsive here—I know that can be hard for some. Also I hope you didn't do anything too crazy to the body, because his mother is beside herself. We're keeping her pretty heavily sedated. She's young, she'll be able to have another when the time comes . . . but it's best we don't complicate the narrative for people. Still." He leans forward. "I'm curious. Tell me more."

"I don't know," I say.

His face falls. "You don't know?"

"No."

I almost add, *Men like you have taught me I'm so unimportant my whole life that sometimes even I don't try to understand what I do.*

It's silent for a long while as he regards me from behind his desk. All friendliness bleeds away from his expression.

"Can I ask *you* something?" I suddenly ask, thinking of the large portrait of his father again. "Are you actually a real doctor?"

"Why don't you come closer and look at my certifications?" The threat in his voice is unmistakable. His face tells an unnerving, dangerous story. There are no good feelings there, at least not for me. I've ruffled him.

He'll hurt you if you go closer to him. But he's also not coming closer to you. That's good. That means he knows he can't hurt you with impunity. He would if he could, but he can't.

That means you have some sort of power here.

But of course I do. That's what coming home does: it gives you power.

I hold the book to my pounding chest and hurry out the door.

40

Hard to Ignore

Home. Home.

I repeat the word to myself like I'm Dorothy Gale. It helps quell the twister in my chest.

Back up at my room, there's a plate of food—looks like an attempt at huevos rancheros—covered with a paper towel waiting for me. I pick it up and bring it inside, all appetite gone. The plate goes on the dresser, by the mirror I'm still very much avoiding.

Burton's book gets tossed on the bed. It lands with a heavy *whoomf.*

Just because I need something to busy my hands, I pick up the small package from the nightstand and yank open the cardboard pull tab.

Inside is a thin, mustard-colored hardback.

Distant Messages Unheard: Poems, by Jane Mayhew.

On the back, another author photo, different from the one on the website. She's wearing a tank top, leaning forward in some sort of yard. Her wine-stain birthmark is clearly visible. It's definitely Jane.

I wonder if that birthmark is a somatic echo of her previous life. Maybe once she was a hunter who was torn apart by a wild animal, starting with her shoulder and—

No. I can't be doing this. I can't be spending time researching her like this. I put the book down on the night table. Her name keeps calling my eye, so I flip the book over. That's even worse: now it's her photo again. I can't think of what else to do, so I stash the book inside the nearest pillow at hand.

Better. I can pretend like it doesn't exist now.

The blue book is what really matters. The blue book is community. Acceptance. Dare I think it, even: popularity.

Oh, Mary, what have you gotten yourself into?

I sit down on the bed, which creaks in such a satisfying way, and open the gospel.

I try to read as much as I can. I really do.

It's just so . . . dense.

And dry.

And the font is so small.

And Burton's father writes like a smart man trying to sound smarter. Which is just death.

I read (well, skim) about the teachings of Elias Cross, the town's original founder, who began to preach that all of man's woes, and I do mean "man's" because he did not appear to be very fond of women, were the results of Azazel, a fallen angel.

Elias based this worldview—correctly, for, how more plainly can it be stated?—on the book of Enoch 10:8, "The whole earth has been corrupted through the works that were taught by Azazel: to him ascribe all sin." He would preach: "Who can but doubt 'twas Azazel who filled the serpent, who spoke with its mouth, who used that weak, hungry vessel of Eve to be poured further into, increasing his own voluminousness with the female's easily-imprinted nature? And does it not say in Enoch 8:1 that Azazel brought unto mankind bracelets and ornaments; and the use of antimony and the beautifying of the eyelids with coloring tinctures. And there arose much godlessness, and they committed fornication, and they were led astray and became corrupt in all their ways! Makeup and the harlot's eye are Azazel's gifts. Superfice! The mask of woman, the false face of Jezebel!"

To pacify the demon, or to cleanse his community, or maybe just for a good ol' time, Elias Cross regularly enforced animal sacrifice. Actual scapegoats. The book doesn't say, but I have a feeling that might be why this little community found itself having to splinter off and find a new home. Especially if they were availing themselves of other people's livestock.

Further on, I read more about the history of the town, essentially corroborating everything the FBI agent mentioned. The town was indeed called Fertile Ground. And the dichotomy the agent mentioned is spot-on: besides the Crosses' newly relocated religious community, the town was peopled by those who'd come to seek their fortunes mining gold, copper, silver, quartz. And, lo, the town I recognize was born.

It takes far too long to get to the first chapters on Damon Cross. I skip a lot to get to him, noting how strange it is to feel selfish for wanting to learn more about another person.

His father raised him alongside Victor, his older brother, with a very clear plan for both: Damon was to be molded into some sort of religious leader, and Victor was to go into politics. He groomed each to focus on their particular path, assuming each boy would take care of the other—and the community—when they were grown.

Then the boys' mother died, and Damon began to have visions. Visions of angels—"from Azazel to Zepar"—came to him and told him the town's sins were too great. There needed to be "regular purgation" if they were to survive in the cruel desert. Rituals. Damon's father encouraged Damon to become an "enforcer of the spirits' advice by purging unto vessels for sin."

"Vessels for sin."

No wonder Barb and Anna-Louise argued my condition was compatible with their belief system. We're all just cups, dipped into the Deep Sea of Life. And how interesting that the desert and the sea are such contradictory images—and yet somehow complementary.

Anna-Louise . . . I should go see if she's okay.

Focus, Mary.

When Damon and Victor's father died, according to Daddy Burton, Damon began to dedicate himself to his final, truest mission: "To cleanse and expiate not just the Fertile Ground on which he lived but the world entire."

Cleanse and *expiate* seem like lofty ways to describe serial murder. But I suppose murder and religion have always been old work buddies.

What surprises me is how . . . empty and convoluted this all seems. Every sentence takes five minutes to diagram and digest, and I'm left no closer to understanding how this all really relates to the Jane Doe Killer in the first place.

Then again, there are pages and pages (and pages) to go. I haven't even gotten to a description of the "harvest" Dr. Burton mentioned or what it means to gather their crop. Hell, I haven't even gotten to the analysis of Damon's texts/my mysterious scribblings. I'm still essentially in the intro.

I try to get comfortable on the bed. This is going to take a while. If I had a coffeemaker in this room, I'd put on a fresh pot.

Something digs into my back. I squirm to reach it, forgetting so quickly that I literally just put a book inside the pillow I'm lying against not twenty minutes ago.

I pull the book out.

Mary. No. Study the blue book. You're being reckless and stupid. Be Good.

But for some reason, that admonishment isn't working on me like it usually does.

I'm just curious. I'll just crack Jane's book open for a moment and, with that itch scratched, get back to work.

I read ten of her poems before I come up for air.

I don't mean to read so many. They're just so . . . easy. Not in a patronizing way—quite the opposite. I find each poem to be complex and layered and worthy of being chewed and savored. It's just, they make sense to me in a way I can hardly express. Like how drinking water is easy.

"Not for nothing"
You said to me
"But I can see why you would want your space."

You always blamed the lonely for their solitude.

"But I can see why you would want your space," you said
And I said nothing
Naught for nothing
For no thing is what I am

I stare at that one for a few moments. Read it again.

Naught for nothing. For no thing is what I am.

I know that feeling. I . . .

I read it a third time. I *really* know that feeling.

I turn the page.

I could have been a Stalin
But I was born with Nadia's body
If you knew how much anger
I had in me you'd say

Thank God she's not a man
She might destroy millions

Thank God the only person she has the power to destroy
Is herself

They're not all the angry words of a woman scorned by the world, though. There's actually quite an impressive variety to her verse. Some of the poems remind me of that one guy who wrote poems about wheelbarrows and plums. Small but profound snapshots of her childhood, her horses, a windchime outside a lover's bedroom.

Other poems are surreal and strange. One in particular is even horrifying, describing her finding a dead skunk on the side of the rode and imagining eating it and carrying its stench inside her like a delicious secret.

Some poems speak more to me than others, but they all say *something*.

Jane, you were so talented. You were so—

Her bloody claws, lunging from the tub, flash through my mind like a visual alarm. I remember just how many ghosts are in this mansion with me right now and—I need to stop.

This time, I drop the book on the floor and scoot it under the bed. No more of that!

But the prospect of going back to Burton's book fills me with overpowering fatigue. If I keep trying to read that, I'm going to fall asleep.

"Not for nothing"
You said to me
"But I can see why you would want your space."

I shake the poem from my memory. I stand up from the bed.
I need to go for a walk.

41

Real Estate

I think I've grown too used to New York City real estate; this house is *bafflingly* large. What does a person even do with this much space?

I mean, this is just the top floor, and it feels like I'll never run out of areas to explore. There are at least ten doors off the main hallway. And then doors within those doors. Rooms, bathrooms, closets. Winding at strange angles, like the wallpapered walls grew from the ground at random.

The crawl space. The walls are strange to accommodate the crawl space.

I am Bluebeard's wife. Only . . . I am also Bluebeard. No room is off-limits to me.

So why do I feel so unsettled?

What I did back in Burton's office was so stupid, making an enemy of the most powerful man in this community. And for what? Just because things don't feel right? What kind of cloudy thinking is that? Things have never felt right for me. Why should they start now?

"You've seen so many incredible things," a voice—Damon's voice, gentle and enticing—speaks from one of the hanging mirrors I pass. "Why can't you be incredible, too?"

"Hmph," I grunt in response.

Here's another bedroom, musty and neglected. Here's a bathroom. I give a quick glance to the bathtub and look away. There's nothing in that bathtub. Nope. Nothing. Certainly not another dead woman.

Here's a closetful of old coats, smelling like a fuzzy sarcophagus. Here's an armoire full of expensive but dull and dusty china.

One room is full of portraits, stored there for future use, I suppose. Then I get a better look at them. Probably *not* for future use after all—all the portraits have had their eyes either scratched or punched or rubbed out. There's something about the methodical nature of the defacement, the way no other part of the canvases were damaged that sends a parade of shivers up my spine. This wasn't some fit of passion; someone sat with each portrait, probably feeling like they were being stared at the entire time . . . until they weren't. Some were clearly done with a knife, some probably with something smaller like a fingernail, some with a cloth . . . or maybe even a tongue.

Another room contains bookshelves. As always, old habits: I have to look at the titles. Surprisingly, I know a lot of them well. Not the particular editions, no, these are very old, some even turn of the century. But I recognize the books. I shelved many of them in the basement of the bookstore for years. Under the section labeled Playscripts. Shakespeare, Shaw, Chekhov, Wilde, the Greeks, as well as less familiar names like Congreve, Wycherley, Behn. I open a few of them up. They're full of notes. Lines circled. Blocking. Questions about motivation. Men's roles and women's roles, with two different sets of handwriting. A phrase I'd frequently see on the bookstore's copies comes to mind: "Acting Edition."

In this same reading room is another armoire. When I open it, at least a dozen wooden crucifixes tumble to the ground in an obscenely loud clatter that makes me think of bones. I quickly stoop to stuff them back in. Like the portraits, I have a distinct feeling these crucifixes used to be heavily featured on the walls until someone decided they'd had enough.

I need to get back to the blue book. I need to read it all before tomorrow. It's important—I can't screw this up, and there are obviously so many things about this house, this family, this community that I need to learn.

But I don't move.

Why don't I move?

Dread comes back to burrow inside me. It spreads out, turning my blood into buzzing lead.

Come on, Mary. This should be exciting! You're getting the opportunity to learn about who you are—in a way few people ever get! Isn't that what you wanted? A deep, annotated dive into your metaphysical inheritance?

Still I don't move.

"What do you know about skinning?"

That voice—*his* voice—comes from yet another decorative mirror on yet another wall.

"If you'd asked me that a week ago," I respond, aware I'm really talking to myself, "I'd have said very little." I remember how Burton and Steve discussed the mangling of Carole's face, what an amateur job it must have been. But then I also think of approaching Nadine, sharp shard in hand, absolutely certain I'd be able to do it . . . and do it well. "Now, I'm not so sure."

The voice from the mirror says, "It requires concentration. Precision. And when you do it right, you can really see what's just under the surface. The truth of things."

"Muscle and blood?"

"Can you think of anything truer than muscle and blood?"

The desert, I almost say. Instead, I ask, "So how do you do it?" I get closer to the mirror, still not looking into it, coming at it from the side.

"You have to have something really sharp. Obviously. And then you have to find a place to pinch. This is hard when you're dealing with something close to the bone."

"Like a face."

"But it's still doable. Especially if the skin is a little loose. Once you've found a place to pinch, maybe by the chin or the cheek, you can slip your blade in . . . ever so gently . . . and from there, you just . . . slide."

I haven't even realized I've left the reading room and am now out in the hallway until I feel the wall against my hand. I press on a panel I somehow know is there, and a small door exposes itself ever so slightly in the wallpaper.

The voice continues from whatever mirror is closest. Or maybe it's just in my head.

"Once you slide carefully enough, you can start to see the truth underneath."

So we slide.

It's easy to fall into a hypnotic state inside the crawl space. The dark is so monolithic, consciousness and its counterpart become indistinguishable.

I settle into it. At first, it's comfortable . . . and then we're running.

The thing about faces, he's saying, *is they're always a lie. Even before they're slathered in makeup. Faces make us different from each other. And we're not—not really. We try so goddamn hard all the time to be different, to be unique. You know what we all just really are? When you strip away the dumb expressions we all practice to try to look a certain way?*

Meat.

We're in the crawl space for hours. I only realize just how long when I emerge, starving and filthy, and feel the silence settled over the house. It's the same silence I felt at another time in my life when I wandered away from the group only to realize they'd all gone home without me. Only this time, I *am* home.

"And now you understand," the voice in the mirrors says.

"Yes," I answer. But do I?

I keep my thoughts and feelings hidden from him. I don't want him to know the swirl of emotions going on within me right now. The confusion, the dismay . . . It feels a strange accomplishment keeping such a secret from a part of myself, but I'm aided by two things: I don't think he's all that interested in my feelings in the first place, and also . . . well, I've always been good at keeping things from myself, haven't I? Rooms within rooms.

"Now go back to the blue book and finish reading," the mirror-voice instructs me. "Prepare for tomorrow."

"I will."

But once again, I don't move. I should eat something. There's got to be a kitchen or pantry somewhere. I'm famished.

I'm also filthy from the dirt and concrete dust and cobwebs—there are a lot of bugs in there. If I didn't already know that firsthand, I was treated to the memory of a little boy hiding in the crawl spaces from his monster father, lasting for days on all the crawlies he could find. No wonder I knew how to take care of myself at that insect museum.

But now I'm an adult, and I need real food.

I half walk, half tumble through the hallways, supporting myself where I can on the walls and banisters. I might have had a restful night's sleep, but I feel more exhausted and drained than ever. The portraits stare down at me disapprovingly. As if they know the truths I'm concealing.

Assuming the kitchen must be on the second floor, I start down the staircase. Halfway down, I look up and see the ghost of Victor standing on the landing where I just was.

"What did you see?" he asks. "What did he show you?"

"Everything," I say.

"He showed you our childhood? He showed you Father?"

"Yes."

"As he *really* was?"

"Yes."

The ghost of Victor Cross says more to me. But this time, I ignore him.

I can't eat yet. I'm too distracted and dizzy. I need to talk things out. I wish I had my Loved Ones with me—I suddenly feel off-axis not having them here—but in the rush of things, I left them at Nadine's. I make a plan to rescue them tomorrow morning, but in the meantime, I need someone to be my sounding board.

My feet take me to my next-best option before my brain catches up, and soon I'm lowering my exhausted body into a chair.

Night lays flat against the hospital room window, as featureless as a coat of paint.

"I can't stay long," I say. "I've really got to eat something or I'm going to pass out. But I've been meaning to stop by and see how you're feeling anyway, so."

The machines in here with us make soft, alien music. Anna-Louise, her face swathed in bandages, sleeps peacefully to their lullaby. Only one closed eye is visible through the layers of white cotton. Her chest rises and falls steadily.

I keep my voice low; I don't actually want to wake her. The irony occurs to me that, thanks to her bandages, this is the first time I can actually have a conversation with her where I don't have to look away from her face.

"Something just happened to me," I tell her. "Something I wish I could actually tell you because I think you would maybe have some insights into it."

I tell her what I saw. I tell her everything.

We ran through the dark together, Damon and I, just like we did when I was hypnotized at Bonnie's house the other night.

"But it was also completely different. Because this time we were looking at his memories, not mine. *My* memories were so small and brief. Like pinpricks in the darkness. His were like museum displays." Actually, my first impression was like shotgun blasts. "His memories just felt so much more . . . vivid. And important. He was almost proud of them. And I kept wondering, *why*? Why do they feel this way? But whenever I tried to question it, he pulled me further into the dark."

His memories were also out of order. There was no sense of chronology to them, so we ricocheted between visions of him as a boy, a young man, an adult, and as my energies began to wane, he dragged me along with the unflagging enthusiasm of a child presenting his favorite toys.

He showed you Father? Victor had asked. *As he* really *was?*

He did indeed.

"Most of what I saw lines up with what Burton has told me, or what I've managed to read in that blue book so far . . . but not all of it. Like, did you know Damon's father was an actor? Or, wanted to be?"

In fact, Jonathan Cross loathed his religious lineage. He didn't want to help lead a fanatical community of isolationists; he rejected all of that. He wanted to be onstage. And yet he never did much beyond dream; he was too scared to leave the comforts of his small-town prominence, and that fear curdled into something dark and equally fanatical.

Then he met the woman who would become Damon and Victor's mother, an actress in a touring show who caught Jonathan's eye. She was older than he; experienced, worldly, confident. She would be his way out—if she put her own career on hold for a few years, bore him children, and waited out the lives and energies of Jonathan's own disapproving parents, they could live their dreams as they wished, with money and freedom.

Damon was six years old when the United States entered the Second World War. Jonathan was eager to fight overseas, thinking the experience would enrich his understanding of the human condition, make him a better artist.

"That was the only time Damon was ever truly happy: when his daddy was gone at war."

But eventually, Daddy came back. And like many men, he came back changed. Moody. Irrational. Violent.

One day not long after, little Damon found himself locked in a room—one of the bathrooms on the third floor. Dumped in the tub was the body of his mother. Stripped nude and dead. Strangled.

I watched as young Damon begged and pleaded to be let out. I heard Jonathan on the other side of the door, saying it was *her* fucking fault, she'd let herself go while he was away, she was too old to be a famous actress now, no one would want to fuck her, no one would want to look at her, not now. She'd ruined everything! Now, Jonathan said, it was going to be up to Damon to become Jonathan's meal ticket. Victor was handsome, sure, but he was too old to properly train. Besides, handsome was boring; Damon had something unique. They were going to have to turn Damon into a great and true artist. Maybe the greatest, and Jonathan would hitch his wagon to that star. I watched as ants began to crawl over the dead woman's skin and Damon screamed. The house had always had an ant problem.

Damon wasn't let out of that bathroom until three days later. Well after his mother began to bloat and leak.

What followed were years of abuse. Horrific scenes of Jonathan torturing Damon, ruining him, forcing him to watch, or sometimes participate in, depravity after depravity with women Jonathan would bring home. All in the name of "artistic research" and "emotional truth." Victor was also enlisted—his duties were resigned more to escorting the women home, making sure they were paid and didn't cause trouble.

Of course, Jonathan's plan made no sense. If he'd really wanted to leave this fundamentalist community, he could have. The man had so clearly lost his mind. And soon, even he seemed to forget the reason he was torturing—"training"—his sons in the first place.

My heart ached for the little boys. But every time I began to feel something like pity, the next memory we would run to would show an older Damon, in his twenties and early thirties, as he began to collect his own victims. Hunt. Skin. Erase.

His father died inauspiciously, anticlimactically, of a heart attack while doing yardwork in the desert sun when Damon was in his teens.

"And it could've ended there," I say. "Damon didn't have to cater to that sick man's whims anymore."

But now Damon had his own whims. His own justifications. His own needs.

Because so many of the women who crossed his path reminded him of *her*. His mother. That old, useless hag who'd made all this torture and torment happen in the first place. It was her fault for displeasing Father. Her fault for getting old. For not being around to protect him. For rotting in the tub.

I watched as he hunted. I watched as he took detailed notes on each target, determining whether she was safe. I watched him get close to her. I watched him strangle her, hard enough to break the delicate bones in her throat with a final *snap*.

I watched as, for the first time, gripped by horror and outrage, he began shredding one of their faces . . . all because an ant was crawling on her skin. It wound up easing something inside of him, a kind of guilt perhaps, and he began covering all their faces afterward.

Victor, too, did his own covering. He, too, had been trained well. He, too, was an actor of sorts.

So, yes. I saw *everything*. But the thing I couldn't say to Victor, the thing I can barely say to myself now, is how . . . boring it all became.

How predictable.

Maybe I wouldn't feel this way if I hadn't listened to so many of Eleanor's podcasts. But the entire endless time, during the cavalcades of horror and heartbreak and justification and misery, I couldn't unsee how repetitive it became. Mommy issues. Daddy issues. Abuse. Revenge. Horrifying though it was, the cycle was so commonplace. There was nothing to earn Damon's preening sense of accomplishment. It ceased being *interesting*. It was only sad. For everyone. Especially the innocent women swept up in it.

The whole time, I kept thinking, *Why are these moments supposedly more memorable than my own quiet life?*

By the time we got to what I knew was Damon's last day, I felt immense relief.

Damon had secreted a woman back to the mansion, as per usual. His reign of terror had proceeded for years with no sign that the authorities were close to catching the Jane Doe Killer. But then, a hideous coincidence: a local sheriff had formed a task force and just happened to be visiting Victor at the Cross House to give him an update.

Good old Victor was the mayor now, and he'd played his part in keeping outsiders off Damon's trail, but even he couldn't stop this impromptu debriefing. No problem there; the house had plenty of quiet, private rooms where Damon could do with the woman (*Meg, her name was Meg*) what he wanted. In fact, Damon found it extra thrilling knowing it was happening under the noses of the so-called authorities.

But he was too curious. Midway through his work, after he'd sliced her fingerprints off, he left old Meg, bound but barely conscious, and went to spy on his brother and the sheriff through the crawl space. His beloved crawl space. He wanted to hear them squirm over his brilliance.

The Greek tragedies in his reading room would've called it *hubris*.

When Damon returned to his work, he discovered he'd left the knife he'd used to carve off Meg's fingerprints a little too close to her. Meg had managed to grab it, cut her bonds, and by the time he got back to her, she was waiting for him.

Even while bleeding and screaming, Meg managed to kick the shit out of poor surprised Damon, leaving him momentarily incapacitated.

She'd noticed the secret entrance by which Damon had come in and out of the room, and she escaped, still screaming, into the crawl space—a violation!

All this commotion had been loud enough to attract the visiting police, even despite the house's size. Damon turned up the radio he kept in the room to mask the noises, but it was too late. They were banging on the door, demanding to come in and see what was going on. It was all over.

So Damon began to scream, too.

At first, he was just mocking the lost, disoriented woman in the crawl space. But then a curious thing happened.

Damon found it felt good to scream.

It felt *right*. Now it was *his* turn to play the victim. To scream in horror and outrage at all the wrongs that had been done to him. Yes. Yes! At last, he had found the role he had been born to play! He was the real victim here! And so he grabbed the radio and, still shrieking, in demented glee more than anything else, disappeared into the darkness of the crawl space.

I indulged him in the self-pity; I was just so glad to have reached the end.

Until I remembered these memories were all out of order, and I was dragged to yet another death, yet another misery, yet another justification. The feeling was very much like being damned.

And now you understand . . .

I don't know how much of this you already know, Anna-Louise." My throat is very dry now—from speaking and from the dust I inhaled—but it feels good to talk this out, to nail this dreamlike assembly of images down with words. "I'm sure you know at least some of it. But there's one moment I saw that I can't stop thinking about. It was maybe the only moment that really shocked me."

Truth be told, it was a moment I found flat-out hilarious. I had to work hard to stifle the laughter it provoked in me. But it doesn't feel so funny sitting here, now.

"He made it all up, Anna-Louise. All that stuff about visions and angels and sin. He made it all up."

It's true. I watched him do it.

It was just a few months before Jonathan dropped so inauspiciously dead. He had found Damon rummaging through an old box of papers, reading some of Elias Cross's old sermons. Jonathan hated all that religious shit, had hid it all on purpose, just as he'd hidden the crucifixes and disfigured the faces on some of those fucking ancestral portraits. He beat Damon badly that day—one of the worst beatings he'd ever given. *Don't you dare read that Christing swill*, he'd roared.

And so, just to get back at his father, Damon started writing fake journal entries about seeing angels. About having spiritual epiphanies in line with his ancestor Elias's preachings.

They were half-baked. Incoherent. Often hijacked by his own obsessive, traumatized ramblings.

They were also all a lie. A fevered, desperate lie. Another performance.

Maybe Damon thought his father would one day read those pages, or maybe they were just private little exorcisms, but either way, Jonathan's heart had vapor locked well before that bridge was crossed.

The humor comes back to me, and I start to giggle as I recount this to Anna-Louise.

"It was just a prank to him. A joke. Can you believe it? And now there's a whole stupid religion about it!"

The machines answer for her. Hiss. Beep.

"I'm sorry, I shouldn't laugh, but . . . God! I need to forget what I saw, right? Go along to get along? Be Good?"

She doesn't have an answer. Of course not; she's asleep. If my Loved Ones were here, they'd know what to say. Tomorrow, bright and early, that's my plan. I'll have them with me for the big day.

"Tomorrow's my birthday, Anna-Louise. The big five-oh. Time sure goes fast, huh?"

It all comes out in a rush, the words as ready to come out as food-poisoned vomit:

"I'm sorry for what I did to you, Anna-Louise. I'm sorry I remembered you wrong. I'm sorry for ruining your life. Probably twice. I guess, what I'm wondering is . . . was it me, or was it him? Do you know what I mean? Where am *I* in all this, Anna-Louise? I've been wandering around all day, looking at portraits on the wall, and I have these twin impulses. One is to say, wow, look at all this; look at what I found out I belonged to! And the other impulse is to say, what the hell am I talking about? I'm not *actually* related to any of these people. I came here to find out who *I* am. And for a moment there, I thought I did! But . . . after today? What if I'm actually further away than ever?"

I stare at my hands. The hands that beat this woman when we were children. That carved off half her face when she was an adult. They're filthy from the crawl space. And they're old. The dirt throws their veins and wrinkles into stark relief.

"I guess, in the end, I should just be grateful I'm here, right? Not a lot of people our age get a shot at a new life like this. I should go eat and try to read that book. Even if it is fiction." I stand up, feeling very creaky and tired. I give a soft chuckle. "Hey, serial killer fiction always did well at the bookstore, so I guess—"

Anna-Louise's one exposed eye is open, staring up at me. Wide and terrified.

"Oh," I say. "You're awake. Did you hear a lot of that?" The frightened squeak I hear in response is just faint enough that it might have been in my imagination.

I lean closer to her. Really close. So I know she can hear me.

"Probably should keep this between us," I tell her. "Who knows what Damon would do to you to keep you quiet?" I softly trace a finger along her bandaged face. "Or maybe it's just me."

Later that night, nestled in a murderer's bed, I have the Dream again.

Darkness. Moving through it. Hunting. A shark in the deepest, darkest sea, only instead of teeth, I have a massive knife in my hand. But there's nothing to cut. The knife, my hand, they thirst in agony.

Then, a corner is rounded and a spotlight suddenly blares onto a figure standing in the nothingness. Her back to me.

She turns around.

It's me.

Finally in the spotlight.

Mary. Plain old Mary. Boring old Mary. Pathetic old Mary, with her slightly tensed shoulders, as if she's always waiting for a blow.

I stare at her. That face, so untenable, so unbearable. I could cut it to ribbons. I *want* to. I have the means.

But I don't. I just stare.

She stares back.

Then she opens her mouth. Is she going to say something? Finally speak up for herself? Tell me what she wants me to do?

Her mouth opens wide. Wider. Too wide for speech. She makes gurgling, retching noises. The effort is hurting her.

Something's inside her mouth. At the back of her throat. Slick and wet, glinting in the light of the spotlight.

An eye.

Her mouth opens even wider.

A finger emerges just under the eye. And another. And another. A hand. It starts to pull her—*my!*—throat open from the inside. Widening the throat. Like stretching a hole in a garbage bag. Not caring that the skin and the cartilage are tearing.

A head begins to push itself out from the straining opening.

I can hear my jaw breaking, harsh, dry-wooden *cracks!*, as this new person is born.

My lower jaw finally rips away, bringing with it my throat, the flesh off my ribs, the entirety of my chest, allowing the person inside to step fully free. My teeth fly out like splinters. Like bullets.

Jane.

It's Jane.

Breathing hard from the effort of tearing herself loose.

She's naked. But she's not a ghost. She's as pure and whole as her author photo.

"Not for nothing?" she says, finally catching her breath. "But . . ."

Then she puts her hand on her own face, sets her nails into her skin, and tugs the flesh free, screaming as the gristle and gore give way in great, red strings.

I wake with a jolt.

No idea what time it is exactly, but the pale light of dawn makes the windows glow in pastel softness.

It's my birthday.

PART SIX

BIRTHDAY

The morning was full of sunlight and hope.

—Kate Chopin, *The Awakening*

Obviously, the investigation was somewhat hamstrung by the lack of any survivors to interview, including the perpetrator. "Do you regret that?" Oprah asked me the day I came on to her show for an interview. "Do you regret the fact that you weren't able to take this evil woman alive?"

I looked her straight in the eyes and said the truth: hell no.

My only regret is I didn't recognize her for what she was the one time I spoke with her in the days prior.

—Special Agent Peter Arliss, *In the Dark with the Devil: One Heroic FBI Agent's Ground Zero Account of the Arroyo Easter Massacre*

42

New Mary

APRIL 20, 2019

The smell hits like a blast of wind. It almost pushes me out of the gloomy, dark house and back onto the dawn-lit walkway. I force my way inside, hand over my nose and mouth. Nadine's body is still on the floor, draped with the blanket from the couch.

I'm going to make this quick. I just want to fill my purse with my remaining Loved Ones and also pack up some clothes—can't wear this tank and these capri pants forever, can I? Today's a big day. Wanna look my best.

Standing in the living room now, though, the question of what to do with Nadine's body hangs over me as naggingly as the smell. Let her rot here? What if that FBI agent comes back? Hell, what if Brenda comes back? Gotta remember to wipe down all my fingerprints, too, don't I? Make it seem like I was never here. That sounds exhausting. No way will I remember every place I've touched.

Just before anxiety gets a proper hold on my chest, the answer comes to me. Of course: *they'll* help me. I'm not alone anymore. I'm part of the flock. That thought buoys me. Relying on others will take some getting used to, but I'll just have to keep reminding myself. I'm not alone. I have all I ever wanted.

Despite the pervasive stench of decay, I walk through the house one last time. Such a different experience from wandering through the Cross House. The sound of my breathing into my palm cupped around my nose and mouth almost makes me feel like an astronaut or a deep-sea diver.

Only takes a few minutes to cover all the terrain. Nadine's room, her closet somehow overflowing despite her limited wardrobe, her bed so tall I still can't believe she was able to climb into it every night, the kitchen, the living room. It's still a mess, papers thrown everywhere, books dumped off shelves. A snapshot of our final fight and my hasty exit.

Finally, I've got nowhere to go but down the hallway to the bathroom and Brenda's room. The smell will be better there, I'm sure, so—I stop. Something's wrong.

The bathroom door is open.

All the spit in my mouth suddenly dries up.

Did I do that? Leave it open? An ominous idea comes and goes:

Jane opened the door when you read her book.

Or when you dreamed of her.

You gave her power.

I shudder and walk very quickly past the open bathroom door—even though nothing's in there, nothing that can hurt me—

(*no thing is what I am*)

—and into Brenda's room. I close the door behind me because it'll cut the smell off, no other reason.

Once my heart and breath return to their usual rhythm, and my mouth no longer feels like it's been stuffed full of cotton, I grab one of my suitcases and put it on the bed.

Before I start filling it with clothes, I sit next to it, press the heels of my hands to my eyes, enjoy the darkness for a moment. *I'm okay. I'm okay.*

Today's a day for being happy, I remind myself. *Don't be an ingrate.*

A few moments later, I'm softly singing to myself—"Happy birthday to me"—while I pack everything up. I try to make the room almost as spotless as it was when I arrived.

Last to go in are my Loved Ones. So few of them left. I could cry looking at them, so innocent, their expressions undeterred by the powder-strewn carcasses of their siblings right next to them on the dresser top. Put on a brave face, little ones. But then again, we all know what faces are, right? I shake that thought from my head and lovingly pack each porcelain statue into the suitcase.

"You're off to meet your long-lost cousins," I tell them as the zipper goes up. Then pause, halfway, to add, "Also, I need you to help keep me from asking too many questions. I need you to remind me to be Good."

What to do with the shattered figurines next? I should just throw them away. But some of the shards are too sharp; they'd rip through a garbage bag. There's a front zipper on my suitcase, one of those pockets I never know what to do with, and I deposit the shards in there for now. Maybe I'll bury my little brokens in the crawl space—that seems kind of fitting.

Next, I blow all that powder off the dresser. That hurts the most; it feels disrespectful somehow. But once the powder has all settled between the dresser and the wall, the pain eases a little. It still hurts, knowing what was there, but it also feels cleaner. Lighter. Simpler. Truer.

Don't forget the ones in the living room.

Right. The ones that came out of Nadine.

I'm not going to try to rescue anymore from her—Nadine is putrefying enough already that the thought of reaching farther into her gullet makes my stomach somersault and plunge like an Olympic high diver. But there are the ones I already pulled out, sitting on the carpet. They're not too far gone.

The smell is, unsurprisingly, worse out here in the living room. I find the Loved Ones in the nap of the carpet and put them in with the other shards.

Then I look at the lump that was my Aunt Nadine, still covered in the fleece blanket I pulled off the couch. She's as lifeless as the rest of the furniture in the room.

That unsettled feeling flutters inside of me again—*I am Bad, I am a monster,* somehow coexisting alongside *I am an imposter, I am a pretender.* I think again of that clean dresser in Brenda's room. That painful simplicity. Then a solution of sorts occurs to me.

Today is a birthday, goddammit. Today is a day for rituals.

Time for a New Mary to be born.

Time to put Old Mary to rest.

And I'm going to do it by burying the woman who helped make her.

This isn't going to be easy. I stare at the covered shape on the floor.

The faint smell of cigarette smoke lingers in the air. A ghost of sorts. That thought sends another shiver through me.

"Okay, how am I going to do this? I should dig the hole first. That's *really* not going to be fun. Oh, Mary, what are you thinking?"

I could swear I hear a cough. I whip around.

Silence. Maybe that wasn't a cough. Maybe it was the bathroom door creaking open even wider. Maybe Jane has decided to finally leave her bathroom prison cell and pay me a—

Stop spooking yourself! Jesus.

If I'm serious about doing this, I'd better do it now, before the day really begins and the heat settles over everything.

First step: the most important one. Location, location, location.

I head out to the backyard, past Chipotle's food bowl and water dish, still both full—which makes me think absurdly of images of Pompeii, tables set for the dead—through the kitchen door with its little doggy flap. I leave the door open to help air out the house.

The gravel and dirt crunch under my feet in a way that feels particularly early morning. Something about how the sound echoes in the quiet, still-damp air.

The backyard is mostly loose rock, but there's a patch of dead grass on the right-hand side: something that could be a sort-of lawn if the homeowner had the time and desire. Nadine certainly had the time, but desire must have gotten lost in the mail. Various shades of dried Chipotle droppings decorate the yard, some bleached as white as bone.

I definitely can't dig a grave in the gravel, so I guess it's got to be the grass plot. Hopefully, it's mostly dirt and not hard rock underneath.

"Last chance to back out," I tell myself. "You really wanna do this?"

I do. Absurd though it might be, it feels right. I did a horrible thing to her. An ungrateful thing. I want to show her this one grace.

"Okay," I sigh, "then let's dig a fucking grave."

It takes a while to find a shovel in the garage.

I finally locate one, tucked away in a corner, the handle draped in spider-webs. Before I reach for it, I notice the black, bulbous body of the responsible spider perched on a strand of web stretching out to the wall. My eyes aren't good enough from this distance anyway, but I have a feeling if I could see the underside of this spider, I'd find a red hourglass.

She's perfect, beautiful, and terrifying. *Like the desert,* I think.

I find a rusty old trowel to sever the threads and slowly, very slowly, pull the shovel free.

My eyes never leave the spider—she's as unruffled as lake water on a breezeless day. She has all the confidence a deadly thing should.

Finding the shovel and moving in deference to that spider takes longer than I would have liked; the day is beginning to really establish itself when I step back outside. Shades of yellow are soaking into the light, and the birdsong in the air is more businesslike, no longer just the gossipy thrill of having made it through another night.

It's probably something like 8:00 a.m. already. It'll start getting hot sooner rather than later. So I'd better get—

At first, I think it's an optical illusion, a sudden shadow on the ground. But my body catches on before my brain. My heart lurches. My knees almost give out. I'm barely able to keep my bladder from suddenly emptying down my leg.

A hole has been dug in the yard. While I was in the garage. Jagged but deep. Like something got down and frantically tore dirt out of the ground. Like a dog. Only it's not a dog.

Standing by the fresh grave is Jane.

Her head tilts slightly inside her bloody cowl; her claws are still flexed from their work.

I've seen other ghost women like her in the daylight before, but seeing Jane, specifically Jane, out of her bathroom, out here in the sun, makes me begin to shiver as if I'm not standing out in an increasingly warm desert day.

The blood cascading down her chest is so very rich, maintaining its shape like a dried stain but never losing the red, glossy sheen of fresh blood. By contrast, the wine-stain birthmark on her shoulder is so much more muted. So mundane. So natural.

Ignore it, Mary. Ignore her.

How can I ignore *this*?!

Immediately, I understand: that must have been her goal.

I look away, eyes too big to even blink, and awkwardly skitter around her to get to the kitchen door. As soon as I'm inside, I close the door behind me.

Okay. Okay, now what?

She's trying to trap me. She's trying to make it impossible to not see her. Maybe reading her poems really *did* give her a taste of a new kind of attention, and now she wants more.

"I know I said it before, but it's *still* not too late to back out," I remind myself.

What gets me back on task is the smell of cigarette smoke and the nascent, but unscratchable, itch that I'd better not give Nadine any proper cause to haunt me. If there's ever a ghost I wouldn't be able to ignore, metaphorical or otherwise, it's hers. I need to see this through. Besides, if it *is* a trap, Jane already had the opportunity to get me for a few good seconds there. Maybe these ghosts are too weak to strike right away.

I can do this.

I disconnect Nadine's oxygen tank and then proceed to drag her heavy, stinking bulk by the ankles, blanket and all, to the kitchen door.

I expect her body to be stiff, like moving a statue, but she must be past that stage. She's floppy, uncooperative, and so, so heavy. It's exhausting work, and I haven't even gotten her outside yet.

It's even hotter by the time I get her into the sun. Still keeping my eyes focused on anything but Jane (*What Jane? Who? Ha ha*), I take a second to catch my breath, rub my complaining lower back, and then continue dragging Nadine over the gravel and concrete to the hole that, I'm telling myself, just happened to open up where I needed it to.

Finally, I roll Nadine's covered corpse into the hole. She lands with an impressively dull *whump*.

She twisted in the fall, so she lands facedown, but one arm is now wrapped behind her back and one leg bends backward up onto the wall of the hole. Something about seeing her veiny and bruised ankle, her practically boneless arm, fills me with more pity than I ever would have thought possible. I think again of that neverending parade of cruelty I saw in the crawl space, in Damon's history, last night. Trauma inflicted, trauma incurred, trauma passed on. The reincarnation of abuse.

I quickly work to push the dirt back into the hole, over the body. I move as fast as I can, not just to escape the growing heat but to make sure Jane-what-Jane never has reason to try to join me.

Once it's done, I'm drenched in sweat. For all I know, I could have had a hot flash during the effort; it would have come to the same effect.

It's not a very subtle grave. In fact, it's pretty glaringly obvious something was just buried here. But it'll have to do.

"You were not a very nice person, Aunt Nadine," I say to the hasty-looking pile. "Then again, what reason did the world ever give you to be nice? Still. I could have used your . . . I don't know, wisdom? Experience? There was more to you than people saw, and I wish we could have found a little peace together." I wipe my hands on themselves. They're gritty and caked with earth. "I hope you're reincarnated into . . . a tobacco plant. Or the Loch Ness Monster." I stop and consider, surprised to find tears stinging my eyes. "No. I hope you're reincarnated into a bunch of big, bright, actually

real flowers. The kind people will want to put in their hair." I chuckle. "And
you'll probably want to have plenty of thorns, too."

The work of filling in the grave was frantic and meditative enough that I
actually did manage to forget . . . *that other thing* for a little while. But now
my body remembers that I'm not fully alone out here. The hairs on my arms
tingle.

Maybe if I don't look at her, if I just act like I'm talking to myself, I'll be
safe enough.

"Thank you," I say to the air around me. "I guess . . . maybe you wanted
to pay your respects, too. I mean, you certainly lived with her long enough."
I swallow, desperately thirsty. I need to grab some water and hit the road.
"I'm never coming back to this house, you know. You're going to be all
alone. So maybe . . . maybe it's time for you to move on, too. Go do . . .
whatever it is you want. Take off that damn hood and, y'know. Have a nice
afterlife?"

I want to say more. I want to tell her how much her poetry meant to me.
But I've said too much. I head back inside.

The house still reeks of death. Or maybe it always smelled this way and I
never noticed.

I feel better, though. Lighter. I'm glad I did this. I put Nadine to rest. I
put Old Mary to rest.

I wash my hands in the sink, then fill a glass with water and promptly
dump that water down my throat. I should probably clean the glass, wipe
down the sink, begin the exhausting work of erasing my existence in this
house—but no. Remember. I have others who can help me with this. I don't
have to do this alone.

I head back to Brenda's room and get my suitcase. Then I stop in the living
room and give one final look to this dark, dank, stinking house. The shadows seem deeper and richer than ever. Time for me to step out into the sun.
Time for me to follow the advice I just gave the dead woman in the backyard
and move on.

"You wanna know the one thing that really pisses me off?"

I whip my head around to see who's speaking and, standing in the bottomless shadows of the hallway by the bathroom door, is a small, squat
silhouette. Its voice is gravelly, low, and poisonous. Smilingly hateful. Even

though it's rendered almost featureless by the gloom, I can still make out the outline of a fake flower in its hair.

"The fact that I had a goddamn genuine paranormal entity in my house and you never fucking told me."

43

Ghosts

"I mean seriously, Mary, do you know how much I woulda loved to'a known something like that?"

She's wrapped in the dark shadows of the gloomy house, her entire body muted and rendered nearly invisible. Except for her eyes. Her eyes glare white in the sooty darkness like bleached teeth in a diseased mouth.

"You're not here," I say after a long pause. "I can ignore you. I can make you go away."

"Yeah, good luck with *that*." She gives a gravelly approximation of a laugh. I can smell the faint rumor of cigarette smoke, can almost see it swirl out of her shadow-mouth. "I gotta hand it to you, Mary, you really fucked everything up good and proper. I mean, I asked you to come out here to protect me, and now . . . !"

"I'm really sorry, Nadine," I say. "I didn't . . . I didn't know what I did or what I was until it was too late."

Nadine's ghost groans. "Ain't that the most pathetic thing? I mean, shit, if you're gonna be a monster, at least labia up and enjoy it. That's what I always did."

"I'm sorry."

"'*I'm sorry*,'" she mimics in a high, whiny tone. "It makes sense *sorry* is your favorite word because that's just how I'd describe you." Her voice has a thinness to it. It reminds me a little of how long-distance phone calls used to sound, back when we cared about phrases like *long-distance phone calls*. There's a faint crackling to her words—like even her sound waves are wrong.

"I have to leave, Nadine. I . . . I'm sorry, but . . ."

I look away for a second, down at my hands, ashamed, pertinent . . . and when I look back up, she's gone. Just regular darkness in the hallway. No shape.

"Aunt Nadine?"

Great. I really am losing my mind.

Then I turn around and see her in the living room. Still almost entirely shadow, like she's knitting herself together out of the house's gloom. She's by her recliner, but she's looking toward the kitchen, the door to the backyard, where Jane is still visible.

"She's a beaut, huh?" Nadine asks. "Look at her. I mean, goddamn."

Nadine stares out almost with reverence. I cautiously step closer to see out the door. Jane is still outside, standing in the sun, looking up at the sky as if basking. What is she doing out there? I imagine it's been a long time since she left that bathroom—maybe she's considering my advice?

"There are a lot more like her," I say. "All around town. Victims of Damon Cross."

"I told my sister to leave this place when all that started happening. But your damn father insisted. Said this was a godly place to raise a family. I wasn't sad when he became a crispy critter."

"Does it hurt?" I ask Nadine from across the room. "Being dead?"

Nadine's shape shifts. It sags somehow, like it's suddenly under a heavy weight. If she were an actual body, I'd think she was leaning on her recliner for support. She doesn't answer for a long time.

"There are feelings you've never experienced before. They don't have words for 'em in any language. Not even the language of nerves." She runs a vaporous hand over the recliner as if she's sampling how it feels in this new state. "But I ain't ready to give all this up yet. Gonna stick around for a while. Explore."

"Is it . . . a choice?"

"Like deciding to float in the ocean or letting yourself sink. Oh, none of those books know *anything*." Her preternaturally visible eyes flick over to her shelves.

"That's something, right?" I say, trying to sound positive. "Like, a silver lining? At least you finally get to know the truth about—"

She's suddenly right in front of me. I smell the plumes of cigarette smoke, but there's an undersmell, too. A burned, ionic kind of smell. Like metal and scorched steak. The sort of thing you smell before a lightning storm.

Her too-bright eyes bulge from their smoky, shadowy murk. I'm gripped by a shuddering fit. My teeth chatter. My entire body begins to tremble; I can't stop. It's fear, it's loathing, it's uncanny outrage. That warning from her books flares in my mind like neon: *Don't let them touch you, don't let them touch you.*

"There is no fucking silver lining." Nadine's voice is low. Full of pain. "I deserved *life*. You had no right to do this."

I can only make a gasping noise in response. My heart jackhammers, and the metallic taste of adrenaline fills the back of my mouth.

Then she's across the room, in a corner, gathering herself into the darkness again—maybe for strength? Security? Nourishment? Her eyes are also wide. I think she even surprised herself with that outburst.

"I deserved life," she repeats with a pout. Then she composes herself. I almost can hear the leather-creak of her smile. "But fuck it. Always make the best of a bad situation. That's my fucking motto. Right? I'm gonna haunt the shit out of this town. Have some fun. Always loved reading about poltergeists. Maybe there's a training program for me."

She gives a cruel chuckle, and I remember what Barb and Anna-Louise said about some personalities being strong enough to stick together like an oil spill.

As that thought trails through my brain, though, it drags a couple more in its wake.

"Why haven't I seen any other . . . *newer* ghosts?" I ask. My voice is shaking. "Like Carole, or"—I gulp—"that little boy?"

"Ohh yeah," Nadine purrs, "you've been busy, haven't you? Bad girl. Bad, bad girl."

Her laugh is horrid. Somehow, when she laughs, that's when she sounds the most dead. I can almost hear the dirt I just buried her in tumbling down her chin.

"Do you remember writing me letters when you were in Clearview? You didn't keep it up for long—I think sooner or later, they learned they just had to keep you nice and medicated if they were gonna get anything done around there. But those first few years, you used to write to me a lot, saying, 'I'll be good, Aunt Nadine, I'll be good, the doctor says good things for good girls, and so I'm going to be good.' I always used to think goddamn I hope she's telling the truth. I hope they force some good into her somehow. But you were never good, were you? Not really. Not deep down, in your squishy bits."

"I used to write you?" This is complete news to me. Of course it is. I only just learned of my being committed.

"I saved the letters for a little while. Threw 'em out in the move. Not in-teresting enough to keep. You were always such a whiner. I never met some-one who was so whiny. And also nosy—so many questions! And so violent! God, it was like there was three or four people in your ugly little head. And I didn't wanna know any of 'em."

Rage begins to bubble up inside me. I welcome it. It gives me something to feel other than fear. I can't believe I ever said I was sorry to this . . . well, I almost said *woman,* but I guess that's not quite accurate now.

Nadine continues, "You wanna know why you haven't seen anyone else like me? Cuz it's another thing the books have backward. People don't *see* ghosts."

"What do you mean?"

"Ghosts *show themselves* to people. When they wanna be seen. It ain't up to you."

"So, like Carole . . . she doesn't want to be seen?"

"She knew she got what she deserved. She's moved on. She's *sunk.*"

"You don't think *you* got what you deserved?"

Another broken-asphalt chuckle. Low. Rumbling. A thundercloud full of phlegm and bile.

"Maybe I did."

"Maybe if you'd shown me a little love and support," I say through clenched teeth, "maybe I could have been different, Nadine."

"Yeah, electroshock didn't cure you, but maybe some ice cream woulda. Get real, Mary."

"That's my plan. For the first time in my life. Really real. I've moved into the Cross House, Aunt Nadine. You'd never believe everything that's hap-pened to me. I'm *special.*"

"I've been saying you were special since day one, Mary. A real Short Bus Extraordinaire."

"You can say whatever you want. It doesn't matter. I have friends now. They accept me. They even worship me."

"Like a huge turd in the bowl you gotta admire before you flush it down."

"You need me, too. You just said so yourself. You're showing yourself to me. Which means you want me to see you. I have the power here. I can make you disappear. Jane taught me that."

"Who's Jane?"

"Oh, I guess you don't know everything! Jane. The ghost who lived in your tub. Who never wanted to be seen by you, but chose *me*." I indicate the backyard where I assume Jane still is now. "Being seen is a choice, but so is seeing. And I can choose to not see you!"

"Jane." Nadine savors the name. An unexpectedly tender moment in the midst of all this acrimony. Then her tone hardens. "You're wrong, y'know."

"No, I'm not! It isn't always easy, but I can do it, I can ignore—"

"About her being a ghost, dipshit. She's not a *ghost*."

"What?"

Another mimicking sneer. "'Oooh, I guess you don't know everything!' I said she's not a ghost. At least, not like you think she is. If she is, it's only a technicality. Like how a shark and a seahorse are both fish. Heh. I'm the seahorse in this equation."

"Then what is she?"

Another chuckle. It takes me a few seconds to realize Nadine is no longer in the shadowy corner. She's disappeared again, and I have a brief moment to really appreciate just how insane this is. I'm arguing with the ghost of a woman I murdered about the classification of another ghost I also murdered but in a past life. Happy birthday to me, indeed.

I turn around and see the barely visible Nadine-smudge is at one of her bookcases. She sweeps a shapeless arm at one of the shelves. Nothing happens. She growls. Focuses. Does it again.

A book falls to the floor. Nadine gives a proud grunt. "Hell yeah," she says to me. "Poltergeist skills." Then she gestures to the book: a nonverbal command.

I pick the book up, not wanting to get too close. One of Nadine's hands sneaks around my shoulder to turn the pages, and I suck air through my teeth. The sensation is appalling; worms and maggots roost in my nerves. She takes me to a specific location, and it's only then that I notice the book I'm holding. I would have expected it to be one of her many paranormal texts. But no.

It's one of her books I never would've thought to consult.

It's one of her books on Greek mythology.

She points an ash-plume finger at a bolded header on the page, and she whispers a word in my ear that feels like an invasion.

"Erinyes."

44

Furies

Erinyes in Greek. *Dirae* in Latin. The Furies. As seen in stories like *The Aeneid* and *The Oresteia*. Vengeful spirits that sprang from blood and punished those who committed the worst kinds of atrocities. Mythological antecedents to revenants in European folklore. Cousins to the onryō in Japan.

Furies.

"But, they're so . . ." I'm not quite sure the word I'm looking for. Meek? Reserved? Passive? I land on: "Shy." Then I remember the dog. "Usually."

Ghost Nadine shrugs. "Maybe they're just used to being invisible. You know how that goes better than anyone, right? Besides. It's not like they're *special*. Creatures born of violence and pain? Might as well be born from bug shit or corn niblets; violence and pain are everywhere."

I consider this. That might explain why Jane seemed so affected when I first said her name. It never occurred to me that maybe she'd forgotten her name, too; hearing it again would have come as quite a shock.

"Are they still . . . who they were?"

"There's part of 'em in there, sure. But they're also something less. Or something more, maybe. Everything's fluid in the Deep Sea, Mary."

"But *you're* still you."

She spreads her thick, immaterial arms wide. "Takes more than some fucking torturous death to get rid of me, you queef." Another smarmy, almost audible grin.

My head is spinning. Ghosts. Furies. Reincarnation.

"What else?" A breathy laugh comes out of me. Dancing on the razor's edge between sarcasm and hysteria. "What about the ants? Are they something, too?"

"Psychopomps."

"What?!"

"Couriers of the dead. Usually it's birds, but, hey, things are always a bit weird out in the desert. And ants got wings when it's mating season, so."

She's loving this. Loving how obviously frazzled, how dangerously overwhelmed, I'm becoming.

I snap the mythology book closed and put it back on the shelf with a fumbling, sweaty hand. I want to sit down. "It's too much," I whisper desperately. "Why is this all so much?"

"Well, I can give you one possible answer for that, Mary. But you're not going to like it."

Cigarette smoke. Burned steak. She's right behind me. I don't turn around when I ask her, "What is it?"

Once again, she whispers in my ear. I don't know if it's what she says, how she says it, or just the very presence of her, but suddenly I'm running to the bathroom and throwing up in the sink. Nadine's cackling laugh follows me.

"Maybe none of this is real and you've just gone cuh-ray-zeeee," she said. Her voice, like a centipede crawling into my skull.

I spit my stomach into the basin, rinse bile out of my mouth, spit again.

"Fuck you," I say, sure she'll hear me wherever she is. "I'm not . . . I'm not *crazy.*"

But I am, aren't I? That's really what I came back to my hometown to learn. I'm just a tragic case of a young girl with some unfortunate mental predispositions who never got the care she needed and learned to suppress some dangerous tendencies, who eventually got old and—who knows why, hormones or boredom—now those tendencies are becoming impossible to keep suppressed. No need to overcomplicate this with Greek fucking mythology and kabbalistic metaphysics and all that nonsense.

"I'm leaving, Nadine."

I quickly walk to Brenda's bedroom to grab my suitcase. Too late, I remember it's actually already in the living room. Nadine has come in here with me. There aren't any shadows in Brenda's room, but my crawling skin can sense her presence.

"You don't belong *anywhere,*" she says again. "And you know it. You're a fucking freak."

Movement catches my eye.

The sheet draping the floor mirror in the corner of the room. It's suddenly yanked off the glass—*She's getting better at this,* I think feverishly—exposing the mirror. I see myself standing there.

"You don't belong anywhere."

My face begins to warp and crumble. Nausea and rage fight for a front seat in my gut. *Useless motherfuck—*

"Here's an idea!" she continues. "How 'bout you kill yourself, and then we can really have some fun. Whaddya say? Go out on top. You've tasted the most acceptance you're ever gonna get, right? And you know I've got sharp knives."

The world begins to lose all definition. I'm falling, falling down a hole a trapdoor a secret entrance into the space between walls into—

I watch myself grab the mirror and yank it forward. The glass smashes on the floor. Shards belch out from underneath, but it's too late—the feeling remains, the vertigo, the disgust, kill, skin, rip, peel, her, you look just like her, *who?*, Mommy, you look just like Mommy, useless motherfuck—

"There you go. Use one of those glass shards and cut open your wrists. Peel off your skin. It's called *degloving*, Mary. Take off your gloves and stay awhile!"

Maybe she's right, Mary; maybe—

I don't. It takes all my effort, every last drop of will I can muster, but I stumble backward and reel out of the room.

The feeling starts to dissipate, taking longer than it ever has before, but its grip loosens. I grab my suitcase, first for support, and then to beeline out of here.

Nadine shouts after me, "Run all you want! I'm not just a ghost either, Mary. I'm your aunt fucking Nadine! We're family! I'm in your blood! And you know what that means?"

I reach the front door, yank it open. How is there still sunlight? How have I only been in this pit for a couple of hours?

And then Nadine's intimate in my ear again, her decaying, shadow-tarred lips pressing lustily against my ear, only instead of moist breath, I feel the freezing vacuum of space itself. "You're never gonna be free of me, Mary," she coos.

I shake her off like a mosquito, but I still hear her delighted voice, even as I run out of the house, even as I stumble through the gate in the chain-link fence and onto the bleach-black road, even as her words spiral into her upper register, cackling with insane, triumphant glee.

"*You're never gonna be free of me! You're never gonna be free of me! YOU'RE NEVER GONNA BE FREE OF ME!*"

45

Routine Maintenance

I'm still shaking.

I feel as if I've been submerged in ice water.

Even the ever-intensifying sunlight can't burn this chill out.

Never gonna be free of me

Never gonna be free of me

Her voice, a teakettle shriek swirling in my head, eddying into subzero tornadoes that make me want to look back over my shoulder in fear even as they propel me forward away from that awful house.

Worse, that encounter just confirmed my fears: I'm not cured of my mirror problems. If anything, the mirror she exposed me to seemed to have affected me worse—and faster—than ever.

I trudge as quickly as my exhausted body will let me up to the Cross House, my suitcase trailing behind me, a tourist lost in a strange, unfriendly land.

There's a sign on the hospital entrance:

CLOSED AT NOON
Routine Maintenance
Come back tomorrow

So brusque, I almost have to give a short laugh. Can a hospital even do that? Just close up shop for the day? I guess, for a community this small, it's not a huge problem, but accidents still happen. Snakebites, broken legs, heart attacks. Come back tomorrow! Your life-threatening injury is important to us.

Mary. Most of the town is already going to be here.

I suppose that's right. I don't know if I've really grappled with the scope of whatever I'm about to participate in will be. How many people did Eleanor say were in this flock?

Even as I ponder that, I walk in to see four people sitting in the waiting room. Just sitting. No visible maladies. No obvious reasons for being in a hospital waiting room.

All their eyes, including Chantelle's, land on me like flies onto rotting food. Every face wears a small, secret smile.

"Hi," Chantelle says, apparently pleased as punch to see me.

"Hi," I say back.

"See you in a little bit," she says as I walk my suitcase toward the forbidden stairs. The eyes all follow me.

The harvest ceremony begins at 2:00 p.m., I was told yesterday. That means I still have a good amount of time, a little over four hours, to finish reading, prepare whatever I might need to prepare, maybe even find a moment to relax. I'd love to try to find an empty bathroom and take a bath. Scrub this horrible morning off me.

Before I can step onto the first stair to the second floor:

"Mary?"

It's Nurse Nancy. Goddammit. I was hoping I wouldn't run into her.

"What are you doing here?" she asks.

"I have a meeting with Dr. Burton," I say quickly. She glances at my suitcase. "He requested I bring some materials for him to look at. That okay with you?"

The grinding steel in my voice throws her. She stammers in a way Old Mary recognizes all too well. Good.

"No, I mean, yes, of course, I-I didn't—"

"I didn't realize I was *banned* from the entire *hospital*."

"No—"

"I guess I'd better not ever get sick. If I do, I'll just have to die outside. Good to know."

Jesus, I can practically hear Nadine coming out of my mouth. Maybe this is what she meant by, *You're never gonna be free of me.*

Nancy doesn't know how to respond, and so we soak in awkward silence for a few excruciating moments. Then she says:

"I was actually hoping to run into you."

My turn to be surprised. "Why?"

"Well, I never paid you for your . . . time here."

"Oh." A sudden urge to tell her it's okay, they don't have to pay me, we're even steven, don't worry about it, almost spills out of my mouth. I swallow it. "Right. That's true."

"I don't want to take you away from your meeting—"

"It's okay." I privately delight in my dismissal, making fake Dr. Burton wait for a fake meeting entirely in my imagination, something I'd never have the courage to do to Burton in real life. "He can wait."

She takes me to an empty exam room where her purse and jacket hang.

"I forget what we agreed on exactly, but here's three hundred dollars for the week. Is that okay?" Nancy pulls several bills from her wallet and offers them to me.

"Is this . . . your money?"

She waves a hand, trying a magic spell to make me forget those pesky details. It doesn't work. My silence gets to her.

"I just . . . I hired you on my own because I thought you needed help, and so it was my responsibility. Don't worry about it."

Once more, I fight the urge to feel bad, to tell her I don't want her money. If I hadn't had that horrible encounter with the ghost of Nadine, I probably would lose that fight. Instead, I fold the money and put it in my pocket. It sits there like greasy food in a sensitive stomach.

"Thank you," I say.

"I'm sorry things didn't work out. I know . . . things are difficult for you right now. With your aunt, and with finances and everything, but I really do hope everything works out okay."

I nod. This is too uncomfortable.

Before I step toward the door to leave, I glance at her face. She looks terrible. Huge bags under her eyes. A tautness to her cheeks. The decomposition begins, and I look away, but there's no mistaking she's in actual bad shape before that.

"Are *you* okay?" I ask myself in spite of my burning desire to get out of here.

She gives an embarrassed, "Oh," then tries another magic hand wave again. It's just as unsuccessful as the last one.

"I'm just tired. I'm . . . very tired. Event-planning stress, that's all." A self-conscious laugh, high and breathy. "But by tomorrow night, it'll be all good."

"Okay."

I turn for the door. She stops me.

"Hey."

"Yes?"

"When you were down in the basement, did you ever hear anything? Like . . . like weird noises?"

I look at her chin. Her neck. "No."

"Yeah, I didn't think so. I think I'm just going a little crazy. I've been hear-ing weird noises in the walls. Like something's in there, crawling around. I even thought I heard, like, crying the other day." Another self-conscious laugh. "This house!"

Of course, it's me she's been hearing, crawling around. I'm the one who should be self-conscious. (*Although . . . crying? Have I been crying?*) But self-conscious is something Old Mary would be.

"You're not crazy," I say. "Maybe the house is just haunted."

Impulsively, I move my eyes up to her face. Her skin continues to recede and melt away. Liquefy. Putrefy. It's a horrible sight. But the rage that usually comes with it is muted now. After this morning, I think I'm too exhausted for rage.

"Riiight." She gives me an askance grin with lips that are cracking and dissolving. "I was thinking more like maybe something got caught in a crawl space or something. But. Yeah. Maybe the house is haunted."

I keep looking. Pustules ooze. Sores form like shallow pools of redness. Bone peeks through. Her eyes go milky with cataracts.

Nancy continues, unawares.

"Anyway. I think tomorrow I might get here early to investigate, before I start setting up for the egg hunt. There must be an entrance I don't know about, you know? Maybe an animal got caught and I can save it somehow."

I'm barely listening. A curious thought has occurred to me. What would happen if I just keep staring? I've never tried that before. Old Mary was always too horrified to keep looking. What about New Mary?

I keep my eyes fixed on Nancy. How far will this hallucination go? Will she become a glistening skull? Will bone start to crumble into dust? Just when I feel like I'm on the precipice of an answer—

Nancy turns away from me to set her purse to rights. The moment snaps in two, and I almost lose my balance.

"Maybe," I say. Although whether it's in response to what she said or the strange new idea I have, I'm not sure.

"You're still going to come tomorrow, right?" she asks, hopeful but cautious. Now it's her turn to be afraid to look me in the face. "It would be so great to have you."

"Wouldn't miss it."

Old Mary would've smiled. New Mary turns and leaves.

There's still time, but I'm beginning to feel the weight of everything I need to accomplish pressing down on the diminishing buffer I've got left.

I make it upstairs, mind awhirl with Nadine's curses, my own anxiety about this coming afternoon, and the new addition of what almost just happened in the exam room with Nancy. If I had just been able to keep looking . . . *Then what?*

I'm not entirely sure.

Safely inside my room, I start to unpack my little suitcase for what feels like the hundredth time this month. I'm about to put my remaining Loved Ones out on the dresser when I notice the mirror sitting there. I stop, midaction, deer in headlights.

It's just not fair. Yesterday, I was feeling confident that I could now start looking into that glass and always find a comforting face. Today?

Thinking of how quickly I almost lost consciousness when Nadine yanked that blanket off the mirror in Brenda's room, I slip the case off one of the bed pillows and, tears welling up in my eyes, slip it over the glass. *Soon,* I promise myself. *Soon, we'll have this all figured out.*

It feels like a fool's hope. No, worse: the hope of a pretender.

An imposter.

I don't belong here.

I am not actually related to anyone on the walls of this house. I am related to Nadine. And I will never be free from (*her*) that fact.

"Shut up," I tell myself, as if I were speaking these admonishments out loud.

I unpack and array my Loved Ones on the dresser. There's so few of them now.

"But there are others down the hall, just outside this room. And they're mine, too. Because I belong here."

They stare back at me, silent. They don't need to agree. They look *right* here, and that says more than enough.

I settle myself on top of the bed, the blue book in my hands, and resume my studies.

God, this book sucks. It's practically unreadable.

It's pompous. And lifeless. And declamatory, in that way only theological texts can be.

Phrases repeat and repeat and repeat, bleaching themselves of meaning, contradicting themselves when their orbits intersect.

For, lo, the angel sayeth, "I am the observed of all observers."

And we are all bound together by the great Eye. Ego. The Great I. Let us see through the great Eye. Let us be the true observed of all observers as we hunt for meaning and purgation.

Mortal life is but an act, and actors are the most loathsome creatures.

Azazel demands it. Zepar demands it. The A–Z of the universe.

Pain is the stream, and rivers can be redirected.

There is only the desert. The desert is pain, and what does pain demand but appeasement?

It doesn't help that so many sentences and ideas keep hearkening me back to that vision I had in the crawl space: Damon purposefully writing religious gobbledygook just to irritate his anti-religious father.

For some reason, this all makes my mind keep drifting back to that exam room with Nancy. What *would* have happened if I'd been able to keep staring at her? I don't know why that question is suddenly needling me, but it is.

I should just skip ahead. I just want to know what I'm in for this afternoon. I don't want to look like an idiot—or worse, get myself in trouble with a bunch of zealots. There's got to be a section on, I don't know, holidays or rituals or something, right? Would it have killed you to include an index, Daddy Burton?

There's a knock on the door.

Even though I know I need to keep reading, I jump at the opportunity for distraction.

It's Eleanor. She's standing there looking ever so like a little porcelain statue, her arms clasped behind her back.

"This is so cool!" she chirps. "I've never been up here before. Do you mind if I—?"

"No, come on in."

"I won't stay long, I promise, just . . ." She takes in the room. "Whoa. So this was his room?"

"It was."

"There are so many things I've only just read about up here. Like those portraits all over the place of the Cross ancestors in the hallway. I heard there's even a room where the faces have all been drawn over and—oh!" She points, keeping one hand still behind her back. "Is that the radio he was playing when . . . when they found him?"

"Oh, I guess so." I hadn't really made that connection.

"You must feel really special," she says. "Staying in here."

"I guess so," I say again, stupid as ever.

"What's that?" Now she's looking at the mirror with the pillowcase over it.

"Nothing. It's . . . nothing."

"Oh. Okay." Her brow knits. A glumness overtakes her. The rapid emotional gearshift only teenage girls possess.

Like you're so different these days, Mary?

No, I suppose that's true.

"Is everything . . . ?" I ask.

"I was just thinking about how crazy it is that you're here. I mean, I know, not *crazy*, but. You know what I mean. A week ago, you didn't know *anything* about Damon Cross, and now . . . It's amazing how they've welcomed you in. I honestly didn't think they would."

"Oh." Is she pouting? There's a sharp edge to what she's saying. Is it jealousy?

"I wish I could be there to see your first harvest today. But nooooo. I'm just a stupid kid, I can't handle it. They have no idea what I can handle, you know. No idea what I can do."

She might be young and embittered, but she's also my best chance for advice on this ritual. Maybe she can give me a heads up on what to expect.

"Eleanor," I start to say, and when she looks at me, her eyes suddenly light up.

"Oh, hey! Duh! I almost spaced on why I came up here." She takes her other hand from behind her back and presents to me a rolled-up piece of paper, tied with a red ribbon. "Happy birthday, Mary."

I accept it and unroll it. Only as my fingers recognize the paper as from her sketch pad do I really begin to process what I'm looking at.

It's a portrait of my face. She drew my plain, unremarkable face.

No, *drew* is too pedestrian a word. She captured it. The level of detail is astonishing. It takes my breath away. Tears prickle my eyes.

No one's ever done anything like this before.

No one's ever thought this face was worthy of documentation, let alone effort. Shadows, sharp definitive lines, an artist's skill, spent on . . . me.

And I want to keep looking, but—it's not fair, it's not fair, it's not fair—I can't, the drawing is too good, it's starting to distort and cause me to wobble just like any mirror.

"I hope you like it. It's just a dumb thing I was working on."

"Don't," I manage to say. I swallow. "Don't play it down. It's incredible." So incredible that I can only look at the blank margins around the image.

"Anyway. Maybe we can hang out afterward, and you can tell me how it went today. Tell me all about it."

"Okay," I say. Or think I say. My knees are weak, and I desperately want to sit down.

"I'll get out of your hair." Eleanor heads for the door. Then stops. "Hey, do you think it'd be cool if I poke around for a while? I figure I can't get yelled at for exploring up here as long as you're around."

"Sure, sure," I say.

"Thanks."

I put the drawing down on my night table and start to come back to myself. Before Eleanor disappears, I call her back.

"And, Eleanor?"

"Yeah?" She pokes her perfect, young face back into the room.

"Don't be in such a hurry, okay? The thing about getting old is it happens sooner than you think."

Running out of time.

Need to concentrate.

First, I should put this suitcase away. Everything else of mine seems to fit, but the suitcase is jarring. Transient.

Best place for it: under the bed. I start to slide it under when I notice the book I threw down there yesterday. Knowing I shouldn't, I slide the book out before pushing the suitcase in.

Just one poem. That's all. One poem and I'll get back to work.

I open the book and read the first poem I turn to.

When I was a little girl my uncle
Was a veterinarian
And I was a little girl who loved animals

I had a cat and a dog

And once I asked my uncle
(who was a veterinarian)
Why does my dog love belly rubs
But they make my cat attack?
I showed him scratches up and down my arms.

He said the thing about cats you have to understand
Is they are predator and prey
They can hunt and pounce and kill
But they're small and light and probably
Delicious
So they take some things very
very
seriously

I was a little girl when he said this
But when I became a woman in this world
I understood what he meant.

"Yes," I whisper. *This* I understand. "Oh, Jane."

I wonder if she's still at Nadine's, staring at the sky. I hope reading that poem somehow gave her the boost to embark on some grand ghostly adventure. Far away from me, of course.

Then I remember something else from my visions. Cross wrote down everything about his victims, didn't he? He took diligent notes on all of them, cataloging their lives so he knew just what to say to get past their lonely-woman defenses. I sit back on the bed and start flipping through the blue book again, suddenly rabidly curious what he might have said about Jane.

But there's nothing. I skim quickly, but I don't see mention of a single victim in here. Just more assertions about the mysteries of life and pain and consciousness, with Burton's blathering on *here's what we take this to really mean.*

"Fine. Goddammit. Focus, Mary. You're running out of time."

Yes. I am. I kick Jane's book back under the bed, swing my feet up, and get back to trying to read the blue book more thoroughly.

One more thing catches my eye. I left Eleanor's sketch out on the night table. What am I going to do with *this*? Ugh!

I pull Jane's poems back out. I'm going to fold the drawing in half and stash it in the pages of the book. Before I do that, though, I just want to take one more quick glance at the drawing, just a peek, just to appreciate its skill and—

Someone's knocking on the door.

"Are you in there?"

A woman's voice.

"Hello?" I call back, my voice rusty and sleep-clogged.

"We're going to be starting in about twenty minutes!" the woman calls. A second later, I realize: it's Bonnie.

Twenty minutes?! How is that even possible?!

I'm on the floor. Jane's book is on the floor. Eleanor's drawing is on the floor.

Oh, fuck me.

I passed out. I stared at the drawing and fainted.

Oh, *fuck me.*

I haven't even changed my clothes. I haven't showered. After a moment, I realize, too, that I'm grimy from sweat. I had another hot flash while I was unconscious. The floorboards are damp with condensation.

Fuck me!

I quickly gather some clothes together out of my suitcase and burst out of the room. Bonnie leaps back—she must have been hanging by the door, waiting for my response.

"I just have to use the facilities; I'll be right there!" I call as I speed down the hallway, hoping instinct guides me to a bathroom.

Eventually, it does. I splash water on myself from the sink and give myself as good a cleaning as I can without getting my hair too noticeably wet. It's only as I'm stepping out of my old clothes and into fresh ones that I realize I'm not alone in here.

There's a corpse in the bathtub.

I pay her no mind. Let her watch me. I'm too busy repeating the same mental litany, again and again: *fuck me fuck me fuck me fuck me.*

Once I'm dressed, I go about making sure I haven't left anything important in my old pants. There's some sort of wad in one of the pockets. I pull it out.

Cash. The money from Nancy.

An errant thought:

This is your last chance, Mary.

I have the money to escape. I could run out right now, catch a ride somewhere safe, hop on a plane, and be gone before sunset.

My heart begins to pound heavily in my chest. The hair on the back of my neck, and on my arms, prickles.

I hear a voice in my head from my previous life in New York. Automated, chiming through the subway. *This is the last stop on this train. Everyone please leave the train.*

Even as I think that, there are noises outside. The small bathroom window looks out onto the grounds below, where I can see dozens of people making their way toward the house like ants.

46

Harvest Time

Bonnie walks me down to the second floor. She hooks her arm through mine, chummily, but it feels as if I'm being shackled.

"Isn't it funny how life works out?" she muses girlishly as we walk. "Who would have thought, after everything we went through as kids, that you and I would wind up becoming so close?"

I stop us. "I'm . . . I'm sorry about Carole," I say. I want to add: *I didn't think I actually did anything to her; I thought I only* wanted *to kill you all.*

"Yes, it's very sad," she says, albeit distantly. She gives a strange sigh. It gives me the impression of a woman at a pawn shop selling a beloved ring or packing away photos of a recently deceased loved one. Compartmentalization.

"I remember you were close, even when we were kids," I say.

"Well. We're not kids anymore, are we?" She emits a high, short, almost maniacal laugh. "Besides, Eleanor was right. Carole had no husband, no children. We're not in the habit of making volunteers out of our own, not anymore, but . . . it's not unheard of. There have been times when the harvest was light and we needed to look inward. I'm sure she would have understood. And on the plus side," her tone brightens artificially as we continue walking, "it brought us *you*!"

Volunteers? I have no idea what she means. I distractedly tug my light cardigan out of the way as Bonnie clings closer to me. I'm wearing this cardigan for two reasons: in case I get cold and for its slightly lumpy pockets. There's a Loved One in one of those pockets. Stupid, I know; but I wanted all the extra support I can get.

I open my mouth to ask for clarification, but Bonnie interrupts.

"Oh, by the way." She puts her head closer to mine. "I did a little digging into our records—our community's records, I mean. I can't believe I didn't know about your parents!"

I look at her for a split second before her face begins to do its thing. I manage a raspy, "Huh?"

"Your father," she says. As if I should know these things. "He was listed as one of the flock. I don't know about your mother—I'm sure the registry listing meant to include both of them—but I can't believe you never told me!"

I told my sister to leave this place when all that started happening. But your damn father insisted. Said this was a godly place to raise a family. I wasn't sad when he became a crispy critter.

If I could talk I'd say, I never told you because I didn't know. I'd say maybe my mother wasn't listed because she never fully gave herself over. She was probably just following her husband's wishes. That's what we're taught to do, right, Bonnie? Follow the man? You're doing it; I'm doing it. It's enough to just have a place and to be protected, isn't it? Any collateral suffering is just the price of admission. We are predators, but we are also prey.

All the same, it's a dizzying thought to consider I might have always wound up here eventually. If my parents had lived, I'd probably have been just as zealous as the rest of them.

Maybe that's why I burned the house down before school one morning. If, in fact, I did. Maybe it was my mom who did it instead . . .

The sudden realization that there are things about my life I'll just never, ever know about sets the world spinning, and now I'm the one clutching Bonnie's arm for support.

"Oh," she says, surprised at my grip.

"Bonnie?" I'm surprised to hear myself speak, in hushed tones. "How are you okay with this? With worshipping Damon Cross after what he did to . . . to women like us?"

She blinks at me as if I'd just ask her to name her favorite ancient Greek astronomer.

"Damon Cross was a great man," she says in her upper register. "All great men have their imperfections. Great women learn to accept that, don't you think?" She touches my hand with something that sounds like pity. "You'll understand after the ceremony. Once you've been purged, it's like . . . nothing can ever weigh you down again."

We reach our destination on the second floor.

Before I can gather my faculties, she opens the door, and then the world spins again. I'm staring at myself from across the room.

The room is one giant mirror.

My eyes immediately fall to the floor, where I'm at least able to get a better understanding of what I've actually walked into.

It's a rehearsal room. I remember it from my visions of Damon's childhood. This is a room his father built for his mother, probably to practice dancing and movement. At least one wall is covered in reflective glass so the performers can always see what they're doing.

I turn to flee, ignoring Bonnie's confused squawk, and run straight into a hulking mass. Meaty hands grip my shoulders in a way that's at once loathsome and strangely comforting—because, I realize in an instant, it takes all responsibility off me.

The world spins again, this time because it's me being spun around like a toy and taken back inside the room. The wood floors squeak.

"Me again," a soft, male voice says to me, and I shudder in either disgust or delight. Then I recognize the unmistakable accent. It's the cab driver. "Oh, by the way? I meant to tell you yesterday: consider your tab forgiven." He chuckles, pleased with himself.

If I was hoping to disappear in the crowd, I'm in for disappointment. I can feel eyes on me, on all sides. Even if people aren't looking at me directly, they're looking at me through the mirror. I'm suddenly aware of my stupid clothes. I wish I had some sort of appropriate outfit for the occasion. Then again, what's appropriate? I have no idea what I'm in for. Why didn't I read that damn book? Why did I look at that damn picture?

"Does everyone here know?" I ask the driver, my voice almost a parody of weakness. "About me, I mean?"

"Well, word gets around," he says. "Probably not everyone. Not yet, at least. But . . ."

"Word gets around," I say. And, even as I do, someone reaches out and lightly touches me. Just a graze, but I can tell it's a gesture of reverence.

Like most things in this house, the dimensions of this room are strange. In this case, it's a mostly rectangular room, but it's far longer than it needs to be—especially if it was built for one woman. A combination of the mirror, the crowd, and the room's length gives it an almost nightmarish plasticity, like it stretches on forever. But now we're on the other side of the room and I'm able to at least put my back to the mirror, thank God.

To my right, made indistinct by lights either burned out or turned off, is a blank wall. Across from me is the door to the room and a long, long wall with occasional curtained windows set into it. Far off to my left, the room just extends and extends until it reaches a thick black curtain. What's behind that, God only knows . . . though I expect we'll find out soon enough.

The room is filling up with people. I see familiar faces from the council among the crowd. Mustache. The heavyset man. Chantelle. I see Pepto near the back. He's chugging another small bottle of neon-pink goo. No Anna-Louise. But there's Barb, barely visible due to her short stature. Steve has joined Bonnie.

Maybe it's the flat, dim lighting, or my own panicked imagination, but every face I see looks deranged. People's eyes dart, they lick their lips. No one is as well put together as I thought—hair is askew, clothes are ill fitting. Absurdly, I find myself thinking of Nurse Nancy, no doubt back at her own home right now, preparing a little holiday party for everyone here, just hoping they all get to know each other a bit better. *They're way ahead of you, Nancy.*

Suddenly, someone is in front of me, a thin and ragged young woman whose disarrayed hair and half-lidded eyes make her seem as if she's just rolled out of bed.

"Can I just ask," she's saying to me, somehow both desperate and disconnected, "where is he? What did you do with him?"

A man is pulling her away now. "Come on, Tania, don't."

Tania stays latched on me as best she can, blinking, trying to will herself to be more coherent. She's young, maybe in her early twenties, but grief has stamped decades into her face.

"I just want to know what you did to my boy. I didn't know we were doing children now. I didn't know we'd changed the rules!"

She's pulled back into the crowd before I can tell her that . . . what, that it wasn't me? That I know the rules probably less than she does?

That I don't really belong here?

I reach my hand into my pocket to feel my Loved One for comfort, and—*ouch*!

I quickly pull my hand away, wincing. A little bead of blood has emerged at the tip of my finger. I suck it away.

Don't tell me I did it again.

I carefully reach back into my pocket, feeling around.

I did. Oh, I'm such an idiot. Once again, I meant to bring one of my Loved Ones with me and once again I'm discovering I accidentally brought one of the broken ones instead.

The last time I did this was that night at Eleanor's. The night with Carole.

I sure hope today goes better than that night did.

Suddenly, I find myself desperate to know which Loved One is in my pocket. The shape feels too familiar. I want to check but there are too many eyes on me. But . . . what if it's Constance? No, that's impossible—Constance is lost somewhere in the desert, bloodied and dulled by Carole's face. But what if it *is* Constance? What did I kill Carole with, then? What if I didn't kill Carole at all? What if I didn't do anything they thought I did? What if this has all been a mistake? What if—

I don't really belong here.

I tamp those thoughts down, hard as I can. Like sitting on an overstuffed suitcase.

The room fills even further with people. A trembling eagerness is in the air. Animals about to be fed.

Many are unwashed, with stringy hair and oily skin—have these people always been this filthy? I can even smell the acrid tang of adrenaline and sweat. There are so many familiar faces from the past week and yet they all look wrong together—because they *are* wrong together. I'm looking at a roomful of loners. In a way, that's the thing that unifies them all.

Maybe I do belong here after all.

It's not a comforting thought.

"You came here from the Midwest," I hear myself say to the driver, realizing something. "You weren't born here."

"That's right."

"How did you find out about this place?"

"Online," he says. "You can find all sorts of stuff online."

"Ah." I don't ask for elaboration.

My stomach churns with anxiety. I don't want to be here anymore. I shouldn't be here. I'm about to witness something truly awful. Something so deplorable it necessitated the shutting down of an entire hospital. And it's standing room only.

Just as I think that, my hand goes back to the dangerous, sharp shape of the Loved One in my pocket—*but which one are you?*

We're all broken here, it whispers back.

For a moment, I hear music. Primal. Percussive. My eyes fall on the black curtain again. What's behind it? What's going to happen?

Then I realize there is no music. It's just my heart thudding in my ears.

The curtain stirs, and Burton emerges. He looks flushed, like he's just had a workout. His ginger beard curls underneath two splotchy cheeks.

He looks at the room.

"It's two o'clock," he says. "Let's begin."

47

Curtain Speech

The lights are turned off, but sunlight still comes through the heavily draped window opposite the wall that's curtained off, and it gives everything a sick-from-school feeling. Muted browns and yellows.

The town clumps in front of Burton. There are no hushed murmurs, only the silent assent of acolytes. The flock.

I try to hug the outer edge of the crowd, remain as anonymous as I can. My eyes keep being drawn back toward that curtain at the far end of the room. What's behind it?

After a pregnant pause, Burton begins a speech.

"Family. Fellow seekers. Fellow believers in the Eye."

His whole demeanor has changed. He's no longer the pissy, distracted, small-town doctor. This is his true calling; there's no questioning his comfort and ease. I wonder if medical school was his own father's way of providing cover—the way Damon's father forced Victor into a life of pretense and acceptability so the family would always have a social shield.

"I know you're all eager. I know you're ready. Every year, it's the same. We gather here to cleanse ourselves. To set our spirits free. Restart the clock until, by this exact point next year, we can barely stand it all over again. Some religions have periods of fasting: days, weeks. Ours is the entire year, save this one day. And this year's particularly special. You can feel it, can't you? Fifty years. Fifty years."

Sighs of agreement roll through the crowd.

"At 2:13 p.m., fifty years ago today, Damon Cross became the victim of horrible luck and cruel timing. Sometimes I wonder, if he'd left his room five minutes earlier, or five minutes later, how different would his story be? And yet we can't mourn, because . . . look what he gave us."

More noises of group assent.

"I've been thinking of a word a lot. *Reincarnation*. And why not? It's what we've always been, isn't it? The next incarnation of our prophet. With one small difference. He was just one man. We are *many*."

He's gearing some of his sermon toward me. My face burns.

"I know it's been a rough time, y'all. We have lost some of our own. We have an outsider among us."

The crowd hisses and grumbles. For a heart-stopping moment, I think he's about to loose them all on me, but then he continues, enunciating each letter with hateful relish: "The Eff. Bee. Eyyyye. I think it's pretty understandable we're all a bit skittish when it comes to big-city lawmen. Not just because of what they did to our prophet. But because of what they represent. The Laws of Man. The Laws of the Outside. But we reject man's government, do we not? We reject the Outside!"

The townspeople roar in approval. The entire room shakes.

"That's right. They'd have us stop our traditions. They'd hunt us down, the way they hunted our prophet. The way they hunted our ancestors. They don't know that we have the desert in us! We are tougher than they! We are as myriad as the sand, and you know how sand can get everywhere; well, we are twice as hard to shake! Now, everybody, turn to the wall!"

The shuffle of bodies toward the mirror-wall jostles me. People push and squirm for a position in front of the mirrored side of the room.

It's dark enough that I can get away with looking at my neck, my torso, anywhere but my face. I'm so packed in among people I don't even think I could look to the side and find my Damon reflection for comfort. And still, so many eyes drift toward me, even just for a moment, aware that I'm here. I wish I wasn't on this side of the room. I wish I were at the back of the crowd now.

Burton continues, purring low and sensuously.

"Behold yourselves. Get a good look. *You!* Live in the harshest environment this world knows, and yet you thrive! You have humbled yourself to the great unblinking Eye of the sun and have not burned! For there is the other great Eye, that is the great I, the Ego, the pure self! The observed of all observers! The hunter! For in our humility we are also strong! The desert does not permit weakness, and it does not permit doubt! No guilt, nor shame, nor fear. That is useless baggage, my brothers and sisters! Deadweight! You must be rid of it to survive another year! Purified! And that is what our prophet has left for us—our means for purgation! Our means to *earn* our survival!"

Again, that roar, that straining excitement among the people. And now I start to understand the appeal. The way Burton's father used Cross and Cross's family to unite this schizophrenic community with personal affirmation, with shared purpose, not in spite of their harsh living conditions but because of them.

But then I remember the curtain.

I remember every strange comment made by other townspeople.

I remember the way they all have responded to a murderer in their midst: with almost giddy acceptance. Dread thrums in my chest; my stomach fills with hot, roiling acid.

"The desert is cruel," Burton continues. "The desert is pain. The desert sings to you, and it is a song of sacrifice. It *demands* sacrifice. And we give it willingly."

I barely have time to remember that phrase, *the desert sings to you*—I wrote something like that in my journal, didn't I, when I first arrived here, in the back of that cab—when Burton says:

"As many of you know, we have a special guest with us today. A new member to our flock. It's been so long since we had a new member—Patrick, that was you, wasn't it?"

A man in the crowd calls out with a chuckle, "Long time ago!"

"Long time," Burton agrees. "Membership is pretty exclusive out here. But we saw fit in this case. Why don't you bring her forward?"

As if they'd been waiting for just this moment, I'm suddenly pushed through the crowd toward Burton.

"There she is," he says as I come forward. I stop at the edge of the group. In front of me are just the doctor . . . and the curtain.

Burton checks his watch. It's an expensive-looking watch—way more expensive than anything I've seen on anyone else's wrist.

"It's now 2:10. Our prophet would have been pursued by the police at exactly this moment. Only minutes left to live. But we know he died pure. The way we intend to die pure. Because he taught us how to cleanse our souls. Every year on this day, we honor his lessons . . . and we finish what he started. For him as well as for us."

Finish what he started?

What did he start?

What did—

"I want to thank our harvesters for finding this year's crop of volunteers. I think you'll all agree, they're perfect. Before we get to it, let's take a moment and thank them for what they're about to do for us."

Everyone's heads suddenly bow, and they murmur a staggered, "Thank you."

Meg.

Damon was caught in the act, and the woman's name was Meg. She got away. Damon didn't get to finish what he started with her.

Burton cracks his knuckles, a quick rat-a-tat of unpleasant popping sounds, like dry tinder in a fire. "Okay," he says. His eyes, like everyone else's in this room, shine with a giddiness that would be at home in the eyes of a rabid dog stumbling onto an unguarded baby carriage. "Here we go."

The crowd begins to applaud. A man or two hoot in appreciation.

The curtain is pulled.

It's so very much like my dream.

My rational brain can see all the ways it's not, but none of that matters. It's enough of a parallel that my breath is gone.

There's a light on. A spotlight. White and insistent. And caught in its glare are three women.

They aren't crowded together in the center—one is more prominently displayed in the light, and the other two are in the periphery toward the back—however, they all appear to be in similar circumstances. They're each stripped nude, and they sit, limply, on the edge of what I recognize quickly as examining tables.

No, *sitting* is not entirely accurate—they look *sat*. Like rag dolls, plopped down definitively and arranged. The tables' backs are positioned all the way up, and the two women in the shadows are leaning against them.

Gravity and her own quavering balance hold the third, more prominent woman up without aid. Her hands hang between her thighs. Her spine curves over itself so that her breasts hang almost onto her lap.

On the outer sides of all three sets of legs, thin, spindly shapes extend from their respective tables. Stirrups.

I see why they would've wanted to turn the Cross House into a hospital. All sorts of equipment, no questions asked.

Each woman's head is draped in a pillowcase.

To the front woman's left, my right, is another table, smaller and simpler. There's an object on it I can't quite make out from here.

The single most disconcerting detail of the whole scene is the simplest.

Underneath everything is a thick plastic tarp covering the floor. For spills.

"Nicholas," Burton says, "you harvested this volunteer. Tell us, Nicholas: Is anyone missing her back home?"

A voice in the crowd: "No."

The exchange is perfunctory, like an oath sworn in court.

"Excellent," Burton says. "Everyone will get their turn with the volunteer to confess and to purge."

Everyone?! There's at least fifty people here. Maybe seventy-five. Hell, there could be over a hundred—

"And I want to remind you all that the two in the back are simply spares in case our main volunteer isn't able to make it through the ceremony. We want to return them to their hospital rooms where we can finish waiting to make sure no one is missing them, if at all possible. We don't want a repeat of three years ago, *Derek*."

Nervous laughter rolls through the crowd. When the curtain had been opened, an appreciative silence had fallen over everyone. Now, there's a palpable, straining, itchy eagerness bubbling up. They're all ready to begin.

"Before that, though," Burton continues.

And then he pushes me forward to join the women in the spotlight.

There are murmurs in the disorienting darkness. *What is she doing? Why does she get to go first?* Not everyone in the crowd is pleased with my skipping the line, no matter how against my will it was.

Burton holds his hands up.

"I know, I know. It's not normal to let the newbie go first. But some of you know why our guest is so special, yes?" His words drip with viscous Goodness. "We've been looking forward to what she has to say—we think she might have some great insight into our traditions. The council saw one hell of a show last night."

The spotlight is too bright for me to see much of the crowd, but I see a blob where I knew Barb to be previously standing, and it's nodding its blobby head. I understand what they're doing with razor-sharp clarity. I'm about to either prove my worth . . . or screw up in the most public way possible and earn pariah status from here on out.

Too bad I never read the book I was supposed to. I don't know what I'm even supposed to have insights *about*.

From the mirror, a disembodied whisper:

It's okay, you'll be safe, I'm here.

Just go along.

Don't. Ruin. This.

Now that I'm closer, I take a few steps toward the small side table to get a better look at the item there. It's a long, thin cactus branch, about eight inches from end to end. Like an ocotillo, with thick, dreadfully sharp thorns. Those thorns cover almost all the branch, except for a few inches toward one end of it, where it's clearly been artificially sanded down. A handle. It almost looks like some sort of . . . examining wand.

"Well," Burton purrs. "Go on."

A voice that sounds suspiciously like Barb's from the crowd: "Don't you know what to do?"

My mouth is uncomfortably dry as I pick up the spiked, brutal-looking wand.

"Tell your sins to the cactus!" someone yells impatiently, to which Burton yells, "Quiet!"

"I tell my sins . . . to this?" I ask stupidly.

"You have much to atone for," Burton says. "We all do, of course. But . . . Carole? Wallace? You need to be purged. You need to be cleansed. We are only granted survival in the desert if we are pure. The desert is cruel, and it demands purgation."

I look at the hooded woman. It's all beginning to click into place. Elias's teachings. Damon's prophecies. "She is the sacrificial animal."

"She has served her use," Burton replies.

The crowd sighs in echo: "She has served her use!"

"No longer the girl, no longer the lover, no longer the mother. Her moon has moved, and this is her final gift to us!"

I put my sins into the cactus, and then I put the cactus . . .

The stirrups.

The cactus.

My God.

We put our pain into her and we are purged," a woman's voice calls; I think it's Bonnie. "We are purified!"

"Then we take her face," Burton says. "We preserve her as thanks for her volunteering to take our pain from us."

"Volunteering?" I ask, although I can barely hear myself.

"By being what she is," Burton replies with the most insidious smile I've ever seen. "This is what our prophet taught us. This is why our people have survived—which your recklessness has threatened. So confess!"

"Confess!" Another voice in the crowd, straining and whiny. "And then we can confess, too!"

For a moment, I look into the audience and am horrified to see so many people there. It's a wall of leering, hungry, demonic faces. More than a congregation; it's an army. Then I understand it's just the reflection, making the crowd seem bigger than it is.

The mirror is a lie.

I repeat that in my mind. *The mirror is a lie.* There's something incredibly important to this revelation. *The mirror is a lie.* Something I've been waiting to finally understand. *The mirror—*

No time to chase the thought now, though. The grunting, straining energy of the crowd intensifies, and I recognize some of it's for me now, to see what I'm going to do next. These people want to be led. They want someone to justify, contextualize, their sickest urges. Some of the men have their hands down their pants, playing with themselves. Some of the women do, too. They have tears rolling down their cheeks—women! Women participating in this? Condoning this? How broken do these people need to be to need something like *this*? But even as I think that, I feel the iron tug of (*go along go along don't you want to belong somewhere don't you want to have a home*) because nothing feels safer than when someone *else* is the victim; especially when the next victim could always be you. The only way to prove you haven't *served your use* is to endeavor to stay as useful as possible, even to a system that hates you. Oh God, do I understand that.

No. Old Mary understood that.

New Mary feels a chilly anger begin to fall over her.

"Why is she wearing this now?" I ask, pointing to her hood. "The hood happens afterward."

Burton blinks in a way that reminds me of his reaction to the out-of-place radio in Damon's room.

"It's simply to prevent any harm from coming to her face," he says. An obvious half-truth. I bet it's so they don't have to look their victims in the eyes.

"And why isn't she moving?"

Barb answers this time, apparently deciding Burton needs help. "We give her a mixture of sedatives. To make it easier f—"

"It's not supposed to be easy." I surprise even myself. *"What you're doing is horrible, and it should be hard."* A brief rattle of laughter follows up from my throat, and I feel more laughs ready to come and join the fun. I try to swallow them back. Now's not the time.

The crowd has gone still and stony. I might have just made a big mistake.

What are you doing?! a voice hisses. *Why are you being so stupid?!*

I recognize it immediately as my great, reprimanding, always hateful and demeaning undervoice . . . but this time it's coming from the mirror. With awful clarity, I realize it's Damon's voice I'm hearing. Have they always been the same? Is that why he always sounded so familiar?

Before I can pursue this thought, I hear yet *another* familiar voice. This one, coming out of my own mouth.

"I need to see her face," I say. "I'm taking her hood off."

I didn't mean to say that. A flush rises to my cheeks. I didn't mean to say that!

Oh God, I realize. *That's not* me *talking.*

Burton is just as surprised as I am. "But—"

"I'm taking it off." Panic grips me. What is happening to me? "Trust me," my mouth says to Burton while I clamor internally for control. "I just need to see her face, and then we can proceed."

My hand—also out of my control—pulls the hood off the woman and drops it to the floor.

"What's her name?" I ask.

Burton: "Why does that—"

But another voice from the crowd answers, "Dana." Interesting. They're starting to ignore Burton. They're starting to listen to me.

Not me! This isn't me! I'm being controlled!

"Hello, Dana," I say, lifting the woman's head up to look at me. Her eyes flutter. Her mouth chews up and down almost imperceptibly with the memory of speech. A line of spittle hangs down from her lips to the speck-led skin between her breasts.

She's probably in her early fifties. Time has done some stamping on her slightly heavyset face. I have a sudden, strangely dizzying feeling I've seen her before. Either at the supermarket or walking around town while I was running errands; I've seen her before and not even noticed.

Behind me, in the darkness, Burton is not happy. "The only name we concern ourselves with is Azazel!" It sounds like he's trying to whip up the crowd. "The only name we concern ourselves with is Zepar!"

I ignore him. I'm too busy trying to take my hands away from Dana's head, to stop looking at her. I can't. I can't get my hands, my neck, my eyes to obey. The only other time I've experienced something remotely like this was when I felt that strange, alien sensation of writing in my journal with-out being aware of what I was . . .

Understanding like a bomb blast: Damon is doing this. He *wants* me looking at this woman. Because . . . when I look at a woman like Dana . . . her face begins to change, and so do I.

Right on cue, all the usual feelings flood me as I watch Dana's face con-tort and dissemble. The rage, the disgust, the eagerness to destroy her. And maybe there's even a little relief at just not having to think anymore.

Her face puffs and splits. Thick, viscous slime erupts from breaking pus-tules. Her dull cow eyes go milky with cataracts, and the bags underneath sag and rip. She makes me want to fucking puke. She's just like mommy.

She *does* deserve this.

She *did* volunteer for this.

She *has* served her use.

Yes.

In a flash, I see myself going through with it. Whispering all my pain and fear and guilt into that cactus and giving it to her, putting it into her, in and out, in and out, rip, tear, hearing her scream with the righteous torture of it all, screaming along with her, because it's so much and it hurts, it all hurts, pain is meant to hurt and hearing someone else scream with *my* pain is the most validating thing in the world, it says I'm right to hurt, it says I'm seen, it says I'm not invisible, and then that pain would finally be out of me, even for a moment, I'd be cleansed, ready to collect it all over again like the desert drinking in all the rainwater it can get in one magnificent deluge. Yes, thank God! And then afterward, I can show them how I take a face! Because I have talent! I'm special! I can be seen and heard and goddamn respected and then—

The vision starts to fade away.

What?! No no no no!

It's like a cramp letting go: the distortions and decompositions lose their vividness. Same with the attendant anger I feel. That moment with Nancy in the exam room earlier today comes back to me. I'd had that sudden, almost revelatory idea: What would happen if I just kept looking? What would happen if, for once, I wasn't too scared to keep staring? Nancy had turned away before I could really find out, but now it seems like I'm getting an answer. Damon got too caught up in the fantasy and left me staring at her too long.

Dana's rotten corpse face simply unveils, fades into, gives way to, the face she always had. More rational thought begins to gain purchase inside me again.

All I ever had to do was not look away. How simple. How absurdly simple! Mary, you absolute dummy!

Burton, meanwhile, continues thundering biblical names. Angels! Demons! He's giving his little speech about great men and the desert: Jesus, Moses, Joseph Smith, Muhammad! The juxtaposition is too much. The giggling starts up again in the back of my throat. And this time, I'm too exhausted to stop it.

Oh no; this is the worst time for a giggle fit.

That's very true, and thus I begin to giggle even harder.

Dana's eyes flicker with the dulled understanding that something is happening in front of her. Oh, Dana, you have no idea.

A fiery sermon of my own swirls and forms in my brain.

So many things I want to say to this pathetic little gathering. You're all a bunch of fakes! You're all playacting, just like Daddy, just like all of them! Damon Cross didn't believe in any of this! He was a sad, horrible, woman-hating creep—the kind podcast hosts like to laugh about because he's such a cliché! He never had visions, there's no greater purpose to what he did! And none of your stupid goddamn religion makes sense! It's all over the place, because it's just an excuse to do awful things! You can't be saved and you can't be purged—you're all just as pathetic and scared as your phony little savior!

I imagine myself saying all this in my little, usually ignorable voice, my brow fixed and serious, gesturing righteously, and now the giggles metastasize into full-on laughs. I clamp a hand over my mouth, but they don't stop. I feel tears pouring out of my bulging eyes. Something inside me is breaking, and maybe it will be whole again afterward, but for the moment, it is a sharp rending, a resounding severance, and the noise it makes as it cracks is *hahahahahaha*!

Then a voice—I think it's Barb—screams, *"Stop laughing, you fucking bitch!"*

I laugh even harder, blinking away tears just in time to see Dr. Burton hurtling toward me.

It all happens very quickly. And yet there's an excruciating clarity, like reading a flip-book page by page.

Burton reaches for me. I know he's going to grab me hard, maybe even choke me. I reach into my cardigan pocket, pull out my Loved One, and swing out with the sharp end like a cat's claw.

I realize in a flash that it's not Constance—it's Cynthia, the Goose Girl. My first ever Loved One. The porcelain tip of the Goose Girl's broken body sinks deeply into Burton's palm. I feel the vibration of its impact all the way up to my shoulder. Then I *pull*.

The figurine rips through Burton's palm, slicing tendons and muscle and all sorts of things that Burton probably knows the names of, until the razor-sharp porcelain edge pops back out again between his middle and pointer fingers. His middle two fingers sag forward like marionettes whose strings have been cut.

I do this. Me. No one else. I have control again.

Then, while Burton is paused in agony, I reach out and grab the cactus branch off its table and swing it like a club, like a fucking aluminum baseball bat, into his face. *This is for you, Anna-Louise,* I think wildly as I watch a cactus thorn disappear into the soft flesh around Burton's left eye. I let go of the cactus, and it stays there, quivering as he moves.

Dana has been sitting, slumped and unresponsive, between us. Glancing quickly at her, I have time for one more instant underthought:

Slash her throat put her out of her misery kill the useless cow.

But I ignore it. If today is a day for history to repeat itself, time for me to make like Damon Cross and run the fuck away.

48

Escape Plan

I have to move fast.

A thousand buried memories jam their hands out of the earth, reaching for me, moments when teachers, my parents, Aunt Nadine, an endless parade told me to shut up, go along to get along, be good, be good, be *Good*—and I'm still laughing despite of the chaos I've undoubtedly just unleashed on myself.

Mary what have you done what have you DONE

I can escape it. I just have to move fast.

My plan: gather my Loved Ones and get the fuck out of Dodge. Hitchhike if I can. If no one stops to pick me up, I'll just keep walking, first to Socorro or whatever town is closest, where I'll hire a car to take me to the nearest airport. If I have enough money, I'll fly back home. If I don't, I'll fly somewhere random and cheap. I'll keep moving. I'll find a way. That's what I've always done. They might come after me. They might send someone, or someones, to get me, but I kind of doubt it. I think they'll be glad to have me out of their hair. I think they value their privacy more than they'd want revenge—and it's not like I'm innocent either, so I wouldn't call the authorities. All I need to do is get far enough beyond their reach. Just me and my Loved Ones, we'll be okay.

And do I even need them?

That thought is so blasphemous it literally stops me in my tracks as I open up a panel to the crawl space.

Leave the statues. Going back for them is a waste of time. It's not like I *need* them. All they do is remind me that I need to be—

"Of course I need them," I hiss at myself. "They're a part of who I am. Maybe the only part left."

Before I can give myself an opportunity to point out how stupid that is, I slip into the crawl space, and the darkness takes my thoughts away.

I make it a few feet before I run into a ghost—*no, a Fury,* I remind myself. She blocks my path. I squeeze my eyes shut, take a moment to convince myself she's not there. Then scooch past her, scraping myself against the wooden walls.

I round a corner.

Another one. Standing in the way. *Nope, she's not, not there, there's nothing there.*

I'm about to push past when she does something I can't ignore. She raises a finger and points right at me.

The gesture sends a shiver through me. And, eeriness aside, it also makes it much harder to get past her now. Walking toward her means walking toward that razored finger—practically *into* it. How am I going to pretend it's not there, perilously at eye level?

"I'm sorry." My voice is a dry, husked whisper. "I need to leave. Please, just let me go past."

The finger remains.

"Please. I . . . I don't want to get involved or cause trouble. I'm sorry for everything I've done so far. I just need to get out of here. I don't have time."

The finger remains. Red. Glistening. A deadly, unmistakable edge. I can remember the awful slicing sounds as Nadine's dog was turned into so much bloody confetti.

"Do you . . . want me to go that way?"

Her bloody cowl nods.

What choice do I have? At least I'm in my safe, secret place. The cultists aren't going to follow me in here. Maybe I have a little more time than I think. I turn around in the direction she's pointing.

"Okay. But please. We have to be quick."

With a hair-ruffling whoosh of freezing air and a faintly astringent smell, almost like bleach and salt and tears, she's suddenly in front of me.

I have to run to keep up with her. My cares are momentarily forgotten in the exhilaration of palms slapping against the wood, splinters and slivers biting into my skin. Don't care. Don't even care about the dust and grit in my throat, or the murderers searching for me on the other side of these walls.

Once again, I'm Tarzan flying on vines. I could trip on a beam or brain myself with a pipe or run straight into an exposed nail—it's so very pitch-black here—but I follow the specter/revenant/Fury/woman in front of me and now we're stopping, and I've somehow made it in one piece.

I know where we are.

I can't see anything, but I feel this house, its geography, in my bones. I've been in this exact spot before. When Victor first took me through the crawl space and then stopped, rattled a doorknob, and muttered that he always forgot this door was here. *I* haven't forgotten. Just as I know that when I reach out and try the knob to the secret door in front of me, it will be locked.

"I don't have a key, I'm sorry," I tell the Fury. I turn around and realize several more of her kind have followed us. Another shiver rolls through me. *Ignore them, ignore them.*

The ghost-not-ghost is now in front of the door. She makes something of a peace sign with two bleeding talons and then points the tips right at me. At my eyes. *Watch me,* the gesture says. Then she inserts a talon from her other hand into the lock under the doorknob. I hear the metal scraped by the spectral claw, and the uncanny sound makes me want to scream. It's like bone and teeth and steel and something utterly unplaceable and wrong. My shoulders lurch in a deep, desperate shrug.

It doesn't work. Not right away. But I remember Nadine trying to knock that book off the shelf. It takes practice. This Fury needs me, needs my attention. She's never been able to attempt this before.

"It's okay," I tell her, still wincing at the noise. "I'm watching. I see you."

Soon, the sound of a latch letting go echoes through the crawl space like a gunshot. The draped head swivels toward me as if in proud astonishment. It worked.

"Well, you ladies are just full of surprises."

49

The Secret Room

The door creaks open into even more darkness. What a strange sensation, hearing nothing open into more nothing. Cooler air sighs toward me.

We step into the invisible room, and my shoes connect with finished flooring. From the sound alone, I can tell we're no longer in cramped passageways between walls, we're in an actual room, one that must have been sectioned off, secreted away, during the construction of the building. A hidden sanctuary within the walls.

"Is there a light?" I ask the dead woman next to me, but even as I ask it, my hand instinctively moves toward a switch.

A bare, yellow bulb frizzes to life.

At first, it's like I've just found my way back to the basement storage room. The featureless sides of a half dozen bookcase-like structures face me. Compact shelving units, all neatly closed up. But in a corner of the room is a large antique desk with a tall hutch. The hutch is stuffed with papers; organized chaos. On the flat surface of the desk are two books.

I don't recognize the book on the left. It's old and incredibly well-read. But the second book is certainly recognizable.

It's my journal.

Someone was doing side-by-side comparisons of these two books. The older book is soft and beaten in the way only a book that has been pored over and over and over again can be. It's sacred in its worn-out-ness. My journal is more like a dissected specimen. Spine broken to splay open. Yellow sticky tabs and Post-its festooned in its guts. A notepad to the right for observations and thoughts.

I get closer for a better look.

The first page of my journal is the first page to have a yellow tab jutting out. "DISCREPANCY" is written on the tab in outraged, accusatory script.

I don't know that I've ever seen a written word be so abrupt and *offended* before. The Mary I was even a day ago would have probably looked at all the DISCREPANCIES here and blushed like a third-degree sunburn. Like she'd done something wrong. New me chuckles.

"Well, excuse me," I say.

There are also huge chunks of pages without any DISCREPANCIES, and that makes me smile, as well, because I can picture Burton sitting here, getting increasingly agitated over the proof, the goddamn inexplicable proof, clinging desperately to every DISCREPANCY just because it makes him feel a little better, a little more secure and Superior, that life raft on which so many men's identities float.

The look on his face and the rip of his skin as I tore through his palm, that was a DISCREPANCY, I bet.

I flip through, curious what specifically of mine has been flagged.

I'm so giddy. I need to focus.

Yes, focus. If my journal is down here, that means they have access to this room. Burton had my journal the other day—he's been down here very recently. They could check this area any minute.

I grab my journal—feeling very possessive of it all of a sudden—and make to head back out into the crawl space.

The dead women prevent me. They're crowded in the doorway. The one in front points behind me. The compact shelving.

"I have to hurry," I start to plead, but she points again: I took you here for *this*.

I quickly scan the room for the controls of the compact shelving. As soon as I find them, the outermost shelf rumbles to life and separates itself from the other units. Flickering fluorescent lights activate above, motion-sensored.

They make the contents of the shelving unit that much more ghoulish and wrong.

Glass display cases. Each one with a thin, leathery oval propped up inside. At first, I think they're maybe organized by color or texture, but no. It's a chronology. The faces simply get clearer, less ragged, less leathery as they proceed from the bottom up.

"Oh my God," I whisper. "He kept them. *They* kept them."

The ones farther into the shelving must look completely recognizable. Because he got better and better and better. Practice makes perfect.

Another ghost woman in the doorway rasps an unintelligible noise. I turn to see her pointing to the desk again. This time, to the pages filling the hutch.

I tear myself away from the display, pull some pages out from the hutch, riffle through them.

"Sylvia Morrison. 51. Likes needlepoint. Reads science fiction novels. Talks with her invalid mother in New Jersey every week. Study up on Asimov, Bradbury, Simack (sp?). Brown hair, stringy, needs dye job, chin work, disgusting dumb bitch needs dumb stories."

"Bethany Carville. 44. Wanted to be a chef. Divorcée. Bad divorce. Lost friends and family. Cheated on husband. Always felt guilty. Needs time to process and be alone. Will respond well to chance to cook for somebody. Put on a lot of weight recently fat whore."

"Donna Brighton. 48. Studied Shakespeare. Wants to recite it to anyone who's in the room. Will take any goddamn opportunity. Wanted to be an actor (fucking fake). Arms too thick. Moved to Cottonwood to find herself. Estranged from daughter."

"Allison Jennings. Won't tell me exact age. Probably 50. Raises dogs. Some professional contacts, must be careful, see how long she goes between contacting them. Had a baby who died of crib death. Boo-hoo. Always wanted to visit Paris—make her jealous, convince her I'll take her there. Too thin. Bad smell. CAN'T STAND THOSE WRINKLED WET FUCKING EYES FUCKING FARM ANIMAL."

The way the handwriting changes, from steady print to jagged, angry scrawl. Even the texture on the paper, you can see he pressed his pen down harder when he was writing—no, overtaken by—the things he didn't like. Like two distinct personalities there on the page.

Unable to help myself, I keep searching for someone specific. I find her a few handfuls of pages later.

"Jane Mayhew. 52. Works at the court in Cottonwood. Writes poetry. Nothing special, about feelings she knows very little about. Study up on contemporary poets to have something to talk about. Grew up on a ranch. Wants to own another one. Proud she's all alone, no family. Orphan. Fucking know-it-all cunt, smug, smug, smug, self-centered. Pathetic poems about her her her, wrinkled witch."

He wrote it all down.

He took notes on all of them.

They all existed. They all *were*. Had names, plans, dreams, and he wrote them all down, but no one thought it was worth remembering, not even the assholes who worship what he did to them.

The hatred for these women practically burns off the page.

I can't help but imagine how my own biography would look among these.

"Mary Mudgett. 50. Just got by. Only interesting thing about her happened before she was born. Yet still an overinflated sense of importance. Asks too many questions. Dried up like a corpse left in the sun. Can't even look in the goddamn mirror, no wonder no one wants to be around her."

But then, again, I find myself thinking of the mirrored wall. The way the flock convinced itself there were so many of them. That phrase: *the mirror is a lie . . .*

"I have to get out of here. There's no time." Still looking at the desk, I speak over my shoulder to the other occupants in the room. "You led me here for a reason, didn't you? You needed me to watch you so you could come in here . . . but you also want me to know all this. Why? What do you want me to do with—?"

I've turned around to ask them, but there's no chance for an answer. Can't even finish the question, because in an instant, the doorway Furies suddenly burst apart like images projected onto mist, and an insane and rageful Dr. Burton barges into the room, hands reaching forward, grabbing me by the throat and plunging a giant syringe into my—

50

Ucking Itch

Darkness.

Familiar darkness. All encompassing.

Hunter's darkness.

Hunger's darkness.

He's coming.

Spotlight hits the black, but this time, I understand: it's not a spotlight. It's never been a spotlight. It's the moon. The moon shining like a gunshot hole through perfectly black cloth.

No victim this time. The light illuminates no one but itself.

Then the moon moves.

Lifts. Like a lid. Like a trapdoor being pushed from the other side. A single segmented leg, capped by a clawed paw, emerges, searching. The claw scrapes against the black, and I hear that horrible uncanny noise of the Fury's talon scratching inside the door lock again, I never want to hear that sound, not even in dreams, and in my flinching, that claw is somehow able to sneak around my ankle. I'm knocked down and pulled into the space behind the moontrap.

Falling.

I land on the hideous, hard back of a giant ant, and now we're burrowing down into the dark, the moon-lid getting farther and farther away.

The sound of digging is unbearably loud, an audible itch that makes me cringe and want to curl up into myself, as if that will somehow protect me, but I'm entirely naked and exposed, and we keep digging until we hit water, the deepest, darkest water where impossible fish have see-through heads and glowing fangs. At some point, the ant's carapace must have also become see-through, turned into a submarine even, because a voice comes to me, muffled, outside glass.

Itch
I do; I itch so badly.
Ucking itch
What?
Crazy fucking bitch.

"You crazy fucking bitch. My father helped rebuild that house. Did you really think we didn't know about the passageways?"

I open my eyes to blinding brightness. Blink. Blink. Everything hurts. What happened, what did they do to—

"You awake now? Look what you did to my fucking hand."

A tremendous, world-echoing *tonk*. Again, that feeling of being in a submarine, only now I'm being attacked by a giant squid like in that old movie. But I'm not in a submarine. My chin rests on hard, dry dirt. And hot sunlight is beaming down on my face. And it's not a squid attacking—although for a moment my disoriented brain still insists the red tendril shape close to my eyes is some sort of sea creature. *This has happened before; I thought this before and it wasn't a sea creature, it turned out to be—*

A hand. The red thing is a hand. Palm out, like a crossing guard telling me to stop. Only this particular crossing guard suffered a massive slash across their palm, and the blood has painted their hand the color of a stop sign.

Directly behind the hand is Burton, one eye covered in gauze wrapped around his head. He's kneeling but somehow looms over me. He looks gigantic.

Where am I? How did I get to be so small? It's like I've been shrunk down to the size of a Loved One—a thought that's so fucking insane I almost start giggling again until I start to realize I can't move. Have I been paralyzed? No, I can still move my neck. I can barely tilt my head down a little, up a little more, and I can swivel my neck left and right. But it's like my shoulders, my arms, have been dipped in concrete. I can *feel* everything, down to my toes, but when I try to move—

I haven't been shrunk. I haven't been paralyzed.

Have I been decapitated? They say the brain stays aware after decapitation for a long time and maybe—

No.

I've been buried.

All the way up to my chin. The yellow-brown dirt of the desert stretches out from the bottom of my peripheral vision to as far as my limited field of vision can see.

"We've never done this to a living body before," another voice says. A woman. Barb. "It might not be great for your skin. But we'll take what we can get."

"It's going to be fine." Burton pulls his hand away, and the bloody ghost of a handprint floats in the air even after he stands up.

I can barely strain my neck to look up at his full height. Besides the bloody hand, particles float around me. Nicks and scuffs caught frozen in midair. What is happening? It's like I'm surrounded by a force field.

"Not that she cares, the heretical cunt," Burton continues. I try to look up at him, but the effort is too great. He's happy to lecture me anyway. "Damon Cross used to leave his skins out in the sun to cure. Not for long, just a day or two to dry them out and make them more durable. We improved his method. We cure with the sun *before* removing the skin. I'm more confident in my scalpel skills than Damon. He was more eager to strip the face immediately. Hey. You probably noticed this, too."

He picks up a handful of sand from the ground and throws it at my face. I flinch, but the sand doesn't hit me. It clatters off the sort-of-invisible barrier on which the bloody handprint is floating.

"Polycarbonate double-layer glaze," he says. "Greenhouse glass. See, this uses the humidity trapped inside to help the skin lift off the bone, while also better maintaining its shape. By the time we peel your stupid fucking cunty face off, it'll be more like a plaster mask coming off instead of some old deli meat."

"Plus it keeps any nasty critters from getting the goods," Barb says.

"The top layer, too—you probably can't see—but it's Fresnel glass. Like they use in spotlights. Directs the sunbeams more efficiently. And the back is coated in reflexive aluminum. It's a pretty brilliant contraption, if I do say so myself."

"Guess who designed it," Barb says, an audible eye roll.

"Normally, we don't bury the body like this. We'll just decapitate and then cremate the unnecessary remains. We don't have that weird compulsion Cross had to stash bodies everywhere, like the fucking Easter Bunny.

Another dumb thing he did that led to him getting caught, right? I think in a lot of ways he actually wasn't that bright."

"What—?" I'm hearing all he's saying, but I'm not quite processing it. "Why—?"

"Are you wondering why we're burying you? Is that what your dumb-cow expression's about? Well, it's because I want you to suffer."

He shoves his wounded hand against the glass again, making the blood-stain larger. He growls at the pain, which only makes him angrier.

"I might never get to perform surgery again after what you did. Your face might be the last one I get to take, so I want it to be fucking stamped with pain. I want it to advertise your slow, painful death like a goddamn billboard. I want people to look at it and say, 'Jesus, what did you do to *her*?'"

The pain in his palm gets to be too great, and he takes it away. Through the bloody film, I see him pull out a bottle of hand sanitizer, pour it onto his fingers, and then massage it into the wound. He hisses in agony, making a show out of it like a Real Tough Guy. Then he pulls a cloth bandage from his back pocket and wraps it up.

"What about the rest of the flock?" I ask. "Won't they be angry about what you're doing?"

"I can't hear you, you dumb bitch."

Barb can, for some reason. "She asked if the others will be angry."

Burton laughs. He laughs and laughs—actual, real laughter. He looks at Barb, then back at me, before getting all the way down on his hands and knees, using the heel of his hand to keep his injured palm off the ground, then onto his chest, into the dirt, so he can have a private moment face-to-face with me. His face fills my vision.

"I'm gonna let you in on a little secret." His voice is a gossipy, slumber party secret purr. "See, the thing you gotta understand about us is only some of us have any sort of spiritual connection to the great teachings of our dear boy, Damon Cross. Half of us think this reincarnation bullshit is a joke. Hell, a whole lot of us don't give one shit about any of the spiritual mumbo jumbo that gets thrown around. We just enjoy the *work*, if you get my meaning. Maybe a little too much, who knows? It's that good old pioneer spirit: people coming from all over the country to this place because they can do things they've always wanted to do without getting harassed by the law. By outsiders. See"—he gets a little more comfy—"you've gotta understand something. Damon Cross? Wasn't shit. He wasn't a great man. You know who was? My father. My father, who took all of Cross's bullshit and turned it into a *religion*. Who knew the hicks and rubes in this town would make him king as long as he gave them permission to blow off a little steam. That's *my* legacy. You ask me if I'm a *real* doctor? If the Cross House is a *real* hospital? It is, but fuck all that. What you really tried to mess with? Is a king."

He grimaces at dirt getting in his mouth and spits a large, wet glob— thankfully off to the side and not right at me.

"As for the rest of the town? The ones who *really* believe, the ones who for some reason think you're remotely special?" He steals a look at Barb, then comes back to our secret little chat. "Well, they can be convinced of all sorts of stuff, can't they? Maybe we'll go and find a newborn baby we can actually train and pretend like it's you again. Or maybe we'll say your spirit entered a potato. Or a pencil. Or maybe—maybe we'll just each take turns wearing your face and that'll be good enough."

"William," Barb calls from where she's standing. "Let's get out of here, please."

"Barb's got the FBI on her mind," Burton tells me. "Another thing we have you to thank for. But we'll be all right. We know how to keep a low profile and wait out the storm. And then we'll saw your head off and leave your body in the dirt where no one will find it for a hundred fucking years."

He rises and brushes himself off.

Standing above me—lording above me, he'd probably like to think—he chuckles. Like most men, he can't resist one final word too many.

"Oh! You wanna know something funny? It was gonna be your aunt this year. We'd already been planning on harvesting her after her daughter left town, and then you showed up and were just the *perfect* addition. We were so excited to have a twofer. You're everything Damon Cross ever wanted in a sacrificial offering. Reincarnation might be bullshit, but let's chalk up a win for fate, huh? Ha! Think about that during your slow, agonizing death, 'kay?"

"William, please!" Barb calls again.

Suddenly, I'm screaming. Deep, rageful, from the bottom of my lungs, which are so buried that it's like my howls are coming from the depths of the earth itself.

"I'll fucking gut you! You fucking dare do this to me. I will come find you and I

will destroy you, you pathetic fake. You coward. You will know nothing but pain and misery. I will carve you down to your fucking soul!"

He responds with a smile and a shrug, cupping one ear with his uninjured hand. "Sorry, that glass is kinda thick. Can't really understand what you're saying."

There's a small, exotically shaped car a few dozen yards away. I assume it's Burton's because it screams Mediocre Man Status Symbol. They both head for it.

Before they get in, Burton stops and shouts, "And happy birthday!" Then they get in and, with a puff of dirt and a roar of the engine, they peel away into the featureless expanse.

I scream and twist and thrash for a while after they're gone. If anyone could pull themselves out of the ground by the sheer force of anger, it's me. Because it's not just me. It's *him,* too. Damon. I can feel it inside me, his absolute outrage at being forced to die like this and—

No, fuck that, I don't need his rage, my rage is enough, it is complete and total on its own.

Eventually, though, even that rage must pass. It burns away. The desert burns all away, and I'm left with a full-body throb from my inability to move, to vent this energy. It's a horrible feeling. Dull and pulsing like a toothache. I cry for a little while. More moisture gone. My tears dry and my face itches in their wake. I try blowing on my cheeks. It doesn't work.

It's growing unbearably hot.

Or rather—I'm not feeling *hot,* in fact my body is quite cold. I'm feeling *heat.*

The top of my head is burning under the concentrated heat of sunlight through glass.

Here's that spotlight I ordered.

Now that Burton and Barb are gone, at least I have a more unobstructed view of where I am.

Nowhere.

I'm nowhere. I'm in the middle of the desert. There's no telling where exactly I am. I'm where specification disappears and the only definition is here. Nothing but mountain and sky and brush.

And sun.

And sweat.

And an itch.

A bead of sweat rolls down behind my ear. And now another itch perks up, this time in my scalp. The two itches sing together in harmony.

Scratch me, scratch me, scratch me.

It's the most persistent, maddening thought. It covers my mind like an old wool blanket. But there are thoughts underneath that blanket. One particularly horrible thought, in fact. I can lift up that blanket and see that under-thought if I want to.

I don't want to. But I do it anyway.

It's an awful thought. Even worse than *scratch me scratch me scratch me*.

I deserve this.

51

All That's Left

Scratch me

Scratch me

Scratch me

Scratch me

Scratch me Scratch me
Scratchmescratchmescratchme

52

Visitors

A gecko makes his way toward me on my left-hand side—if I still had hands. He sprints a little bit. Stops. Sprints a little bit more. Stops. Tilts his head this way and that with robotic jitters. I scream at him. It doesn't deter him in the slightest. My voice is mostly a wheeze now anyway.

My screaming turns into song.

"I don't remember what day it was! I didn't notice what time it was!"

What time *is* it? The sun is definitely on its way down now it's so bright in my eyes.

Might go blind.

Tanned and cured skin with bleached eyeballs that's how they'll find me like someone carved out my eyes and stuck two ivory marbles in their place and then my skin will slip off like a loose-fitting T-shirt all done for the day.

So bright.

Maybe I'll just close my eyes and

"—of loving you! with each day comes a new way of loving you! I love you more today than yesterday! But not as much . . . as . . ."

I stop singing.

I need to preserve my energy.

Hahaha. For what? I try to move my shoulders again—nothing. Not a millimeter. And that's because this is where I belong. I was always going to wind up here. Alone. Dried out. Dusty. A mummified corpse in training. A Victim with a capital *V*, ready for Eleanor's portfolio. I even have my own bloody head covering—only mine's made of glass! No pillowcase for me! My face is on display, a carnival curiosity for anyone to see . . . if anyone were around to notice.

Well, *someone's* around to notice. The gecko continues his tentative approach. Finally, a few moments later, he's walking impossibly up into the air in front of me, scaling an invisible wall and showing me his soft underbelly. That loose, vulnerable flesh says scratch me scratch me scratch me almost as loudly as my nose, my burning scalp.

I'm so hot. But the joke's on them. I can stand being hot.

I keep drifting in and out and in and out of consciousn

My Loved Ones are all standing a few yards away, watching me. "Oh, hello," I say.

As always, they just stare, but unlike always, they're not motionless. They blink. They breathe. They swallow. They sweat under the desert sun. They're flesh and blood.

The animals that accompany some of them shift impatiently in place or sniff their surroundings. One of them, Hildegard, munches away on an enormous baguette. I can hear the crunch of the outer layer, the chew of the soft innards. Flakes of crust sprinkle to the dirt below.

"Sorry," I say. My favorite word. I want to say more, but I don't know what, and also my throat feels as if it's merged with the dry dustiness of the dirt enclosing my neck.

"This is your fault," Petunia, the girl with a basket of wilting flowers, says.

"This is what you get for thinking you were special," says Effie, the little girl holding a squirming fawn.

"For thinking you deserved to be worshipped," says Lloyd, the little boy on his way to school.

"You should have just been quiet and Good," says Cynthia, only a head bleeding in the sand, pecked at by geese.

"I'm scared about what happens next," I tell them. "Will you stay with me?"

Tommy, the redheaded scamp with skinned knees and a slingshot, says, "You could have killed yourself when you had the chance and let him move on to another life. You only think of yourself."

He picks up Cynthia's head, and they all turn to walk away.

Something's in here with me.

My blood freezes. An insect? Something that burrowed up from the ground? I don't feel it with my nerves—they've finally given up the ghost, ha ha—but I sense its presence all the same. Panic. I can't turn around. Is it going to bite me? I imagine razor-sharp jaws scissoring into my flesh, depositing venom, awakening my nerves and lighting them up with electric agony. I squeeze my eyes shut.

Nothing comes. Nothing happens.

Nothing is in here with me.

Wait. Yes. I see.

It's him. It's his presence I sense. I open my eyes, and his reflection is just faintly visible in the glass.

He refuses to look at me. He's furious with me. Fine. Let him hate me. Let him resent my failure. We're both in this together. Only . . . are we? Are we twinned destinies, never able to be separated? Or was that just a fairy tale I was telling myself to feel less alone? If I die out here (*when I die out here*), it will just be me, won't it? It'll be *my* death and no one else's, won't it . . .

"Something's coming," he says. I look up, and he's disappeared. But far off, in the distance . . .

A cloud of dust piling up on itself. A car? Coming fast.

Oh, thank God.

Maybe it's Dr. Burton, having a change of heart. Or someone else from the town, come to remedy what Burton did.

Eleanor! Or no! It's the FBI agent! Yes! It must be! What's the point of there being an FBI agent in my story if he's not going to stage some sort of last-minute rescue? He found out what's happening and is coming for me! That's why the dust cloud is approaching with such urgency! My unlikable knight in squirmy armor!

The yellowish cloud of dirt gathering on the horizon begins to curl around itself. Whoever's driving is turning in a circle. No! Don't go! Don't leave me here! Notice me! I try to scream.

The cloud curls some more. They're coming back. No. Wait. What—

Why are they going in circles?

It's not a car, you stupid, useless idiot. Just a dust devil. Gone as quickly as it arrived.

Ha. Hahaha.

I'm still screaming. I let it turn into a song again.

"Every day's a new day of loving you! With each day comes a new way of loving you!"

The quality of the air seems to have changed. The colors—and there

are a lot of them because of that magnificent desert sunset—have intensi-
fied. Everything is oversaturated. Another little dust devil whirls itself into
oblivion in my peripheral vision. Wind must be picking up outside of my
little cube. Wouldn't that be nice to feel the breeze again? I'll never feel
fresh air on my sweaty, burning face, my raw scalp again.

What is going on out there? Am I hallucinating some more? Why has
everything gone so yellow and brown?

All at once, a sudden memory: the back seat of the taxi I took into Arroyo
a million years ago.

We get some big whaddya-call-'ems? Haboobs.

"That's a funny word," I say in my little glass cube.

A haboob is coming my way.

The cloud gets bigger. And bigger. No mere image of a car approaching—
now it's like an army of gigantic, stampeding horses. Tiny, incidental dust
devils preparing the way, joining hands to become a dust inferno, mercifully
blocking out the sun for entire moments, turning the world into a thick,
brown, undulating sludge of grit.

It's coming for me. It's coming to swallow me.

Yes.

Swallow me.

Break this glass. Destroy my face. Give them nothing they can use.

I keep singing. "I love you more today than yesterday! But not as much
as tomorrow!"

Now it's like a hailstorm of earth against the glass. Tickettytickticktak-
taktaktaktak.

The dark cloud reaches me. Overtakes me. All is nothingness and noise.
I'm in a new crawl space and the world around me is static and hell and I'm
screamsinginging along with it in my breaking voice, *yarfyarfyarf,* I am Demon Dog in the Dust Devil, swallow me up and take me to the Deep Sea this
is my death this is my experience these are my nerves this is mine mine *mine*

The sky is a bruised pink. The storm has passed. The glass remains. At least
the wind and scour took most of the bloody handprint away.

Only a few minutes of daylight left. I'm going to spend a night out here
in the wilderness, unable to move, now even unable to scream. It'll probably
break what's left of my brain.

The mountains are black construction paper. The world is a rotted mouth, with bloody gums and stained, broken teeth, only turned upside down. Or maybe this is just the point of view of something being chewed up.

I'm so thirsty. I'm so tired. I'm so uncomfortable. It's only been hours—there's no way I'll make it through another day of this.

Perhaps that's why I'm not surprised when a piece of the darkening sky detaches itself and starts to trickle down the glass.

Because it's not sky.

It's an ant. Crawling on the cube covering my head. Come to collect me.

And off in the distance, a figure is approaching against the setting sun.

More movement, off to the side.

Another ant. Two ants. Three ants. Gathering around the base of my glass cube.

The silhouetted figure is now close enough for me to make out more details. Her hips, her shoulders, the top of the pillowcase covering her head.

"Jane," I say. Or maybe I just think it. My throat is too raw to make actual speech.

The dead woman makes her way toward me, led by a thin train of ants, until she stands before me. So strange to see a towering figure, standing between me and a sunset, and yet she casts no shadow.

She looks regal from this vantage point. Like the most powerful creature in any God's creation. Her dead-skinned feet, her veined legs, her thighs textured with pebbles and divots, she exudes pure, awesome *power*, it's the only word my brain can conjure. I feel like, if I weren't literally buried up to my neck in the ground, I would be bowing at this woman's feet regardless.

"Jane," I say again.

Look what they've done to you, her head tilt says.

"Look at *you*," I say. "Out in the world. You left that awful house. I'm so proud of you."

An ant walks up the face of the glass like a caress.

"Did you come here to say goodbye? Or . . . just to stare? Are you even really here? Doesn't matter. Whatever. It's nice to see a familiar . . . Ha ha, I was going to say *face*, but . . . ha . . ."

I swallow and it's like a dozen razor blades tumble down my throat.

"I'm going to die, Jane. And I think I'll just sink. I'm not strong enough to be born again. I'd try to be a ghost, but . . . no one would ever see me, and I've had enough of that already . . ."

Her feet crawl with ants. They run up and down her filthy, purple toes. She stands there for a moment as the sky darkens. Then I watch as those feet begin to turn around. Even she has had enough. Of course she has. I use the last vocal power I can possibly summon to call out.

"'Not for nothing,' you said to me, 'but I can see why you would want your space'!"

She stops. Turns back toward me.

"And I said nothing, naught for nothing, for no thing is what I am. I loved your poetry, Jane. I just wanted to tell you that. I should have said it back at Nadine's."

Her feet shuffledrag back toward me.

"Can I ask you something?"

She doesn't respond, obviously, but I'm used to talking to things that don't respond to me.

"Were you ever actually trying to hurt me? You, or the others like you in the Cross House? You weren't, were you? If you'd wanted that, nothing would have stopped you. Am I right?" Her head tilts ever so slightly. Her claws twitch. "Yeah. I thought so. You were all just trying to get my attention—in the bathroom, in the basement. Is that right? It'd been so long since you'd had any attention. You probably didn't even want to do that to Aunt Nadine's dog! Or maybe you did, I don't know, that dog sucked. I know I apologize too much, but I'm sorry I ignored you. I thought I could see you because I had *him* in me. Now I know I could see you because I'm *me*. You chose to show yourself to *me*. Thank you for choosing me. I'm sorry I messed it up. I mess everything up."

A few more ants, thick and black, make their way across the glass cube, probably sensing the ghost of Burton's blood smears.

"But, Jane, I'm so glad you left that house! I hope I'm not imagining you and that you don't *need* eyes on you anymore! Because I'm not going to have eyes soon. I'm going to die out here, and I won't be able to see you anymore. Ohhhhhh, Jane."

I'm starting to get very dizzy. The earth is getting ready to start tilting again, this time to bring me all the way into the dirt, swallow me whole. It makes me a little giddy, the vertigo. Like I'm drunk.

"I hope you go on some glorious adventures! I hope you keep walking and find something amazing to . . . to stare at, or whatever you do. It's never too late to make a change, Jane! Hahaha. If you ever make it to New York, there's a bookstore with a pretty good Personal-Growth section in the basement, I highly recommend flipping through some of those books for some tips!"

I honestly don't know if I'm laughing or crying now.

"Go have fun! Go be a Fury!" In spite of everything, the pain, the dehydration, the damage already done, now I'm actually shouting again, eyes squeezed shut as if I'm singing the best part of a song. "And I hope one day you're brave enough to take that stupid fucking pillowcase off! You don't need that! That was *his*! It's not *you*!"

The sobbing laughs come louder now. I'm giving up all my water. Fine. Let it be done. Let me empty out and become one with the dust.

I don't have any more energy to shout. My head tilts forward, and I mumble words into the ground.

"Victor told me that you couldn't hurt me as long as I ignored you, and I hope you know that means you have all the power, Jane! Because once you decide you want to be seen anyway? They'll never be able to stop you."

I don't know if my words have reached her, but I sense movement and, summoning all my effort, I force my head to look up again.

There in the glow of the desert sunset, Jane reaches up and pulls the pillowcase from her head.

I stare at what remains underneath.

I expect horror. I expect gore. And I suppose on one level, I receive both. But with the sun at her back, what I really notice are . . .

"Your eyes. You have such beautiful eyes, Jane."

She really does. They shine like . . . like white shells in dark ocean silt. Her hair, ruffled by the static and pull of the fabric, rises toward the sky.

"Thank you," I say. "Now you can really see me, and I can really see you."

I know she doesn't have lips, but it really looks like she's smiling at me, her teeth curving upward in an ever-so-subtle grin. And that's nice. A nice feeling to go out on.

"Okay," I say, head falling forward, too heavy. "I'm gonna go now. Time to go swimming. And maybe when I'm gone, you can bury my body like we did with . . . Nadine . . ."

Wait.

Wait a minute.

Nadine's makeshift grave . . . How could I have forgotten?

"Jane?" I lift my leaden head back up. Is she gone? Did she leave me? No. Jane's still here, still looking down on me. Still flexing her blood-colored claws.

"*Did* you like what you did to that dog?"

She nods. Oh yes, she did. She's a Fury after all. Her grin feels even less incidental now.

"Do you want to do it again?"

Another nod.

I remember the Fury who unlocked the door to the secret room in the Cross House; who'd probably been waiting to do that for a long time.

"I'll watch you, Jane. If that's what you need. I'll give you all the strength you need."

In a flash, she begins doing something I wouldn't have expected in a thousand lifetimes. She needs no prompting. It's very much as if she was just waiting for my offer.

She gets down on her knees and starts digging. Frantically. Her razor fingers tear through the earth. She looks like a fevered animal now, furrowing the ground as if its life depended on it.

"Jane," I gasp. "Yes."

But the earth does not want to give me up. It's too dusty, too diffuse, too loose. It's not like the ground of Nadine's backyard.

"Get closer," I urge her. And then I shriek in pain as her claws rip into my flesh. She draws back.

"It's okay. Try. You can hurt me."

She tries again and, in her frenzy, cuts me again. I can't take it. I beg her to stop, and she obeys. I tell her to keep digging around me.

If only I could twist my shoulders or move any part of me, to reach the furrows she's digging, to help break up the earth.

I'm trying, Jane. I'm trying.

But it's no use. I can't help. It was a glorious idea, a beautiful idea, but no, it's too hard, it's too hard.

"I'm sorry, Jane. But thank you for tr—"

A sensation.

So familiar, yet forever alien.

Somewhere in the center of my chest:

Click, click, *fwoom.*

I didn't think I'd have any more laughter in me. I begin to guffaw, in gratitude, in amazement, in actual goddamn joy.

I'm starting to have a hot flash.

My skin begins to radiate heat. A few minutes later, I feel myself begin to slicken with sweat. I can actually feel the dirt around me change with the warm moistness.

I try shifting my shoulders again, and maybe it's the easily broken, thin mud beginning to form or maybe it's the intense heat, but I move. A millimeter maybe. Same in the other direction.

Jane keeps digging, and I keep squirming and sweating and laughing.

It's well past sunset now and, even though it's dark, it feels as though the world is glowing. The stars are so bright. The dust storm has scoured the sky clean. Steel wool against cast iron.

It's taking me a long time to get anywhere. My legs feel as though they were left behind in my would-be grave. My feet are bare, and the rocks cut at my soles. They buried me without clothes, and my naked skin is a crusty jelly of dirt and sweat and I think urine as well, I don't know: not only does my body not feel like *my* body anymore, it doesn't even feel like *a* body. I feel like pure consciousness being slowly shuttled forward through alien means.

The direction I'm heading is entirely instinctual.

Well. Instinctual *and* led by a single ant.

Jane keeps pace, just behind me, comfortable and confident. I can tell she's looking at the world, the night sky, differently now. I bet the air feels like a blessing on her skinned face. She chooses not to put her pillowcase back on, just drapes it over one arm.

Eventually, we see the Cross House high up on the hill and the first signs of Arroyo.

No one is out in the streets. I have the town to myself.

Well. That's not entirely accurate.

I look behind me.

I smile.

It's a small smile because I'm so exhausted. But it's genuine. Ecstatic, even.

By the time I get to the foot of the hill, there's something like ten dead women behind me.

By the time we reach the top of the hill, it's more like twenty. And I can see more looking down on us from the windows as we slip into the crawl space entrance.

PART SEVEN

BLOODSPORT

She was becoming herself and daily casting aside that fictitious self which
we assume like a garment with which to appear before the world.
                                        —Kate Chopin, *The Awakening*

And why Easter specifically? The resurrection metaphors are perhaps too
obvious to need explaining, right?
              —Special Agent Peter Arliss, *In the Dark with the Devil: One Heroic*
                  FBI Agent's Ground Zero Account of the Arroyo Easter Massacre

53

Homecoming

I proceed through the crawl space to the secret room. The tunnels are lined with women. They've come from every direction imaginable. Even though the way is cramped, they're not crowding me. There's room enough for me to pass, and the sensation I get as I move toward—through—them is a pleasant chilliness.

They all have different head coverings, but that's not what makes each interesting. It's their bodies, their shapes, the way they stand, the stories I know they have to tell. Those stories are rimed with tragedy, but not defined by it—I begin to understand the injuries and disfigurements many of them bear are defense wounds. Even facing death, they fought back.

Now that I really picture the layout of the house, I can place this secret room as near the exact middle of the mansion's two primary identities: the school and the hospital. As I step into the room, that fact makes a strange sense to me. This room of horror exists as a sort of nexus—between education and innocence and science and death. It's as if those all of these things are truly just words. Facades. Because they all wind up here, in the place where victims are tabulated and where gory trophies sit in unseen display.

As before, though, the women stay gathered in the tunnel and entrance; they don't come farther into the room. Why won't they come in? It's like there's something in here they're scared of.

Then a man's voice speaks next to me.

"This is where it happened."

I whirl around. Hiding in the shadows of the room is handsome Victor, the former mayor, the caretaker of the Cross House, the great and powerful enabler of Damon Cross. Damon's face, as it were.

"Back before the renovations," he continues, "this was just a small, random part of the crawl space. Nothing special. But this is where they finally caught up with him. This is where his body lay. He couldn't run fast enough. He'd run through these halls so many times, I guess he thought he could keep away from them forever. But they smashed down a wall and got him."

The sound of gunshots, the smell of acrid smoke, linger in the air like cobwebs.

"Of course, you know *where* they hit him," he says, and the spots on my body suddenly ache and burn. Somatic echo. My hands go to my throbbing birthmarks, and I realize—as if I somehow forgot—that I'm totally naked. No, not totally; I'm coated in a layer of mud and dirt. I resist the urge to cover myself further.

"So, the flock keeps this area special," I say, half to myself. "But I bet only Burton has the key. Just another little gesture of dominance?"

Victor shrugs. "Hierarchy is important. There's a natural order to things."

"Right."

"But look at you," he says, unexpectedly changing tone. "You *survived*." His handsome face breaks into a huge, dimpled smile. "You saved him. I'm so proud of you."

He approaches, beaming, and envelops me in his arms. It's unlike any ghost encounter I've had so far. Warmer. Not the sensation of corporeal arms around me, but inside. Validation.

"This is so good," he continues in my ear. "They'll have no choice but to worship you now."

He pulls back from our embrace.

"Here's what you should do. Go to Bonnie first. She thinks you're old friends. She believes in you. She can gather a meeting with the rest of the flock, and you'll tell them all what Burton did. He'll put up a fight, but even he will be stunned you survived. You might never win him over, but the rest will see it as confirmation that you are what you are." Ever the political strategist at work. "I'll be there to help, always. And, of course, so will *he*."

That other (*under*) voice speaks up in my head. That voice I now know has always been with me and always been his, cold and critical when it wants to be, loving and gentle when it *needs* to be. It's so loud and present it's as if another man has entered the room and is standing right behind me.

"It's not too late, Mary. You can still take your place and be adored."

Hands wrap around me from behind. They move all over me. But these hands are different from Victor's. These hands are real.

They're *my* hands.

He's moving my hands. Damon is in control again, and . . . it's so very *nice*. He catalogs, caresses, the various parts of me, like a man feeling a treasured possession rescued after a house fire. I feel that warmth, that slipperiness, spread in my lower belly.

"Isn't that what you want? It might take some time, but that's all you have anyway. Why not spend the rest of it as a celebrant? You don't have to like them. You don't have to believe in what they're doing. Just let me do the talking and, soon, we might even be able to get revenge on Burton himself, get him out of the way, and actually have this flock to ourselves. The way my ancestors intended. Step into the spotlight, Mary; it's finally your time."

My eyes have closed in the rush of sensation, but they open now and land on an object on the floor: my journal. I must have dropped it when Burton barged in. A word flashes behind my eyes:

DISCREPANCY

I remember all the notes Cross took on his victims. All the things he said to them versus all the things he said about them. I immediately understand what he's doing.

"But that spotlight is for victims," I say.

My hands stop where they are. Guilty.

"What?"

"You're trying to seduce me. Like you seduced them. So that I'll do what you want. Next you'll probably be asking me if there's 'anyone missing me back home.'"

I break away from him. From myself. My nerves groan in frustration: *no.*

I turn around, and I'm alone in the room. Nothing but ghosts and voices in my head.

"We know there's no one missing you back home, Mary," Victor says at last. "That's the point. That's why we're *here. This* is your new home. And *they* don't know they miss you. Yet."

I look at him, thinking of how Victor never participated in his brother's slaughters, but he *knew.* He probably sat up in his room and thought about it all, playing with himself, living out his fantasies of proxy power. So much misery in this world just to give a few cruel men a quick spurt.

Damon's voice in, under, outside my head again: *"What I want? What about what you want, Mary? Do you even remember what that is? What brought you here to begin with? I do. You want love. You want to matter. And more than that. You want to hurt. You want to maim. You want to peel. I know you. I know all about you."*

"You wanted me to go through with the harvest ritual," I say. "I felt you taking over."

"That was for our safety! We need to stay on their good side and indulge their nonsense. There's so many of them. And we're"—my hands grab my body, pinching loose skin with disgust—*"just not strong enough to fight them all off. I'm sorry, that's just a fact."*

"We both know that's not the only reason, though. You like the worship."

"But so do you."

"Except they're not worshipping me. They're worshipping you."

"They're worshipping us."

I remember the cactus wand, the stirrups, imagining that invasion. Burton's cruel, mocking voice telling me how it could have—would have—been me. How men are allowed to forget what it's like to have a body.

"What's my favorite song?" I ask abruptly. "What's my most cherished memory? When was I happiest?" Silence. "You don't know. And you don't know because . . . I don't know. And I don't know because—"

"Maybe you just haven't had your most cherished memory," he purrs. *"Yet."*

Oh, he's good. I can see why someone lonely might open herself up to him.

"No," I say. "That's not why I don't know. I started to understand this in the crawl space. Your memories were so much brighter than mine. Then, during the ritual. The way they all gathered in front of the mirror like that. It wasn't just to look at themselves; it was so that they felt like there were more of them. It was so they felt like they were an entire army."

"I don't—"

"The mirror is a lie." I begin wiping the dirt off me, trying to expose more and more of my naked self.

"What are you doing?"

"I want you to look at me, Damon. Really look at me. My body. Me." I keep wiping the dirt and mud away. It leaves smears and stains on my skin, but my nakedness becomes more and more apparent. Undeniable. There's a riot in my head—childhood taunts, laughter, jeers, and also cries of disgust, of annoyance, this is stupid, this is gross—but I refuse to let that stop me.

"Beginnings are hard," I say, "but I know when all my problems really started. It's when *you* stopped liking what *you* saw in the mirror. But the mirror is a lie. It never shows us the truth. It's always backward. Whenever *I* looked in the mirror, it was always through your eyes. Never mine."

I look down at myself. I can see all sorts of imperfections revealed in the dirt, as if I were an archaeologist digging up a specimen. Behold, the Middle-Aged Woman, with her cellulite and soft belly and spotting skin and gray hairs. But are they imperfect? Or is that just what *he* thinks they are?

I feel Damon's panic and loathing pulse through me. He wants to run. That's always been his instinct. But this time, there's nowhere to go.

From the corner of the room, Victor's voice: "Stop this. You're being crazy." I almost forgot he was here. "Stop! You worthless idiot!" He thinks I can be driven away like the Furies. But none of what he's saying is new to me; I've had his brother's voice in my head my entire life.

"Look at me," I say to Damon. And I close my eyes.

I'm in darkness now. But his face is there, floating in front of me. I'm putting it there. Me. Mary. He's trying not to look at me, but I force him to. I use my nerves to make his eyes lock onto *me*. That familiar wooziness overtakes me. I've never felt it outside of looking at a mirror before. I can feel how I transform in his eyes—his undereyes—into a hideous, decomposing horror. I can feel his rage—my rage—growing, hotter than any hot flash.

I want to tear my goddamn flabby, veiny, wrinkled, stupid skin off, my fat, my flaws, my failures as a woman, my—no, I just have to get through it, *I just have to get to the other side of these thoughts*, like with Dana.

The feelings start to crescendo, but I can sense myself, my *real* self, there, waiting to be knitted back together. Yes! I can do this! I feel a moment of preemptive triumph and then—

My legs give out.

I slam down to the ground, banging my already injured knee in a white nova of agony. I'm losing consciousness. I'm about to faint.

I have to open my eyes and make it stop.

"You dumb fucking bitch! You ugly, useless cunt!" Victor is screaming at me, impotent but delighted. "You're so stupid!"

And I *am* stupid. There's a huge flaw in my plan. I was hoping I could get past it, the way I was able to get past it looking at Dana during the harvest—I didn't remember there's a built-in fail-safe when it comes to looking at *myself*. My mind literally can't take it. I'll pass out before I get to the other side. And who knows what sort of mercy I'll be at while I'm unconscious?

But I can feel him inside me. He's also winded and dizzy. This is affecting him, too.

In front of me is the doorway full of women. Jane is toward the front.

"I need your help," I tell them.

"No, no—fuck off!" Victor yells with sudden fervor, not at me but at them, and I realize with cold fear that even if his taunts don't work on me, they might work on them. They're conditioned to flee. "Fuck off, you ugly, dumb cows, you worthless shits!"

They twitch, ready to disperse.

"Don't listen to him," I say. "I see you. And I need your help." They look at me. They're listening. "I need you to keep me from falling. And I need you to . . ."

Jane steps forward. She holds up two of her claws at my eye level, tips pointing toward me.

"Yes," I say, heart thudding. "I need you to carve his eyes out."

Inside my head, he begins to laugh. *"You can't do that! You can't hurt me! I'm you!"*

I answer him with a laugh of my own. "Darling. If there's one thing this world teaches someone like me," I tell him, "it's how to hurt myself."

I start to walk toward Jane's claws.

He tries to keep my legs from moving. My feet are dipped in concrete, and my ligaments lose their will. He uses my own hands to beat at me, but joke's on him, I'm too weak to do any real damage.

"Get out of here!" Victor is screaming at the hesitant ghosts in the hallway. *"Go! You dumb, worthless bitches! You don't exist! You're nothing!"*

"Help," I beg them.

Two women tentatively step forward, into the room. It costs them great effort—but before I can thank them, they're lifting me up and pulling me like a battering ram toward Jane.

I close my eyes, and the last thing I see before Jane's razors sink into my skull is *his* face, eyes locked onto me, really seeing me, mouth open in an outraged scream.

The pain is indescribable.

Only screams can articulate it.

No no no NO don't make me no just like her you're just like her why did you have to be this way why did you have to grow old i don't want to get old i don't want to fall apart i'm scared i'm so scared

He thrashes. He sobs. He begs for mercy. He receives none.

I feel razor tips enter the soft jelly of my eyeballs. Exquisite. Excruciating . . . but somehow not physical. I understand that much as it's happening. It takes a little longer to fully realize . . . she's stabbing *through* my eyes.

I don't know on what level or plane I'm being operated on. Spiritual. Metaphysical. Metaphorical. Jane's claws go into me, through me, the spaces between atoms. I have seen them be corporeal, destroying dogs and dirt, and also ephemeral, bursting apart into vapor when Burton ran through them. They can be—do—many things. They're still learning, same as I am. As if to prove this realization, the other two Furies keep me bodily upright, as sure and steady as crutches, even after my legs turn into water.

Damon screams even louder in my head as the first slashes rake into his face. But eventually, he shuts up. Because he has no tongue. Or eyes. Or nose. He is a floating, shredded, featureless mess of meat. A delightfully, deliciously, magnificently amateur skinning. There's not even enough of a face left to take and preserve—it's like it never existed. He deserves nothing better than this botched practice job. He was a learning tool and nothing more.

And I feel calmer. Clearer. Quieter.

I'm gently put back down onto the concrete floor, and I stumble backward, finding my balance. I open my eyes—my physical, real eyes—and am amazed I can still see.

Victor is standing there. Once again, I forgot all about him. He looks as panicked as I've ever seen a person look. Which I guess is a little funny, considering he's not a person.

"What have you done?" he keeps repeating, over and over. "What have you done? What have you done?"

I look back at the Furies in the hallway. "You can come in," I tell them. "He can't hurt you."

That snaps him out of his little fugue state. He stares at me with deep, seething hatred. "You're nothing without him. You're just a weak, pathetic little vessel. Dried out and empty and worthless. You can't do *anything*."

The Furies begin to stream into the room. My God, there are *so many* of them.

"Do you know what today is?" I ask Victor. "Today is the day Damon Cross died. And today is my birthday."

"Oh, fuck you!" Victor blubbers as he retreats. His back finds the wall. "You're going to die. You can't do anything without him. Hell, you couldn't do anything *with* him. With your stupid, weak, disgusting body. You're *fucked.*"

I'm surprised to find this hits me in a place of wounded pride. I can't do *anything*?

"Tell that to Carole," I say. "Or Wallace. Or Nadine."

He surprises me by starting to laugh. Great, snotty yuks. "Oh, wow! You killed some old invalid shut-in! You didn't even know you were doing it!"

"Carole wasn't an invalid. And neither was—"

"You didn't kill Carole!"

The room is filled with dead women now. All waiting. All eager. But I'm interested now. For the moment he has my attention.

"What are you talking about?"

He's shaking his head, either out of pity or loathing. "You idiot. You're so fucked. You're dead, you stupid, worthless, useless—"

"Are you going to tell me, 'It was Damon who killed Carole,' or something like that? Because I've had enough metaphysics for the time being."

His laughter stops, and he pins me down with a hateful glare. "Damon would never be so impulsive and stupid. And he would never kill a child either. You fucking *dolt.*"

"Then who killed Carole?"

"Fuck you!" If he were corporeal, I'd be covered in spittle. The veins in his neck bulge. I bet if he could, he'd disappear through the wall behind him, but it occurs to me, in sudden understanding, that he never bothered to learn how to do things like that. Even as a ghost, he coasted.

"Who killed Carole?" I ask him again.

He only answers me with more laughing, more cursing. I begin to grow bored with his resistance—and so, too, do the Furies who are now so packed into the small room that they almost blur together.

I step aside.

Victor's laughs turn to whines of terror and then falsetto shrieks as the Furies approach him, ready to shut him up—and I give them all the strength they need with my attention. He tries to muster up curses to deflect them, but he can't put any real effort behind it as they begin to carve away at him.

First his clothes. He stands there naked, covering himself . . . until his hands are lopped off at the wrists. Another Fury grabs his penis and testicles and, with a quick squeeze of her razored fist, makes them disappear in a spray of blood. Talons rake his eyes into viscous rivers of semen-like jelly. His jaw is forced open, and his teeth are sliced off above the roots like niblets of corn off a cob. Lastly, his face is shorn away with a few skillful flicks of the wrist. They've learned so quickly; it's much better than what they did to Damon. Fitting. Victor was the handsome one.

The Furies back away to give him the tiniest bit of space and, as they do so, I watch as ants begin to crawl their way up his body and make a hungry pilgrimage to the pulpy, pulsating ruin of blood-seeping muscle that remains on his skull.

As a coup de grâce, Jane takes her pillowcase, which she's carried in the crook of one arm, and pulls it over his head. His fresh blood quickly rushes to join the already-extant stain.

I turn away, satisfied, wondering what to do next, and I see my journal still on the floor. I pick it up and turn it over in my hands. All those DISCREPANCY tabs. They start on the very first page. The first words I wrote in this little book.

I am.

"Huh," I say to the room. "You know, I never noticed it before, but . . . that's a complete sentence, isn't it?"

All this time . . . I never considered that.

I toss the book to a nearby Fury. She shreds it into nothingness. A single yellow tab dislodges and floats to the ground like the world's smallest autumn.

Another Fury goes to the desk and destroys Damon's original. Poof.

I wade through the women and make a show of pressing the buttons on the compact shelving. The unit shudders and groans as the first shelf opens up. While they inspect the contents of these first shelves, I head over to the desk and begin looking through the pages. All their names are here. His old hunting ledgers. And his acolytes'.

We go shelf by shelf. Each woman steps forward when a face calls to her. They all pay a sort of homage. Some reach a hand out or touch their chests. Some react angrily. One swipes at a glass case, and it drops to the floor and shatters. A few even pull their faces off the shelf, remove them from their cases, and place them on their own. The physical sliver of skin falls through them, onto the floor with a soft lunch meat *plip,* but their spectral selves take on the look of the reattached faces. It doesn't sit naturally on the skull, but they find a certain comfort in having it relatively back in place.

Most, however, move on once they pay their respects. They've had time to understand they can't go back to what they were. They're not these people anymore. They're something new. Something *changed.* What's important is they were seen and acknowledged.

I don't call them beautiful. It's not that they're *not* beautiful—my God, they are—but that word has too much baggage. It's an outsider's word and it was weaponized to render these women invisible in the first place. They are full of so much more than beauty. I tell them they're amazing. Powerful. I tell them they're *here.* I will learn all their names in time. Tonight, we are just beginning. Baby steps, as the books in the Personal-Growth section liked to say.

The unimportant slivers of skin remain, like their bloodstained wrappings, in the room behind us as we all move on.

54

Council, Again

I don't use the crawl space now. I just walk straight down the hallways of the hospital. It's late enough that no one's milling around to see me. A shame: just this once I would have been quite noticeable.

I suspected Burton would be awake and in his office, but I'm surprised to find the council is there with him—not the entire town, just the selectmen and -women who were at the meeting at Bonnie's the other night. The ones who pulled my clothes away and judged my birthmarks.

I stand in the back of the room and wait for someone to notice I'm there.

Have they been here all night? Did they all go home and enjoy a nice, comfortable meal while I burned alone in the wilderness? Did they even finish their ritual? Probably not, with Burton's hand injured—if he can't participate, I bet no one can.

They're clearly in crisis mode. Who knows how my outburst affected the town, already tense and stressed due to the presence of the FBI agent? Maybe some are even berating Burton for what he did, arguing on my behalf?

I decide I don't care.

Whatever their arguments, and whether they stayed home or came here in the Cross House, tonight will end no differently for them.

Someone on the outer rim of the group sees me first—or more likely, smells the sweat and the blood and the dirt—and makes a choked inhale. The realization ripples across the room. Burton, sitting behind his beautiful, shining, cherry oak desk, is among the last to receive it. His argument, whatever it was, dies like flash paper on his tongue.

A lot of questions come all at once, and none of them are asked with much energy. Mostly fragments—*but, how, is, did, where, whuh*—not one sentence completes itself. Until one does.

"He's come back to us."

I don't know who shouts it first. It's such a surprise that I don't even really register that it was really shouted. It skips straight to echoing in my head, like a dream noise that jolts you out of a sound sleep and then rings in your ears after you're awake.

"He's come back to us."

"He is here."

"He found us again."

He's nothing, I try to say. But no thing comes out. My voice is too wrecked. It's okay. We didn't come here to talk anyway.

Show them.

I watch as one of the Furies, a woman named Renate who was fifty-three and who fell into accounting because she was desperately afraid of financial insecurity after having been raised by a father who survived the Depression, who never fully loved her occupation but who also never failed to feel good whenever she helped save a struggling family a little extra money come tax day, steps forward and stabs her fingers into the biggest neck in the room. The driver's. She probably gets him right where his tattoo sits on the other side. Right through the Eye.

The driver makes a sudden gagging noise.

I can only imagine how this must look to everyone else in the room: as if the massive man's throat has suddenly exploded outward—or maybe like an invisible hook had been placed into his neck and then yanked in the other direction. I'm sure it's pretty surreal . . . which means what happens next must be simply unfathomable.

Renate flicks her hand up, slicing the driver's head into two vertical halves, rooted at the neck.

Before he can drop to the floor, that's when she *really* gets to work.

I have a brief, incomprehensible memory of a movie many years ago about a poor boy whose hands were blades and who began to find success with topiary—seems too strange to be real, but that's the first connection my brain makes to what's happening now. Only Renate isn't trimming a hedgerow to look like an animal, she's shredding a massive, human man into literal nothingness. Even his clothes are reduced to spider silk strands. Two other Furies lunge forward and join her. Their efforts lift his rapidly diminishing body off the ground—I don't even think his knees got a chance to buckle. Bits and pieces of him plop and drip across the room, quivering with the impact and with the life still spasming through them. The blood spray is most impressive.

The rest of the room scatters, the council running for every exit. The Furies lop off the leg of one person as they try to flee, but the rest succeed in getting out of the room. Some get through the main door, some through a door set on the wall behind Burton's desk, which leads to a bathroom and then another hallway. Burton himself disappears through a secret entrance to the crawl space.

I look at Jane, who's standing next to me. I smile.

"See what you can do?" I say.

She does see. They all do. They strain like hounds to be let loose.

"Go. And know that, wherever you go, *I see you.*"

The screams from the pursued are loud and delicious. It's only when I think again of Carole and Wallace that my smile begins to falter.

Why did Victor say that? If I didn't kill them, who did? Was he even telling the truth, or was that just something designed to get under my skin? Look how much power I can wield—how could he doubt what I'm capable of?

Still, I look around for someone I can ask for more information. It appears I might be too late. The room is mostly empty save for a few scenes of random dismemberment.

I make my way past three Furies cubing the body of the recently delegged man—oh, it was the man with the faint auburn mustache—into smaller and smaller chunks.

Hot blood sprays across my skin. Not only did I forget to ask about Carole, I seem to have momentarily forgotten I'm completely nude. I'm not self-conscious about it, but I am a little chilly.

I decide to go put on some clothes.

I start on the journey upstairs to my room, trying to boost my mood again with thoughts of how there's no reason to be preoccupied about what Victor said. That was all in the past anyway. It might as well have been in another life.

55

Loved One

The screams filling the hallways of the mansion make me think of tire screeches at a racetrack: the loud, persistent sound of sport encircling you. These idiots aren't even screaming because they're in pain. It's a totally illogical impulse, they're only calling attention to themselves, making them easier to find.

I can hear them even now in my bedroom upstairs. It's bad acting. They're performing the roles of the Pursued in some cheap drama.

I go straight for the dresser and pull out some clothes to change into. My eyes stay on my Loved Ones, though, and, after tossing the clothes on the bed, I pick two of the little statues up.

I'm surprised to find the feeling inside of me is similar to when I first stood in the hospital waiting room and looked down at the town below me: distance. The socket where a memory once was.

These little statues that I was so compelled to collect, that reminded me to be Good, be Normal, that I used to speak to because I was so lonely . . . They're just porcelain.

It's a sad feeling. Like sitting down at a favorite restaurant only to discover nothing on the menu looks appetizing anymore.

I smack one of the statues against the side of the dresser. It cracks in two. A little powder. A few incidental shards.

We invest so much in certain objects, don't we? More vessels, dipped into the waters of life, holding identity inside. Which I guess just goes to show how little of what we think of as identity is really real.

How can you leave us? their perfect faces ask, their voices growing faint. *How will you remember who you are?*

Because I'm still in the process of learning who that really is.

Something else occurs to me. I've gotten so used to ignoring mirrors I completely looked past the one right here on the dresser. The one I covered with a pillowcase.

Am I ready to do this now?

"I'm going to have to try it sooner or later."

I take a deep breath—screams still wailing elsewhere in the mansion, giving me an encouraging feeling of not being alone—and pull off the pillowcase.

"Oh."

The woman in the mirror has been brutalized. Her face is caked in blood and dirt and sweat, a makeup job from hell. To call her hair disarrayed is to call a hurricane gusty, a tsunami a little damp. Her eyes are wet and gummy with trauma and maybe even madness. Her skin is scratched and burned; it's puffy, it's ringed, it's sunken, it's peeling.

But she's looking at herself.

I breathe a soft, probably inaudible, "Wow."

I stare at her for I don't know how long. There's no distortion, there's no trembling over the precipice of consciousness. There's no nausea. And there's certainly no decomposition. I can stare at this face all I want.

Because it's mine.

The tears come surging out of me in big, wrenching, cathartic globs. I can't help it. I bend at the waist, clutching the dresser. I want to sit on the bed, but, no, I want to look again. I lean forward across the dresser and touch my face in the glass. I can barely believe it. Me. It's Mary. I missed you. I—

Movement behind me.

Someone's in the room.

Standing by the door on the inside—I must have walked right past her and she's been standing there watching me this whole time. It's Eleanor. And she has the old radio from the floor in her hands. She's lifting it high above her head as she quickly walks toward me.

I want to tell her she needs to be careful with that thing; it's so heavy, and it almost looks like she's about to bring it down fast against my—

The crack of the radio against my skull won't stop.

How is that possible? It should have been over in an instant—a *smack!*, and then darkness, maybe even death. But, no, it's like it keeps coming down on me, like I'm stuck inside an infinite echo, *smacksmacksmacksmack,* pain

pain pain, and a high-pitched ringing in my ears. I'm Dorothy, spinning and spinning and spinning in a twister ripped in time, *smacksmacksmacksmack*.

There goes Auntie N, cackling, "Holy shit, am I glad I came to see this!" No little dog, though; that's my fault.

Finally, finally, the vortex slows . . . and slows . . . but it doesn't stop. I'm aware enough that I was only actually hit once, I'm just swirling and swirling and—

No, Nadine's not really here can't be.

But why do I smell cigarette smoke?

Why do I hear her laughing?

Traumatic brain injury and doesn't that serve you right.

The sound of Nadine's laughter changes. Echoes in on itself—

No—it's another voice. Speaking. Not laughing.

"Okay. Okay. Okay," the voice is saying, self-soothing. I try to focus my eyes.

One of my Loved Ones has come to life. She's standing over me and ready to revenge herself on me for letting so many of them shatter. Which one is it? I can't remember the name I gave her! Mabel or Emily or, or—

Oh no, she bashed her name out of my head.

I don't realize I'm on my hands and knees until my right arm gives way and I fall farther onto the floor. I groan and try to push myself back up. No longer Dorothy. Now I'm a newborn calf.

"Shut the fuck up," my Loved One snarls at me. It sounds like she's speaking to me through a tube of paper. Is that just because her throat is hollow porcelain? "Stay right where you are."

She starts to pace. She's clearly upset. With me? Or maybe with herself?

"I don't know what you did or how you did it, but you ruined everything!"

Meanwhile, the impact against my skull, the ringing in my ears, continue to stretch on, and I really do think I can smell cigarette smoke.

I look up at the girl again. Her skin is so slick and flawless.

Is that sweat? No. It's porcelain.

Her name starts with an E, what the hell is it?

"You bitch," she says. "You thought you were so special, huh? You thought you could just come back here and mess everything up?! End our way of life?!"

She's got a phone in her hand now—of course she does, all my Loved Ones have little props, sometimes it's a lamb or a bird or a kite or a radio or a cell phone. She's tapping something into it. The other Loved Ones, smaller and less lively, stand on the dresser, watching. Coconspirators. They were all planning this attack. Another betrayal.

"Come on, pick up, pick up, pick up," the girl is muttering, putting her phone to her ear.

I start to speak, but then I cough. I cough so hard I puke a little. A thin stream of bile trails out of my mouth.

She notices, too, and grimaces in disgust.

"Jesus. Shut the hell up!" she barks at me.

Bark bark. The boy with the puppy's name is Anthony. What's her *name??* *Enid? Ethel?*

The radio, my head, the ringing, the pain, still caught in a looping swirl.

"No one to answer the phone," I mutter. "They're throwing me a birthday party. Hahaha. Erinyes!" Oh! Was that her name? No. No, but close. I cough and spit up some more. Nothing in me. When was the last time I ate?

"I heard them talking about you all night," she's saying, trying her phone again. "I had to listen through the door. They said you ruined the harvest but that they took care of you, so you shouldn't be alive! I came back up here while I still could, to spend a little more time up here, because *everything is ruined*!"

She's so young. My God, she's just a baby. Petulant and frustrated little—

"Eleanor!" I shout. It finally came to me!

In case I had any doubt that that's her name, she pauses what she's doing and looks at me, her precious, perfect face fixed in a frown. It all comes flooding back, my poor, probably condemned memory mansion, generator whirring and smoking.

Poor little Eleanor, who feels like she's always left out; she just wants to be included.

I start to put everything all together: Eleanor heard the screams of the flock. She got scared because she didn't know what's going on. She hit me in self-defense. She doesn't know I'm not going to hurt her!

She's my friend. My only friend.

I slowly get to my knees, supporting myself with the bed.

"Eleanor," I repeat. Her name helps me steady the world. "I'm not gonna hurt you! Come on, let's get out of here. You and me. We can start new lives and, and, and be whoever we want to be!"

It all plays out in an instant in my mind. I see us in some new small town.

We find odd jobs and pay our way. People will wonder if we're mother and daughter, or May–December lovers, and we'll delight in their confusion. They will always try to condense our complexities into something simple and dismissible, because that's what being a woman is, being too much for definitions and being defined anyway, out of fear, and my God, will we be fearless!

She stares at me for a beat, seeming to not understand what I'm offering. Did all of that come out of my mouth? Am I like Anna-Louise now? Did I speak gibberish?

Then Eleanor laughs. Her little sunrise eyes, her adorable dimples. She's so perfect.

"Are you seriously this dumb? Do you not understand who I am?"

"You're perfect," I say, reaching out to her. "You're a little perfect porcelain d—"

She reacts, revolted, away from my hand. "I was just marking you, you dumb fuck. I was just trying to do what Damon Cross did and learn everything about you."

"What . . . ?"

"I'm so goddamn sick of this town treating me like a child! I wanted to show them I could handle harvesting, even though I'm a girl. I wanted to show them how useful I could be!"

"W . . . what?"

I'm still lost.

Eleanor laughs, high and desperate, and cups her mouth with her hands like a megaphone. "I was going to kill you, Mary!"

"But . . . but . . ."

"I didn't mean for things to get so fucking weird and complicated. I just thought you were this lonely, crazy idiot. I even threw that idea out there about you being one of his victims because I thought that was kind of funny. I should have just killed you first." She starts pounding on her head with the heels of her hands. "I shouldn't have practiced on Carole. And I shouldn't have told Barb about your journal. It was just exciting and strange and I was a part of something and now it's all gone to shit and it's all your fucking fault, you useless, crazy bitch!"

That word.

"I'm not crazy," I say through gritted teeth.

"It was *your* advice, you know! You said I shouldn't wait, that I should show them what I can do! That's why I killed Carole! Also, let's be honest, it was your whole fucking existence, too. Because there's no way I ever want to let myself become someone like you. Pathetic and weird and alone and fucking *old*."

I'm not crazy . . . but I think she is. Was she always? Yes, I suspect so; either I just didn't notice or she's become an expert at hiding her madness behind her gee-shucks cuteness. Probably it's a little of both. But the gleaming in her eyes—no longer that charming twinkle but the cold, shining glint of a blade—is utterly crazy. There's no other word for it.

A thousand cluttered thoughts storm through my head. How can I reach her? How did someone so young become so unhinged? Nature? Nurture? What did they teach her in this town? What goes on in that school? And another, even more chilling thought: Is this what I would have become if I hadn't been sent away? I think maybe so.

"Eleanor—"

But she's too worked up to listen. She reaches into her pocket and pulls out what I guess is her weapon of choice. Something small and easily concealed. Something she probably already had lying around her house because she's a child and couldn't buy something on her own.

A box cutter.

She doesn't know why this is funny-not-funny to me, but it makes me think of my bookstore and of all the young coworkers I've ever had who ignored me and treated me like part of the furniture.

"Eleanor," I say again. "You need to calm down and—"

She kicks me, and I fall backward against the dresser. I hear the Loved Ones sitting on top rattle and fall.

"Stop fucking saying my name like you're my mother!" she yells. "Don't fucking patronize me!"

She kicks me again. Pain flares across the world.

Why don't my Furies come and save me? But of course they're too busy with their assignment. Their fun.

I try to grab at her leg, but Eleanor kicks me in the gut. All the air rushes out of me.

Now she's on top of me. She wraps her hands around my throat. "This is how he did it, you know," she says. "He liked to strangle them first. See the lights go out in their dumb cow eyes. He was a great man. He deserves better than you, you fake."

I try to tell her he's gone.

I try to tell her I carved his face off and the ants have him now.

I try to.

But this isn't like the struggle with the Cross brothers in the hidden room. This is purely physical. And she's younger than me. Stronger than me. Crazier than me. I don't have a chance.

The world begins to go dark. Not the encroaching gray of when I used to look in the mirror but a pinhole blackness like an old movie drawing to a close. My fingers scratch at the floor, looking for purchase to pull myself away. They scratch at her arms, her elbows, her face, but I don't have claws, I'm not a Fury, not yet at least. She's too strong, too young, and now my arms begin to fill with sand, and that sand hardens into concrete, and I just don't have the energy to lift them anymore.

Her face has frozen into a scowl. A poignant enamel portrait of concentration. A little girl taking a difficult exam. Her eyes shine with rapturous tears.

My hand finds an object on the ground. A little porcelain statuette. I grab it and slam it as hard as I can into the side of Eleanor's head.

She winces in agony and lets me go. I scoot myself backward as far as I can get, but the dresser is in the way and stops me from getting far. I stretch my neck upward, gasping for air . . . and again I could swear I smell cigarette smoke.

The pinhole expands and I can see a little bit more. I can see Eleanor looking at me, seething, blood beginning to run down from her temple.

And I can see the box cutter in her hand, which she's bringing up and . . .

With a swipe of her arm, Eleanor slashes the blade across my throat.

I don't see it as it slices me.

But I feel it.

I feel a mouth open up in the flesh of my neck.

And then that's it.

That's the end of me.

56

A Ghost

So.

Here I am.

My body is crumpled in a heap against the dresser and I'm a ghost.

Now what?

I didn't sink, the way Nadine described it. I didn't feel much of a choice one way or another. And I know I told Jane I didn't want to become a ghost, but despite being dead I appear to be suffering from a real persistent case of sense of self.

To be totally honest, death hardly feels different at all. It's pretty underwhelming. Mostly, it just aches. I want to escape this throbbing, uncomfortably wedged body. I want to get out of this room, where an incessant buzzing noise won't leave my ears alone.

But I can't quite float away yet. I guess I just need to practice.

Mary.

We can't all be fast learners, like Nadine.

Mary!

Great. Even as a ghost I still have voices in my head. How wonderful.

You're not dead, Mary.

But of course I am. My throat was slit! I can feel hot, sticky blood pouring down my naked chest and—

If you can feel it, that means you're not dead. And it isn't so much pouring *as it is . . .*

Dripping. Leaking.

I move my neck a little. The pain is immense . . . but it's not quite *deep*, is it? Swallowing is excruciating, but everything still feels connected. And I've lost blood, but not in pumping, arterial spurts. Maybe I *am* still alive.

I begin to piece together what must've happened. Eleanor's cut managed to miss all the major arteries and veins in my neck. The wound is just super-ficial enough. I almost have to laugh. I bet if I'd been younger, if the skin around my neck and chin had been as tight as it once was, maybe Eleanor would've had a clearer shot.

And what's that buzzing noise? I focus a little and realize it's words. El-eanor. She's jumping up and down in the middle of the room, gripped by manic glee, a surge of adrenaline and triumph too much for her adolescent body to handle. If she were a little more mature, she would've noticed what she'd done—or failed to do.

She's celebrating too early. She's just too young not to. And she's talking to me, to the room, the way I would often talk to my Loved Ones.

"God! It was so frustrating hearing them talk about how you must have killed Carole! I wanted to tell them so bad! That was the whole reason I practiced on her, so they'd see what *I* could do! Me! I mean, I was happy to let you take the blame for that FBI guy showing up, but still."

As she waves and gesticulates with the box cutter, I notice it's not entirely a miracle that I survived. The blade looks gummy with skin and blood al-ready. She probably used this same weapon on Carole and didn't think to put a new, sharp, clean blade in.

Kids' stuff.

"They should've taught me how to do it better. They should've been teaching me for years, not this dumb meek-and-mild crap. There are more ways to be useful than having babies! But *you*? Ha! You could never have done what I did! You're a weak fucking useless worm. You're—"

Her eyes lock on mine.

"Are you . . . Are you still alive? God*dammit*!" She stamps her feet. "How—?"

She looks at the blade, makes the same realization I did.

Then she looks back at me. A smile curls her lips.

"Good. I want a little more time with you."

She looks for something to clean the blade with. She doesn't want to use Damon Cross's precious bedspread, but she finds my clothes and makes a show of snapping my shirt open and wiping the dried flesh and blood off the box cutter.

I try to speak, to say something in my defense. I can only manage a whis-pery wheeze. Maybe her cut wasn't as harmless as I thought. Maybe she severed a vocal cord or two? My already quiet voice might be a whole lot quieter after this.

If I survive. Which is very much not a guarantee.

Cigarette smoke hanging in the air.

Why am I still smelling that?

Eleanor throws my shirt aside and points the box cutter at me.

"He deserved so much better than you," she says, dripping with hate. "He deserved to be reborn as a strong man who could've changed the world like he *deserved*. Or, at least, he should have been born as someone like me! Someone who appreciates and understands him. Someone who *loves* him. You don't deserve to be here!"

Now she's screaming.

"You don't deserve this room! I do! You're an outsider! You tried to end our way of life! And I don't care what you think you might have been in a past life, that all ends now. With me. *By* me. And I'll start everything from scratch if I have to!"

She's advancing on me. I've got nowhere to go—my back presses against the dresser. And it won't matter that her blade is dull, because she's got *intent* in her eyes. I hold up my hand that's not clutching my throat in weak defense. Tears are streaming down her face now.

"You think you're so fucking special, huh? Well, I've got news for you, Mary. You. Are. *Not*—"

A muted metallic *clang* rings through the room.

Eleanor staggers, suddenly dazed. She blinks rapidly, touching a palm to her forehead.

A voice cries, at once present and from very far away: "Fuck yeah!"

A shadow voice.

Carried on the stench of cigarette smoke.

From my peripheral vision, I see there's a smudge in the room. A smudge with a very familiar shape. It gives another muffled and distant shout: "Fuckin' poltergeist *skills*!"

Then the smudge-shape swings her smudge-shaped oxygen tank, and it connects with Eleanor's head. Rather than pass through Eleanor like smoke, there's another muffled (smudgy?) *clang!* and Eleanor stumbles backward and collapses to the floor.

"The Bell Witch can lick my fucking taint!"

I look toward the chuckling ghost of Nadine. Turns out it's easier to see her in my peripheral vision; looking straight on, she wavers like a mirage, like ripples off a hot highway.

"Aw, don't look so dumb, Mary. What's going on in this house is a fucking hoot! Ain't no way I was gonna miss it. It's even better than watching people jerk off—which is also a thing I've gotten a kick outta doing lately."

I give a voiceless laugh. Life is amazing—the actual force of living, in all its dizzying, horrifying, hilarious permutations.

I try to ask her why she's saving me. I barely manage a hoarse "Why" before I have to clutch my bloody throat. She seems to get my meaning, though.

"I told you you'd never be rid of me, didn't I?" The shadow-ripple gets closer. "But I gotta give you credit, Mary. You're more fun than I woulda thought."

We look down at Eleanor, who's moaning dully. I wait for Nadine to gloat, to point out that she was right about this town, these people, all along.

Instead, she grunts, "Youth is always wasted on the young," and I think she might be referring to me as well as Eleanor.

Then she adjusts what I assume is a ghost flower in her hair. "Now, if you'll excuse me, I got some fun ideas of my own I wanna go try. You gals have fun."

And just like that, her presence disappears from the room.

Eleanor is starting to blink now, gathering strength. I have to act quickly. But first I hurry to my purse and retrieve something I stashed in there for emergencies. My period has been so erratic and unpredictable lately, it would've been plain reckless to not be prepared. I unwrap the pad from its pastel paper pouch and then grab another of my T-shirts from their drawer. I stick the pad to the shirt and then tie the makeshift giant Band-Aid to my throat. That'll have to do for now.

Eleanor has raised herself onto her elbows. I quickly (well, relatively quickly; we're both badly banged up here) get on top of her and lock her arms down under my knees. I have something I'd like to say. It's easier to speak with my bandage in place, but I have a feeling I'm going to pay for the effort. These might be the last words I speak for a long time—maybe ever.

What comes out of my mouth is so ragged, so voiceless, so airy and whistly, I can't help being reminded of the noises I heard sometimes from under the Furies' hoods.

"You all tell me I apologize too much. But I'm so sorry. Sorry I didn't live up to being Damon Cross for you. Sorry I got older and didn't do what I was supposed to with my life. I'm sorry I was never Good, and I'm also sorry I'm not the monster you wanted me to be. But, Eleanor, sweetie, the thing you all never understood was . . ."

I pick up the box cutter from where it landed, pull one last strand of old flesh from its blade, and look Eleanor in the eyes as unapologetically as I've ever looked.

"That doesn't mean I wasn't still a monster all along."

57

The Observed of All Observers

Once I'm finished with Eleanor, I wipe my hands clean on Damon Cross's bedspread.

I could grab more clothes from the dresser but I decide not to. I like being naked. I like this feeling of freedom. I even like how I looked in the mirror as I moved about the room. I might never put clothes on again. This body has survived so much trauma and bloodletting—more than any man's could have. It deserves to be celebrated.

However, while I left my clothes—in fact, all my belongings—in that room, I did take one souvenir with me. I'm holding it tightly in one hand now as I step out into the hallway. I don't have a plan for it; I just want it with me.

I almost can't believe it: my confrontation with Eleanor barely took any time at all. Has it even been a half hour? I was halfway expecting to see morning light coming through the windows, but it's still night. The house is still full of commotion and screaming.

This is doubly surprising because I spent what felt like a long time with Eleanor's body. I did more than I intended to with her. She'd been so invested in trying to make me feel small and worthless, I guess I wanted to make something of a statement.

Now I pad quickly down the hallway. There's something I want to see, and I think it might be time-sensitive. However, for the briefest of moments, I pause at the top of the stairs.

What about Wallace?

Eleanor admitted to killing Carole. But did she admit to killing Wallace? Has anyone?

That's an excellent question, but I shrug it off. Maybe Eleanor did it. Maybe I did. Who cares? I know who I am and I know what I'm capable of.

That's why I carved those words into what was left of Eleanor.

I didn't take her face—that's somebody else's trademark. I tried a few new things. And I left the opposite of a suicide note. My own little manifesto, in case anyone doubts my sense of self again:

"I KNOW"

I make my way to the hospital rooms, moving as fast as my brutalized body will allow. The door to Anna-Louise's room is just slightly ajar. I hope I got here in time, but I have a bad feeling about what I'm going to find as I push it open all the way.

Yup.

Darn it.

Anna-Louise's bed is a ruin of red. The sides of my mouth pucker in disappointment.

I'm sorry, Anna-Louise. You deserved better than this. I should have told them to spare you.

But would they have listened?

For the first time, it occurs to me that I may have started something I have no way of controlling.

Oh well. Can't worry about that now. Not tonight.

Carefully juggling the item I carried with me from the bedroom, I go about grabbing some gauze and bandages and make myself a proper dressing for my wounds.

I am the observed of all observers.

I make my way through the mansion, finding clues and piecing together what's happened.

I find a severed hand with a big gash in the palm. This must have once belonged to Dr. Burton. Farther off, I find bloodied bits of his clothes, as well as a closed door. A ring of keys dangles from the lock plate like earrings off a well-to-do earlobe, and a splash of blood crests across the door.

I add it all up: Burton was about to attempt an escape into yet another secret room before a Fury caught up with him and made quick work of his body. Too bad, Doctor. Hey, maybe it's just hormones. Textbook.

I turn the key, put a hand above the blood spray, and push the door open. It's impenetrably dark, but my hand finds a light switch.

A semi-opened curtain attempts to bisect the room. On the other side of the curtain is a hospital bed flanked by a few monitors and IV stands. Next to those is a familiar figure: a woman slumped in a wheelchair. I recognize her from the Ritual earlier. Dana.

There's an IV jammed into her arm: either something to knock her out or maybe pump her full of calories and water while she's incapacitated. They didn't kill her yet. Burton probably wanted her alive to work out some of his frustrations with how the day went.

I tuck my item from the bedroom under my arm and pull the IV from her. I have no idea when she'll be able to move on her own accord, but I lean down and whisper to her in my ragged ghostvoice:

"You don't have to stay here if you don't want to."

I lean over toward the bed and grab a pillow. One of those thin, papery pillows in an unimpressive blue slip. I remove the pillow and toss it back onto the bed before putting the pillowcase on her lap.

"Put this on and they'll leave you alone," I say. Then add, "Probably."

Because I don't know for sure.

Once when I was young, I had to walk through my school naked. It was, quite literally, the stuff of nightmares. But now, like most childhood fears, I'm finding it feels much different as an adult.

I walk with a skip in my step and a song in my heart. It plays as loudly as if it were blaring over the PA system for morning announcements.

Every day's a new day of loving you!

A small object on the floor: a little pink bottle of Pepto, oozing equally garish gloop. I kick it away like Gene Kelly splashing a puddle.

With each day comes a new way of loving you!

The screams aren't as loud here. Maybe there's more insulation in the walls, but I suspect really it's that there are fewer vocal cords remaining to scream.

I make my way in and out of the small classrooms. I never really explored this part of the mansion before. Expectedly, there aren't pictures of George Washington or Abraham Lincoln or dinosaurs hanging up in the rooms.

There are portraits of Burton's father. Elias Cross. Other stern, old white men I don't recognize. They all look very disappointed in me.

I wonder how scared Mrs. Burton was when the Furies found her. I hope she tried to *tsk* them before they disintegrated her.

There's a whimpering coming from behind one of the hallway closet doors. I open it up. A few mops clatter to the floor like prop trees toppled by an invisible giant. Someone's hiding in the back of the closet, and she bursts through, screaming. I think she's trying to startle me and buy time to escape, but she trips over her own feet and spills to the ground.

It's Bonnie. Not as good at ambushing as her daughter.

Fear has driven her insane. She's babbling incoherently, eyes rolling, teeth gnashing, swatting at me as she tries to get to her feet or, failing that, make a speedy getaway on her butt. If this were a Gothic novel, I think, her hair would have turned white, but I don't think Bonnie's hair color is natural to begin with.

"They all—disappeared—ripped apart—thin air—"

Suddenly, she looks at me and quiets, her tear-streaked face making some sort of computation. She swallows. "Have you seen my daughter?" she gasps. "Where's Eleanor?"

I give her a sad smile.

"Did *they* get her?"

I shake my head: no.

"But she's gone?"

I nod: oh yes.

She blubbers a bit more. "I'm so scared to die," she sobs.

I shush her with a finger to my lips. She obliges. I trace my free hand up against her cheek. I want to tell her not to fear death. I want to say it's just another Change. Women our age know all about the Change, right? Change is the only thing life promises us. I want to tell her that, above all, death must be one thing: useful.

But her daughter sliced my throat with a box cutter, so I don't say any of these things.

Instead, I look up and see a Fury moving quickly down the hallway—she must have sensed Bonnie's presence, maybe even through me. The Fury's feet drag against the floor as she speedily floats toward us.

I give Bonnie a goodbye pat on the cheek and walk away. Bonnie, not knowing what's quickly headed her way behind her, calls after me, *"I'll worship you! I'll love you! Please just tell me what to d—"*

Then her quickly extinguished scream, which lasts longer as an echo than as actual noise.

In another classroom, there's a wealth of decorations and party favors piled and ready for deployment. Everything Nancy was preparing for tomorrow. A trove of shining pastel. Banners and goody bags and so many colorful plastic eggs. I feel a tremendous pang for her and all her efforts to be seen, to be welcomed. I'm sorry, Nancy. It's never enough. The more you try, the easier it seems it becomes for them to ignore your efforts.

Another thought occurs to me while looking at the decorations. Eggs and bunnies: this was always just another fertility ritual, wasn't it? A celebration of reproduction. So many cultural rites to celebrate birth, adolescence, adulthood, reproduction. Why isn't there any sort of ritual to celebrate the *other* side of fertility? Why isn't there a holiday for middle age?

Some of the eggs begin to move. A pile of them scatters to the floor. Once again, the dim smell of cigarette smoke.

"Always hated this holiday," a gravelly shadow voice chuckles. "So cute 'n' cheery."

More of the eggs begin to float in the air.

There will be plenty of time to learn what Nadine's up to. Maybe even lend a hand. Plenty of time to learn all sorts of things from her. For now, a table near the back of the room catches my eye, where there's an array of chocolates and other sweets.

I suddenly realize how famished I am. I rip open bags. I tear off the foil from peanut butter–centered chocolate globs, the cellophane from sugar-dusted marshmallow ducks, the plastic sacks enclosing caches of jelly beans, and devour their insides with all the speed and fury of, well, one of my new friends. The chocolate most of all tastes like pure, radiant joy. Oh my God, has chocolate always been this delicious?

There's a large, hollow chocolate rabbit. Ignoring the sound of plastic eggs scraping across the floor, I take a bite out of her face and then thank her for being such a miracle.

Around the corner and down another hallway and there's Jane. Her mouth is lipless, but I know her smile is genuine.

"Maybe we should pay a visit to the rest of the town," I tell her. My voice would be inaudible to any living ears, but she's able to hear me. "Everyone who lives here is sick. At least everyone with one of those tattoos. Would you be up for that?"

Her claws flex in assent. They are still hungry. I can understand it. They've gone so long being unnoticed.

"Don't forget every copy of that blue book you find. Erase them off this earth."

Within moments, I watch as Jane and a handful of other specters make their way out of the house. They'll be speeding their way down the hill and toward the sleeping town in no time. They're becoming so independent already. I wonder how many people will wake up in the middle of their handiwork and how many will wake up at all.

Perhaps those people will wake up in new bodies, with new lives, and new chances to find their real selves, I muse. That's a nice thought. Life goes on, doesn't it?

The moon hangs in the sky like overripe fruit, pendulous and ready to burst with sweetness. I bet if I could reach up and bring it down to my teeth, it would taste of white chocolate and citrus and run down my chin.

How beautiful is this night air! This placid dryness. This un-insistent chill. It's made for naked skin and revelations.

I stand in the playground, basking in the moonlight as a stream of Furies leaves the mansion and zips down the hill, eager to join Jane and the others. There haven't been screams in the Cross House for a number of minutes now.

Perhaps I hear screams down in the town—or maybe that's just the wind. Hard to say. That's actually fitting; death really is just the wind in the end. Another childish anxiety. Like skeletal shadows on the wall that turn out to be tree branches. Or nightmares of being naked at school.

Poor Death! Such a sad, small, silly thing. Death never wins. There is always more life. Always. In the baseboards of every dingy basement. Within tunnels plunging through the earth. At the bottom of the deepest ocean. Life goes on and on and on. It *Changes*. Death can't win against an adversary like that. It's so easy to think of life as short, but no, that's not right, life is very long—the longest thing there is—it simply moves in one direction. It makes hairpin turns. Life goes this way and that, swings and roundabouts, as natural as the moon tugging on the tides. The moon moves. The moon *Changes.*

And in the meantime, I think I've done all I can do here.

Because the night is so quiet—not just the night but my mind—I'm able to hear the faint rustle in some of the foliage a dozen yards away along the side of the mountain.

A giant cat emerges from the bushes. Her eyes catch the moonlight with an eerie, copper glow. Her lithe, muscular body blends into the mountain, as if to say, for all that talk of how cruel and deadly the desert is, it's hospitable, too. For those who know how to call it home.

Of course, it's not unheard of to spot one of these magnificent creatures in the mountains from time to time. They're mountain lions after all. Cougars. It feels like a miracle all the same.

She must have smelled the blood and meat. She must have sensed the unnatural quiet.

If I could call to her, I'd warn her to stay away; they're not big fans of animals in that house. She might be a predator, but she's also prey.

She senses it anyway. She sniffs the air and then promptly turns around and disappears. She won't be seen by other human eyes for a very long time, I'd wager.

I look at the ineffably deep night sky and imagine myself lost in its boundless wonder.

How marvelous that I get to bear witness to such darkness.

Who am I, to see such miracles?

That question, plaguing me for so long. So simple, yet so inexpressibly difficult to answer. The reverence and awe of the moment almost demand it.

Who are you? the nothingness inquires.

I open up the item I took with me from the bedroom, the thing I've been carrying since leaving what remained of Eleanor.

She really was talented, that wannabe serial killer little creep.

My portrait.

My face.

I stare at it for a long time.

The world doesn't tremble. I see no hallucinations. I hear no voices. I feel no physical resistance. I just see the face of a woman with a lot of life left in her, if she's so lucky. There's a song in my head, and it seems to capture how I feel about her pretty well, all things considered.

I love her more today than yesterday.

But not as much as tomorrow.

Who *am* I?

I am just a story written in present tense.

We all are. We are never finished.

I am life and I am alive, I tell the night sky. And life, with all its Changes and joys, with all its cycles and surprises, goes on.

And on.

58

And On

From In the Dark with the Devil: One Heroic FBI Agent's Ground Zero Account of the Arroyo Easter Massacre *by Special Agent Peter Arliss, copyright 2020:*

The first family to show up was the Snyders (real names withheld). "I have a bad habit of showing up to things early," Brett Snyder, a GI Joe of a man who'd been living in the neighboring town of Socorro for a handful of years, later told me. "No one was outside to meet us, so we just sat in the car. I thought it was weird that there weren't any tables or anything already set up. But I could see there were some eggs lying around in the yard." His unease began to grow the longer he, his wife, and his two children sat there, waiting. "I just had a feeling, you know? I served two tours in Afghanistan, and there's a feeling you get that something really bad has just gone down. It's not a smell, but you feel it in your nose. The air's vibrating."

Another family, Tessa Avalon (real name withheld) and her six-year-old son, arrived next.

"We didn't go to church that morning or anything," Tessa said. "We're not really church people—although I tried for a year or so, and you wouldn't believe the condescending crap I got for being a single mom. But this sounded like a nice way to keep Max occupied for a couple [of] hours."

By the time one other family showed up on the early side (they declined my request for an interview), people began to get nervous. Finally, Mr. Snyder decided to enter the building.

"If I was getting flashbacks [of combat] before, walking into that mansion was like walking into a time machine. One time just outside of Mazar-e Sharif, my unit had to clear out a house where a bunch of wild dogs had been slaughtered. One of the worst gigs I ever pulled over there. I never thought I'd smell blood and guts just sitting in a house ever again."

Snyder called the police while still inside, trying to further assess the situation.

Unfortunately, outside, a larger crowd had begun to show up: families who were planning on a fun diversion for their kids on Easter morning. Some coming from church. Some coming from home. All of them, unwittingly, arriving at the scene of a massacre.

Ms. Avalon describes, "It was just one of those things where too many people showed up too fast and the word couldn't spread in time. Folks were pulling in, kids were shouting and screaming and running around. Before we knew it, kids were out looking for eggs. It all happened so fast."

From Page A16 of the New York Times, *April 22, 2019:*

SMALL TOWN IN ARIZONA SITE OF SURREAL EASTER HORRORS

From In the Dark with the Devil: One Heroic FBI Agent's Ground Zero Account of the Arroyo Easter Massacre *by Special Agent Peter Arliss, copyright 2020:*

According to the interviews, it appears the first several eggs discovered weren't necessarily as horrifying as the scene would later become. It's easy to forget that now, in light of the other eggs that captured more of the media's attention.

"Madelyn ran up to me and said, 'Mommy, Mommy, look what I found!'" Tabitha Oliveira says. "She was holding a couple [of] eggs, and I was telling her, 'Baby, you weren't supposed to go looking yet. There's probably going to be an announcement.' I just got so distracted by that guy yelling from the entrance that I didn't see she'd run off and started searching. They move so quick, you know? Anyway, I looked at the egg she was holding out to me. She said it sounded like the 'candy went hard' in there. She rattled it and, yeah, she was right, it sounded like stone or something. I got annoyed—I was already pretty mad about how in the middle of nowhere this place was and we just came because I was desperate to have something to tire Madelyn out—so I opened the egg up. And now Maddy's yelling at *me* for doing something too early—'We're supposed to wait, Mommy!'—if you can believe it. I almost didn't hear her because I was so creeped out by what I was looking at. The face of a little porcelain kid. One of those figurine statue things, like the kind my gramma used to collect. Someone smashed one of those figurines up and put it in the egg. Creepy. Maddy had three other eggs with her. We shook those, too. Sounded like there was more porcelain in two of them. When I shook that third one, though . . . God."

"I thought maybe it was a joke," Tessa Avalon remembers. "Like, a bunch of punk kids. I was in high school when that Columbine thing happened in Colorado, with those trench coat kids. I remember kids like that in my own school; I figured kids like that were responsible, putting Halloween props in a bunch of Easter eggs."

They weren't props.

I wasn't there to witness this part of the chaos, but I've imagined it many times.

The ripple of confusion and then screams spreading through the crowd as more and more children opened up eggs to discover pools of blood, ragged flaps of flesh, bisected eyeballs, the tips or middle joints of fingers, other unspeakable mutilations of body parts. One egg contained the head of a penis. And, most inexplicably, shattered ceramic statues. Little figurines, clearly indicating the perpetrator's psychotic hatred of children. The killer wanted to break these children's minds, their innocence, as literally and figuratively as possible.

But the truly surprising thing was that this killer wasn't far, far away by this point. The monster was closer than any of us could have dared imagine. With her latest victim, no less.

Yes. Her.

Up to this point, I still thought the killer would be a man. In some ways, my own innocence was shattered that day, too. Or at least a kind of naïveté.

So how did we end up catching her?

Fifty years ago it was dumb luck, and I suppose it has to be said that history repeats itself a little bit.

From the Papers Found in the Wastebasket at the Residence of Nancy A. Ruiz. Admitted into Evidence as Exhibit C-1 in the Proceedings, <u>State of Arizona V. Nancy Ruiz (Deceased)</u>, and Currently Held by the Phoenix Police Department:

TO DO
Get into the walls (Bring Dad's big knife)
Set up the snack tables
Put out the gift bags
Pack the eggs
Hide the eggs
Never do this again

Carmen and Sofie arrive at 10:15 to help!

Transcript of "Truthexposer: Truth Exposed About Arroyo Easter Massacre: What the Media Didn't Report," YouTube, Commentary by Jason "Jay" Dixon, March 27, 2020 [Url Withheld]:

Because you know there's a reason they wrapped that case up so quick! They knew there was something about it they couldn't explain unless they got in front of it, you know? Jump right in front, explain it away, wipe your hands, sell the story, cash the royalties. That's exactly the sorta thing they do when something goes too deep. They get a patsy, and they run with it, man. Took two days to wipe Oswald off the map after he "shot" Kennedy. Two days, man! Whatever freaky government experiments they were up to in that town, it wiped everyone out, and the only way to get us all from asking questions? Blame it on the *chica.*

From In the Dark with the Devil: One Heroic FBI Agent's Ground Zero Account of the Arroyo Easter Massacre *by Special Agent Peter Arliss, copyright 2020:*

When I reached the scene, blasting my favorite song (the Hollies' "Long Cool Woman in a Black Dress"—refer to chapter 3, "My Process," for a refresher on why it's the perfect song for an investigator to have on repeat), there were several patrol cars parked, several staties pulling up, two ambulances, two fire trucks, and a competition between the screaming families and the wailing sirens to see who could drown the other out.

I knew it was going to be bad because the officers coming out of the hospital entrance looked just as horrified as the ones coming out of the school entrance. This was before we even knew about what had happened to the sleeping residents of the tiny town at the bottom of the hill.

I chose the hospital entrance.

My first thought was: vandals. Someone had come and spray-painted the insides of the hospital red.

I made my way down hallways, taking notes and photos, doing the dance all federal agents have to learn where you both supersede and stay out of the way of the local police—I had a superior officer at Quantico who always called it the *jurisdictional do-si-do.*

I was jumping out of the way of a local officer who I believe was rushing out to vomit, and I hit my shoulder hard into the wall on accident.

This is where the dumb luck comes in. Two things happened at once. I noticed that the part of the wall I hit was hollow . . . and I heard someone talking on the other side of the wall. The inside. The voice was faint. Whoever was speaking wasn't directly on the other side—in fact, they could be very far away—but because I was close enough to an amenable structure, I heard it.

Dumb luck only gets you so far, though. I had also studied up. I remembered what happened to Damon Cross: the pursuit into the crawl space. And I already figured we had some kind of sick copycat on our hands. In that moment, I realized exactly what was going on. I felt along the wall for what seemed like minutes, and then . . . a hitch. I could pry the boards open just wide enough to slip through. A secret entrance.

Perhaps I was reckless in not enlisting any backup. But I wanted to be nimble. I wanted to be swift. And I wanted to be quiet. A copycat killer can be particularly wily. I was on their home turf, trying to play along to sheet music they'd memorized.

Luck, intuition, *and* knowledge. That's what makes a great detective. That's what enables you to face the devil and survive.

From *Deadline.com*

LIONSGATE BEGINS PRODUCTION ON "EASTER MASSACRE" TRUE CRIME THRILLER

From *Entertainment Weekly (Ew.com)*

OUR TOP TEN CASTING CHOICES FOR REAL-LIFE HERO AGENT ARLISS!

From In the Dark with the Devil: One Heroic FBI Agent's Ground Zero Account of the Arroyo Easter Massacre *by Special Agent Peter Arliss, copyright 2020:*

It was as dark as a Montana midnight in there, but I had my Maglite. I immediately wished I'd brought bread crumbs, or maybe some string like in that Greek myth about the Minotaur, so I could find my way out again. I desperately wanted to be out of there—all my warning signals were flaring red. But I pressed on. Call it bravery or duty, I pressed on.

Then I heard a voice.

My sidearm was drawn and practically glowing hot in my hand. All my fear was gone now. My job had never been clearer.

I rounded a few more impossible, invisible corners. The corridors were narrow and unpredictable, but there were clear footprints in the dirt. Someone had been running through this area very recently. I turned my Maglite off once I felt like the suspect was close enough to surprise. This is around when I began to think, *That voice, it sounds female.*

I brought up my Maglite, along with my sidearm, a Sig Sauer P226 9mm, because if you're going to administer justice, do it loudly . . . and then I clicked the light on.

There she was.

The monster I'd been hunting.

The mad butcher copycat.

She had a small, filthy child in her arms. Even in the beam of my flashlight, I could see this kid was in terrible shape. Later, when I visited him in the hospital, the doctors told me he was severely dehydrated and starving. He'd been in the dark for several days. It was a miracle he was still alive. All because of this monster's sick, senseless worship of Damon Cross.

In one of her hands was a large hunting knife.

As long as I live, I will never forget the look in her deranged, hysterical face. Her hair was wild, her eyes were bulging, she wore no makeup, her clothes were disarrayed, and she was screaming at me in a high, almost-screeching voice:

"There's no way out! Lost! We're all lost!"

I shudder now, even typing those words. She was clearly ranting, a haunting, existential accusation. A nihilist's prayer.

I identified myself and told her to drop her weapon. I saw the knife twitch, throwing a beam of light back at me from my Mag. She was going to stab one of us, either me or the kid first. Later, our investigation was able to piece together more proof of her unquestionable guilt, such as the blue nitrile hospital gloves—nurse's gloves—found on the scene of Karen Hoff's murder (see chapter 14, "Evidence"), but in the moment, that knife was all the confession I, and my Sig Sauer, needed.

Yes, I took some heat later on for the exact number of bullets I fired as she ran toward me, spouting her deranged reverie. I don't feel the need to rationalize what I did—I followed protocol when facing a clear and present danger. She was about to do something awful, had clearly done *a lot* of awful very recently.

I think about this moment all the time, though. Her words, most of all.

We're all lost.

There's no way out.

She sounded almost triumphant.

I think if she were still on this planet, behind bars, serving a well-deserved, Macy's Thanksgiving Day Parade's worth of life sentences, I'd say to her: Lost? No, we are absolutely not.

Not as long as there are men like me, good men ready to enter the dark corners and flush out the bad guys. We are not lost, Nancy Ruiz, you sick, crazy monster. We're not lost because we came into your dark lair and *found* you.

Incidentally, the little boy, Walter Shopkins (a pseudonym) is doing well. I go and visit him sometimes. He says he wants to be an FBI agent when he grows up.

Transcript of Interview Conducted with Wallace Shopsin, April 21, 2019:

Q: And, Wallace, can you tell us what you were doing in there?
A: I got pushed in, and I couldn't get out.
Q: You must have been very scared.
A: It was really dark. So I tried to sleep.
Q: But what did you do for food, Wallace? And water?
A: There were puddles. Some were gross. Some were okay. And there were lots of bugs! I ate a lot of bugs. Did you know you can eat bugs? The lady told me how to do it.
Q: Which lady?
A: There was a lady on the playground. She told me how to eat bugs. Can I have a Snickers bar?

The Front Page of the Arizona Republic, *Published April 23, 2019*

THE WOMAN BEHIND THE ARROYO EASTER MASSACRE

GOP Claims Vindication for Anti-Immigrant Policies; POTUS Promises to "Step Up" Efforts

From Buzzfeed, *"Questions Abound in Arroyo," Published September 25, 2021*

As of this date, FOIA requests are still mostly being denied or litigated against. I will say, it's strange to encounter so much resistance to investigating what's been described as an "open-and-shut case."

Cover of Book Sold at 7-Eleven in Aguila, Arizona, off US-60, Eagle Eye Road Exit

The Arroyo Easter Massacre: How MS-13 Got Away with Kidnapping & Murder

Cover of Book Sold at Harmony Holistic Crystals and Books, Jerome, Arizona

Vanished in the Night: Documented Proof of Alien Mass Kidnapping in Arroyo

Transcript of the Podcast Inexplicable Crimes with Jordie and Jameela, *Episode 405:*

JORDIE: Thanks again for coming along on this ride with me, J.

JAMEELA: Oh, well, I can't say it was a pleasure, J.

JORDIE: No, it was pretty gross, wasn't it? But you know you love it.

JAMEELA: Guilty as charged.

JORDIE: And just to remind you, Crimers, this four-part series looking at Nancy Ruiz, the Copycat Killer of Arroyo, was sponsored by Parachute Bedding. We love our Parachute sheets here at *Inexplicable Crimes*—

JAMEELA: And Lord knows we need all the help we can get, getting to sleep after studying all this stuff for you.

JORDIE: That's right! So use the code INEXPLICABLE for 20 percent off your first order and enjoy your time in bed before, y'know, you wake up to a crazy woman standing there, staring at you.

JAMEELA: Oh my God, I hate you.

JORDIE: Next week, we'll be taking a crack at exploring the crimes of another favorite female serial killer, Aileen Wuornos. And until then . . .

TOGETHER: Keep smiling and no criming!

JORDIE: Stay inexplicable, y'all!

and glossy magazines—probably a big fan of books about girls at the window on the train with tattoos—before settling in to watch the most popular shows on her tiny, unremarkable TV. Police procedurals and sitcoms (whose laugh tracks are made up of dead people, don't you know). There's nothing wrong with any of this, of course, you don't mean to judge, she's just not as unique or interesting as you, that's all. Not everybody can be interesting. We'd never get anything done.

She's read this FBI agent's book twice now and will probably read it again. It makes her angry. She's fueled by anger.

Strange things have been happening in the city lately. The population has been decreasing. Thinning out. Screams have punctured through the bubble of din that usually surrounds everything and everyone.

The police don't know what to do. They don't know whether to investigate the disappearances or the incidents of inexplicable, spontaneous mutilation. Just today, a man was sitting comfortably on the subway, and maybe his legs were spread a little too wide, but it's not like he was really hurting anybody, if you don't like it you can get up and move, but then suddenly a hole appeared in his thigh and his femoral artery began spraying everyone nearby.

Or what about the woman who was going through her busy day, talking on the phone, maybe a little too loud, and maybe she wasn't paying attention and didn't acknowledge the person who held a door open for her, and then a few feet later, her arm suddenly came off and fell onto the sidewalk, phone still in hand?

How do you investigate something like that?

How about that bookstore down in the Village that one afternoon was just suddenly empty? It wasn't a particularly busy day, but there were certainly employees inside . . . until suddenly there weren't.

If this phenomenon doesn't stop, the woman in the empty apartment muses, she might be the last person left on this entire island. That doesn't sound so bad to her. Her companions are getting better and better at not leaving any traces, so everything is just getting simpler and nicer.

Her attention turns back to the book.

"Poor Nancy," she says. She remembers a conversation where they commiserated about loneliness. Nancy had made a point about how some kinds of women are only invisible until somebody needs to be blamed. It appears as though Nancy was correct. It makes the woman mad.

EPILOGUE

Afterlife

The city atmosphere certainly has improved her. Some way she doesn't seem like the same woman.

—Kate Chopin, *The Awakening*

NOW

You've seen her before. Maybe even a dozen times today and not even noticed. A shy, unremarkable, middle-aged woman whose ordinariness edges right up to extraordinary, but never really steps over that line.

It's not your fault you don't notice her; she doesn't do much to call attention to herself. Often, she keeps her head down, as if she's facing some sort of strong breeze. Sometimes she's muttering to herself, which might be interesting elsewhere, but in this city, it's nothing to write home about. Her voice is well-nigh inaudible anyway, so you don't even get to hear anything interesting. And she always wears scarves or turtlenecks so you never see the jagged scar across her throat that she let heal on its own.

If you do happen to pay her a wayward glance, you might idly wonder: What does she do with her time? How does she fill her days?

Every person is different, of course. We all have our secrets. We all wear masks.

This particular woman comes home to her apartment. It's an empty apartment—a bookcase in the living room sporting bare shelves is a particularly strange detail—in an empty apartment building. She appears to be the only resident . . . but she doesn't live alone. There's a lot of life there, whether you see it or not. If you stop and try, you can feel it. You might even see . . . what, shapes? Shadows? Figures in the corner of your eye? No. It's probably just your imagination.

Is she a smoker? Is that why the faint smell of cigarettes hangs in the air?

There's a book on the unremarkable coffee table in front of her tiny, unremarkable couch. A currently omnipresent bestseller. Written by an FBI agent claiming he fought with the devil.

Of course, you might think; she's precisely the sort of person who reads bestsellers like that. She probably takes her reading cues from celebrity gurus

Furious, even.

She sits in her empty apartment, surrounded, looking at the book, and frowning. It's so quiet now, especially since the construction next door ceased. Another strange case of inexplicable disappearances. Finally, she breaks the silence.

"Who wants to go on a trip?" she asks. She turns the book over, revealing a wealth of advance praise, then opens the back cover to look at the author photo and bio. The suburbs of Virginia, the last line of his bio says. That must be right by Washington, D.C. "I've never been," she says, imagining the nation's capital, its historic sites. "We can see an old friend and then go be tourists for a little while."

She smiles, and she feels smiles around her. Lipless smiles.

She's read enough stories to know how tales like these eventually end. One day, they'll turn on her, too. She's certainly spilling enough blood. Some of it is assuredly innocent. If there really is such a thing.

That's okay. When that day happens, she'll understand. Every day is a gift after all; that's why all the books in the Personal-Growth section of your local bookstore say to live in the present. That's exactly what she intends to do. And if you don't know what a local bookstore is, ask your parents. Ask about Blockbuster Videos while you're at it.

In the meantime, this woman's got traveling to plan.

After D.C., there are so many places she's never seen. Cities. Towns. Places full of truly interesting people like you. People who might swear they've seen her before . . . if they even notice her in the first place.

People who will never see her coming.

Why would they?

Why would anybody?

It's like she doesn't even exist.

Afterword
—or—
What's This Asshole Doing Writing a Book About Menopause?

I first wrote this book when I was thirteen. Before you get too impressed, though: when I say *"book,"* really, it ran about a hundred pages. And when I say *"wrote,"* well, at that age I was more preoccupied with finding grown-up-sounding synonyms for commonplace words than any sort of narrative flow. (True story: once, a character "fell down," and little me tried to fancy it up by describing them as "metastasizing to the floor." All hail Shift + F7.)

Precociousness aside, though, I thought it was a pretty neat concept: What if a serial killer was reincarnated as some unassuming lady who had to fight for control over her personality? It was a sort of werewolf story . . . written by someone far too young to understand the implications of stories about cycles and the moon.

Now I'm three times thirteen and, over the years, I've developed something of a reputation as a prolific story generator. I write *a lot*—books, movies, teleplays, stage plays, audio plays. Say what you will about my flaws as a writer (just don't tag me when you do), but a scarcity of new story ideas has never been one of them. Yet for some reason, despite plenty of other options, sooner or later, I'd always find myself coming back to this weird almost-book I sorta-wrote as a teenager.

I'd always come back to *Mary*.

I broke the story again and again—as a novel, a screenplay, a radio play. I still occasionally find notes with the word *MARY* circled and some random idea or observation underneath, tucked away in old paperbacks I was reading five, ten, twenty years ago.

A surprising number of things about the story have remained consistent through its various permutations. But that's not what I want to talk about now. What I want to talk about in these final moments with you, the patient and curious reader who indulges afterwords in the first place, is what's changed.

Because a lot has. Particularly about myself and the world around me.

One such change is a growing awareness of who can—or perhaps *should*—tell which stories.

Simply put, despite my long history with this story, it wasn't until just a few years ago that it occurred to me: Do I even have a right to tell it? I'm a cisgendered man in my late thirties. What makes me think I can—or *should*—tell a story that's not just explicitly from a perimenopausal woman's point of view but where the experiences of perimenopause are a major factor in the telling?

That this question took so long to occur to me can't just be blamed on my being young, by the way. While I have no doubt certain clear-thinking individuals would've asked this question no matter when this book came out, I *do* think there's also been a cultural blind spot to these sorts of matters for a long time, and the zeitgeist has only recently, at long last, begun taking them seriously. After all, like I said in the Author's Note earlier, I was most inspired to write this book by *Carrie,* another iconic horror story about menstruation . . . also written by a cis dude.

So, yeah: Was this a story I should have pursued? Or should I have let it scratch in vain inside the haunted trunk of ideas that sits inside every writer's brain? I've been thinking about this a lot, and the answer I've come to is:

I don't know.

Okay, thanks for reading. Good night, everybody!

I kid, I kid. I *do* have a few things I want to say. First being: I think this is a valid question. Complex, but valid.

I'd be remiss not to mention that above all, this book is intended to be a horror story: scary, entertaining, and diverting. While it definitely has *themes*, it's not a thesis paper—but even pointing that out feels like a dodge because I have made it my life's work to defend and revere my genre *specifically because* of its unique ability to allow us to address larger issues under the cover of entertainment.

So I want to offer up this afterword as an acknowledgment of the issue and as a conversation starter. Because, kidding or not, I honestly *don't* know the answer. And I don't know the answer because I actually don't think it's for me to say.

Art, and the creation of it, is supremely fucking difficult and complicated, and we don't always get to pick the stories that call to us, let alone the ones we're able to carry over the finish line. All I can really do is present this story as effectively as I'm capable of, honoring the material with all the humility, curiosity, honesty, and due diligence possible. In this particular case, that meant reading several books on peri/menopause, watching countless videos, running the manuscript by several of my friends who've experienced it, and, of course, putting my trust in my brilliant editor and her candor to keep me in my lane whenever I might start showing my ignorance.

Is that enough? Again: I don't know. That all just feels like the bare minimum, really.

Here are some things I *do* know.

Menopause is an incredibly important topic of conversation, and, like many topics involving bodily functions—doubly so if they're so-called "women's issues"—our culture avoids it with an effort so concerted it borders on panic. This, despite the fact that menopause is something pretty much every person with a uterus, or who had a hysterectomy, or is transitioning, or a half dozen other scenarios, will experience; and it's something every person *with* a person like that in their lives will experience secondhand. It's a challenging, fascinating, nuanced, vital biological rite of passage and, hell, I *very much* agree with Mary when she makes her offhand comment about how sad it is we don't have a cultural celebration for middle age. A second puberty? This time while navigating bills and adult responsibilities and relationships? That shit's intense, and it deserves some goddamn honor and respect.

I also can't claim to know what it's like to live through this world as a woman, but I'd like to venture that I at least share a common anger with the women in my life. I share it as a son who watched his mother (a single mother with a degenerative disease who had to raise two children on a part-time income) fight for her due respect in her professional and personal worlds. I share it as a husband who, literally while writing this novel, watched his wife deal with a mysterious, occasionally debilitating chronic pain and was witness to innumerable doctors' appointments where her discomfort was dismissed in a way mine would never, ever be. I share it as an actor who has heard horror story after horror story from my female peers who have dealt with the slimiest, most demeaning, frightening shit I could ever imagine.

And, actually, on that note, I think *that's* ultimately what I drew upon to really allow myself to feel comfortable writing this book. Not that I'm a man with female friends and loved ones (gosh, that term hits differently now). Not that I've been witness to How Bad It Can Get. But precisely *because* I am a man in this world.

The bulk of *Mary* is narrated in first-person present tense because I wanted access to the voices in the titular character's head. But the most harmful, poisonous, insidious, domineering-yet-dastardly subtle voice actually isn't *hers;* it belongs to the serial killer Damon Cross, a man who (not so subtly) represents the violent patriarchy we're all of us inheritors of.

I felt I could write this book because I know *that* voice.

I have been around that voice, and I have *been* that voice. I may not know what it's like to be Mary Mudgett, but after thirty-nine years as a man in this world, in my darkest, most uncharitable thoughts, in the hardwired, misogynistic training I've received both concertedly and unconsciously and am working hard to unlearn, I sure as shit know what it's like to be a Damon Cross. To judge women for their youth, their solicitude, their convenience, their "use." I think we all do, on some level, and we've got to own up to those instincts, those poisons, if we're ever going to fucking change things. To crib a lyric from one of the greatest songwriters of my generation, Sufjan Stevens: in my best behavior, I am really just like him.

That's why the book has to end when Mary finally gets that horrible voice in her head to be silent.

That's the point at which this stopped being my story to tell.

That's why the scariest thing in this parade of ghosts and blood and razor-sharp claws . . . is a mirror.

Nat Cassidy
New York, 2021

ACKNOWLEDGMENTS

Any book this long (and this long in the making) is a team effort. I am greatly indebted to the writers' groups of which I'm a member and which facilitated the writing of this story in all its different permutations. Thank you to Kari Bentley-Quinn, Don Nguyen, Laura Pestronk, Meredith Packer, Jonathan Alexandratos, Tyler Rivenbark, Jason Tseng, Kristine Reyes, Lisa Huberman, Scott Casper, Ray Yamanouchi, and Mrinalini Kamath of Mission to (dit)Mars, and to Jordana Williams, Sean Williams, and Mac Rogers of Gideon Media, for first workshopping various episodic scripts of *Mary;* and most of all, my invaluable Table of Discontents, Matthew Trumbull, Stephanie Trumbull, and Brian Silliman, who read chapter after chapter after chapter (after chapter) of this book as it slowly took shape.

I'd like to thank Kristen Vaughan, who recorded the first demo versions of this story when it was still attempting to be an audio drama and who first gave Mary a voice; Tandy Cronyn, whose delight in Aunt Nadine changed the character; Adam Gomolin of Inkshares, who got me to finally finish a new outline; my readers over the two years of writing this manuscript, who gave feedback on either parts or the whole megillah: Samantha Wyer Bello, Jennifer Gordon Thomas, Sarah Lahue, Jim Lawson, Morgan Zipf-Meister, Eric Gilde, Ellen Adair, Anna O'Donoghue, Pete Boisvert, Brian Pluta, Angela Hamilton, Mark Sussman, Heidi Armbruster, Lauren Jost, Zach Jost, Jeff Wills, DeLisa White, Annalisa Loeffler, Nick Hammer, Karen Sternberg, Montserrat Mendez, Anne Heintz, Stuart Bousel, David Young, Clay McLeod Chapman, Dr. Frances Auld, and Dr. Gina Wisker.

Thank you to the authors whose works were invaluable in inspiring some or all of this book: the nonfiction of Dr. Tara Allmen (*Menopause Confidential*), Dr. Rosemary Leonard (*Menopause—the Answers*), William Walker Atkinson (*Reincarnation and the Law of Karma*), James Matlock (*Signs of Reincarnation*); and the fiction of Frank de Felitta (*Audrey Rose*), Max Ehrlich (*The Reincarnation of Peter Proud*), Shirley Jackson (*We Have Always Lived in the Castle*), Stephen Gilbert (*Ratman's Notebooks*), Elizabeth Engstrom (*When Darkness Loves Us, Black Ambrosia*), Michael McDowell

(*Katie, Toplin*), Dan Wells (*I Am Not a Serial Killer*), Ken Greenhall (*Elizabeth*), Peter Straub (*Julia, If You Could See Me Now*), Diane Johnson (*The Shadow Knows*), Naomi Alderman (*The Power*), Bari Wood (*The Killing Gift*), Carmen Maria Machado (*Her Body and Other Parties*), Barbara Comyns (*The Vet's Daughter*), Caitlin R. Kiernan (*The Drowning Girl*), Tade Thompson (*The Murders of Molly Southbourne*), Jane Chambers (*Burning*), Iain M. Banks (*The Wasp Factory*), Eric C. Higgs (*The Happy Man*), Bentley Little (*The Ignored*), A. J. Finn (*The Woman in the Window*), Sarah Pinborough (*Behind Her Eyes*), Sara Gran (*Come Closer*), Oyinkan Braithwaite (*My Sister, the Serial Killer*), Catriona Ward (*The Last House on Needless Street*), and most of all Ramsey Campbell (*The Parasite, The Face That Must Die*), and, of course, Stephen King (*Carrie, The Dark Half*).

Thank you to my agent, Alec Shane at Writers House LLC; my managers at Circle of Confusion, Daniela Gonzalez and Lawrence Mattis (and their heroic assistants, Casey Minella, Jane Riegler, Thomas Heegaard); my lawyer, Joe Dapello.

And supreme of all these, the woman without whom this would've been impossible on a whole host of levels: my brilliant, patient, incisive editor, Dr. Jen Gunnels.

Lastly, to my wife, Kelley: Yes, we can go get lobster now. I love you.

About the Author

Kent Meister

NAT CASSIDY writes horror for the page, stage, and screen. His critically acclaimed, award-winning horror plays have been produced across the United States, as well as Off- and Off-Off-Broadway. He won the New York Innovative Theatre Award for Outstanding Solo Performance for his one-man show about H. P. Lovecraft and was commissioned by the Kennedy Center to write a libretto for a short opera (about the end of the world, of course). As an established actor on stage and television (usually playing monsters and villains on shows such as *Blue Bloods, Bull, Quantico, FBI, and Law & Order: SVU*), Cassidy also authored the novelization of the hit podcast *Steal the Stars*, which was published by Tor Books and named one of the best books of 2017 by NPR. *Mary: An Awakening of Terror* is Cassidy's Nightfire debut, with a second original horror novel on the way in 2023. He lives in New York with his wife. Visit him at natcassidy.com.